THE LAKE ESCAPE

ALSO BY JAMIE DAY

One Big Happy Family

The Block Party

THE LAKE ESCAPE

JAMIE DAY

ST. MARTIN'S PRESS
New York

This is a work of fiction. All of the characters, organizations, and events portrayed in this novel are either products of the author's imagination or are used fictitiously.

First published in the United States by St. Martin's Press, an imprint of St. Martin's Publishing Group

EU Representative: Macmillan Publishers Ireland Ltd, 1st Floor, The Liffey Trust Centre, 117–126 Sheriff Street Upper, Dublin 1, DO1 YC43

 For information, address St. Martin's Publishing Group, 120 Broadway, New York, NY 10271.

www.stmartins.com

Designed by Donna Sinisgalli Noetzel

The Library of Congress Cataloging-in-Publication Data is available upon request.

ISBN 978-1-250-35819-6 (hardcover)
ISBN 978-1-250-35820-2 (ebook)

First Edition: 2025

10 9 8 7 6 5 4 3 2 1

For Melisse Shapiro, aka M. J. Rose—

a shining star in our community, gone too soon.

Thank you for your light.

There are no beautiful surfaces without a terrible depth.

—FRIEDRICH NIETZSCHE

THE LAKE, *SPRING*

The lake slowly rouses from its winter slumber. Each gentle wave against the shore is like a *tap, tap,* encouraging the earth, the forest, to join in its slow revival. Wildlife stirs, leaves reach for sunlight. But the lake is hungry. As it awakens, so does its need, its desire. Life blossoms, but danger lurks . . .

Excerpt from the *Burlington Standard*, Vermont's Largest Independent Newspaper

APRIL 13

A construction crew unearthed human skeletal remains while excavating a parcel of land several miles from Lake Timmeny in northern Vermont, the District Attorney's Office reported. Workers notified police of the grisly discovery around midday Wednesday. According to the DA's office, investigators scoured the area, and the Chief Medical Examiner's Office was at the scene to ensure all the bones were recovered.

The medical examiner will work with law enforcement to identify the body. Presently, in the United States, more than 15,000 people reported missing have not been found, 106 of them originating from the state of Vermont.

Chapter 1

Julia

The newly built house was a monstrosity: three stories tall, made almost entirely of glass, and partially blocking what was once Julia's cherished view of the lake. She had spotted the towering eyesore halfway down the long driveway that many visitors mistook for a road.

For months, she'd been eagerly anticipating her annual summer vacation to the lake house where she'd spent her formative years—but now everything was ruined. Ten minutes ago, it was a different story. From the passenger seat of their brand-new Land Rover Defender—which they couldn't afford—Julia had been composing her vacation kickoff Instagram post.

Finally arrived, let the relaxing begin!

Or better: *Be back never.*

Maybe . . . *Collect moments, not things.*

She could come up with a hundred of these and never run out.

Julia kept her posts simple, engaging, and heartfelt, but how fun it would be to write the truth for once: *My ass is saddlesore from the three-hour ride north, Christian and I are going broke, oh and our neighbor just royally screwed us over. #blessed*

It wasn't until Julia exited the vehicle that the magnitude to which they'd been screwed fully registered.

"You've *got* to be kidding me . . ." She trailed off, unable to find the words to describe the visual assault before her.

Julia didn't stick around to help Christian, her husband, unload.

Instead, she trotted to the adjacent property, where she proceeded to circle the perimeter of the new house in a daze. Her eyes raked the gaudy glass structure from top to bottom. *Unbelievable!* It looked as though a UFO had crash-landed in the forest. It was a scar upon the land, a sacrilegious affront to the otherwise pristine surroundings.

Lake Timmeny deserved better.

"What on earth was he thinking?" Julia muttered to herself. The *he* was David Dunne, the homeowner, not to mention her lifelong friend—or ex-friend, depending on how this went down.

Julia knew that David was renovating, but he conveniently neglected to mention that the work involved demolishing the house his grandfather had built and erecting a structure that was more than twice the original size. The new building was modern and sleek, in stark contrast to the two charming, rustic neighboring homes—one belonging to Julia and the other to Erika Sullivan, the third musketeer in their lakeshore trio.

The state forestry service was supposed to protect the surrounding woodlands, which had managed, up until now, to keep the natural beauty unchanged. So how had David skirted the zoning issue, clearing enough trees to make the Lorax keel over? Even the birds were less chirpy. But the air hadn't changed. Lake air had a particular freshness—the smell of clean water mixed with pine needles from the surrounding forest—that always made Julia's heart soar. But not today. She doubted anything could lift her spirits.

Julia turned her head in disgust only to have her gaze settle on an obtrusive lawn sculpture—a giant round orb made of reflective bronze. It was one of many such geometric objects scattered about, all probably meant to be artistic, but to her they just screamed "trying too hard."

Nutmeg, their older Lab mix adopted from a shelter years ago when Julia and Christian were on the cusp of divorce, came loping over, sniffing the ground, savoring the new smells that had accumulated since last season, oblivious to the galling insult looming above.

The lucky dog had no idea that David's home now completely blocked the old path to the lake. It used to be that Julia could walk out of her house and head straight for the shoreline. Now she'd have to take a roundabout way just to put her feet in the sand.

What angered her most was that it looked like the view from her kitchen's bay window was forever changed. Julia had always enjoyed watching sunsets over the water, a chilled glass of wine in hand, and music playing as she prepared dinner. Thanks to David's glass-fronted castle, she'd be able to see into his kitchen to know what *he* was cooking.

The three dwellings were built close together, facing the water, but not in a perfect row. David's plot of land was in between and in front of Julia's and Erika's respective homes. In the past, his simple two-bedroom cottage wasn't an obstruction. Julia believed she still had a clear line of sight to the lake from some rooms in her house, but Erika wasn't so fortunate. David's creation appeared to block her water view entirely.

What the actual fuck?

It was possible David used his newfound wealth to bribe his way out of the standard permitting process. She could only imagine how Erika, her hotheaded friend, would react. A fiery redhead who was one of the most sought-after defense attorneys in Connecticut, Erika was no-nonsense in the courtroom as well as in her personal life. She had trouble leaving work at the office, which had been an ongoing source of tension between her and her husband, Rick, a professional hunting and fishing guide. Rick had quite a collection of guns—so if Erika couldn't beat David in the courtroom, Julia briefly entertained the crazy notion that he might solve the issue another way.

Julia's daughter wandered over. She looked striking in her cut-off jean shorts and flattering red top—the perfect summer attire. A rising high school senior, Taylor was something of a teen boy's dream, with long blond hair and an aloof manner that guys her age found irresistible. Except for her hair color, she was a mirror image of Julia at that age. And now that clothes from way back when were in fashion again, her daughter's outfits reminded Julia of her own wild and carefree days, many of which had been spent at this lake with David and Erika.

"It's soooo ugly," declared Taylor in a drawn-out voice, echoing Julia's sentiments exactly. The cold, boxy structure was devoid of character—like three doctors' offices stacked on top of each other. Even the furniture, which Julia could see through the plethora of windows, was fittingly austere, like a mating between Ikea and OfficeMax.

The back of the house faced the water, and Julia made her way there. A wraparound deck on the second level was large enough to host a flag football game and featured a steel railing thick enough to contain cattle. From here, Julia noted the only carryover from the old house—a stone chimney that poked through a sharply angled roof. But really, it was the windows that galled her. Everywhere she looked, there were windows.

"This makes our place look like David's outhouse," noted Taylor, scrunching her nose.

Nutmeg barked as though in agreement.

Honestly, it was a relief to hear Taylor voice an opinion about anything, positive or negative. For the last month or so, she'd been as gloomy as an overcast day. Nothing got a rise out of her. Christian chalked it up to the pressures of senior year and a college decision on the horizon, but Julia remained unconvinced.

Aside from her poetry, which Taylor wrote in an old-fashioned leather-bound journal, their daughter had lost interest in most things—including their annual two-week vacation to the lake. But bearing witness to this glass injustice energized her like a wilted flower in the rain.

Christian approached from the direction of their house (or the outhouse, in Taylor's parlance). Technically, it was Julia's home, after her parents had gifted her the deed that came with the responsibility of maintaining the property. She and Christian put the house in a trust that Christian oversaw, so the lake home could eventually be given to their daughter.

"I'm telling you, the new car made the drive here feel like nothing," Christian marveled. "The way she glided over the logging road—she's really a dream."

Julia flinched ever so slightly. *Even his cars are girls,* she thought. She'd once caught him caressing the leather seats lovingly when he thought nobody was looking. It reminded her of a man in the throes of infatuation. *Oh, how easily a married man can be distracted by a shiny new toy.* And sometimes those "toys" could talk, laugh, and order drinks at an airport bar. It was hard not to dwell once the reminder took hold—his mistake . . . and hers.

Julia gave Christian the once-over like he was being dim. "Really? You're talking about your new car and not this *house*?"

Christian peered up, finally acknowledging the giant fish tank. He took a step back, as if the slight change in his perspective might alter his assessment.

"That's a big surprise, all right," was all he said, which annoyed her. Such a bland, middle-of-the-road comment put the burden of outrage entirely on Julia.

"Christian, he's blocking our view." She pointed through David's house into their kitchen to prove her point.

Christian defended his occasional golfing buddy. "There's nothing we can do about it now, Julia. I get that it's not ideal, but it is his property. He can build whatever he wants."

Julia eyed him with contempt. "*Not ideal?* Oh, please. It's too close to the shoreline. There's no way a building inspector would have approved this," she said. "This was definitely done under the radar and probably under the table, not to mention he didn't share any plans with his abutters, meaning *us*."

Christian looked away.

Julia glared at him. "Did he share plans with you?" she asked, all fired up.

"No, not really," said Christian, shaking his head. "He told me what he told you, that it would be a modest addition."

Julia was relieved. Christian keeping secrets would trigger her lingering doubts and set back all their progress. He'd been eight years sober, and his affair was finally in the rearview mirror. How the marriage had survived his brief fling with some woman he'd met while on a business trip defied logic. It certainly wouldn't have lasted if his drinking had continued.

"It's hardly a small addition," said Julia, stating the obvious. "This is the kind of house a clueless rich asshole would build just to show off."

"He made one smart investment, so he gets to do whatever he wants, including being a rich asshole. At least *someone* around here is making money."

Christian's remark earned him a stern, albeit silent rebuke from Julia. Taylor wasn't privy to their financial struggles, and with her mood in free fall, it was best to keep it that way.

Julia's phone buzzed in her pocket, as if she needed any more reminders of their precarious position. She grimaced in a Pavlovian response while playing Guess the Bill Collector. *Electric? Landlord? Franchise?* She decided not to look. Everyone wanted their money, yet here they were, ready to vacation, having arrived in Christian's overpriced tax deduction he drove off the dealer's lot before Julia had a chance to object. What an absolute disaster.

"At a minimum, this is deeply unfair to us, but even more so to Erika and Rick," said Julia.

"What do you want me to do about it, Jules? Throw rocks at the windows? He's built the damn thing. All we can do now is adjust. Just relax. Everything is going to work out."

Julia winced. "Last time you said that, we bought a gym."

Christian returned a wan smile. Naturally, she wanted him to back her, but she also understood why he kept his rose-colored glasses on. It's how he saw life after he found sobriety. Every minute was a second chance, and every day was a new opportunity to experience something amazing. Exuberance and blind zeal had replaced his nightly scotch and soda. He'd become a whirlpool of a human, always churning up new ideas or get-rich-quick schemes with enough force to suck her down with him.

Even though it was Christian's idea to buy a VR Gym franchise—

the nation's only all–virtual reality fitness studio—Julia had signed on the dotted line as well. Nobody forced her to leave the job she loved at a prominent nonprofit devoted to child welfare, which boasted a former First Lady of the United States as a supporter and a brand ambassador, to help Christian run his new business.

Julia jumped in headfirst, her heart full of optimism and her head abuzz with dreams of an early retirement. How naive she had been. In some ways, Julia missed the drunk Christian—the salesman who was too fuzzy and hungover to turn any of his ideas into reality. Now what could have been uneventful days became an endless adventure on a trip to nowhere.

"I'm going to put the groceries away," said Christian. "Just remember that we're all friends, Jules. We're only here for a short time, so let's make the best of it."

At least he didn't quote his favorite AA aphorism about accepting things we cannot change.

Everything had changed with this one ugly building.

Christian might be fine with it, but Julia wanted to kill David—and she knew Erika would feel the same. Her friend was due to arrive any minute. Only one question remained: Who would get to him first?

Chapter 2

Izzy

Being a nanny is not a cush job. Absolutely not. It is a serious business that demands care, focus, and know-how. You have a huge responsibility. As the nanny, you are in charge of the most precious, sacred, and meaningful part of someone's *entire* existence—their children. You can't just kick back and coast through the day. Oh no, no, no. To be a high-caliber nanny means being on top of your game, always on your toes, eyes everywhere—back of your head, top of your head, you name it, you *must* have eyes on the prize. But it's more than just being watchful. This is a job that requires great skill, caring, the compassion of a saint, and most important, cunning.

Naturally, a prerequisite of a quality nanny is to love the company of children. This is not something that can be faked. Children possess an uncanny ability to sniff out inauthenticity, so joy for the job must be genuine, and should emanate from the nanny like sunbeams on a cloudless day. But love is not enough to guarantee success. To provide one's charges with age-appropriate experiences, a quality nanny must also be familiar with the stages of childhood development. After all, the CDC (that's correct, the Centers for Disease Control and Prevention—that's how important this profession is) publishes guidelines, so there's no excuse for ignorance.

And while organization, self-motivation, and sound judgment are mandatory for the job, a nanny must remember to keep a level head at all times. Unfortunately, emergencies do arise.

It is advised to keep a stocked first-aid kit in your car and a smaller one in your shoulder bag. And don't be afraid to use 911—you're not a miracle worker.

Now, it goes without saying that your references must be impeccable. Never burn a bridge. Remember, fire can easily spread, burning you instead. And above all else, a nanny must always be honest. Trust is *everything* in our trade. The family is counting on you, so please be up-front about your experience, qualifications, and abilities.

Which is precisely why I *shouldn't* be a nanny.

You see, I've never done this job before. I never even babysat in high school. Everything I know about being a nanny I've learned from Google and watching *Mary Poppins* so many times I have the whole movie memorized. I've filled a notebook with my research so I could absorb the information and embody my new persona with as much authenticity as possible. In a way, I'm like a method actor. If I think I'm great at my job, pretend to be in charge, project utter confidence, then everyone will believe it.

I'm not lazy, so my new employer doesn't have to worry about that. As soon as I could legally work, I had a job bagging groceries at the supermarket where my father was the store manager. I'm in college now, a journalism major heading into my sophomore year. My new boss knows my age—I can't hide that—but he thinks I'm studying early childhood development. That's far more nanny-like than journalism.

He certainly wouldn't be pleased to know that I don't really like kids, and I'm pretty sure I have zero maternal instinct. Well, maybe not zero. I just don't feel a need to become a mother. Children are annoying, loud, and full of snot. I'm not a big fan of messy eaters, either, or drool, and forget diapers. Luckily, the five-year-old twins I'm going to look after are beyond that stage. I definitely can't deal with babies.

But I do need this job, and for a very good reason—though not one I can be honest about, which is why I had my roommate (and best friend) pretend to be my last employer.

When the call came for a reference check, I listened in on the conversation with the father and his girlfriend, who'd be joining us on vacation. It helped that Meredith is a theater major. She was brilliant on the phone.

"Oh, Izzy is simply the best," she crowed. "Our youngest, Gabe, had a speech impediment, and by the end of the summer, you'd think he learned his English in *England*."

Okay, that was over the top, but they *were* impressed.

"And Sylvie couldn't have loved Izzy more."

Sylvie? I mouthed to Meredith. To this day, I don't know where she got that name.

"She's our picky eater, and just the other day we went out to dinner and she had *sushi*—honest to God, sushi! And even more shocking than that—she actually liked it. I swear to you, before Izzy came into our lives, we couldn't eat at a restaurant that didn't serve elbow macaroni bathed in butter sauce."

My eyebrows shot up. I was nervous she was overselling me, but Meredith, who every guy on campus has a crush on because she's cuter than a teddy bear and as tough as a Navy SEAL, held up a hand to assure me all was under control.

The rest of the conversation sped along because these people were *desperate.* They had a vacation coming up and their nanny had left them high and dry. No reason given.

After the call ended, Meredith voiced her concern. "You don't know a thing about this guy."

"I know his name is David Dunne. I looked him up online—he has no criminal record and he has kids. How bad can he be?"

Her look was telling. "You're a journalism major who loves crime shows. I think you can answer that question."

She had a point, but I couldn't back out now. I had set up a Google Alert for Lake Timmeny, hoping for a scenario just like the one that hit my inbox. It was the chance of a lifetime, a paid one at that.

"I'm not worried," I assured her. "You know I *need* this job."

That was true. Meredith is one of the very few people aware of my story. She understood what I was doing, and more important, why. "There must be a reason the last nanny left them so suddenly. You are walking into a potentially dangerous situation with blinders on," Meredith warned.

"His girlfriend will be there. Another woman in the house should put your mind at ease," I suggested. Mer's look told me she wasn't buying it.

Now that I've been out of school for a few weeks, back home living with my mom, Mer's words keep tumbling in my head, anxiety nipping at me. I examine the suitcase on my bed one more time. It's all packed. Socks. Shoes—sandals, sneakers, and hikers, probably overkill. Same with the bathing suits (packed three). I'm bringing an excess of hair products to tame my mane of curly light brown hair. In middle school I was anointed the unfortunate nickname Frizzy Izzy, a self-explanatory moniker that stuck with me through high school graduation. I'm as ready to go as I'll ever be. All my clothes are very practical, nothing too revealing.

I'm just about ready to leave to meet David for the drive to the lake when the smell of frying eggs and bacon draws me into the kitchen. My mother's standing at the stove, cooking up a storm. She gives me a cheery smile. My heart swells with love. I don't like keeping things from her, but she'd worry. She always worries. We're close in a lot of ways, but my mom's anxiety often discourages me from being open with her.

She's still wearing her bathrobe and fuzzy slippers, her hair tucked behind her ears. She's in her fifties, but has an ageless look with her pixie face, short-cropped blond hair, sweet little nose, and a bright, loving smile. Oversize glasses, the same dark frames she's had since I was a baby, magnify her sparkling blue eyes. Outwardly, she radiates the pleasant charm of a down-to-earth Vermonter.

She has friends, a good life here, but I know what others don't. Sadness lurks beneath the surface. She thinks she does a good job of hiding it, but I can see through her mask. It's not the divorce that's responsible for dimming her glow, and we don't have money issues.

It's the memories reflected in the family photos hanging on the wall in our living room that continue to haunt her dreams.

"Izzy, hon, do you have time to eat before you go?"

She knows I'm leaving for a couple of weeks, and I know a gently disguised order when I hear one. I plop myself down on a seat at the same kitchen table where I did countless hours of homework. Mom's already got a place setting for me. I take a sip of orange juice that she's poured into my favorite glass from when I was little—a blue tumbler I thought looked like a sapphire. I wouldn't drink my juice unless it was poured into the sapphire glass—such a bratty kid.

I wonder if the twins I'll be watching will be equally annoying. I get the sense that Mom picked that glass on purpose. She doesn't like that I'll be away with people she doesn't know. It makes her uncomfortable. Mom likes order. She wants everything to be as predictable as a tide chart. The hearty breakfast and my childhood dishes are her way of saying that she's still holding on to me, even as I'm slipping away.

I get it. I'm her only child. She wants to protect me from the monsters she knows exist in the real world. I can't bring myself to tell her that sometimes I hear her cry in her sleep. I try to put her mind at ease.

"Everything is going to be fine, Mom. There's *nothing* to be nervous about."

Nobody, but nobody, could worry about nothing better than my loving and devoted mother, Lauren Greene.

The corners of her mouth crinkle with concern as she plates my eggs. "I know, honey. I didn't even say anything."

She has a defensive lilt to her voice, an upward trill that all but confirms my suspicion. "You didn't have to." I smile up at her, hoping to convey how much I appreciate her love and caring, though I wouldn't mind punctuating it with an eye-roll emoji if I could.

"I'm nineteen years old," I remind her. "I can take care of myself."

She does the eye roll instead. "Two weeks in Burlington all on your own is a lot. Are you sure the newspaper has housing arranged for you? I really would like a phone number of someone I can call in case of an emergency."

"I *am* that someone," I insist. "And everything's arranged, Mom, just relax. Who knows, maybe I'll even meet a cute guy, so I won't be all alone."

And I'm sure I will. I just don't tell my mom that the cute guy is only five years old.

"Like that's supposed to ease my mind."

Mom kisses the top of my head, and I take in her familiar fragrance. If I could bottle up that apricot scent, I'd put it on whenever I'm in need of a warm embrace. But for these next two weeks, I'll be on my own.

I glance at my phone discreetly, nervous I'll be late for the car ride to the lake. Mom can't provide a lifeline during this venture because I've told her I'm attending a prestigious two-week journalism internship at a Vermont newspaper my mother knows and reads.

"We gotta go. I don't want to miss the bus," I say.

But there is no bus. I'm being picked up by a man I've never met, to be driven to a lake I've never been to, in a car I've never seen.

I hate that I have to lie to my mother as well as to my new boss.

I'm usually an honest person. Lying is not something I do easily. But some secrets are too dangerous to share.

Chapter 3

Julia

Julia loved the ritual of waking up the house at the start of vacation. She went from room to room, pulling back curtains, clearing dust, putting sheets on the beds, and opening windows, inviting the rejuvenating lake air to fill her home. Even the presence of David's glass house couldn't spoil the joy of this tradition.

Everything appeared to be in relatively good shape after the long winter, which was a relief. The roof shingles were intact. There were no signs of leaks. All the plumbing still worked, and Julia didn't pick up any mildew smells.

If only her business could withstand the test of time as well as the lake house her grandfather had built in the 1950s. While the first few years of owning a VR Gym franchise exceeded expectations, enrollment had been on a steady decline. Once the novelty wore off, membership started to tank, especially in the warmer weather months when people preferred to exercise outdoors.

To make matters worse, the computers powering the virtual reality cycling, running, and rowing machines broke down at a rate far above projections. And the headsets caused dizziness for many members. In the early days, VR gyms had tons of press coverage, and they still had it now, but for all the wrong reasons. She supposed the glass house was good for one thing: plummeting revenues from her failing franchise no longer seemed like a top concern.

When all her chores were done, Julia took a moment to call her folks from the screened-in porch her father had added long before she was born. All was well, though of course Dad complained about the food at their Florida retirement community, and her mom complained about her dad. Some things never changed. Still, they were happy to hear from her, and delighted she was enjoying the house, just wistful that they weren't able to share in the family vacation. She missed her parents coming to the lake. The place felt a little empty without them.

"Maybe next year," Julia said to them, though no doubt she'd make the same pledge the following summer. Her mother's lack of mobility after the double hip replacement would turn any vacation into hell week, and her father didn't have the stamina (or patience) to deal with airports and long car rides. Besides, his heart might give out if he saw what David had done to his family's homestead.

Not only had the lake houses been passed down through the generations, the friendships had as well. Julia's grandfather bought his plot from David's grandfather, and the two became thick as thieves. Next on the scene was Cormac Gallagher, Erika's father, who was just a young man when he purchased his parcel in the 1960s. He traveled from New York to Vermont on weekends while his house was being built and became friendly with his neighbors, who were fifteen years his senior.

Cormac waited until later in life to father a child, which worked out in Julia's favor because she and Erika grew up like sisters, separated by only a couple of years. Sadly, Cormac always said motherhood didn't suit his wife, who ran off with another man when Erika was still very young, leaving him on his own to raise his daughter.

But the kids always had each other. Even now, a whiff of sunscreen steered Julia back to those youthful summer afternoons when the strong sun baked the ground dry and the lake beckoned them to play in the cool water.

The question on Julia's mind now was how the David from way back then had become the glasshouse-building jackass of today. If Erika was like a sister to Julia, David was her protective brother.

One time, when she twisted her ankle on a hike, it was David who carried her home on his back, refusing to put her down even when his legs buckled from the strain. That was the David she knew and loved—the boy who fancied himself a budding biologist. Julia often accompanied him on his shoreline patrols, using nets to capture freshwater minnows, tadpoles, and other critters they could study in water-filled glass jars. Erika occasionally joined in, but she preferred watercolors and her drawing pad to those fishing expeditions.

One thing they all agreed on was their love of the raft moored out on the lake. They would swim to it while their parents paid only partial attention. They had a favorite game—King of the Raft—that involved tossing their opponents into the water until two players decided they'd had enough, and a winner was declared. The trio were all strong swimmers, but it was David who usually won the title of King. Still, he would sacrifice victories here and there to keep the game interesting.

Of course, with the good times came the bad. David's father died in his forties after a fall off a ladder while replacing shingles on his lake house roof. David was just fifteen, and he was the one who found his father unconscious on the ground, a fast-moving brain hemorrhage draining his life away. The loss was devastating for David, and heartbreaking for all. David's mother succumbed so deeply to grief that it was as if she'd abandoned him. Thankfully, Cormac had stepped in and became a father figure to him, and in turn, David became the son he never had.

Thinking back, maybe that was a turning point, when David started looking for something to shield him from the pain of his loss and trauma. He spun a self-protective chrysalis, cocooning himself within. It wasn't a coincidence that he never let Julia or Erika win King of the Raft after the funeral. Anger cloaked some of his natural sweetness. Bravado became a substitute for humility. Distance and self-absorption put space between him and the potential for another loss.

But there were always flashes of the old David to keep Julia from pulling away. Like that time two years after college, when she broke down somewhere off I-87 near Albany, returning from a family reunion in Poughkeepsie, of all places. It was David, her only contact in New York, who drove two hours north to get her and brought her back to Manhattan to stay with him. They spent the weekend exploring Greenwich Village, indulging in Indian food and too much alcohol, and when the car repairs were done, he drove her north again, insisting she not take the bus. It was the old David, her surrogate brother, carrying her on his back once more.

As adults, Julia, Erika, and David always made it a point to coordinate their schedules so they could meet at the lake and enjoy their vacation together. These reunions reinforced a bond that began almost from the time of their births—one she believed was unbreakable. Until today.

How could this be? They shared birthdays, graduations, new jobs, new lovers, ex-lovers, marriages, deaths, kids, and a divorce (David's from Debbie). While his marriage didn't last, David did get Brody and Becca out of the deal—twins who were now four, or maybe five? The years were a blur, but the Lake Gang remained a constant in her life.

Julia and Christian.

Erika and Rick.

And David and his lady of the moment.

In true David fashion, he didn't mourn his marriage for long, probably in part because he didn't have much of a history with his ex. He and Debbie had tied the knot within six months of meeting, and the twins were born a year later. Divorce papers were served by the time the kids took their first steps. He had joint custody, which came with the usual headaches, but he always had the funds for a part-time nanny.

Julia and Erika both agreed they didn't miss Debbie. She was nice enough, but in a distant and *appropriate* way. She said all the right things, but lacked the warmth to make it feel genuine. She was pretentious, coming from money and carrying herself with a superior air Julia found off-putting. David insisted he married for love, not money, and he signed an ironclad prenup as proof, which left him with no claim to Debbie's family wealth.

Rich as she was, Debbie loved David's family cottage, with all its quaint charm. No doubt she would have been appalled to see what he had done with the place. She'd likely shake her head and say something along the lines of, "*This house belongs in the Hamptons.*"

Too bad Debbie wasn't still in the picture—she could have paid to move it there.

Taylor appeared while Julia glumly stared out her bay window into David's kitchen.

"Is the house still there?"

Taylor's quip coaxed a slight smile out of Julia.

"Unreal, isn't it?" she lamented.

"Yeah, it is, but Dad's right. It's built. What can you do?"

"I dunno. Erika is the attorney. I'll ask her."

"Speaking of, are she and Rick here yet?" Taylor wanted to know.

"No, not yet."

"And you're sure Lucas isn't with them, right?" There was a nervous twinge to Taylor's voice that caught Julia off guard.

Lucas was Erika's eighteen-year-old son and, like Taylor, was beginning his senior year in the fall. Julia had high hopes the next generation would carry on the vacation-together tradition, but that was now in question.

"Erika told me that he's got some gigs booked with his band, so I don't expect him to be here. What's up with you two, anyway? You always got along so well."

Her daughter ignored the question. It wasn't long ago that Taylor went away for a weekend with Erika and Lucas to tour a couple of colleges that both kids were interested in. At first everything seemed fine, but now she was acting like she didn't want him around.

While this new friction was cause for concern, getting her tight-lipped daughter to open up might take a miracle. Chances were, only her journal knew the truth.

Julia thought Taylor's poetry hobby was a healthy outlet for expressing her inner world, and Taylor was actually quite a good writer, but she couldn't make a living at it. Julia attempted to sway her in the direction of business or finance instead. Life had enough pitfalls without digging your own trench.

Enough is enough, Julia decided. She would put her parental struggles, David's house, and her financial worries on the shelf to soak up these two weeks of doing nothing. She was going to vacation *hard.*

There was so much to do and so little time to fit it all in. Boating, swimming, hiking . . . she wanted to savor the rose-colored sunrises and orange-dappled sunsets, to spend her evenings lounging in the hammock, with the fire roaring and her favorite chardonnay within easy reach.

The sound of car wheels approaching pulled Julia from her daydream. Nutmeg barked an alert and followed Julia and Taylor as they stepped outside to greet the new arrivals.

She saw a sparkling midnight-blue Mercedes SUV pull to a stop in back of David's house. The passenger door opened, and a young woman with curly light brown hair, who could not be much older than Taylor, emerged from within. *This must be David's new girlfriend,* Julia figured, the one he was so gaga over. They were a relatively new couple, together three months or so, but from what Julia heard, they were already hot and heavy.

She was petite and perky, unassuming in jeans, flip-flops, and a simple white T-shirt. Young and pretty had always been David's preference, but this cherub didn't have a wrinkle on her youthful face. Menopause was as distant as Mars.

David had told Julia the name of his latest fling, which began with an F—Fern, Flora, something like that—but he had failed to mention that she'd get carded at most liquor stores.

The young Miss F paused to send Julia a pleasant smile and a brief wave before helping Brody and Becca out of their booster seats. A moment later, out stepped David, flashing a huge smile, as if he were on top of the world. He gestured with open arms at his creation.

"Amazing, isn't it?" he said with a dimpled smile.

Brody and Becca bounded over to Taylor, whom they revered like a deity.

David's new woman stayed back and watched. She looked so young, it seemed as though she were playing house with real kids. And David, with his dark hair, olive-toned complexion, and Roman nose, fit the role of the handsome older man quite well.

Julia went to him with lips pursed, eyes narrowed, and brow furrowed.

David looked surprised that she was anything but happy to see him. "What, you don't like it?" he asked, pointing to the house.

Christian came over and shook David's hand as if everything was fine. *Men!*

Brody and Becca were getting along fabulously with Taylor, while David's young fling remained silent as a mannequin. Julia felt uncomfortable being the only one to express her disgust, but she stood her ground. "Are you out of your mind?"

David folded his arms across his chest. "This is prefab construction from one of the world's most renowned manufacturers of luxury modular homes. I thought you'd be more impressed."

Julia's mouth fell open. Because it was David, and they had a history, she tried to make excuses for him. She told herself that all the new money must have shut down part of his frontal lobe. But she wasn't about to give him a full pass.

"You're blocking our view," she told him, directing his attention to the new part of his home that jutted out past the original construction. "And Erika's . . . all I can say is that I hope you've kept up with your life insurance payments. She's going to flip."

David's smile broadened again. "Oh my god, Julia, relax, will you? I thought that all through. The windows in the front and back line up, so it's not obstructing anything. And I cleared out a bunch of trees, so the view should be even better than you had before."

Christian perked up. "Right, so to see the lake, we just have to look *through* your house?"

David held up his hands, like a magician performing a stupefying trick. Leave it to him to come up with such a ludicrous explanation and expect everyone to buy in.

"It'll be like admiring the lake through your own window," he insisted.

"Yeah, with your hairy full moon in our view," said Julia bitterly.

David slipped extra charm into his boyish grin, which even Julia wasn't immune to. "Pants always, anytime I'm in the living room. That's a promise."

"And a shirt," said Christian, eyeing David up and down. "You're looking jacked, bro. I don't want Julia getting any ideas." Christian offered up the uneasy laugh of someone who was only half joking. After his divorce, David had gotten into working out, posting CrossFit photos of his daily WOD so often that he tempted Julia to unfollow him.

She drew David's attention to his pretty, young companion and said quietly, "Please tell me she's old enough to drive."

David belted out a hearty laugh. "That's not Fiona," he insisted.

Fiona, that's it! Julia felt bad that she hadn't remembered the new girlfriend's name, but keeping track of David's love life took a lot of effort.

Before she could respond, a gleaming red Porsche barreled down the drive, pulling up alongside the Mercedes. A blond woman with a fair complexion and legs that had no end emerged from within.

Julia wasn't sure if it was envy or a hot flash that made her feverish. Christian did a double take when the woman lowered her sunglasses to reveal striking blue eyes. Yet, despite all her natural beauty, she gave off the same cold vibes as David's new home.

She wore a low-cut tank, cropped trousers, and statement sandals with leather straps circling her ankles, as though giving a fashion nod to the Romans. In her left hand she carried a white Saffiano leather wallet with a gold shoulder strap, an odd choice for a lake accessory. Julia doubted she'd ever be caught dead carrying a foam noodle.

The woman moved to David's side. He slipped his arm around

her slender waist. The other young woman joined them as well. Julia almost gasped. Was David in a *throuple*? Well, if Erika killed him over her obstructed view, at least he'd die a happy man.

"Julia, Christian, this is my girlfriend, Fiona," said David, gesturing to the woman with the captivating ice-blue eyes. "And this is Izzy, our nanny. She's helping out with the twins for the next couple of weeks."

Izzy's mouth crested into a shy smile. "Nice to meet you both," she said, extending her hand.

The hot girlfriend and the alluring nanny. Julia had heard this story before, and it seldom ended well.

Chapter 4

Izzy

It's amazing how two children could turn an hour-long drive from Burlington to Lake Timmeny into an eternity. We've arrived at the lake, but I'm not sure if my hearing will ever return to normal. If there's one thing five-year-old twins are not, it's quiet.

I couldn't wait for that car ride to be over.

At first it seemed like a good idea. David had offered to pick me up, and we arranged to meet at a Starbucks near the bus station where my mom dropped me off for my fictitious ride to my internship. Fiona, his girlfriend, wanted her car, so she was driving separately. I wasn't too worried about being alone with a stranger, since his kids would be with us, but for obvious reasons I couldn't have him come get me at home. I made my lack of transportation sound like a benefit: "It'll be a good opportunity to get to know the children," I explained during our phone call.

I waited for David curbside, coffee in hand. He was punctual, which made a good first impression. I liked his smile, too—friendly and relaxed. He was attractive for an older guy, with his dark complexion and a touch of gray flecking his hair, but he went heavy on the cologne. His skin had the outdoorsy glow of an active person. Parenting didn't seem to fluster him in the least. There wasn't a strand of his thick dark hair out of place, and I didn't notice any food stains—the marker of a harried parent—on his blue polo or dark gray shorts. This was a man in control of his life (and children). Or so I believed.

"Brody, Becca, it's so nice to meet you both," I said, shaking their tiny hands before getting settled into my seat. "I'm Izzy, and I'm going to be your nanny during vacation."

Brody stuck his tongue out at me.

"I don't want a babysitter," he declared with a pouty face that matched his voice.

David corrected the behavior gently. "Brody, we don't speak that way, it's not polite. Izzy's here to help you both have fun and we're going to treat her with kindness."

I was pleased that David had my back.

"I DON'T WANT A BABYSITTER!" Brody screamed before tossing a plastic container of Goldfish all over the immaculate carpeting of David's Mercedes.

"THOSE WERE *MY* GOLDFISH!" yelled Becca, to which Brody declared loudly that he didn't care and he wasn't a baby and he didn't need a nanny. Thick hot tears streaked down his plump, ruddy face.

Oh. My. Good. Lord.

I had no idea that two precious creatures, with angelic faces, soft brown eyes, and matching hair—an adorable ponytail on one, sweet bangs on the other—could be so impossibly loud. If David's car came equipped with an eject button, I might have deployed it. Instead, I plastered on a tense smile and assured my new boss that I had the skill and expertise to win them over.

I almost believed myself.

"This is going to be the *worstest* vacation ever," whined Brody.

"Worst vacation," corrected David tersely. "And it will be if you don't start behaving."

In the rearview mirror, I could see Brody attempting to turn me into stone with his stare. A minute later Becca screamed at the top of her lungs: "DADDY, HE STOLE MY STUFFIE!!!"

"Did not," insisted Brody, who didn't seem to care that he held the evidence (a fluffy stuffed tiger) in his lap. And this went on until David was forced to pull over, issuing a string of warnings that I could tell had zero chance of being effective.

He used all the threats I remembered from my childhood.

You're both going to be in big, big trouble.

I'm turning this car around this instant if you don't start behaving.

And . . .

When we get to the lake, you'll go straight to your rooms.

Becca screamed, "*That's not fair!*" Brody chimed in, echoing her protest against this grave injustice.

I was left thinking: *What have I gotten myself into?* I entered into this arrangement fully aware I didn't love children, but could it be that I actually *loathe* them? Either way, I wasn't going to sit passively, lamenting my plight while my eardrums burst.

Thankfully my survival instincts took over. I recalled a useful tidbit from a blog I had sourced about dealing with recalcitrant children.

"We're going to play the Quiet Game," I announced in a clipped, officious tone. "First one to talk will have to forfeit their iPad for the remainder of the drive to the lake. That is non-negotiable. Ready? Quiet Game starting in . . . one, two, three . . . *now.*"

It was as if someone hit the mute button on a TV. The decibel level went from a million to zero in a flash. I sat up straighter in my seat. Admittedly, I felt triumphant. Maybe this wouldn't be so bad after all.

David gazed at me, astonished.

"It works because it's a consequence they can understand, and it's something that will happen immediately. Add in a little competition, and you have cooperation."

David's grin stretched ear to ear. "Lucky for me you're very resourceful and extremely practical," he said, which almost made me laugh.

If I'm good at anything, it's being *impractical.*

I realize that's not something I should be proud of. Honestly, it's caused me all kinds of grief.

I always strive to do the right thing, but occasionally, my impulsivity leads me astray. Like when I went to a party and used lighter fluid to ignite a bonfire that nobody could get started. My approach proved so effective that the fire department showed up to extinguish the blaze. Or when I chopped off all my hair to donate to Locks of Love without telling my mother first. She came into the bathroom and thought I had adopted a Persian cat, until she realized what I had done. No big shock—she was horrified with the result. Then there was that time my freshman year in college, when I spent all my summer savings for textbooks on a bus ticket to New York to go to a rave with a hot guy from my journalism class. My date turned out to be a dud, but the rave was epic.

I don't do a lot of self-exploration, but I think my impulsivity is rooted in anxiety, which runs in my family. In my mother's world, a cold is pneumonia, you can drown in a tablespoon of water, and a stray dog *must* be rabid. She's a wonderful person, and I love her dearly, but with her, the glass is always half-empty and about to topple over. I've read about generational trauma, and I think she's passed her worries on to me. But instead of becoming immobilized by fear, I get so flooded with adrenaline that my rational mind shuts off.

Practical or not, it was a relief that the kids took the Quiet Game seriously. Both were silent as church mice while lost in their electronics.

"The drive seems to get harder each year," David lamented. "I wish we lived closer to the lake, but their mother is still a New Yorker, and I don't want to be far from them."

Bonus points for being a caring dad.

"Where in New York do you live?" I asked. I'm thinking Long Island, based on his accent. When you're a Vermonter you get to know the dialects of your New York neighbors.

"Manhattan, Upper East Side, near my ex," David said. "Hate the neighborhood. It's full of obnoxiously rich people."

Funny, I had assumed David was one of them. He owned a fancy new car, and when we spoke by phone, he went on and on about his massive lake house renovation. Which made me realize I had no idea what he did for a living.

"I'm a talent scout for the entertainment industry," he said in answer to my question.

"Oh, you don't need to live in LA for that?"

He brushed my assumption aside with a wave of his hand. "Nah, New York is a gold mine. TV, movies, advertising, modeling, you name it, we scout it." He looked me over in an assessing fashion. "There's actually a screen-like quality about you," he said. "If you get headshots done, you know where to send them."

Yeah, I think. *One Creepy Lane, P.O. Box Ina-pro-pro.*

Maybe it was a harmless comment, a genuine compliment, but it was a good reminder to keep my wits about me.

"But you better hurry if you're going to take me up on my offer," he added. "I might not be in the business much longer."

He smiled cryptically. I could tell he wanted me to ask the logical follow-up question, so I obliged.

"Why is that?"

"A friend of mine started a company that imports electronic components—the stuff big tech companies like Oracle and Amazon use to make hardware. He knew a semiconductor shortage was coming and had first dibs on a huge supply of these high-demand parts. He was looking for an investor to help purchase them, and I jumped at the opportunity. Let's just say, my bet paid off . . . and then some. Now I make a cut of the company profits, which is how I paid for the lake house remodel in cash. At this rate, I may be able to retire by fifty!"

And this is where David came into sharper focus. At first I put him in the Silicon Valley tech mogul category, but he's more boastful than savvy. I sense he's got street smarts, like a hustler who finally struck gold. That's not a bad thing; he's certainly a lot more down-to-earth and relatable than a Wall Street financier worth untold millions. But he seems to be something of a contradiction. He's rich, but unrefined; well-dressed, and yet somehow rough around the edges. He's definitely charming, I'll give him that. But at the same time, I get the feeling he might also play dirty.

The rest of the car ride wasn't too bad. The kids behaved for the remainder of the trip, even after Brody lost the Quiet Game twenty minutes before we reached our destination.

I texted my mother as we pulled into the driveway. I told her that I got here safely (true). Housing is fine (also true, and big and glassy). There's a great coffee shop near the office (aka the kitchen). Mostly I'll be working and it's an amazing learning opportunity (true as well). And it's also amazing how easy it is to justify my deceit.

Since Mom follows me online, I won't be posting any pictures to social. I still feel terrible lying to her, but she'd never have allowed me to come here, not in a million years.

But here I am.

The moment I get out of the car after that long ride, eager to stretch my legs, a woman standing nearby shoots me a judgmental look that can't be misinterpreted. She eyes me up and down as though the front of my shirt reads "Hussy" and the back of it "Ho." This must be Julia, with her daughter, Taylor. David gave me the rundown on the lake crew before we arrived. While Julia glares, Taylor is oblivious to my presence. That's because Brody and Becca are all over her like excited puppies.

I know I should introduce myself, it's the polite thing to do, but I feel intimidated (not to mention judged) by these wealthy people. This isn't my scene: new home, fancy cars. Yikes, I'm the classic fish out of water. Maybe that will change with time. We have two weeks together, and it would be nice to make a friend, though it certainly won't be with the woman who has already decided I'm a slut.

I keep a close eye on Brody and Becca, but from a distance. They're safe, having fun with Taylor and the sweet lab I'm assuming belongs to one of the families here, but already I'm stressed about the water. Pools have enclosures; the shoreline here is wide open and full of peril. I must remember to ask David if there are chimes on the doors to notify me if someone goes outside. A creeping sense of dread works its way up my legs. I give myself a little pep talk, remembering all the research I did in preparation for this role.

While I'm lost in a sea of worries (okay, a lake of them), David is busy showing off his new home to Julia, who is clearly unimpressed. With hands on her hips, she looks ready for a gunslinging standoff. I don't know what it looked like before, but obviously the changes are enough to incense David's neighbor and longtime friend.

I step back, instinctively removing myself from the line of fire, when I hear a car speed down the drive. It's Fiona in her fancy red Porsche, driving too fast for the dirt road and the presence of children and pets. She comes to an abrupt halt and gracefully steps out of the vehicle, approaching with the swagger of a starlet. She momentarily draws everyone's attention away from the glass house.

I haven't had time to get to know Fiona and David as a couple, but I don't get the sense that they're in it for the long haul. And it's not just the evident age difference giving me that impression. Fiona greets David with a light squeeze of his arm. There's no big hug, no beaming smile, no *reunited and it feels so good.*

"Julia, Christian, this is Fiona," says David. I swear I catch her flinch, ever so slightly, when he wraps his arm around her, as though claiming his prize.

I don't like to judge by appearances, especially after Julia did that to me, but I understand David's interest. Fiona's quite the beauty with pouty lips, luscious long blond hair, smooth skin, and high cheekbones—qualities that David *should* scout for his talent business. Elite New Yorkers constantly invade Vermont, so I'm familiar with the women who wear brand names like armor and change cars the way I do shoes. Fiona's not from that world, unless hip-hugging pants and tight-fitting halter tops are now Upper East Side staples.

She's got sandals with Roman laces on her feet, which is hardly a sensible choice for the woods, but hopefully she packed more location-appropriate garments in the purple wheelie bag she drags behind her.

When David introduces me as the nanny, I almost look around for another Izzy, someone who is exceptional at time management, maybe speaks a foreign language (it's *so* good for the kids), knows how to cook, and can turn a ball of yarn into an age-appropriate craft project. It takes a beat too long to realize *she is me,* but I extend my hand in time. It goes first to Judgy Julia and then to Christian, who seems friendly and easygoing enough. But at this point, the dog has my vote for best member of the family.

"We got super lucky with Izzy," says David. "Our last nanny quit without warning. Left us in a real pickle. Thankfully, Izzy answered our ad. We've only got her for vacation, but we're hoping she'll stay with us for the rest of the summer."

I smile at David like it's a real possibility. "Why don't I take the twins inside and get them settled," I say, hoping I sound like someone who has an actual clue.

David's eyes light up. He takes out his phone and presses some buttons. A noise emanates from the house, as if the structure is talking to him.

"The home is fully remote," he boasts. "Heat, AC, alarms, locks, lights—everything is controlled by an app."

He presses another button that lowers a massive cellular shade halfway down one of the large windows overlooking the lake. It's pretty cool, though I suspect that shade costs half a semester's tuition.

Julia is less enamored. She stands up straighter, glaring at David. "So much for our view through your windows," she snips.

Wait, did my new boss knowingly block Judgy Julia's view? Who does something like that to his friends?

David reverses the blind. "I'm not keeping it down," he says. "That's a promise. But Fiona and I need *some* privacy from time to time . . . if you know what I mean."

He punctuates his unnecessary comment with a lecherous wink, which is repugnant, but perhaps not out of character. I recall the look he gave me in the car. I can't help but wonder about the circumstances surrounding my predecessor's sudden departure.

I decide to vacate before things get weirder. "Becca, Brody, let's go inside," I call out.

But as I look around, I realize the kids who had been jumping all over Taylor a second ago are nowhere to be seen. My heart leaps into my throat. Taylor is there, engrossed in her phone, but the kids are no longer with her.

I endure another stab of panic, thinking they've wandered off to the water. A nightmarish vision of a massive police response three minutes into my job—boats dredging the lake—momentarily hijacks my brain. But it's quickly dispelled by a loud honk from Fiona's Porsche. Everyone jumps, eliciting laughter from Brody and Becca, who had snuck into the car unnoticed by me—their ever-watchful nanny.

I rush over to them, throwing Fiona a sheepish smile. I encourage both children to exit the vehicle before they're inspired to press the horn again, or worse, hit the ignition button.

"Hey, Brody, Becca . . . let's go inside. You must be hungry after the drive. I'll fix us a snack." David hired some local gofer to stock the fridge, so there should be plenty of options.

Both children follow me indoors without protest.

Before I go digging through the pantry, I pause to look around. The furniture is primarily light-colored, all whites and light grays. *Great. The whole place is like a stain magnet.* I won't let the kids snack on the pristine new couch, not that they'd even want to. The cushions look like they're made of cement. What little art there is on the walls looks generic. Even though it's a warm summer day, it feels cold and barren inside, with the AC set to Arctic Blast.

A scent in the air reminds me of being in a furniture store. It's that just-opened, freshly unwrapped odor, as if the entire house is off-gassing. This is in stark contrast to my home, which is warm and inviting, full of worn, comfortable chairs.

At least David took his children into consideration. There are a pair of beanbag chairs in front of a television, perfect for munching on the cheese sticks, apple slices, and graham crackers I plate for them. Just when I'm praising my nannying skills, the chilly air gets even colder as Fiona barges through the door, striding toward me in a huff.

She comes to an abrupt stop, her frosty blue eyes somehow fiery, mouth pressed into a thin, tight line of disapproval. "Please do not allow the children to use my Porsche as a toy," she orders.

"But . . . but I didn't," I protest, unable to remove the shake from my voice. "As soon as I saw them, I brought them inside for a snack."

"They shouldn't have been in the car in the first place," she snaps back. "A nanny should always be ahead of the game. If you'd been paying proper attention, this wouldn't have happened."

Fiona storms off before I can offer an apology. I'm left feeling assaulted, like she slapped me across the face. The nerve of that woman! She acts like she's the expert on parenting, when I know for a fact she doesn't have kids of her own. And she's not even my boss. I work for David, but I guess she's marking her territory, and I just got sprayed.

A door closes softly to my right. Turning, I see Taylor setting down a couple of suitcases.

"Sorry, my mom wanted privacy to tear into David, so she asked me to help unpack his car. I didn't mean to intrude." She offers an apologetic half smile that tells me she overheard the whole embarrassing exchange with Fiona. Taylor adds, "For what it's worth, she seems like a total bitch. If you ever need to get away, come visit us—anytime."

"Thanks for the offer," I say, meaning it. "At least with all these windows you'll see if she tries to murder me in my sleep."

We both laugh, lightening the mood.

"I'm Taylor," she says.

"Izzy," I return. "Really nice to meet you."

And while I'm still reeling from Fiona's lashing, I feel a small sense of relief that I might make a friend here after all. I just can't get so close that she figures out my real reason for coming to the lake.

Chapter 5

Julia

Julia placed her suitcase on the floor in the bedroom next to the Shaker-style dresser her grandfather had crafted from the same wood he had used to build the house. She plopped down onto the four-poster bed, nestling into the feel of the soft, aged quilt made by her beloved aunt Lorraine. Everywhere she looked, memories of love and family surrounded her, stretching back to her earliest days.

The ceiling's exposed beams made Julia feel like she'd stepped back in time to *The Waltons* or *Little House on the Prairie* (aka the saddest show on television). Even the beautiful stained-glass lamps were from another era, and the colorful folk art Julia had collected from local artists added to the room's charm.

What Julia loved most, however, was the porthole window cut into the wall over the bed. As a little girl, she'd relished coming into what was then her parents' bedroom. To see the lake through the round window, Julia needed to stand on her tiptoes. Looking out at the water, she'd imagine herself in a ship, traveling across a vast ocean to a distant land inhabited by pirates, fairies, and princes.

When she peeked out the porthole now, she still had a view of the water—but also of David's jarringly modern house.

"*You can see the lake through my windows,*" she said, mocking him.

Julia fully intended to turn her indignation into a passive-aggressive assault once their annual Scrabble night commenced. She'd do all she could to make each word a rebuke of David's thoughtlessness.

Aghast. Dismayed. Sickened. Perturbed (that would score big). *Betrayed.*

There. That summed it up.

David might not get the message, but Julia would take pride in her clever revenge.

While they were outside, she'd asked David what on earth had prompted him to build a house more than twice the size of his previous home. His answer, no surprise, proved unsatisfactory, not to mention mildly manipulative.

"You know my father, Mr. Fix-it. He always wanted to add an addition and have lots of grandchildren to fill the space. Now his dream is a reality. How beautiful is that? He may not be here to enjoy it, but I know he'd be impressed with what I made for Brody and Becca."

There was so much to unpack in that little soliloquy that Julia had been rendered speechless. She was supposed to sacrifice their view so that a *dead guy* could be impressed? *Oh, give me a break.* But of course, it did pull at her heartstrings because she knew how much the loss of his father had affected David. And true to form, he had flipped the narrative around to make himself look like a hero.

"And just think what a nice modern house will do for *your* home's value."

Julia could hardly stifle a laugh. But he was trying—she gave him credit for that. She always felt conflicted when it came to David. He had his grand ego, but she also knew his softer side. David had his kids later in life than Erika and Julia, so he had been like an uncle to Taylor and Lucas.

It was David who bought Lucas his first guitar and set him up with lessons. And when Taylor got a concussion playing field hockey, David called in a favor from a top neurologist, who agreed to take the case on short notice. He never failed to recognize the kids' birthdays, sometimes with extravagant gifts, but what mattered most was that he treated them like family. And while you might not always like your family, more often than not, you love them.

Sigh. At least she was here, in her happy place, and all she could do was wait until Erika arrived. Then she'd have someone to commiserate with, as Christian was too busy fawning over David's newfound wealth to be supportive in that arena.

Julia climbed from the bed, shaking off her annoyance. There was nothing to be done about it now, other than to stop obsessing. *Good luck with that.*

In the hallway, she paused to listen. All was quiet, unsettlingly so. In times past, Julia would have heard Taylor's fast-moving feet racing up and down the stairs, or drawers slamming as she rummaged for her bathing suit. Julia and Christian had planned on having two children, but almost ended up divorced over his drinking. Even when Christian got sober, the marriage remained strained. It had never felt like the right time to bring another child into the picture. While she didn't regret the choice exactly, had she understood how quickly time passed, how fast *small* would grow up to be *tall*, she might have overlooked some of their marital fissures to have more days with tiny feet and little hands.

Christian appeared at the bottom of the stairs on Julia's way down. She recognized the excited look in his eyes. It usually spelled trouble.

"Honey, check this out," he said, thrusting a pamphlet into her hands before she reached the final step. "I found this in our mailbox. It's from a company called EcoCitizen. They're offering a burial service where you convert your ashes into a tree through a biodegradable urn."

Julia gave the pamphlet a cursory once-over, squinting as she puzzled it out. "Wait, is this something you actually want to *do*?"

Christian nodded vigorously. His eyes went big. "Yeah, I want to do it," he said emphatically. "A surplus of coffins can't be healthy for the environment. It might even be a good business for *us* to start."

Great, another venture to go down the drain. Julia groaned. "So, what you're telling me is that I have to worry about watering you and keeping you alive even *after* you're dead?"

Christian returned an uncertain nod.

"That's gonna be a hard pass for me," she said.

Before he could protest, Julia heard the sound of car tires approaching. She and Christian exchanged a knowing glance. *It might be David who'd soon be turned into a tree.* She led Christian outside through the front door.

Erika and Rick Sullivan emerged from a gleaming silver Audi. They'd arrived from Greenwich, Connecticut, where Erika's thriving legal practice was based and Rick worked nearby as a hunting and fishing guide. Considering them as a pair, Julia couldn't help but think of that Donny and Marie song about her being a little bit country and him a little bit rock and roll. Only it was Erika who sparkled with city vibes. Her pale skin reflected the light on account of the copious amounts of sunscreen she'd applied.

Opposites may attract, but they don't always mix (hello, oil and water). While they had an enduring marriage, Rick and Erika doled out compliments to each other with the stinginess of misers. If you asked Erika, she'd say her husband didn't really have a job, but rather a modestly paying hunting hobby, and he was too hard on Lucas for trying to do the same with his music. Rick's biggest gripe about Erika was that she didn't have an off switch when it came to work. He wasn't wrong.

No surprise, Erika was on her phone. She and her job were a toxic couple: a relationship built on arguing, combined with an unwillingness to leave. She held a finger up to Julia—*done in a second*—like she was initiating a countdown to vacation.

She got out of the car, Rick trailing behind her. He was the handsome, outdoorsy, blue-collar type with strong arms and an equally strong jawline. Here was a man who could get a honey-do list done, and done well. But he was still a local yokel who'd grown up on the lake, honing his skills as a fisherman and hunter.

Also, he loved guns. He loved buying them. He loved shooting them for fun, which never made sense to Julia—not that hunting did, either. Who would shoot a defenseless little deer and call it a sport? Erika's husband, that's who. A few years back, he'd killed a buck and brought the frozen meat to their annual vacation, where he roasted venison that everyone felt obliged to sample. It tasted like everything the poor creature ate—mainly leaves, acorns, and grass. Julia preferred having less of a connection to the food she consumed, a stance she understood was full of contradictions.

Rick arrived ready to relax, dressed in ripped jeans and a boxy gray T-shirt. The physique he had honed working outdoors had turned doughy from his softer lifestyle, thanks primarily to Erika's high salary and his evident love of beer. *Middle age gets us all.* But he was a loyal, committed family man, which made him more attractive. His tan baseball hat partially covered a receding hairline, which he compensated for with a beard that had become like a tangle of weeds, partly obscuring his best attribute: his charming smile.

In contrast, Erika showed up dressed for a fancy brunch. She wore the cutest navy chambray shirtdress, which deepened the color of her luscious red hair. She opted for comfortable slide-on sandals adorned with gold studs that matched her hoop earrings. Her Hollywood-style sunglasses concealed her green eyes, providing an air of mystery.

When Rick and Erika first had a fling at the lake as teens, nobody expected it to last the summer, let alone nearly twenty-five years of marriage. In contrast, Julia and Christian appeared to be a perfect match. They had met in college, both studying some form of business. Julia yearned to get into nonprofit work—she wanted to make a difference in the world. Christian's focus was finance, but ultimately he found work in sales using his natural enthusiasm and likability.

They came from similar backgrounds and shared a vision for their future. No one would have doubted their compatibility, yet they were a couple that had survived infidelity, addiction, and more. Their marriage had been on shaky ground for years, whereas Erika and Rick appeared to be a more typical married couple—resigned to a destiny of togetherness, warts and all, without any grand upheavals to shake the foundation.

Erika finished her call with an exasperated exhale, put her phone away (that wouldn't last long), and breezed over to Julia. As she and Rick approached, Julia was struck with an unwelcome thought about the pair's intimacy. It would be like a songbird mating with a grizzly bear. She banished the visual from her mind. Despite the odd coupling, they'd had a child, Lucas, whom Taylor dreaded seeing for unknown reasons and who wouldn't be at the lake this year—or so Erika had said.

But (surprise, surprise) the information Julia had relayed to Taylor proved incorrect. As Rick and Erika approached, Lucas slid his lanky frame out of the car, standing almost as tall as his father. Like his dad, he wore a baggy T-shirt and loose-fitting jeans—"casual cool" was how Julia would describe his style.

He had been shy and introspective as a child, but found his voice when he started playing guitar in middle school. Years later, he was proficient in the instrument and had become a good singer as well. He had that long musician hair that drove girls wild, along with brooding eyes and an inscrutable expression that made him even more intriguing. He gave off artist vibes, and Julia often wondered if he was composing music in his head while everyone else was chitchatting.

Erika had gushed about the kids collaborating on a song during the college tour, with Taylor using her poetry as the lyrics. *What happened between then and now to make Taylor so fretful of seeing him?* Julia wondered if music could repair their friendship. Perhaps they could create another song together at the lake. It was a nice thought, but one tinged with idealism.

Oh, if only people could sort out this world with clever wordplay and angst-ridden melodies. Julia was aware that Lucas wanted to pursue music full time. It wasn't her place to say anything. He would learn on his own that mortgage payments, car loans, and dead-end jobs could make every note ring sour. Or maybe not. Christian, the dreamer, seemed to have missed that life memo.

Lucas collected his suitcase and guitar from the car and dragged behind his parents. Julia searched for Taylor, but she was nowhere to be found. Probably for the best—*one drama at a time, please.*

At least Julia didn't have to warn Erika that she was in for bad news. David's new home loomed before them like a giant see-through abomination. Julia expected a full-blown explosion. It was obvious even from a distance that David's goliath would be blocking Erika's precious view.

But instead of a fit of rage or the threat of a lawsuit, Erika opened her arms wide and wrapped them around Julia so tightly the embrace momentarily took her breath away.

Erika pulled back, keeping her hands affixed to Julia's shoulders, a broad smile brightening her celestial face. "Oh my god, it is *so* good to see you," she said, still beaming. "I'm ridiculously happy to be here, and I can't wait to do absolutely *nothing* for a couple of weeks."

She let out a weighty sigh, suggesting Erika had been doing too much of everything for too long. Now it was time for cocktails, sunsets, and lazy paddles in the canoe. But all that should have taken a back seat to the glass house. Erika was petite, but she had the warrior gene, which many prosecutors in Connecticut had come to know firsthand. She could grow ten sizes taller when she was battling injustice, and David's new showpiece certainly fit the bill.

"Aren't you freaking out?" Julia asked, casting her thumb over her shoulder.

Erika startled as though she'd been plucked out of a daze. "Oh, well, yeah . . . it's a lot bigger than I thought."

Julie blinked incredulously. "That's it? That's your take—bigger than you thought? Erika, he's blocking your fucking view."

"Maybe, but we're always down by the water anyway. That's all I need, especially after dealing with the worst case of my career."

Erika wasn't prone to hyperbole, except when discussing her law practice, where every case was brutal and every judge had it out for her.

"It was a BUI case—boating under the influence—and unfortunately the judge is a sailor herself. In pretrial she basically insinuated that my client was guilty because nobody would chart a course like he did *unless* he was drunk. Absolute rubbish, so naturally, we won. But the whole thing was ridiculous."

"I'm glad you won, and if I'm ever in legal hot water, I certainly know who to call. But, Erika, it's crazy what David did."

God, how she wanted an ally, or even a dollop of validation. She might not have received the expected reaction from Erika, but Julia anticipated that Rick would reset the tone. He could blaze hotter than his wife when aggrieved. He did kill things for a living, after all. She braced herself for a Rick tirade—thunderous voice, pounding fists, and ominous threats.

Instead of a rampage, Rick shrugged as he set his suitcase down. "It's not that bad," he said. "Lots of windows. Dave was right about that. And look at all the trees he cleared. That's one less problem we have to deal with."

Julia was stunned. "You *knew*?" she asked.

Rick and Erika exchanged glances like two people trying to get their stories straight. Rick attempted to explain.

"My folks checked on the progress, gave us some early reports, saw a lot of land cleared, so we knew it would be big. Honestly, I'm surprised how fast it went up. Modular homes have become really sophisticated."

At least one part of that story made sense. Rick was close with his parents who stayed in the area after they sold off their nearby camping ground. Julia understood they were his inspiration for getting into the fish and game business. Rick was a basic sort; there weren't a lot of layers to his onion. He was a what-you-see-is-what-you-get kind of guy. But what Julia saw baffled her. Where was the shock, the fury?

Christian spoke up. "We all knew Dave was doing an addition, honey. It shouldn't be a surprise that he went a little over the top. His company is on fire . . . unlike *ours*."

Julia picked up the jealous undertones, but what galled her was the side-eye he gave her. On top of suggesting she was overreacting, somehow, without words, Christian managed to make Julia feel responsible for their business's downward trajectory. Then again, taking responsibility wasn't something that came easily to him.

"David said he was keeping you in the loop," Erika said, sounding too much like a defense attorney for Julia's liking. "If you were upset, we figured you'd have called. I guess we assumed everyone was accepting of it. And you know how David is—he never goes small."

That was true as well. David's creed was if a little was good, a lot must be better.

But Rick and Erika perplexed Julia beyond measure. There simply had to be more to the story than they were letting on.

But what?

Chapter 6

Izzy

So this is what a two-week lake getaway looks like. There's a roaring blaze in the stone firepit, fresh air bathing my skin, waves gently lapping the shoreline, a happy dog bounding about, the kids running around with sparklers, and the smell of burgers and hot dogs sizzling on the grill. Kenny Chesney is playing through portable speakers, but not loud enough to drown out the haunting wail of loons calling back and forth, or the pleasing hum of night critters. I'm accustomed to beautiful star-drenched summer nights, but tonight the sky looks incredibly full, like someone spread a bag of shimmering diamonds across a velvety black cloth.

My mom would disapprove of the DEET I've lathered on, but I'm desperate, and she's not here to protest. As a family, we've had some nice vacations together, but we always kept it simple (and cheap). We're working-class Vermonters, not the second-home, ski-trip types. Mom is an elementary school teacher, and my father runs a grocery store. He started behind the deli counter, worked his way up to manager, and then became a regional manager for a new supermarket chain. Unfortunately, that meant he had to move to Arizona. At least we have FaceTime, and we visit each other a couple of times each year.

My parents have been doing better since the divorce. Well, my father is, anyway. He's dating a woman who took his blood. No, she's not a vampire. She's a Red Cross volunteer. They hit it off at a local blood drive. He's got a thing for bad dad jokes, and told me the one that made her laugh.

"A priest, an imam, and a rabbit walk into a blood bank. The rabbit says, 'I think I might be a type O.'"

I admit that made me chuckle. The phlebotomist accepted his dinner invitation only after Dad had a cookie and some juice to ensure he wasn't delirious.

The three couples here are enjoying plenty of laughs themselves. Fiona has planted herself on David's lap in a territorial way. She has coconuts for boobs, too round to be true, contained inside a string bikini top, her bottom half covered in a red satin wrap skirt. She looks hotter than the fire.

Rick operates the grill, while Erika plates the food. Those two act like a well-oiled team, as do Christian and Julia, who lounge in adjacent Adirondack chairs, chatting pleasantly and sharing intimate smiles from time to time. But not all are joyful. Taylor and Lucas don't want to play in the same sandbox. She's off by herself on her phone, and he's doing the same thing on the opposite side of the beach.

And I'm struggling with the twins. My parents' divorce hasn't soured me on the idea of marriage, but these kids are a cold-water bath to my future prospects of becoming a mother. I'm stunned the day isn't over yet. It feels as though I've been on the job for a week. I can't count the number of squabbles, outbursts, and breakdowns I've already refereed.

Brody dropped his hot dog on the ground, and the way he cried, you'd have thought he broke his arm. Once he understood that we could make another, he settled.

As I was roasting him a second dog, Becca started in on her string of questions. At first it was cute. *Where are you from? Where do you go to school? Are you married? Do you have a boyfriend?* It kept going from there: *How hot is the fire? What are marshmallows made of?* (I didn't have the heart to tell her about gelatin.) *What's that star? And that one? And that one? And . . .*

This went on until I wanted to rip the hair out of my head one follicle at a time. And talk about fussiness. Becca turned her nose up at everything I tried to feed her. *It's too hot. It's too cold. That's too slimy. It's too yucky. I don't like that, or that, or that . . . no, no, and no.*

I found myself using the same ludicrous threats as David.

"Then I guess you won't eat anything ever again," I said, as I tossed her paper plate—which was filled with enough food options to qualify as a buffet—into the trash.

I fear I am not experienced, capable, or tolerant enough to keep these two in check for the duration. I might have to leave early for the sake of my mental health, ashamed and embarrassed. Even worse, that would mean abandoning my reason for being here, which I could sum up in two words: true crime.

I started college as a psych major before switching to journalism to pursue my passion. I doubt there's a true crime podcast I haven't met. *Bone Ranch. Dr. Dead. Crime Addict.* I've heard them all, though I certainly didn't put my obsession with serial killers on my nanny application.

I think my compulsion is rooted in fear. It's all about staring down the dragon from the cushy comfort of my bed without being directly in the line of fire. According to a psychology professor I interviewed for a feature story about our cultural fascination with murder shows, controlled exposure to something frightening gives us a safe way to subconsciously develop coping mechanisms.

When I saw the story about human remains found not too far from here, I had to come and investigate. But where was I going to stay? There are not a lot of jobs that provide housing, and what I needed to accomplish couldn't be done in a day or two. Luckily, my Google Alert for Lake Timmeny delivered the answer directly to my inbox.

This is more than a job, it's a calling. I remind myself that I can endure anything, even a sibling squabble that amounts to two humans screeching back and forth at each other: "Am not!" "Are too!"

To halt the ruckus, I deploy a secret weapon of the nanny trade: sugar.

"Let's make s'mores," I say, with a clap of my hands that gets their attention.

Brody takes tremendous pleasure in turning his marshmallow into a flaming ball of burning goo. He swirls it around like he's doing a Hawaiian fire dance, while Fiona keeps her reproachful eyes on me. *Letting a five-year-old play with fire?* But so be it. Fiona and I don't have to be best friends. We don't have to be friends at all. I've got a job to do.

Unfortunately, I don't appear to be doing it very well. While Brody captivates me with his pyrotechnic skills, I completely lose sight of Becca. My eyes go to the lake and my mind to the darkest place imaginable. My panic is short-lived when David approaches with his daughter in his arms. She kicks outward in a playful struggle to free herself from his grasp as I prepare myself to be fired.

"Not to worry," David says following my string of apologies. "This one's quite slippery, especially when she wants her iPad."

"I won't let it happen again," I assure him, knowing full well I've just given a piecrust promise: easily made, easily broken. That's lifted directly from *Mary Poppins.* There is no better training for the nanny trade than Mary, and I think this quote is as astute as it is self-explanatory.

Becca squirms in David's arms until he sets her down. I notice how she has a blue glow stick bracelet wrapped multiple times around her slender wrist. It makes her easier to spot in the dark. David probably came up with the idea, based on experience. Since he didn't tell me she was a roamer, I try not to feel too bad about my slipup. But still, piecrust promise or not, I *must* be more vigilant.

"I'm really sorry," I say again. "I was so focused on Brody and the hot marshmallows, I just . . ."

David places his hand on my shoulder. His fingers gently touch my skin. I don't know what to make of it, or how to respond. A tingle of apprehension zips through me. It could be benign, but it could also be totally inappropriate. I think of my predecessor who quit so unexpectedly. No wonder Fiona is on the defensive, though I suspect she may be blaming the wrong person. I guess it's not just Becca I have to keep my eyes on.

David releases his grip. "She's a wanderer, but doesn't go far and knows to stay out of the water," he assures me. He grabs a beer from a six-pack on a table, twists the top before taking a long swig. "Fiona, on the other hand—now that's a different story."

I perk up. *What does that mean?*

David can read the question in my eyes. "She sleepwalks," he explains, and takes another drink.

"I've never known anybody who did that," I say.

"I guess it's happened off and on for most of her life," says David. "But it's gotten worse since she started taking Ambien for her insomnia. Her doctor lowered the dose, so it's better now, but not entirely cured."

I'm fairly certain Fiona wouldn't want us discussing her medical history, and I can't help but wonder what other boundaries David feels comfortable crossing.

He continues, as if we're talking about the weather. "Usually, she just goes to the fridge for a midnight snack, which she later denies." He says this with a chuckle, but if Fiona is consuming extra calories, they sure don't show on her figure.

I turn my attention to the children. They make a great excuse for exiting an awkward conversation. Becca is trying to ride the poor dog like she's a pony. God bless Nutmeg, who basically allows it. Before I have a chance to make my getaway, the music shuts off and Erika's lilting voice draws all eyes to her.

"Everyone, everyone!" she calls out. In her hand, she holds a pitcher filled with glowing blue liquid, like Becca's bracelet has been turned into a drink. "The Lake Escape cocktails are ready. Come and get 'em!" She holds the pitcher high to a rousing caterwaul of hoots and hollers from the adults, with Fiona's voice the loudest of all.

David leans toward me. "It's one of our many lake traditions," he explains. "We always kick off vacation by toasting with Erika's famous specialty drink, the Lake Escape, served only on the first night. She invented it in the Shack." I can hear the nostalgia in his voice. There's a story here.

"The Shack?" I ask.

"It's a one-room clubhouse we found in the woods," he explains. "Someone built it before our time, but left it abandoned, so we took it over when we were teenagers. It was pretty run-down, but we didn't care. It was a good place to party. And to make up drinks like the Lake Escape, thanks to the booze we snuck from our parents' liquor cabinets. Turned out rum, peach schnapps, a hearty splash of blue curaçao, and Sprite made quite the cocktail." His face lights up as he smiles at his youthful indiscretions.

"I haven't been there in ages—don't even know if the Shack is still standing." He pauses. His excited look returns. "Maybe I'll take you and the kids on an adventure to see what's left of it," he says. "They'll think it's awesome. Should be easy enough to find. It's down the road, a half mile tops. There's a path that leads to it, near an old knotted oak tree."

"Sounds great," I say.

"But no drinking—you're on the job." He laughs at his own lame joke, then brightens some more. "There is a nonalcoholic blue punch version of the Lake Escape if you want to try it."

Considering that the drink reminds me of something radioactive, I pass. Though I notice that Erika fills Christian's cup from the nonalcoholic pitcher David had offered me.

Interesting.

The frosty dynamic between Taylor and Lucas hasn't thawed with or without the booze. I haven't seen Taylor drinking, but surprisingly Erika has no qualms serving her son from the alcoholic pitcher. He drinks it greedily before going for a refill.

"Stop trying to be the cool mom," Rick scolds.

"It's better if you know what they're drinking and where," Erika bites back.

Interesting as well. I haven't been here long, but I can already tell there are three couples and three sets of problems, with a big glass house in the center of it all.

I redirect my focus to Lucas. He arrived carrying a guitar. With his long hair and band T-shirt, I'm thinking he's a rocker with a burgeoning substance abuse problem. Unfortunately, that's my kind of guy. He certainly gives off warning signs like they're pheromones. Be still, my heart.

Taylor stays close to her parents, sullen and disengaged. We haven't had time to talk since she overheard Fiona scolding me. I'm curious to know more about her and her obvious discomfort with Rocker Boy.

I can certainly see how he'd get to her. He's captivating. Given his brooding intensity, I'll bet anything he's a songwriter. What I know for sure is, if I wasn't working, I'd be following him around like a drooling groupie. I might be in college, but I'm only a year older, so age isn't a big factor. Even so, I know it's wise to keep my distance.

Something tells me Taylor is exhibiting signs of a recent breakup: gloomy, removed, and detached. I wonder if she's nursing a broken heart and Lucas is the cause. When I get a moment away from the twins, I'll reach out to see if she needs someone to talk to. She was kind enough to offer me a safe haven from Fiona, so I should return the gesture.

But first we gather around the stone firepit, our faces strangely lit by the flickering flames.

"Cheers, everyone," says Erika, hoisting her drink high. All join in, even Taylor, who can't seem to find her smile.

Becca and Brody are essentially glued to my leg, each with a juice box in hand. They're both dirty and smell like smoke. They'll need baths, I suppose. I can only imagine how that will go. Washing cats might be easier.

"I can't tell you how happy I am to be together again," Erika continues. Her hair is the color of the fire, and her eyes sparkle. "I'm so grateful to be here with my best friends. I know our lives are busier than ever, but I think it's wonderful that we still prioritize one another and our lake vacation. I know my father would be happy that we're here together. I can't believe he's been gone seven years now." Erika pauses as she raises her glass higher toward the heavens. "Cheers to Cormac—I miss you, Dad—and cheers to lifelong friendships."

I don't want to break the solemnity of the moment, but Brody is bouncing on his heels and I'm certain he needs to pee. I alert David, who nods, and off I go, back to the house, both kids in tow.

When we return, the scene has shifted, with everyone gathered at the lakeshore. The air has taken on a tension that wasn't there before. As I near the water's edge, I see three Roman candles buried in the sand. Christian and Julia stand by one; Erika, Rick, and Lucas by another; and David and Fiona are at the third. Taylor keeps her distance, earning a frustrated look from her mother.

"Come on, sweetheart," Julia encourages. "It's tradition. The youngest in each family lights the candle."

"They have to be old enough to use a lighter," David says for my benefit. "We're not letting the twins play with fire anytime soon."

I cringe inwardly, hoping he didn't see Brody with his burning marshmallow.

Tradition or not, Taylor isn't budging. She's dug her feet in the sand, more like a stubborn child than a senior in high school. If her mother paid closer attention, she'd know it was a statement, probably in protest of Lucas.

I'm now certain there *was* a romance between these two, and someone got hurt, but it doesn't seem like Lucas is pining. He's *that* guy—the one with the sexy hair, slender torso, pale jeans that hug his hips just so, eyes cool like moonbeams, a mouth meant for kissing, someone with a touch of the bad boy who could draw you in, spin you around, and leave you breathless and dizzy.

Eventually Julia gives up and lights the candle herself, while Lucas and Fiona do the same. They step back a safe distance as the cardboard tubes spit out colored orbs that arc high into the night sky. The fireworks cast a brilliant light over the smooth water before extinguishing on contact.

I watch the fireballs disappear, one by one. But it's strange. This ritual that's meant to symbolize the exciting start of a summer vacation leaves me feeling like something has come to an end.

Chapter 7

Julia

Everything was in place. Julia had her specialty drink in hand, and after her second, perhaps all her worries would melt away. But this night, the top contender for most inebriated was undoubtedly Fiona. She sucked back Lake Escapes with the urgency of a kid downing a Slurpee. Her full, heart-shaped lips were tinged blue, like a goth girl's makeup. It was how a recent college grad would behave—which Julia figured was only eight years ago for Fiona, not twenty-eight like the rest of the adults. Not that she should judge. She already had lingering guilt for having made assumptions about Izzy. *Points for self-awareness?*

The bonfire was roaring and the background music was perfect. The set list Christian curated was just the right blend of classic and modern, country and rock. They had plated the burgers and dogs, toasted to Cormac, fired off the Roman candles (albeit without Taylor's participation). Vacation was officially on—yet the knot of tension at the back of Julia's neck wouldn't go away.

Julia chided herself. Here she was, at the lake with Erika and David, a scene so familiar it felt like home, but she was unable to relax. If only she could recapture the magic of the past. They were some of the best times of her life. Julia's mind catapulted her back to age fifteen, when she was younger than Taylor.

. . .

It was after midnight, and they'd swum out to the raft on a dare. She couldn't remember if it was David or Erika who had issued the challenge, but all were game.

The swim was invigorating. The lake water felt holy, like Julia was immersing herself in a spiritual cleanse. She opened her eyes underwater. The blackness should have frightened her, but it felt oddly comforting. She used the raft to press herself up and out. The water was warmer than the air, causing her skin to prickle, but soon David was lying on his back to one side of her with Erika on the other, and their wet bodies stuck together, providing welcome heat. But it was more than that. In the dark, she could barely make out the contours of their forms. It was hard to tell where she ended and they began. They were one being.

The trio gazed up at the dark sky, awed by the sprinkling of white lights above them.

"The next closest star after the sun is four point three light-years away, but you can't see it with the naked eye because the light's too low," David said.

"I don't get how far that is," Erika confessed. "I mean, I know it's far, but, like, what does that really mean?"

David pointed to one of the brightest stars. "That star there is Vega. My dad taught me that."

All were quiet for a moment. David's father had died the year before, in the spring, and the mere mention of him felt fraught, the wound still fresh.

"That star is twenty-five light-years from Earth, meaning the light that we see right now is actually older than us by a decade."

Erika exhaled. "I feel so small," she marveled.

Julia could relate.

"The ancients knew to revere the heavens," David said. "They understood that our lives are fleeting, but the universe is vast and powerful."

For someone who could be egotistical, pushy, and loved making inappropriate sexual innuendos, David often surprised Julia with his depth.

"Let's make a wish," Julia suggested, "to that star, and in twenty-five years, when the light finally reaches us, it'll come true."

"Oooh, I love it," Erika cooed. "I'll go first. I wish—"

"You can't tell everyone your wish," David cut in. "Then it won't come true. Everyone knows that."

But they weren't separate people, not in Julia's mind. Tonight, three had become one.

"We belong to each other and to the lake," she said, her words coating them like the droplets of water clinging to their skin.

"Fine, fine," David relented. "But I'll go first. I wish to be a millionaire."

"How unselfish of you," said Julia with a laugh. "You sounded so deep a moment ago."

She meant it as a joke, but her comment struck a nerve.

"People are unreliable. Money is not," David retorted, a catch in his voice.

Julia reached for his hand, thinking maybe it was the loss of his father, the shocking reality that our lives are transient, that made David yearn for riches. It was certainly a safer choice, offering endless adventure and distraction, and never leading to heartbreak.

"In twenty-five years, I'm not sure how far a million will get you," said Erika. "What about you, Jules?"

"Me? . . . Hmm . . . I'll go for world peace."

David chuckled. "I think we need a star over a thousand light-years away for that to come true."

They all laughed.

"Now you, Erika," said Julia.

Erika fell silent. In the quiet, Julia connected to the rhythm of the night, the soothing sound of the wind through the leaves, the brilliant hum of life, the air cool and rejuvenating. But mostly she felt gratitude for her friends, the people who meant the most to her, outside of her parents.

"I wish that, twenty-five years from now, we're just like this," Erika said, burrowing even closer to her friends, her voice brimming

with hopefulness. "Together. That we'll always be here for each other, no matter what. That we won't let each other down, not ever."

Now look at them. David was off with Fiona, all over her as if clinging to a life preserver.

Meanwhile, Erika and Rick kept to themselves, continuing to behave as though nothing was amiss. They lounged on chairs, wrapped in cozy blankets, sucking down their respective drinks, and chatting quietly.

This wasn't how the first night was supposed to go. They should be in a circle, trumpeting like a gaggle of geese as everyone played catch-up. Even Taylor and Lucas had caught the bad mojo. Those two kept their distance like a divorcing couple. Julia always thought Lucas carried a torch for Taylor, but maybe her daughter had to douse the flame and now it was awkward.

Christian set his drink down, his lips forming a grimace. "This thing tastes worse each year," he said. "A fly would find it too sweet, especially without the booze."

Julia agreed. The cocktails weren't as good as she remembered. Had the recipe changed, or had they? She stood up—enough was enough.

Erika smiled as Julia approached. She tipped her glass from her chair. "Coming for a refill?" she asked. Her cheery expression implied life couldn't be more perfect.

Julia put on a happy face as she plopped herself down on a stump that doubled as a seat. "No, just coming to say hi. Such a beautiful night."

She directed her gaze skyward and drank in the air, inhaling that unique lakeside fragrance, while Erika savored a sip of her syrupy blue concoction.

"I can't tell you how much I needed this," Erika said. She stretched her legs out long, dug her bare feet into the soft earth. Even her ubiquitous phone was powered down and put away.

This is simple, Julia decided. *Just be like Erika and let go. Vacationing is supposed to be easy. That's the point, isn't it?* She sipped her drink, and to her surprise, it tasted better. *See? It's all in the mind.* Julia allowed her shoulders to soften, and her whole body followed suit.

"Rick, how have you been?" she asked, aware that small talk worked best with him.

"Better now that I'm not teaching city boys how to tie a uni knot."

Erika laughed on cue, whereas Julia's reaction was delayed as she pieced together that he'd made a fly-fishing reference. Julia and Erika were regular chatterboxes, but she always found herself at a loss for words when conversing with Rick. Mostly she avoided it. It was better to let him boast about his ammo-making skills to Christian, not to her.

Speak of the devil. Julia felt Christian's strong hands press down on her shoulders. He kissed her on the ear in a way that sent a shiver of desire racing up her spine.

"Happy to report, this city boy can tie that uni knot with his eyes closed, thanks to you," Christian said to Rick as he dragged over a chair.

He leaned into Julia. "Maybe later," he whispered.

When their eyes met, she knew what was on his mind. A teasing smile lifted the corners of his mouth.

Julia perked up. He looked sexy as hell in his white linen shirt. The creditors could take a back seat for a while. They needed this time together, just to be a couple.

Fiona (who had topped off her drink—again) and David soon joined them. He sat next to Julia, their legs nearly touching. Julia felt a pulse of anxiety at being so close to him, and it wasn't just because of the house. She let the feeling pass through her like a breeze. The power of compartmentalization never ceased to amaze her.

And look at that. One little shift in her perspective, and it was like old times again. No more Debbie Downer! *This life lesson should go on Instagram.* Julia could see the clever captions in her head, earning her new followers as though she were an influencer: *Be in the moment. Relax and enjoy. Don't try to control, just let it roll.*

David, never at a loss for words, jumped into the conversation. "It's funny, I was just telling Fiona about our last hunting trip with Rick," he said. Clearly he'd overheard them talking. A satisfied gleam entered his eyes. "I had a good kill, but nothing like our fearless leader."

"Personally, I think it's cruel," said Fiona. "Animals have families, too. It's just mean to shoot them for a stupid trophy. Sorry, not sorry." She was on the cusp of slurring, but that didn't dampen her impassioned plea.

Julia was all smiles. Perhaps she'd misread Fiona. Add another life lesson to her influencer feed: *The only way to tell if it's a chocolate-covered raisin or a truffle is to look on the inside.* Not bad, but definitely not her best work.

Rick waved off the criticism. "We certainly don't need more hunters with poor aim, so the fewer the merrier." He offered a barrel-chested laugh, but then turned serious. "And just so you know, we eat what we kill. That's code. Also, we help with population control, not to mention the wildlife conservation efforts our hunting licenses fund."

"Great," Fiona answered with sarcasm. "Save the animals so you can shoot them later. How noble of you."

"The animals aren't going to kill themselves to prevent overpopulation," said Rick with another laugh before downing the rest of his Miller Lite. No more blue goo for him.

Fiona stiffened. Julia caught her reaction, which was more than perturbed. She was downright incensed.

"You shouldn't joke about suicide, not *ever,*" Fiona said bitingly.

Nobody was sure how to respond.

"Forgive him, Rick doesn't mean to be an ass—it just comes naturally," Erika said, sending her husband a chiding look.

A brief, awkward silence ensued before the song on Christian's playlist changed to a T-Swift tune.

Fiona's mood shifted instantly. She shrieked in delight. "Oh my god, this song is awesome!" she exclaimed.

Her fast reset was jarring, but lightened the atmosphere instantly. It was impossible to look away as she bebopped over to the firepit, a spring in her steps, her face beaming. Not a drop of her drink spilled as she twirled in front of the roaring blaze. She tilted her head back, singing with drunken ebullience about leaving with some hunky criminal in a getaway car.

"I love this song soooo much!" Fiona howled, spinning around three times as her skirt billowed out from her dancer's legs, catching the breeze. Eventually she lost her balance, but to Julia's astonishment, Fiona kept herself upright. She didn't miss a step as she resumed her song and dance routine.

Sweat glistened on Fiona's body as the fire heated her golden skin. She swayed her hips provocatively, everyone entranced with her movements. She shook her head to the beat of the music, flipping her hair like a coquettish minx at a casting call for a 1980s music video.

Julia remained mesmerized. At that moment, Fiona was divine—a wild nymph clutching her glowing blue drink as she shook and shimmied in uninhibited revelry. In her tiny top, it looked like she was acting out a scene from a fantasy film, a precursor to a weird sex ritual honoring a mythical goddess.

Judging by the look on Christian's face, Fiona *was* the goddess.

She danced her way back to the group, approaching David with a swing in her step and a seductive glint in her eyes. She put her back to him before lowering herself onto his lap, still moving her hips with unabashed intensity, giving him what was unmistakably a lap dance. David looked remarkably uncomfortable for someone who often boasted about his prowess in the bedroom. He pushed Fiona off him with a grunt of annoyance.

"Get control of yourself," he said.

Fiona didn't care. She kept on dancing as if nothing had happened.

"I wouldn't pass that up," said Rick, chuckling as he flashed a hungry smile.

Fiona focused on Erika as if seeking her permission, to which Erika acquiesced with a shrug. "I'm not saying no," she said. "That guy should get a thrill *somewhere.*"

Julia was shocked. She'd never let Christian do the same. There wasn't time for second thoughts (or common sense) to take hold. Fiona grinded into Rick's lap, moving her body in ways that kept the men transfixed.

Before the "dance" could escalate to the level of a live sex show, the music ended, and a new song came on. The spell was broken.

Fiona peeled herself off Rick, only to plunk herself down in the seat beside David, who couldn't bear to meet her eyes.

"Yowza, Dave, you've brought us a real live wire," Erika said, taking delight in her husband's cheap thrill.

Do they have an open relationship? Julia didn't think so, but honestly, that could explain how their unlikely marriage endured.

David cleared his throat to dislodge his discomfort. "So," he said, addressing nobody in particular, "any updates on the discovery up north?"

It made sense he'd want to redirect away from Fiona's escapades, but he'd sure picked a grim topic.

"I don't think the bones have been ID'd yet," Erika said as she bowed her head in respect.

Confusion washed over Fiona's face. Her near-flawless skin took on the pallor of the moon. "Bones? What bones?" she asked.

"Someone bought land a few miles from here, started construction on a house, and dug up some bones," Christian explained. "At first they thought it was a deer—until they unearthed a human skull." He turned his attention to Rick. "Hey, wasn't that near your family's hunting grounds?"

"Close, but not our property, thankfully. My parents don't need that kind of stress." He grimaced. "They're just hoping for a happy, quiet retirement."

Julia exchanged wary glances with Erika and David. Firelight danced in their eyes as if the past were flickering within. She knew what they were thinking. They'd grown up hearing the warnings from their parents: *Keep your eyes open. Make sure someone knows where you're going at all times. And don't wander off alone.*

Fiona was about to get indoctrinated.

"It's hard not to wonder . . ." Erika wrapped her arms around herself.

"*The lake takes them,*" said David, his voice ominous and drawn out, as though he were about to spook everyone with a ghost story. Fiona huddled closer to him.

"That folklore is just silly campfire nonsense," Rick said.

"Wait, I'm confused," said Fiona, looking to David for answers, but Erika spoke up.

"*The lake takes them,*" she said. "That's the legend around here."

Julia felt the need to elaborate. "Two women disappeared from Lake Timmeny thirty years apart."

"First, it was a young woman around nineteen named Anna Olsen," Erika said. "That was way back in the mid-sixties. The police had no leads, and her body was never found."

"Then it happened again, *exactly* thirty years later," said David in a hushed voice, as if the spirits of these two women might be listening. "Another young girl named Susan Welch—we called her Susie—disappeared from her home while on vacation with her family. No sign of forced entry or a struggle of any kind. Two young women, both around the same age, go missing without a trace, no evidence, no apparent motive . . . just poof—gone." His voice trailed off dramatically.

"The police searched the area," Erika added. "Divers looked in the water, but no luck. Susie simply vanished. No note. No body. No clue what happened to her. Same as Anna."

All fell silent.

Eventually Julia spoke up. "After Susie went missing, the young kids in the area started the lore . . . they said, 'The lake takes them,' like it was an evil spirit or something. I think it was just a childish way of coming to terms with what happened. But it caught on and became our version of the boogeyman. We were teenagers back then, just like Susie." She pointed to herself, then David, and next over to Erika. "We all knew her, not well, but well enough that it was a serious shock for us."

"Susie and her family's house was right over there," said David. He pointed to the opposite side of the lake. "We'd canoe to her place once in a while to hang out. She wasn't part of our lake gang, since she lived on a different shore, but we were all friendly." He pointed somewhere south of Susie's house. "Anna Olsen lived down that way, on this side of the lake. There may not be a connection, but there were enough similarities between the two cases to make you wonder."

"And when was the last disappearance?" Fiona asked, and David cited the year like it was burned into his memory.

Fiona's expression turned grim. "Don't you get it?" Her tone implied that everyone was missing something important.

"Get what?" Rick chased the question with a sip of his beer.

The worry in Fiona's eyes deepened. Turning to Julia, she said, "The two disappearances were both young women, and they happened thirty years apart from each other, and it's been *exactly* thirty years since the last one."

"That's right," said David, as if he was proud his partner could perform feats of basic logic and reasoning.

"I don't know if I'm being paranoid, but, well . . . where's Taylor?" Fiona's brow furrowed.

Julia whirled around, searching in all directions.

Nutmeg was there, playing with the twins and the nanny.

Lucas had returned and was sitting nearby, staring at his phone.

But Taylor was nowhere in sight.

Chapter 8

Izzy

Alarm cascades through me. Everyone is frantically calling for Taylor. It sounds like a search party, with Julia's voice ringing loudest. Immediately I go into panic mode, because that's what a well-trained, highly skilled nanny would do. My heart's thumping like I'm at a rave. Even though Taylor has apparently gone missing, my first concern is for the children. *Where are they?*

As it turns out, both are standing in front of me. I wrap my arms around them, not for their comfort, but for mine.

But where is Taylor? And why does everyone sound so crazed?

It's pitch-black out here. You enter a void as soon as you step away from the bonfire. I power on the flashlight feature on my phone only to shine the bright light directly into Brody's eyes like I'm his optometrist.

Becca clutches my hand tight enough for my fingers to tingle.

Julia runs over. She moves like a mouse, quick and haphazard, desperation leaking out of her.

"Izzy, have you seen Taylor?"

Before I can answer, a voice calls out from the gloom. It's Taylor. I hear Julia's loud exhale. Even though I don't fully understand the crisis, a wave of relief washes over me as well.

"What is going on?" asks Taylor, who seemingly manifests out of the dark. The twins latch onto her like Velcro monkeys.

"I just gave myself a scare, that's all." Julia sounds embarrassed.

"Over what?" Taylor wants to know.

I catch Julia's subtle nod in twin's direction. Whatever the problem was, it's not for young ears.

"Hey, kids," I say, sinking to their eye level. "Why don't you each make one more s'more before bath time? Go get them ready, and I'll help with the toasting."

My nanny game is strong as I make it sound like the best, most exciting, wonderful idea in the whole wide world. I lead them back to the fire, where they collect their sticks, already lacquered in marshmallow gunk. At least that area is well-lit, so I can keep an eye on them. Before I can offer a single word of caution to mind the fire, Fiona steps in, ushering the children away from the flames like she's just saved their lives. I happen to notice that she's wobbly on her feet, holding a cocktail in one hand, so she can't exactly lay claim to being a paragon of childcare.

Even so, she holds her head high, sending me a scolding stare that I mostly ignore. She can think what she wants about me and bad-mouth me to David if she chooses. I just need these two weeks, so job security is low on my priority list. I'm not attached to the kids, and I'm *certainly* not going to ask for a reference.

But as Fiona shuffles them away, the children send me pleading looks, like they would rather be with me than her. Have they actually taken a liking to me? Now I feel bad about leaving them with sour Fiona, but not enough to rescue them when my curiosity is piqued. I need to know why Julia was so distressed.

With the little ones out of earshot, she explains, "When we couldn't find Taylor, I got nervous that it happened again."

Taylor groans. "Oh my god. You thought I became part of the lake lore?"

In tag-team fashion, Taylor and Julia take turns giving me the skinny: two disappearances from Lake Timmeny, exactly thirty years apart, both young women—first Anna Olsen, then Susie Welch—and it's been exactly thirty years since the last woman went missing.

"I guess we all got caught up in the coincidences—like the lake had come to claim someone new. Ridiculous, I know." Julia tries to laugh off her overreaction, but she sounds slightly unhinged.

Taylor directs her attention to the cocktail in her mother's hand, her eyebrows arching. "Really, Mom?" She shakes her head, then shrugs it off.

But not me. I can't let it go.

Julia offers another apologetic smile.

"It's okay. Just try not to be such an alarmist next time," says Taylor. They hug it out, and Julia looks like she never wants to let go.

"Sorry to cause such a panic," Julia says. She slinks off, drink in hand.

I watch her go, thinking of my mother. Guilt nags at me. Like Julia with Taylor, my mom is just trying her best to protect me, and here I am lying to her, and now potentially putting myself in danger.

Perhaps sensing my unease, Taylor elaborates. "Susie lived over there, across the water from our house. My mom, David, and Erika actually knew her. They were about the same age and I guess they hung out sometimes."

I follow her finger into an endless darkness. Taylor can't see my eyes go wide or feel my chest tighten. It's as if an invisible pair of hands is squeezing my ribs. I know plenty of similar stories from my true crime podcasts, but this hits a little too close to home.

"Sometimes I would just sit on the shore and think about her—think, what if that happened to me, all the life I wouldn't get to live, the experiences I'd never have. It inspired me to write a series of poems about the lake lore. I submitted them for a writing award, but I haven't heard back yet."

"Whoa, that's cool. Do you have the poems with you? I'd love to read them if you don't mind?" Hearing them, I think, will ground me in the tragedy.

Taylor hesitates, perhaps embarrassed.

"Maybe later," she says. "I get shy about sharing my work, even though it's what I love the most. I'd really like to study creative writing in college, but my mom doesn't think it's a real career path. I'll probably end up in marketing, selling toothpaste or something stupid like that."

Lucas comes loping over to us. Though the light is dim, I can see his relieved expression. It's genuine, but Taylor ices over the moment their eyes meet.

"It's all good, just a minor freak-out," I tell Lucas.

He appears to shrink, likely knowing he shouldn't stand this close to Taylor.

Meanwhile, my heart rate hasn't settled. Peering out over the still water, I think about a young girl living on the other shore. I try to envision her final moments before vanishing into nothingness, as though it's my responsibility to carry some of that burden.

What happened to her? Did she wander off and get lost, never to be found? Unlikely. And if she drowned, her body would have eventually surfaced or been found by the divers.

The lake takes them. No, not the lake—a person, it's *always* a person.

I feel a hand on my shoulder and jump, giving a panicked cry of fright. It's Lucas. The light from the campfire ignites the emerald-green of his irises, drawing me into his world. I go willingly, for just a moment.

"Where'd you drift off to?" he asks. His smile is meant to be disarming, but I remain on guard.

"I was thinking about the poor girl who lived across the lake," I answer.

When our eyes meet, I feel my knees go weak. This guy is not just good-looking; he's downright beautiful. He has a chiseled jawline that hints at maturity and strength, but his soft, full lips, the gentle curve of his nose, and his vibrant eyes, so alive with a youthful boyishness, all make you want to get closer, to reach out and touch his soft skin. There's something otherworldly about him, like a male version of a temptress.

I peer at Taylor, who observes the exchange between Lucas and me. I catch something in her eyes, a fleeting expression that lasts no longer than the flap of a butterfly's wings. Her sharp eyes narrow.

That's when I know with certainty that if looks could talk, hers would say: *Get away if you know what's good for you.*

But I don't. Boys like him are my kryptonite. I sense that Taylor's not wounded or jealous. No, this is a warning look. I think she's afraid *for* me. Instinctively I step back from Lucas. He glances toward Taylor, but her face has shifted, morphed into a blank canvas. Now his beautiful smile chills when he looks my way.

"I'm glad to see you're making friends," he says with a deepening smirk that has lost all of its charm. "But be careful; that one's fickle," he adds, looking at Taylor.

He straightens and pulls his shoulders back, walking away with the arrogant strut of a rooster. I watch him fade into black, as though he was never there.

Believe it or not, I have been keeping an eye on the twins through all this, and I see that David is making the s'mores with them. It's a nice family moment that also allows my attention to remain mainly on Taylor.

Her eyes drift toward Lucas, who's moved over by the campfire. "I don't want to pry, but were you and Lucas, like, a thing? Was there a bad breakup?" I press. "If you ever want to talk—"

Taylor's expression hardens. "Bad breakup?" she asks with an edge. "No . . . no, it's *way* worse than that."

And with that cryptic remark, she skulks off toward the house, looking like she's carrying the weight of the world on her shoulders.

The first bedtime with the twins plays out like an endurance sport for which I am ill-trained, ill-equipped, and thoroughly unmotivated. I'm stunned at the difficulty I have getting them to simply put on their pajamas. They're like two wiggly worms, writhing as though they've been electrocuted.

"Haven't you done this before, like, many times?" I ask. "Your arms and legs and head go through the holes, and after that, you go and brush your teeth."

"My dad says I don't have to brush my teeth," Brody insists.

"That's fine," I retort. "They're all going to fall out anyway."

"You're mean," Becca tells me, frowning.

"Well, you're not listening," I say with an impatient tone. I lower myself to their eye level and say, "Listen, you two." I give them my best low, growly voice. "You know what happens to the Hulk when he turns angry? Well, the same thing happens to *me.*" I cast a look that shows I'm teasing, but I'm also losing my patience.

Maybe they don't know the superhero reference, but I'm delighted (and surprised) that they decide to play along. With no further prompting, they're cooperative almost to a fault. These twins are like chameleons—belligerent one moment, endearing and compliant the next. It's maddening.

After I get the little monsters cleaned up and into their jammies, after stories are read and teeth are actually brushed, and the dears are safely tucked into their beds, I decide to take some time for myself. I slip outside onto the wraparound deck on the second floor for a breath of fresh air. I lean my hands against the steel railing and peer down at the adults gathered around the fire.

My focus soon drifts to the dark shore beyond, where Susie Welch once lived. With a meditative prayer, I pay my respects.

Notes from a guitar break the spell. The music is coming from the neighboring house. I move to the other side of the deck, where I see Lucas below, sitting outside on his patio, strumming his six-string, lost in the moment. I stay and listen, imagining that he's serenading me. I don't recognize the song. Could it be his original composition? If so, he's pretty talented, which doesn't surprise me.

He's like a pied piper, for I'm not the only one lured toward the music. Out of the dark, Fiona comes staggering toward him. Nobody at the bonfire seems to notice that she's no longer part of the group. While they're busy chatting and drinking, Fiona sits directly across from Lucas. Even seated, she seems unsteady, moving her body in a way that could be in rhythm with the music, or could simply be part of a drunken stupor. She appears mesmerized. Her elbows rest on her knees, hands cupping her chin, gazing dreamily at the musician across from her who doesn't seem to care that he's acquired an audience.

"That's so beautiful," Fiona says, but it sounds like *b-ba-beautiful,* like she's having trouble making the *b* sound. If anybody else hears her, they don't seem to care. Lucas's mother should certainly be concerned—I've got the feeling her son is in the presence of a mantis, a nifty bug that bites the head off its partner after it mates. Lucas doesn't appear to sense the danger.

"Can you write a song about me?" Fiona asks, the *me* coming out like a hiss of air. Her body falls forward in her chair, but before she topples over, Fiona braces herself against Lucas's leg. Even though she regains her balance, she keeps her hand on him, leaning forward, her face past the danger zone of being too intimate. I feel guilty being a voyeur, but it's impossible to look away.

"Just sing me a song . . ." she insists.

Asking a musician to play is like asking a fish to swim, so I'm not surprised when I hear Lucas strum a new melody. But this time, he adds vocals. His rich, warm voice draws me in. It has the same effect on Fiona, who rests both hands on his knees while he plays.

She's still in her barely there outfit, but Lucas isn't paying attention to her body. He's lost in his song. A band of moonlight escapes from an overhead cloud as if to shine a spotlight on his performance.

His melodic voice proves too much for Fiona. She pulls his hand away from the guitar, stopping the music abruptly. She puts a finger on his chin, pulling his face toward hers. Before he can speak, she presses her lips against his. He freezes, then instinct takes over. Their mouths open as the kiss deepens.

What the hell? Stepping back in surprise, I slink into the darkness where they can't see me. No need to watch. I know what will happen next.

Chapter 9

Julia

Julia expected to be bone-tired after their first day of vacation. The packing and long day traveling should have worked like extra-strength melatonin, but she was nowhere near sleepy. The temperature was perfect, the crisp summer night air just right for snoozing. It caressed her skin like a soothing touch. So why wasn't she in la-la land?

Christian dozed peacefully beside her. They'd made love quietly, because the house amplified every sound. Her lucky husband . . . his release had put him out like a light, leaving Julia more jealous than satisfied. She could read, but she was in that in-between state of being just groggy enough not to make the effort. She knew looking at her phone would be counterproductive, but did it anyway. Her last post of the bonfire had received quite a number of likes. *So stupid. So vain.* And yet, so real. Her caption wasn't the best, but it got over fifty comments anyway.

Love it!

OMG, just perfect.

Enjoy every minute.

Have the best time ever. You deserve it!

It went on from there.

What would happen, she wondered, if there were such a thing as a what-they're-really-thinking filter, one that automatically converted all sentiments into some version of the truth?

We get it . . . you're having fun. Good for you.

OMG, a real fire. Never seen one of those before.

Only sort of care. Off to the store to buy hemorrhoid cream. Enjoy!

While this thought brought a smile to her lips, it raised a larger issue. What *was* the point of all this social sharing if people weren't willing to be authentic?

Oh, whatever. She played the game like everyone else, and it was probably better to question less and post more. So she composed one with a picture of the moon, which she took through the little porthole window over the bed. Her caption was short and sweet.

The magic here never ends. Good night, everyone.

Click. Post. Lie.

Good night, my ass. She was back under the covers, staring at her phone and not sleeping. She worried she already had a hangover and considered getting up for a glass of water when she noticed she had a voicemail message. Wireless could be spotty at the lake, so missed calls weren't uncommon.

Julia pushed the button to listen, instantly knowing she might not get a wink of sleep all night.

"Hi, Julia, this is Clare Roundtree with financial services at the Purdy School. I hope this message finds you well. I'm reaching out regarding Taylor's tuition payment for the upcoming semester, which appears to be past due. We understand life is busy and it may be just a simple oversight. If you have already remitted the funds, please accept our apologies and kindly reach out so we can rectify our records. If not, we'd appreciate you making the payment at your earliest convenience. Please contact us to discuss any concerns or potential arrangements—"

She disconnected without listening to the rest. Nothing went right anymore. There was always some screwup. Of course the payment had been made. Christian had told her as much. Even so, she knew it would be pointless to attempt to sleep until she saw the confirmation. Julia tried her password on the school website, but it didn't work. She'd need Christian's email to reset it, so she nudged her husband awake.

He came to with a groggy moan. "What? Huh? Everything all

right?" He sat up, looking about with alert eyes. The jolt of adrenaline sucked the sleep right out of him.

"I need to log in to the Purdy payment portal."

"For what?" he asked, clearly annoyed.

"I got a call from financial services. Apparently, our payment didn't go through."

Christian fell back on the mattress, looking unperturbed. "Ah, shit, Jules. It's fine; there's just a delay with the transfer. It's no big deal. I'll sort it out in the morning."

He rolled onto his side and would have fallen asleep if Julia hadn't pulled him back by the shoulder.

"That's what you said about the phone company, and I don't think that bill's been paid, either. And if that one doesn't get squared away soon, it's going to a debt collector. You know, the other day, I had to pay off a tampon repo man from my own pocketbook."

Christian sat up again. "What are you talking about? What tampon repo man? There's no such thing," he said, rubbing his eyes.

"But there is. I chased down some guy who'd gone into the women's room at the gym. I found him unscrewing the dispenser from the wall. It turned out he was from Billings Vendors and, apparently, we're four months behind on our payments. And I can't get a repairperson to service our treadmills until we make our franchise payment. Christian, what the hell? I'm dealing with all the marketing and member recruitment and retention programs, and it's *your* job to make sure our bills are getting paid."

Christian's head lolled from side to side like a tendon had snapped. He didn't have a shirt on, so she could see his stomach muscles tighten. Was that because he was straining to concoct some kind of excuse?

"They *are* getting paid," he explained. His sigh made it painfully clear Julia was wasting his time, not to mention keeping him awake. "The franchise knows our summer receivables are lower than the fall. I'll catch up in September. And besides, we're on a payment plan with them. It's all 'left hand not talking to the right' nonsense. Same with the school. It's no big deal. I'm on it."

Christian rubbed his temples. She was quite familiar with his tic, a relic from his drinking days that kicked in anytime he and the truth were at odds.

"Show me the tuition payment," she said, offering him her phone.

He shoved it away, groaning. "I've got it all under control. Trust me."

"So, what then? I can't see it?"

"You can. But it's not there."

"You said it was taken care of, left hand not talking to the right. Was that a lie?"

"I said I'm working it out with them." Only one hand went to his temple, so perhaps that was a half-truth. "Obviously, the person I'm in touch with didn't update the system, but it's fine. We have until September 15 without a penalty. I'll call the school tomorrow and get it sorted out."

Julia's head sagged forward. Christian was the numbers guy and better at managing the investments. Still, he gave her all the passwords. She could log in to any account of theirs anytime—except for Purdy. Or could she? When had she last checked their bank balances—or their investments, for that matter? She'd been so busy trying to drum up new business that she'd taken her eyes off the ball. *Well, no longer.*

Christian rolled back onto his side, pulling the blanket up to his chin like a force field.

Screw him. She accessed the Fidelity website using her phone and keyed in the password. They had an algorithm based on Taylor's initials and birthday, one password for all accounts to make it easier. Julia quickly got a return message that her credentials weren't accepted. She tried again. *Fat fingers. Just a typo.* But no luck. Same message.

Next, she went to the Ameritrade website. Same result.

She jostled her husband awake once more. "I can't get into any of our accounts," she informed him as he blinked his eyes open.

"Julia, what are you talking about?" he mumbled.

"You changed all the passwords and didn't tell me. Why?" Her voice was sharp enough to cut glass.

Christian tried to bury his head under a pillow, muffling his displeasure. "I clicked on something I shouldn't have and was worried I downloaded spyware," he explained in a muffled, somnolent voice. "I changed all the passwords as a precaution. It's no big deal. Please, just get some sleep, or at least let *me* sleep. You're worrying too much."

"You're not worrying enough."

Christian didn't take the bait, and Julia wasn't in the mood for a fight. Their arguments always went the same way—the angrier she got, the calmer he became, trumpeting AA platitudes like they were going out of style, until it felt like he was a therapist talking to a crazy lady. It was maddening.

She let him sleep. What good would it do to keep rehashing it all? Besides, it was the middle of the night. She couldn't do a thing about it now. Come morning, she'd ask again for the new password and she'd try not to assume the worst because Christian said he was on top of the bills, and he was her husband. They were a team, meaning there had to be a baseline level of trust.

Trust.

The word was enough to bring back the memory of *that* day. It was years ago, but any reminder made the wound feel fresh again. The seismic upheaval nearly sank their marriage. She didn't see it coming, but isn't that the cliché? She'd had no suspicions. There were no warning signs of any kind. There was, however, unfortunate timing—or fortunate, depending on one's perspective.

She had been looking for her phone, which she often misplaced. She was forever asking Christian to call her number to help her locate it. On this particular afternoon, Christian was out in the yard, and in her search, she found his phone at the exact moment he received an incoming text message.

I can't stop thinking about you.

Julia's legs had gone weak. She was standing near a vase full of fresh-cut hyacinths. It was funny how, to this day, the smell of hyacinths still made her knees buckle.

The message didn't stay on the screen, but it didn't matter. The words were seared into her mind.

Can't. Stop. Thinking. About. You.

She found him in the garage, putting gardening tools away. She thrust the phone into his hand.

"Who is she?"

Christian did the expected tap dance routine.

What are you talking about? Who is who? It's a wrong number. Nothing happened. Then . . . *It was only a onetime thing.*

He begged, cried, pleaded, and eventually—after many sessions with a therapist, some difficult soul-searching, spiritual counseling, and a heart probably too forgiving for her own damn good—they were able to salvage their relationship. They both agreed the old marriage was over—it would never be the same. The question remained: Could they make a new and even better one?

After some time, the answer appeared to be yes. Christian quit drinking and left his sales job. No more booze and hotel bars meant no new chances to get into old trouble. He let her monitor his phone as they continued with counseling. Eventually she allowed him to crawl back into her heart before inviting him into their bed.

Along with their new marriage came their new business. But before all that, Julia got her revenge—a little tit for tat that Christian didn't know about, and that Julia regretted to this day.

Now she feared they were sliding backward. Had she misplaced her trust once again?

That was the beauty of social media. She could use it to fool herself into believing that every moment of her existence was caption-worthy. But real life was complex, like flirty Fiona—sometimes it was beautiful, but other times it was just a hot mess.

Julia made her way downstairs. It was late, but already she had a handful of likes on her moon picture. How lame that she cared.

Before she knew it, she found herself outside, wrapped in a scratchy blanket that had been in the family longer than she had. This time last year, she'd have seen the moonlight dancing across the rippling water from the screened porch. She could still see it, but only through David's windows, just as he'd promised.

What a shit.

The view was basically ruined. Julia was about to return inside when a piercing sound drew her attention to the water.

It was a female voice, perhaps a cry of distress.

Julia froze. She listened intently, leaning into it, and heard it again: "Let go. You're hurting me."

"Just get back in the house."

That was David's voice, sharp enough to crack glass. After Fiona's display at the bonfire, Julia could imagine what they were arguing about.

Fiona again: "I said, let go of me!"

A light went on inside Erika's home. Fiona threatened to wake the whole lake.

"Keep your voice down," David said.

Julia didn't like how aggressive he sounded. He had a temper that could ignite with a lot less provocation.

Instead of letting the lovers quarrel, Julia intervened. Instinct told her that silence would be a choice she'd later regret. She had to walk around his house to reach them, using her phone's flashlight to avoid tripping over one of David's pricey new lawn sculptures.

Julia reached the back of his house, horrified to see David clutching Fiona's arm. Even in the dim light, she could tell his grip was firm.

She called David's name, which had an immediate effect. He let go, backing up a step, though he continued to face off with Fiona like they were combatants readying for the next round. He was dressed like a boxer, too, in a black satin robe—a look nobody could pull off, even back in the seventies when it *was* in style.

His chosen opponent was out of her bikini top and wearing a white silky tank with spaghetti straps that paired well with her loose-fitting pajama pants.

"What's going on?" Julia asked hotly.

"Why don't you ask her?" David said, his face mere inches from Fiona's, who held her ground. Good to see Fiona was no shrinking violet.

"I just warned David he was going to drive another nanny away if he tried to fuck this one as well."

"Please, just leave us alone, Julia," David said. "Fiona's still drunk."

"Oh, so what if I had a little too much fun . . . you sure weren't showing me a good time. You were too busy ogling the nanny."

Julia thought: *And you were busy giving Rick the lap dance of his life. Pot, meet kettle.*

David snorted in disgust. "I put my hand on Izzy's shoulder to get her attention. That's all. You're being insane."

"I saw the way you undressed the last nanny with your eyes, and who knows what else you did when I wasn't around."

David stiffened, casting a hateful glare at Fiona, who again did not back down.

Erika emerged from the dark. Her voice broke the standoff.

"What's going on?" she asked, flicking her focus between Fiona and David.

"It's just a little lover's spat," said David, finding his genial smile too quickly to be real. "Let's go inside, we'll sort it all out."

David reached out his hand as if extending an olive branch, and to Julia's astonishment, Fiona took it. They walked back to the house together, leaving Erika and Julia dumbfounded. Fiona seemed rather pleased with herself as she departed. She held her head high, walking with the pride of someone who came out victorious.

But Julia knew something about David that Fiona did not: for him, losing wasn't an option.

Chapter 10

Izzy

I don't know how long Brody's been tugging on my arm, but it's definitely too long for him. He's grown impatient and he's practically pulling me out of bed. *OML, it's too early for this.* I roll over, eyes fluttering open, and I hear a frightened squeak that makes me bolt upright. Becca must have crawled into bed with me at some point during the night, and I inadvertently squished her. Without complaint, Becca grabs for her stuffed tiger and pulls the blankets over her head while I address Brody.

With a croaky voice, I ask, "Is everything okay? Is there an emergency?"

"I'm bored," he says, as though this is a crisis that requires my immediate attention.

Becca nestles close to me. Clearly, the twins aren't on the same page.

"Go back to bed," I instruct.

"No," says Brody, stomping his feet. "I won't. I'm hungry and bored, and you're the nanny."

Oh, shit. I suppose he's right. I suggest we go downstairs and do an art project.

As soon as the words are out of my mouth, Becca is out from under the covers. Clutching her tiger, sleepily rubbing her eyes, she says in the tiniest voice imaginable, "Me too?"

Of course, the answer is yes. These might be budding Van Goghs, and I certainly don't want either of them to feel left out, or worse, wake Fiona with their pleading.

It's 7:30 A.M., I'm still in my pajamas, I've had no coffee, my hair has curled into a poodle's coat, I've no idea what I'm doing, and I'm seriously questioning my life decisions. At least I know I picked the right college major. Early childhood education is *way* too early for me.

But at least I'm prepared. I put the arts and crafts box in the downstairs closet when we unpacked—no problem. I take out the construction paper, childproof scissors, glitter, and nontoxic glue. I've read an article on this subject, and I know it's not just play.

The free-form process of creating with their hands while simultaneously exploring color, form, texture, and composition enhances cognition and coordination and bolsters self-awareness. The nanny's role is to encourage creative exploration without clouding the child's experience with judgment or extensive instruction. Now, go make something that comes from the heart!

Or something that looks like a glittery mountain of glue.

I'm not exactly sure what Brody has made, but he's damn proud of it. Or at least I thought he was—right up until he balled up his masterpiece and threw it on the floor in exasperation.

Great, he's already a temperamental artist at five years old.

I try to think of something Brody can make that might lead to less frustration. I get out more construction paper, washable markers, and a pair of googly eyes. Brody watches intently. I draw a big head around the eyes and add two misshapen ears along with a goofy grin.

"I want to do that," Brody declares.

"Me too," Becca chimes in.

Before long, we're all drawing funny faces with googly eyes. There is no fighting, no complaining. It's the sweetest moment we've shared yet.

Becca is pressed up against me, warming herself like I'm a blanket. Brody's face beams as he delights in showing off his creation—a caterpillar or a lion, it's hard to say which.

"That's really great!" Becca is so sincere it hurts.

"This is the most fun I've ever had—*ever*," Brody says, beaming at me in a show of thanks. His earnest eyes flood me with emotion.

I clear my throat. "I'm glad everyone is having fun," I say, realizing that I am, too. *What's up with that?*

We create for a while until everyone gets hungry. I get up to fix the children's breakfast, which basically amounts to chocolate milk and sugared cereal (I know how to keep my status as the best nanny in the world). I have my back to the little ones for no more than two minutes, but apparently, that's all it takes.

I hear a mischievous laugh, a chair topples over, and then there's a scream that could be playful or—

I spin around, chocolate milk sloshing out of the carton, to see Brody and Becca engaged in what can only be described as a preschool wrestling match involving glue and copious amounts of gold glitter.

What . . . the . . .

"Nooo!" I shout, not caring that I'll wake the house. "Calm down, everyone! Brody, sit in your chair. You too, Becca. Now!"

Luckily they listen, but it's too late. Becca's dark brown locks are coated in glitter. Clumps of Brody's hair are glued to the side of his head, scraps of construction paper affixed to the front of his light blue PJs.

I see Brody readying a tube of green glitter like a mortar round. I lunge forward with a quickness that belies my lack of athletic ability. Although I retrieve the glitter tube before any more is released, the damage has already been done. Not only do the children look like an art canvas gone awry, but the table and floor are strewn with a sea of clingy gold flakes that are insidiously small, as if designed specifically to torment me.

Fearing Fiona might emerge in a tizzy, I usher the children into the bathroom off the kitchen. A trail of glitter follows them like a map of my mistakes. Thank goodness, the glue is not only nontoxic but also washable. The sink isn't ideal for cleaning them, but it's effective enough. Luckily, the laundry facilities are also in this bathroom, so I find a quick change of clothes for both kids before plopping their messy pajamas into the machine.

Crisis averted.

In a cheery voice, I suggest they sit with their breakfast and watch a show on Netflix. While the kids are occupied, I scrub down the kitchen and bathroom, doing my best to remove the remaining evidence. Though I've listened to hundreds of true crime podcasts, I've given little thought to how hard it is to clean up a crime scene. If blood were glitter, it would be downright impossible.

I'm fighting a losing battle with the dustpan when Brody, of all people—the same little twerp (I mean love) who dragged me out of bed and created this mess—comes to my rescue. He sneaks up from behind, startling me with a tap on the shoulder.

"Just use Play-Doh," he says. His voice is so soft and tender, any lingering frustration I feel melts away on the spot.

"Play-Doh?" I repeat. It's a good thing we have a ton of it.

Soon enough, Brody, Becca, and I are crawling on our hands and knees, pressing the moldable clay onto any surface covered in the shiny stuff. We even make up a song while we work, which we sing in whispered voices. As luck would have it, nobody comes downstairs, and the glitter disappears. Mostly. I spot one last clump of gold flakes on the kitchen counter, but unfortunately, we're fresh out of Play-Doh.

No worries. I wet a paper towel and set to work. As I'm dabbing away, the front door opens and David walks in, lathered in sweat and breathing hard. He's wearing a gray T-shirt, stained dark in the front, and sweatpants as mud-spattered as his Nike sneakers.

The kids come running like Santa Claus just showed up. It's a heartwarming scene. I try to give them a moment of privacy, but everywhere I look, I see their shiny, happy reflections in the windows. I can't seem to adjust to all this glass. It's like living in a weird art installation.

The kids don't care that Dad is sweaty from what I assume was his early morning run. Good for David for taking care of his health. I run only if chased.

Soon, the magnetic pull of sugary cereal, chocolate milk, and cartoons lures the children away from their father. Meanwhile, I try to act nonchalant, like I don't have a care in the world. I'm just the happy-go-lucky nanny, picking up this and that, ensuring my eager beavers are busy and well cared for. I'm hoping I'm somewhat invisible, but David takes notice of me anyway.

He saunters over with a self-satisfied smile, maybe on a runner's high. He makes a beeline for the fridge. Out comes a carton of orange juice. He's mere moments from putting said carton to his lips, something my mother would have objected to sternly, when I thrust a glass in front of him.

"I'm sure you were about to ask for one," I say with polite professionalism.

David runs a hand through his tousled wet hair, fixing me with a lopsided smile. He approaches, his eyes stamped to my face. A nervous pulse spikes through me. He inches closer, using a clean dish towel to dry his hair. He strips off his shirt right before me, exposing his torso with the ease of peeling a banana.

I'm in shock, trying not to look, but it's hard to avert your eyes when your boss is half-naked in front of you. He's a shirtless man who clearly likes his physique. No big deal, right? He rubs the towel over his chest and abdomen. A gnarly blanket of chest hair cushions a thick gold chain that belongs around the neck of a rapper. *Eww.*

"Great run," David says.

Of course he doesn't notice—or maybe even likes—my uneasiness, how I'm bouncing on my feet, trying to inch away. He leans his hand on the counter, taking long, purposeful sips from his glass of OJ.

He tosses his sodden shirt and towel into the hamper in the bathroom.

"What's on your face?" he asks. He leans in close, giving me a strong whiff of his musky odor.

He touches my cheek. I try not to gasp. He shows me flecks of glitter on the tip of his finger, the same gold color as his chain.

David surveys the counter, and I see now that my cleanup job could have been more thorough.

"What happened here?" he asks, brushing the area with his palm. Sweat makes the glitter stick to his skin.

"Oh, we had a minor mishap." I try to laugh it off.

"Ah," says David, his dark eyes brightening, "I bet anything that was Brody's doing. He's a rambunctious one." He says this lightheartedly, with no indication of reprimand.

"I'll get it cleaned up straightaway," I tell him.

David's gaze lingers on me a beat too long. "It's no problem, I got it. Glitter patrol wasn't in the job description." He grabs a paper towel off the roll.

I stand there feeling pointless as he sets about the near-impossible task of cleaning up the remnants of our morning fun.

"How do you like the lake so far?" he asks. He's totally relaxed and seems geared up for a lengthy conversation. Meanwhile, he's standing so close I can count his chest hairs.

"It's peaceful here. I just love it," he adds, turning his body so that he's either admiring the view or his reflection in the towering picture window in front of him—probably both.

Thank goodness Becca summons me from the TV room. Whatever she wants, she can have it.

"Duty calls," I say, and slip away. I feel David's eyes on me as I go. I turn around long enough to see him making his way up the stairs, hopefully to put on some clothes.

Is this how it begins? A toe over the line to test the waters? A tap becomes a touch, which becomes something more. What comes after shirtless? I shudder at the thought, but then I tell myself I'm only here for a short while. I just have to keep my wits about me and avoid being alone with him, which I think I can do.

My roommate, Meredith, would be irate to see me giving David a pass. But I need this job for something far more valuable than money. The truth. And I'm too close to my objective to let some sweat-lathered seal scare me off. I'm here to stay, and Becca would gladly second that decision. She bats her imploring, puppy-dog eyes before requesting more chocolate milk.

"Can I have more, too?" asks Brody.

His eyes stay glued to the TV as he extends his cup toward me. He hasn't even drunk half of what I poured.

"Finish what you have," I say like a good nanny should, and down it goes in one hearty swallow. He thrusts the cup back at me, a chocolaty residue dripping down the sides.

I'm returning to the kitchen for refills when David reappears from upstairs. He's changed out of his running clothes into beige shorts and a fresh blue T-shirt (half-naked no more, thank goodness). The shirt has some meaningless logo printed on the front. He tosses a second T-shirt at me with no warning. All I see is bright blue fabric streaking toward my face. I snatch it out of the air with my free hand.

"A gift for you," he says as I set down the cups and unfurl the shirt. The logo is for a company called NewPulse, which I've never heard of.

David looks at me like I should know what this is. "It's my new company I told you about," he says. "You mentioned being interested in entrepreneurship in your application and wanting to know more about my work."

I did? Oh, Meredith. Right.

"Yeah, cool," I say.

"Do you run? You can come with me next time."

"The kids," I say, glad to have an easy out.

"Fiona can watch them," David says. "Speaking of, where is she? Did she go out somewhere?"

I tell him I don't think so, that I haven't seen her. No, there's no way. I would have heard her leave.

"Strange," David says, glancing about. "She's not in the bedroom."

He goes out back, and I watch him through the glass as he scans the lakeshore. It's still early morning. A cool mist rises from the water, as if the lake is actually breathing.

David returns, but something has shifted. His eyes are worried. He goes to the front of the house, but he doesn't need to open the door to see that Fiona's Porsche is still in the driveway.

He bounds upstairs, calling Fiona's name, and returns moments later, looking dejected.

"She's not an early riser," he assures me, his voice nervous. "But she must have gone for a walk."

I nod in agreement.

"Yeah, it's hard to sleep when the sun comes in. I probably missed her leaving when we were cleaning up the glitter." I don't believe it myself, and David doesn't seem to believe me, either.

Chapter 11

Julia

M*orning coffee should set everything right,* or so Julia told herself as she poured a cup in Erika's kitchen. She drank her coffee with cream and sugar, which always meant starting her day with a stab of guilt, but some things in life were non-negotiable.

On this fine morning, the sun's ascent brought a kiss of perfection to the new day. The leaves shimmered under a coating of fresh dew. Bright flowers spread their petals wide to catch sips of sunshine while the birds flittered about. Everything about the moment was idyllic, from the soothing sound of lapping water to the graceful butterflies riding atop the aromatic breeze.

Taylor was out walking Nutmeg. Christian and Rick had taken the canoe on the lake for a morning fishing excursion. Lucas played guitar upstairs, sounding quite good. Evidently he'd been practicing. All felt right in Julia's world.

But it was also a veneer, she knew. Nature's beauty was a mask covering harsher realities: Taylor and her distance, Christian and their money woes (not to mention his possible lies), and David and Fiona's distressing fight.

Right now, what was most troubling Julia was what was *not* bothering Erika.

Here she was, standing in her friend's kitchen, sipping the coffee that was always made to perfection, and not seeing (at least not in an unobstructed way) the damn lake. If she looked through three sets of windows, two of which belonged to David, she could just make out the water dappled with golden sunbeams.

Heck, if she squinted, Julia could even guess what cereal the twins were having for breakfast—Apple Jacks. That green box was unmistakable. "I really can't believe you're okay with this," Julia said, nodding toward the glass house.

Erika looked out the window from her seat at the kitchen table as she drank from her Love Lake Life coffee mug without a care in the world.

"What can I do about it?" she asked.

"You're the lawyer, not me."

"Which is why I know it would be a long, expensive legal battle, and even if we won, he might not be forced to tear it down. He'd probably be fined, but we'd have bad blood and still have to live with it. It's not worth the fight."

Erika might not be outraged, but Julia was pissed enough for the both of them. She considered her options . . . perhaps a bulldozer? At the very least she could give David a good hard slap on the face. But the more Julia thought about it, the more helpless and hopeless it appeared.

Erika went to the fridge, took out fruit for their lunchtime salad, and handed Julia a mango. Of course she'd give her the most slippery, difficult thing to peel and cut. That was typical of Erika, always sending a little "fuck you" with love.

But block her precious water view, and it's laissez-faire, mon frère? Really?

"I just thought you'd be more upset," said Julia, pointing to David, who was absorbed in his phone from an armchair in his living room. "It's like the worst remake of *Rear Window* ever."

Julia feigned a yawn to try to get a laugh, but Erika wasn't biting. She was too busy cutting off the heads of strawberries, her knife a blur. She was quite the chef and would have been far better at dissecting the mango, which Julia was turning into porridge.

"What good is anger going to do me?" replied Erika, as flat as a Stepford Wife.

"Oh, I'm sorry," Julia said. "I didn't realize aliens had abducted my friend."

Still no smile, though Julia remained determined to coax one out.

Erika switched from cutting strawberries to kiwi, using a paring knife to peel the skin with the fine motor skills of a surgeon.

"I happen to be working on myself," she said. "The law is a meat grinder, and the stress was getting to me. Rick's been on my case to dial it back—my doctor, too. I guess my blood pressure is up. So I've been meditating, working on mindfulness, learning to let things go."

"You?" Julia stifled a laugh. "Queen of the Grudge has turned to New Age spiritualism?"

At last, Julia got the smile she had been after, but it was cryptic.

"What can I say?" Erika waved the knife. "People change."

When they were kids, Erika could give the silent treatment like it was nobody's business. The grievances were often over little things. Julia remembered a borrowed sweatshirt she returned marked with a drip of mustard that went unnoticed until the stain had set in. Erika refused to speak to Julia for days until her father got involved, orchestrating a peace summit at the picnic tables. That afternoon the girls were back together, laughing and splashing in the water as if the crisis had never been. It helped that Cormac Gallagher wasn't the sort who took no for an answer.

Julia had no memories of Erika's mother—she wouldn't have been able to help a police sketch artist render her if she tried. Her face was lost to time. Her photos had all been thrown away because of a long-standing vendetta, this one between Erika's parents. *What mother abandons her young child for a new life with another man?* The cruelty astounded her to this day.

Julia long suspected that Erika's edge, her take-no-prisoners attitude both inside and outside the courtroom, stemmed from this early trauma. It was a defense mechanism, just as David's overinflated ego helped protect him from the pain of his father's death and his mother's bereavement. Erika had a big heart, but it was surrounded by fortifications the military couldn't break down.

"Tell me more about this Zen way of being," said Julia. "I sure could use it." She wasn't ready to dive into her crumbling business empire or the debt collectors hounding her. She needed another few days of vacation before she'd sign up for that pity-fest. She also didn't want to be like Christian, who was prone to bouts of jealousy, but here she was, enviously admiring Erika's recently renovated kitchen. It was straight out of *Magnolia Journal.*

As a young girl, Erika fancied herself a budding artist, and she could draw quite well. She'd talked about going to art school, but she must have gotten the same lecture from Cormac that Julia gave Taylor about her creative writing pursuits.

Julia figured Erika would find some sort of creative profession—advertising, perhaps—but she surprised everyone when she took the LSAT and applied to law school instead. Like her choice in husbands, Erika becoming a lawyer never made perfect sense to Julia, though it did fit her warrior persona. She won nearly every argument she got in, never backing down from a challenge. That trait definitely worked in her favor; her career became quite lucrative. Looking around her lake home, Julia supposed the house was now Erika's canvas, a way to express her innate but underdeveloped artistic ability.

The reclaimed beams and Douglas fir cabinets, along with a breakfast bar featuring a soft gray concrete countertop that perfectly complemented the oak barstools, were the stuff of dreams. Erika had even installed the ultimate farmhouse-chic status symbol—a skirted sink below the bifold windows that fully connected the indoors and out. While Erika's kitchen was most definitely the heart of the home, Julia's was the heartache. It was dark and cramped, and probably had mold from shoddy insulation and wet winters.

Julia didn't have the money to remodel her primary residence, let alone fix up the summer house. No wonder she felt a stab of envy as she followed Erika into the well-appointed living room adorned with country-themed furnishings, none of which came from Ikea. Julia didn't begrudge Erika her financial security. She'd worked hard for her money and was also fortunate to inherit a nice nest egg from her late father, who could be generous to a fault and paid for everything in cash.

The remodeling work had taken place over time, done drip by drip—less upheaval, with just a project here and there. And lo and behold, everything had come together seamlessly. Julia was no longer inside the same house where she had played as a little girl. This home had new floors, new windows with fresh window treatments, a modern kitchen, new rugs, and all updated furnishings.

But not everything had changed. Erika kept the oil painting portrait of her late father hanging above the fireplace.

Although he was a salesman by profession, in that portrait, Cormac Gallagher, posed in a wingback chair and dressed in a crisp navy sport coat with a white shirt underneath, had the regal air of a sea captain. His shock of silver hair and stern expression bolstered that comparison, as did his weathered face, rendered as though the wind and waves had carved the many crevices into his flesh.

While he appeared stern and humorless in the painting, Cormac could be personable and engaging, with a magnetism that helped earn him plenty of girlfriends after his wife absconded. But even after he took David under his wing, he still intimidated Julia. His geniality felt like thin ice, apt to crack under the slightest pressure, exposing something cold, dark, and treacherous just below the surface. Julia felt his stony, reproachful eyes—even rendered in a painting—following her every move.

The many candid framed photographs scattered throughout the living room showed his more affable side. Here was Cormac at the lakeshore, frolicking in the water with Erika when she was a toddler. Another showed him with his close friend, a man Erika called Uncle James, even though he wasn't technically family.

Julia's attention shifted from the pictures to an ornate rug in the center of the room. It was made of striking red, orange, and blue dyed wool, handwoven into an intricate pattern.

"Hey, you finally got rid of that ugly brown rug!" Julia exclaimed.

Erika nodded. "I felt bad because my dad picked it out, but I never really liked it. I'm happy it's gone. This is more my style."

Julia agreed, though not only because of the aesthetic improvement. She'd genuinely *hated* that old rug for reasons she couldn't explain. That ugly brown rug unsettled her almost as much as Cormac's steely gaze boring down from his gilded frame.

Even with the new, fancier floor covering, the room gave off a hunting cabin vibe. Several mounted deer heads, all Rick's personal kills, decorated the walls. Julia put the heads in the same twisted category as a serial killer's mementos.

"Oh my god, those things are awful," Erika said, catching the disdainful look Julia directed at Rick's majestic trophies. "But Rick loves them. And everyone in his family is a hunter. He learned to shoot a gun before he could ride a bike." She gestured to a gun rack mounted on the wall that showcased three hunting rifles.

"What about Rick? He must be pissed about the house. You might be meditating, but I have a hard time picturing your husband burning incense and ringing a singing bowl."

The notion made them both chuckle. "It's technically my family home, so he follows my lead when it comes to this place," said Erika.

"David should be grateful for that." Julia eyed the guns again. "Doesn't look like any of those are locked up. Are you sure it's safe?"

"Absolutely," Erika confirmed. "The ammo is stored separately. My house, my rules. I'll live with a couple deer heads on the wall, but that's where I draw the line. Besides, Rick is building me a bar." Erika pointed to the future site of her in-house speakeasy, which would go right beneath a handsome buck with an elaborate crown of antlers.

"If I have to look at those hideous things forever, at least I'll have a buzz on," Erika quipped, setting her coffee down as she plopped herself into an armchair.

Julia found a seat on the couch. From her vantage point she couldn't see the glass house, which felt like a minor reprieve, but she could still hear Lucas playing his guitar upstairs. He must have inherited some of his mother's creativity.

"He sounds really good," Julia commented, and it was true. "Is he planning to study music in college?"

Erika went still, like one of those poor frozen deer mounted to the wall. "I don't think he wants to go anymore," she said.

"What?" Julia did a double take.

"Yeah, he's all about his band these days, doesn't see the need for college, thinks it's just a waste of time and money. I mean, kids these days." She rolled her eyes.

"He was so happy to do the college tour with Taylor," Julia said. "Any clue what happened?"

Erika kept a straight face, though Julia heard her sigh quietly. "Not really. It took Rick and me both by surprise. I mean, his music has always been a priority, but we didn't think he'd put off college for it. But what are we supposed to do? We can't force him. That's my take. Rick and I have been fighting about it quite a bit. To be candid, we don't see eye to eye on much. We come from two different worlds. But I'm not forcing Lucas, or punishing him like Rick wants to do. It's not our life to live, so I guess he'll need to get a job, and that's that."

Erika slumped forward in her chair, nearly releasing a splash of coffee onto her new rug.

"I'm sure it will all work out," said Julia, trying for empathy. She hadn't shared anything about Taylor's apparent issues with Lucas, not that Julia knew what to make of it herself.

When they were young, she and Erika told each other everything, but over the years, that happened less and less. Julia couldn't pinpoint exactly when that individuation began. Was it college? Was it marriage? Perhaps that was just the normal evolution of childhood friendships, staying close, but not so enmeshed.

Erika knew about Christian's infidelity, but not the heart-wrenching details or Julia's revenge. Many of her deeper struggles Julia had kept to herself, having difficulty sharing hard truths even with her therapist. Besides, they saw each other so infrequently these days, Julia didn't feel right tainting their precious time with her negativity.

Erika cut into her thoughts. "Did Taylor say anything to you about Lucas? I wonder if he opened up to her."

"Funny, I was going to ask you the same question about Taylor. She's been hard to understand recently." Julia highly doubted their kids had had a heart-to-heart, considering her daughter didn't want to see Lucas at all this summer. Of course, she couldn't say that to Erika. "Look at us, guess we're both clueless. Par for the course when you have a teenager."

"Right," Erika laughed. "It would probably be weird if they *did* tell us what was going on."

Julia grimaced. "I'm sure you're right. But maybe we should pry a little more."

Before they could hatch a plan of attack, the door flew open. David stepped in, looking like a man on a mission. He was dressed casually, but there was nothing relaxed about him.

"Hey," he said, running a hand repeatedly through his hair, "has anybody seen Fiona? She seems to have disappeared."

Chapter 12

Izzy

Being a nanny means you're always on the go. It's ten past ten in the morning, and it seems I've been up since sometime last year. David has been out of the house, searching the woods for Fiona. I hope there isn't a tragic story unfolding.

I help David by keeping the kids out of the way. So far I've made breakfast, cleaned up from breakfast, done the dishes, folded laundry, picked up the bedrooms, and found more glitter to vacuum. Now, I'm trying to convince everyone to take a swim.

"It's cold and wet," Becca complains.

"Um, that's kind of the point, isn't it? It's supposed to be refreshing."

Becca's frown makes it clear my efforts are falling short.

"I don't want to swim, either," declares Brody, his duck lips cementing his sibling solidarity.

I sigh. I suppose there's peace in allowing people to do what *they* think is right, even if said people can't pour milk into a cup without spilling it. Instead of a swim, the kids play with LEGOs on the living room floor, while I'm in desperate need of an energy boost. Who knew that such tiny creatures could suck the marrow straight out of your bones? Since blood doping for nannies isn't really a thing, I settle for high-caf tea.

David returns to the house as I'm cleaning the kitchen (again!). He looks more frustrated than fearful that Fiona didn't return in his absence.

"Should we call someone?" I ask as I'm emptying the dishwasher, silently adding: *The police, perhaps?*

"She'll turn up," David assures me. "She does this sort of thing after we fight—plays weird games to teach me a lesson. It's either that or she took a walk and fell asleep under a tree somewhere. Goodness knows she had plenty to sleep off."

Or sleep*walked* it off, I think, reflecting on our conversation last night at the bonfire. I remember other things, too, like Fiona and Lucas locking lips, and all that dancing, the scene she had made—her endless flirting with all of the men, not just the hunky, mysterious, and *very* young rocker.

But what I remember most clearly is: *The lake takes them . . .*

"You've been working hard," David tells me as he gets a glass of water. "And you're really great with the kids. I can already tell they adore you. We're lucky to have you."

I give him a faint "Thanks." I don't want to linger in the kitchen because he might go shirtless again. There's nothing wrong with his praise. It's appropriate, and I should appreciate it. But the look he sends me, like he's checking me up and down, makes me cringe.

He knows how to play it. So far he's kept his little hints, subtle winks, and ambiguous gestures to just the right degree to keep me from running out the door. And even though he seems the type to reduce women to their physical "offerings" over their actual selves, he's maintained a friendship with Erika and Julia for decades. Perhaps he hides this side of himself from them, because my misogynistic asshole radar won't stop pinging. I can't help but wonder if he's applying the same just-enough tactics to keep from looking suspicious about Fiona's mysterious vanishing.

David heads out to search again, certainly acting the part of the dutiful boyfriend. Do I believe it? Let's just say I have my doubts.

Everyone on the lake must have heard them fighting last night—I sure did. I couldn't hear what they were arguing about, but the tone of their raised voices was distressing. David sounded aggressive and more than mildly threatening. And Fiona was combative as well, in that sloppy drunk way.

The kids don't seem overly concerned, which I guess says something about their relationship with Fiona. While I understand that a high-quality nanny must remain vigilant, I take advantage of the relative calm (thank you, LEGO) to crack open my laptop and do some investigating. After what I've learned about the lake lore, and with another missing person in our midst, my true crime obsession has kicked into overdrive.

Since I can't solve the Fiona mystery, I settle for the next best thing—a trip back in time, via my laptop. I step into the mysterious, still unsolved disappearance of Anna Olsen, last seen at Lake Timmeny on June 9, 1965. Good thing the internet is a digital time capsule. A few keywords in a Google search bar and I'm transported to the era of Elvis and the civil rights movement, Beatlemania, and the Vietnam War.

"She was my older sister and I loved her. We were very close," Grace Olsen told a reporter for *The Boston Globe*. The quote was cited in an article commemorating the tenth anniversary of Anna's disappearance, twenty years before Susie Welch would go missing from the very same lake.

Grace also had an older brother, Tom, but she was closer with Anna, only two years her senior. "We were inseparable," Grace told the reporter. "Nobody's life was perfect, but ours felt as close to that as possible. We loved coming to the lake every summer.

"We would swim all morning, and then we'd go hiking in the nearby hills. The lake and forest were our playground. With our father's help, we built a fort in the woods from plywood and leftover roofing shingles. It became our magical hideout. I don't go in there anymore, but I can't bring myself to tear it down."

I suspect that the fort must be the Shack that David told me about at the bonfire. He'd mentioned taking the kids and me there for an adventure, but I think I'd rather go exploring without him. I file that tidbit away and go back to my research, landing on an archived article from the *Rutland Herald*.

According to the article, the Vermont state police investigated

Anna's disappearance. Public Information Officer Captain Daryl Greenwood told the *Herald* that Anna Olsen had last been seen "sunning herself at the lakeshore, and all seemed perfectly well. No signs of physical injury or emotional distress. It was an ordinary summer day."

Just like this one, I think with a peek out the window.

Greenwood told the reporter that they'd found various items belonging to Anna on the beach, including blankets and other personal effects, but there was no sign of the young woman.

Numerous searches had been conducted. "We combed the entire beach, dredging the lake in case of drowning, and we searched the grounds north of the bog," Greenwood said. "All the nearby cottages were checked as well, as were the trails." But Anna was never found.

I shut down the laptop, deciding I've had enough gloom for one beautiful summer day, and the children need a breath of fresh air.

"Little ones," I say, interrupting their play, "let's get our shoes on. We're going for a walk."

Neither budge. Brody actually groans, so I improvise. My Mary Poppins training kicks in like a well-honed muscle. Mary doesn't order, she *invites.*

"Children," I say, giving myself a slight British accent, "I've just discovered there's a secret fort hidden somewhere in these woods, and who knows what treasures we might find within. But first we must go outside and start looking. So I invite you both to get your shoes on and meet me at the door. The sooner we get there, the sooner we can have the brownies I've packed for our journey."

With that, I stuff a box of store-bought brownies into my backpack (who has time to bake with these two running around?), head for the door, and wait.

The plan works. In no time flat, two eager children greet me with shoes on (not tied, but I help Brody with that), ready to explore. I'm so amazed at my own effectiveness that I fail to notice until I'm outside that I've grabbed Fiona's sun hat by mistake.

Warm sunshine and a soft breeze greet us. I see Taylor across the way, tossing a ball to Nutmeg in the yard. As soon as the kids notice her, they take off in her direction, their little legs running at high speed. Nutmeg wags and barks excitedly, then rolls in the grass as she soaks up their attention.

Taylor takes out her AirPods as I approach. "Hey," she says, with a friendly smile.

"Hi there." I wave. "We're off to find an old clubhouse I heard about. David said it's off a path marked by a knotted oak tree. Any idea where we can find it?"

"Oh yeah, I know that place. I guess it was the teen hangout back in the day. There's a path through the woods we can take. I haven't been there for ages, but I'm sure I could help you find it if you'd like."

"Would you?" I say, and the kids nod eagerly.

"I need to walk Nutmeg anyway, so sure, let's go."

Taylor clips a leash to Nutmeg's harness, but the dog tugs so hard, she unhooks it. As soon as Nutmeg is free, the pup races ahead, but doesn't go too far. The kids keep pace with the dog, while I keep my eyes on them.

Taylor is like a walking body lotion ad. Everything about her is pert and perky. Her Daisy Dukes and revealing white top make it hard not to notice her figure. I feel protective of her—David better keep his eyes and mitts off.

I probably shouldn't look, either. Envy is a terrible trait, but I'd love to have long, luxurious hair like hers. I'm sure I'm not the only one who's come across a picture on Pinterest that I've taken to a hairdresser, had my hair cut the same way, and gotten home only to hate the way it looks. Then I hate myself. Next, I'm wallowing in self-pity with ice cream. And that's such a terrible cliché that I hate myself even more. Alas, this is my cycle of hairstyling, as unbreakable as my stiff, unyielding, wiry follicles. Taylor undoubtedly would have ignored Frizzy Izzy if we'd gone to high school together.

I let these petty thoughts go. The bottom line is that I like Taylor and I can tell by her smile that the feeling is mutual, though my friendly expression is short-lived.

"We still can't find her," I say, glad we have enough distance from the twins to talk freely.

"Can't find who?"

I guess Taylor isn't up to speed, so I catch her up quickly, though I omit the part about seeing Lucas and Fiona canoodling. We fall into step together, trudging along a path parallel to the lakeshore. A canopy of trees provides much-needed shade from the unrelenting sun, which is good because I, the ever-vigilant nanny, forgot to apply sunscreen to the children.

"That's really weird," Taylor says, following my debrief.

"I know," I say. "And it's triggering my obsession." I decide to confide in her to a degree. "I love murder shows," I reveal, whispering like it's something to be ashamed of.

Taylor squints. "Like mysteries?"

"More like true crime," I say. "Stuff that happened to real people."

I expect to be judged. It's a grim hobby, peering into the misfortunes of others, using their suffering for my entertainment. It's a deeply personal fascination, but Taylor doesn't need to know all that.

To my delight, she smiles back at me. "Oh yeah, I know those shows. They're everywhere these days. Do you listen to podcasts or something?"

"Not *or something,* I love podcasts," I say. "Like, obsessively love them." I could leave it at that, but since I'm sensing a kindred spirit, I spit out a list of all my favorite shows, name-dropping random producers and recalling victims and the grisly crimes visited upon them like I'm Death's librarian.

Taylor listens intently.

"I want to produce a show myself one of these days," I tell her. "Like *White Lies* or *Tom Brown's Body,* one of those."

"Well, you've come to the right lake if you're looking for a mystery," she says. "I mean, we don't just have one missing person—we have two." The spark in her eyes dims. "And if Fiona doesn't come back soon, that'll be number three—all women who have gone missing *exactly* thirty years apart from each other."

I shudder as if cold fingers are tickling the back of my neck.

"It's always women," I answer, feeling a lump in my throat and a pang in my heart for all the wives, mothers, and daughters who woke up one day not knowing it would be their last. "And it's not because we're weaker than men," I'm compelled to add. "It's because we intimidate them. They can't control us, so they demean, punish, and sometimes kill us out of fear. They're afraid of our power, so they try to extinguish it."

Taylor meets my gaze, and something passes between us. We're both at that in-between stage of our womanhood, awakening to the reality that life isn't always fair, equitable, or even safe.

"I think you just gave me an idea for a new poem," Taylor says glumly. "I put a lot of my difficult feelings into poetry. It doesn't change anything, but it's become something of a compulsion." Her head is bowed, making me wonder what else she expresses in verse. For someone who seems to have everything, there's a darkness about Taylor I have yet to understand.

Changing the subject, she asks, "Tell me more about yourself. Do you have a boyfriend?"

"No. I attract the unavailable types, and that works for me." I don't explain that I learned through my mother how to erect walls that keep the Big Bad Wolf from blowing my house down. Good guys are a gateway to a broken heart. When a derelict dude lets you down, you can't say you never saw it coming.

"What about you?" I ask, thinking she'll say something about Lucas.

"Nope, I'm unattached," she says, and leaves it at that.

Despite the somber reality of Fiona's absence, I can't help but take in my surroundings, appreciating the woodsy smell and fresh lake air. Nutmeg seems to be doing the same. Every few steps she stops to sniff something—trees, the ground, rocks, a pine cone—which gives me a flash of inspiration, or more likely just a dumb idea. I take off Fiona's sun hat, which I don't need on account of the shade.

"I grabbed the wrong hat by mistake on my way out," I explain to Taylor. "This belongs to Fiona. Do you think Nutmeg might be able to sniff her out?"

Taylor's not getting it, and I should probably let it go, but in for a penny, in for a pound—canine pun intended. "There are instances where dogs have solved cold case murders," I elaborate.

Taylor gasps. "You think Fiona might actually be *dead*?"

"No, no," I say, backtracking. "But dogs have a great sense of smell, like ten thousand times better than ours, or something like that."

"You think she can track Fiona? She's really only demonstrated an aptitude for cuddling and playing fetch." Taylor smiles tenderly at her aging pup.

"Worth a shot?" I ask, which earns a shrug from Taylor.

The kids are busy running around the path, chasing each other while keeping half an eye open for the elusive fort. I call Nutmeg, shoving the hat in her face. She sniffs it before taking it in her mouth. And just like that, we've entered into a game of tug. But then she releases her bite, and all of a sudden, she's off like a shot. She leads us down the path with urgency, like a bloodhound hot on the trail.

"No way," I exclaim. "It's working!"

This goes on for about two minutes, with Taylor and me in the rear, the kids in front, and Nutmeg, nose to the ground, sniffing with purpose. And then, just like that, she stops abruptly.

Taylor and I look about. The ground here is thick with vegetation, lots of ferns and small, prickly bushes that I pray to God won't have a hand sticking out from underneath. But there's no body, and soon enough, I realize that Nutmeg's days as a super sleuth appear to be short-lived. She's found what she was really after: a good spot for a poop.

Taylor and I burst out laughing.

"Oh well," I say, feeling mildly relieved that we won't need a body bag.

It's then I notice a house in front of us. It's a rustic cabin that looks like it's been there so long it's become part of the forest itself. The exterior is tinged with moss. Vegetation grows around the perimeter like an invading green army. The lake is nearby, but this house is built away from the shoreline.

"Does anyone live there?" I ask Taylor, intrigued.

"Oh, yeah," she says. "That's Grace Olsen's place."

The name is familiar, and I realize I was just reading about her. "Anna Olsen's sister?"

Taylor' s eyes widen. "Wow, someone's been doing their homework," she says. "That family has been here as long as the lake. But seriously, Grace is a mainstay, one of the few residents who lives here year-round, even in the winter. No thank you!" She shudders at the thought of the dark, cold woods.

"Wow, is that place even insulated?" I wonder aloud.

"It must be. But Grace keeps to herself, so I've never been inside."

My interest is piqued. Perhaps the reclusive Grace Olsen would be willing to talk to me like she did that reporter years ago.

Chapter 13

Julia

Gone? Can't find her? Julia shivered. David sounded *far* too cavalier. If Christian went missing like that, she'd be in a total panic.

David tried to rationalize the situation. "She likes to play games when she's angry," he said. "I told Izzy I wouldn't put it past her to pull a disappearing act just to get a rise out of me. She can be overly dramatic, and the bigger the reaction she gets, the better. It's either that or she took a walk, passed out under a tree, and she's going to wake up to a helluva hangover. I'm not trying to freak everyone out. I was just wondering if she came over for a visit."

Julia squinted at him. "Why would Fiona come here?" she asked.

"Just to be friendly or maybe to apologize," David suggested. "She was a wreck last night."

Julia thought: *That's putting it lightly. And David hasn't exactly been a shining star, either. Fiona wasn't fighting loudly with herself.*

Julia asked the obvious. "If she's not home and not here, where could she be?"

Nobody answered. Julia entertained a dark thought. "What if she took an early morning swim to clear her head . . . and *drowned.*" She elongated the word, giving it the gravity it deserved.

Erika rubbed her hands up and down her legs, discharging nervous energy. "Did she take anything with her? Any luggage? Is her car still here? It would be a relief if she just left you, David. And understandable. You were a blue-ribbon ass last night. But what if . . .

what if she did drown?" Worry lines creased Erika's face. "Have you tried her phone?"

"Of course I've tried her phone," David snapped. "It goes straight to voicemail."

"Maybe it's powered down or the battery died," Julia suggested.

David shrugged at the possibility. "All I know is the Porsche is still here and so is all her stuff. And she didn't go for a swim in the lake. It's not her thing," he insisted. "I can't count how many times she's told me lake water grosses her out—the mucky bottom, the fish, algae, all that. She'd never go in the water."

"Could she have gone for a hike?" asked Erika.

David answered so quickly it sounded rehearsed. "She doesn't like to hike. She hates bugs," he said.

"She doesn't like lakes, hiking, or bugs. Why on earth did she even come here?" Julia wanted to know.

"Nobody likes bugs, Jules, and just so you know, I had to talk her into coming," said David. "It's a lot of time with the kids in a setting she doesn't particularly care for. But I thought it might grow on her."

"Maybe she went home," Julia suggested.

"Without her car?" Erika reminded everyone.

"Hitchhiked?"

Erika turned her nose up at that one.

"So what then?" asked Julia.

"I don't know." David sounded rattled. "I went out for an early morning run and did my usual six miles."

Of course, he was out running and has to announce it to all, thought Julia. She was surprised he hadn't already posted his workout to IG. *#girlfriendismissingbutdamnIlookfit*

"The nanny was up early as well," David continued, adding details as if he were concocting an alibi. "And she didn't see or hear Fiona leave."

"Are you *sure* she was in bed when you went for your run?"

Julia's question hung in the air. She couldn't purge the image of Fiona twirling around the bonfire like a music box ballerina in risqué attire. Now she had a vision of her quietly sneaking out of the bedroom, to go where? Perhaps off on a rendezvous, but with whom?

David did one of those rom-com double takes, looking like a man with rapid-onset indigestion. "Are you thinking she snuck out on me while I was sleeping?" he asked.

The deer heads gazed down with knowing eyes, as if they had the answer but weren't telling.

David rolled his neck. He was obviously stressed. Or was it all an act?

"She sleepwalks," he said, clearly relieved to have an explanation for Fiona leaving his bed that didn't involve an illicit tryst. David's self-image couldn't withstand such a blow. "I'm not sure how alcohol and Ambien mix, but it can't be a good combination," he added. "Either way, I bet she's sleeping it off somewhere and she's going to wake up confused, maybe with a few mosquito bites, but no worse for the wear."

"Or she sleepwalked right into the lake." Julia's voice broke slightly as she sent Erika a worried look.

"That settles it," said Erika definitively. "We're calling the police."

But David pooh-poohed the idea with a grimace. "She's quite touchy about her sleepwalking. She'd never forgive me if I made a fuss about it. The nanny's watching the kids. Let me keep looking. I'm sure I'll find her."

Maybe. Or maybe not, thought Julia, gulping down her growing apprehension. Again, she entertained the dark notion that David had nefarious reasons for wanting to delay the police as long as possible. But that was crazy. He might be a womanizer, but he'd never been violent. Still, her intuition told her something didn't add up.

"David, look, let's not ignore the obvious," said Julia sternly. "You didn't have a quiet night with Fiona after the bonfire. I'm pretty sure the whole lake heard you arguing."

Erika leaned forward in her chair, her elbows resting on her knees, a cagey look narrowing her eyes. "Fucking the nanny, David? Really? How cliché of you."

David's smug expression did little to defuse their suspicion. "Fiona and alcohol do *not* mix," he said emphatically. "And Fiona and your crazy blue concoction is even worse. She was out of her mind last night. You all saw her." David's eyebrows shot up in horror. "It was cringeworthy, the whole thing," he continued. "Then, when we're getting ready for bed, she starts going off on me, spouting all kinds of accusations. I have no clue where she got that insane idea about the nanny."

Julia cleared her throat uncomfortably. "From what I overheard, it sounded like she got it from your behavior."

"And you don't think she could have misread something innocent? These days you touch a young girl on the arm, and you're suddenly a rapist. Obviously, I wasn't sexually harassing the nanny—and I certainly wasn't sleeping with her." His top lip curled. "Good God, I hope you two don't think that of me. You've known me my whole life." He sought reassurances from Julia, who kept her expression inscrutable.

Erika squinted. "I just hope you don't have any incriminating internet searches, David. I might be a defense attorney, but I know how prosecutors think. And they'll look at the twins' iPads. Just saying." Her accusatory stare came across like a stab.

David's posture stiffened. "What are you even suggesting?" he asked. "I didn't do anything to harm Fiona, if that's what you're getting at." His voice carried an edge, but it only made him sound less trustworthy.

"I sure hope not," Erika said.

Julia wasn't jumping to conclusions about David, but she was certainly worried about Fiona. Who knew where she could have gone, what danger she might be in?

This whole thing was too weird to ignore. Someone had to call the police.

"Why *did* the last nanny quit suddenly?"

David picked up the innuendo, returning Julia's question with a defiant stare. She found that quite telling. Good gracious, the things he thought he could get away with because, well, he was David. All those young girls hoping to be the next big thing, sending him their headshots, praying he'd make the right connection to this producer or that director—always someone important that David claimed to know. Did he use this power to coerce some of these women into his bed?

Julia had no doubt.

He saw, he wanted, he took. He was a child in that way. She had always known this about him, but it was strange how it never failed to surprise her. Who was this man who felt so entitled? Julia could only laugh at herself. She knew damn well who he was. And yet she still kept him close to her heart. Childhood bonds were like that, she supposed. It was easy to look through the distorted lens of time and see David as he once was, with the wistful hope he could be that person again: someone who would carry her on his back, drive far out of his way to rescue her, treat her kids like he's their devoted uncle—not the self-obsessed caricature he'd become.

"I told you both, nothing happened with the last nanny," David said in a huff. He turned to go, but stopped himself, standing up straighter and more self-assured.

"She up and quit," he added, if he were playacting his own attorney and Julia and Erika were the jury he sought to convince. "Put us in a real bind. Gen Zers don't take work seriously enough, in my opinion." David seemed satisfied with his retort.

Julia began to construct a mental list of ways David appeared guilty of something heinous. It was all there, a police detective's dream: minimal eye contact (except when he gave empty but impassioned speeches about the prior nanny); his answers at the ready, too practiced and well versed; an overly confident, cocky demeanor; known to have a temper. And last but not least: David had a colossal blowout fight with the missing person the night before she disappeared. None of this looked good.

In her head, Julia composed a truth-telling post for social, wondering how many likes and comments she would get if she dared share it.

Possible captions:

Hey all, this is my hunky, maybe murderous neighbor, David Dunne. Wanna come over for tea? #lakelife #TheGuyNextDoor

or

What's missing from this picture? Hint: it's this guy's girlfriend who we can't find. And PS, they got into a BIG row last night over the nanny, who he may have shagged. #handthatrocksthecradle

If the sordid scene playing out in her mind had been an Instagram Reel, she would probably have racked up a thousand views in an hour. Instead, she had a headache and a sinking pit in her stomach.

"I'm making the call," Julia announced as soon as David departed.

Before she could summon the police, in a move that would undoubtedly earn her David's ire, Lucas emerged from upstairs. His long hair curtained his face, so it was impossible to read his eyes as he shuffled past them without offering a hello. Julia didn't know the musical group depicted on his T-shirt, but she recognized the ripped jeans as a fashion trend that wouldn't go away.

"Hey, Mom, we're out of Dr Pepper," he moaned from the kitchen, his voice muffled, his head most likely buried inside the refrigerator.

We may also be out of time, Julia thought, imagining Fiona at the bottom of the lake or bleeding out after a bear attack.

Erika was quick with her response. "I believe you have a driver's license, Lucas, and you know how to get to the store. We're kind of dealing with a crisis here."

"There's no chips or anything good to eat," he called out.

"I *said* we're dealing with a crisis." Erika practically shouted her reply.

Lucas ambled into the living room, munching on an apple—a far healthier choice than soda or chips.

"What's the problem?" he asked.

"Fiona's missing," Erika said.

Lucas did not react. The name Fiona seemed to mean nothing to him. If she suffered a tragedy, she'd be nothing more than a story to tell his friends. It was sad. Fiona was a person with a life and dreams, and his blank reaction was . . . distressing? Alarming? Deeply concerning? All of the above?

Holy shit. It was really sinking in for Julia. Fiona was gone. She had vanished with no explanation. Julia felt overwhelmed by a sense of unreality—almost dissociation—when Erika interjected something surprising, bringing her back to the moment.

"I saw Fiona head toward our house while you were outside playing guitar. Did you two talk?"

Lucas tossed the half-eaten apple into a wastebasket meant primarily for paper. His mother didn't bother with a reaction, perhaps because she already had a disapproving frown plastered on her face. Lucas stuffed his hands inside the pockets of his torn jeans, looking unsure of himself, like a guy who wanted a guitar to hide behind.

"No," he said blandly. "I haven't spoken to her once since we got here."

Abruptly Lucas turned his back to his mother and headed upstairs. As Julia finally placed a call to the police, she couldn't help wondering if Lucas was telling the whole story.

Chapter 14

Izzy

We're just past Grace Olsen's house when Brody bursts out, "Hey, is that the tree?"

He points ahead to what could be the correct arboreal marker for the path to the Shack. Sure enough, there's something of a trail that's slightly overgrown, but not so much that we can't follow it.

"Good job, Brody," I say, ruffling his hair.

He beams at me appreciatively. There's so much joy in his eyes that I briefly forget all the grief he's given me since I started this job.

We make our way single file, with Nutmeg in front, me right behind, and Taylor bringing up the rear after the twins. Before we get far, I see, through the trees, several police cars zipping down the road. The whoosh of their wheels tells me they're in a hurry.

Taylor and I have a silent exchange, both of us apparently sharing the same fear.

Did someone find Fiona?

I turn around and tell a white lie: "Hey, kids, I just realized I left the brownies for our picnic on the counter. Let's head back and we'll do this again and bring your father. Brody, I know he'll be so excited that *you* found the path!"

The fort doesn't matter as much to Brody as the praise from his dad and the promise of brownies. Luckily, Becca is on the same page, her eyes brightening at the mention of the sweet treat.

We head back at a relaxed pace. There's no crisis as far as the kids are concerned, though I'm full of dread. Nutmeg didn't have any luck finding Fiona, but could someone else have stumbled across her body? I can't help but imagine the worst. Then again, I am my mother's daughter.

Two police cars are parked in front of David's house when we arrive, but no ambulance, so no gurney for a body. I suppose that's a good sign. Regardless, I'm still on the clock, and I need to manage this situation with the kids to the very best of my ability—which means making it up as I go.

I'm stuck because I can't simply ignore the scene before us. Police cars with flashing lights aren't exactly subtle. The kids are naturally curious, but my burgeoning nanny instincts tell me that in this case, less is more. Taylor sees that I've got my hands full. She and Nutmeg depart with a brief wave goodbye, leaving me on my own to figure something out.

I dig deep, thinking back to my psych classes and my nannying research, and I reach the professional conclusion that I need to gaslight the children.

"What are the police doing here?" Brody asks, pointing to a burly officer who stands joylessly beside his cruiser. He has the hat, gun, blue suit, and shiny badge that would attract any young boy's attention, but I make nothing of it.

"Well, obviously they were called here," I say blandly. "The police wouldn't show up somewhere without being summoned."

Brody is so busy puzzling out my non-explanation that he neglects to ask the most obvious follow-up question: *Why would someone have called the police?*

"Come, children," I say, taking their hands. "Let's go upstairs and build a blanket fort! We'll have our picnic there."

Brody and Becca are befuddled enough for me to whisk them inside without protest or further inquiries. *Success.*

As we head for the stairs, I notice that David is off in a corner of the living room talking with a woman who looks official, but she isn't wearing a police uniform. She might be a detective.

He eyes me with concern as I pass by. I respond with a dutiful nod that conveys I have everything well under control. I escort the children upstairs, and suggest they start on the blanket fort while I get the brownies.

Downstairs I go. The scene before me is emotionally charged, which matches my inner state. David talks in a low voice to the detective, who scribbles in her little spiral notebook.

It's one thing to obsessively listen to murder shows and something else entirely to be in the midst of one. Not that I think Fiona is dead. Missing is different—unless you are Anna Olsen or Susie Welch, with prolonged absences that leave no other possible explanation.

The lake takes them . . .

I fear the detective will want to speak with anyone who has information about Fiona's whereabouts. Not only have I been in Fiona's presence, I'm technically living under the same roof. But I don't know anything. I have nothing to offer. So why is my heart pounding like a bass drum?

The detective peers at me over her shoulder. I find her assessing stare unnerving, as though she can read my thoughts with a glance. She is rugged and durable, with a head like a block of granite and eyes that wouldn't smile even if you held a puppy in front of them. She's in her early thirties and has short hair that's styled in a way that suggests she doesn't care much about hair.

She's dressed in a tailored dark pantsuit with subtle pinstripes that enhance her air of authority. Beneath her blazer, she wears a crisp white button-up shirt open enough to reveal a small sapphire pendant attached to a discreet silver necklace. Her black leather ankle boots are speckled with mud that she may have acquired while searching for Fiona.

David's nervous energy is palpable. His gaze lands everywhere except on the detective, who is still focused on me.

"Hey there, I'm Detective Ruth Baker. Are you the nanny?"

Oh, shit. Now I know how a cornered fox feels. Supposing Detective Baker is even remotely good at her job, she may figure out I fabricated my way into my current position. *She who does the lies also does the crimes.* I'm only nineteen, but I think I've just had my first hot flash. "Yes, I'm the nanny," I squeak.

Even my job title makes me sound guilty of something.

"Can you stick around? I'd like to talk with you after I finish here." Baker sends a stony stare, and I know an order when I hear one. The good news is, I don't have to strain to eavesdrop on David's interview.

"How long have you and Fiona been together?" the detective asks. Her voice matches her appearance—gravelly and joyless, different from how she spoke to me, a lot less friendly. Is David already under suspicion?

"About three months now," he says. "We met at a coffee shop near my home in Manhattan. She forgot her wallet, so I offered to pick up the tab."

"How chivalrous," mumbles Baker, staring at her notepad. "And Fiona—what's her last name?"

The detective has pen to paper, ready to jot down the answer, but interestingly enough, David seems to have drawn a blank. His mouth opens, but nothing comes out. I don't know Fiona's last name, either, but I'm not the one sleeping with her. The pause lasts long enough for us all to squirm. Finally, it clicks for him.

"Maxwell," he spits out. "Fiona Maxwell. Sorry, I'm just a bit shaken by all this."

"I bet," says Baker, her pen scratching something on her notepad that's probably not in David's favor.

"Do you have a picture of her?" Baker asks.

David takes out his phone, and the detective gives his screen a cursory look.

"Pretty," she notes.

"Yeah, she is," David agrees.

"And *young,*" Baker adds with emphasis.

David's posture stiffens. He's the talent scout who doesn't like to be on the receiving end of scrutiny, especially from a woman.

"She's in her thirties." He sounds defensive. "She's not a kid."

Detective Baker utters an ambiguous "uh-huh" while giving the home interior the once-over. "Nice place you have. Appearances are important to you?"

David's eyes narrow. "I'm not sure what you're getting at, Detective, but I'd certainly like Fiona to *appear* back here," he answers testily.

I have a feeling he doesn't realize who he's up against. Baker is shrewd. She knows showy people like David Dunne wouldn't hesitate for one second to tell a lie to safeguard their veneer of perfection.

"So, you two are close?" Baker asks.

David screws up his face. "She's my girlfriend," he says, as if that's answer enough.

The detective's eyebrows arch questioningly. I'm watching her watch him. Did she catch him lick his lips or run his hand through his hair? Something tells me Baker sees all and then some.

"What I'm really wondering is if you two had any recent arguments or relationship troubles?" Baker continues. "Anything that might make her *want* to take off without saying goodbye?"

I'm thinking: *Hell, yes,* but David's blank expression veils his emotions.

"No, not really. I mean, she drank a lot last night. She wasn't herself, so we had a little heated discussion outside, but it was no big deal."

I figure the detective will pounce on the fight that David tried to downplay, but to my surprise she goes in a different direction. It's almost like I can hear alarm bells ringing in her head.

"From my experience, alcohol and water do not mix," Baker says gravely.

"She hates lake water," David says. "She'd never go swimming."

"When people drink, they often say one thing but do another. We need to search the lake—now."

Baker gets on her cell phone.

"Hey, Tom," she says. "I'm at the Dunne residence following up on the missing person report." She gives the address. "We need three divers on the scene ASAP to search for a body in the water. Yeah, that's right. The missing woman is Fiona Maxwell. Last known whereabouts were this address. Evidently, she had a lot to drink last night and may have gone for a swim. The boyfriend says he's called the cell, and it goes to voicemail, but let's try to get a last known location on it—you know how to do the paperwork. And send a K-9 unit, too. Maybe we get lucky, and she had enough common sense to stay on land."

Baker ends the call, but her expression remains somber.

"I'm sure you're worried, but let's have faith. We need to let the search teams do what they do best and hope we find Fiona alive and well. Do you know how to reach her family? Someone should let them know what's going on. And who knows, maybe she's been in contact with them."

David draws his mouth into a straight line. He appears to shrink before me. "No . . . I've no idea about her family," he admits.

"What about where she's from?"

"She's got a place in New York. That's all I know."

"Are you even Facebook friends?"

David shook his head. "I don't think she's on social media."

"I see," says Baker, but if she thinks like I do, she finds it odd that a young woman would have no social media accounts. "What about an employer?" Baker continues. "Anybody she might check in with?"

Again David shook his head. "She's self-employed, so no."

Baker pauses, waiting for him to elaborate, but David leaves it at that. Based on his earlier responses, there's a good chance he has no idea how Fiona makes money, and he probably doesn't care.

Baker is as unimpressed as I am. "I see," she says, looking at her pad of paper, but she has very little to write down. "You mentioned things got a bit heated last night. Can you tell me more about that?"

David shifts his weight uneasily from one foot to the other. "It was nothing. Just a little misunderstanding, that's all."

I cough. It's a reflex reaction. I didn't mean to call attention to myself, but bullshit doesn't go down easily.

Detective Baker whirls around. I try to make myself invisible.

No shocker, it doesn't work. I'm frozen like a thief caught in a spotlight.

"Did *you* hear anything last night?" Baker asks, stepping toward me.

From over her shoulder, I catch David's eyes harden.

My heart skips a beat. I'm afraid to say the wrong thing. I still need this job, but I have no interest in protecting my boss or endorsing his lies with one of my own.

"I mean, no, not really." I hate how my voice shakes. Even though I'm telling the truth, I fear I sound deceitful. "I was too far away to pick up their conversation, so I can't say what it was about, but they both sounded kind of upset."

Upset. There. Now, that's a fine word choice. I could have said *infuriated, wrathful,* or *irate,* which would have all been accurate. But *upset* says enough. David can elaborate from here, and Detective Baker isn't going to let him squirm out of it.

Unfortunately, Baker's not letting *me* off the hook, either. She advances, holding her little spiral notebook out in front of her like a Taser. I take a tentative step in retreat. The air has chilled a few degrees. David advances, falling into step behind the detective.

"She's just the nanny. She doesn't know anything," he says. "Fiona was drunk and being ridiculous. It was nothing serious."

Baker gives David a sidelong glance. She's not buying it, and now I'm all revved up. *Just the nanny, my ass!* Suddenly I don't feel so bad about disclosing last night's tumult. I may not be experienced at my job or entirely truthful about it, but I am working hard to care for this man's children. You'd think he'd show some respect.

"We all had some drinks," he adds. "But whatever Fiona and I were arguing about, it wasn't important enough for me to even remember."

"But it was loud enough for others to overhear it," Baker counters. "So, Just the Nanny," she continues, "I assume you go by another name."

Her smile is meant to be disarming, but I remain on edge. I tell her my full name, Isabelle Rebecca Greene, and that I'm called Izzy for short, without mentioning the Frizzy Izzy nickname that's followed me since middle school. Then I wait for the worst, consumed by an irrational fear that Baker is going to call my mother, who will demand I come home.

She asks for my ID, but that's up in my room and Baker would rather keep talking.

"What do you think happened to Fiona?" she inquires.

I sense no prejudgment in her question. She's inviting me to be open, but David's cold stare could turn me to stone. I might as well have "She knows more than she's telling" emblazoned across my forehead.

"Well, Fiona did drink a lot last night," I croak. My knees feel weak. My legs are as sturdy as pipe cleaners.

"That much I gather," says Baker. "And you heard a fight but didn't hear what it was about?"

I nod, though not emphatically.

"Anything else?" Baker sounds hopeful. "Did you see anything unusual? Something to explain where Fiona might have gone or what could have happened to her?"

In typical Izzy fashion, without thinking, I vomit out the unvarnished truth: "She was pretty wild, kind of out of control. She came on to Lucas."

"Who is Lucas?" Baker asks.

"Lucas?" shouts David in disbelief. "Like, the kid next door, that Lucas?" He appears dumbfounded.

A shiver of fear slips down my spine. I should have kept my mouth shut. I don't know where I got the knee-jerk reaction gene, but it keeps getting in my way.

Baker interrogates me with her eyes. "And what exactly happened between Fiona and this boy next door—Lucas?" she asks.

I don't want to be involved in this, but I lie only when absolutely necessary. "I was up on the deck last night after I put the kids to bed, and I saw Fiona and Lucas kissing on his patio," I confess.

"What do you mean, you saw Lucas and Fiona kissing?"

The new voice draws my attention to the front door. It's Taylor.

My breath catches in my throat when I see that Julia and Lucas's mother, Erika, have also entered the house at the perfect time to hear my story.

Taylor goes pale, covering her mouth with her hand. Julia stands in stunned silence. But if looks could kill, Erika's would be inflicting bloody carnage.

Chapter 15

Julia

Julia spun on her heels, but wasn't quick enough to stop Taylor, who fled out the door. In a flash, her daughter was gone.

At least David's massive windows were useful for something. She could watch her daughter's rapid retreat back to the house.

Everyone was understandably surprised about the Lucas and Fiona bombshell, but why would Taylor care who Lucas was kissing? If anyone should be in a tizzy, it would be Erika, who just found out her child (still technically a teenager) was locking lips with a much older woman. And who knows what else they did?

Julia knew of no romantic history between Taylor and Lucas. So why was her daughter acting like a jilted lover? When the answer finally came to Julia, it was so obvious that she felt foolish and, even worse, like a bad mother. She had it all wrong from the start. Taylor didn't reject Lucas—it must have been the other way around.

She'd been so self-absorbed, the endless heap of financial worries piling up like snow in a blizzard, that she'd overlooked what would have been apparent to anybody with a drip of common sense. Taylor and Lucas had a secret romance, and her daughter got burned. That had to be it.

Did this romance blossom on the college tour? Was there a big fight? Something else?

Julia let the thoughts go as Erika strode across the room, her footsteps heavy, and an accusatory finger aimed at the nanny.

The young nanny's complexion was dead white.

Erika leaned forward, closing in fast. "What did you say? You saw them doing what?"

In a voice abuzz with anxiety, Izzy repeated her confession. "I went onto the deck to get some fresh air and saw them below. Lucas was playing guitar on your patio, and Fiona came over to him . . . and well, yeah, they kissed. I saw it."

Erika's attention swiveled to David. "Did you put her up to this? Ask her to lie for you to make my son look bad?"

"Ask Izzy to lie? Are you out of your mind?" David came out from his corner like a fighter hearing the bell. The detective held up her hand, halting his advance.

"I did no such thing," he went on, while keeping his distance. "Tell her, Izzy." His tone was firm. "Tell her I didn't ask you to lie for me."

"Oh, like *that's* not intimidating," Erika shot back.

"Whoa, whoa," said Baker. "Let's all take a deep breath and relax."

David did the opposite. His shallow breaths were ragged and quick. "And why would I want Izzy to concoct some wild scenario in which I end up being painted as the jealous boyfriend?" he wanted to know. "If anything, I'd want *less* suspicion put on me, not more."

And here it was again, David's temper catching like a match to a pile of dry kindling. His face flushed, his top lip curled into a snarl, his eyes narrowed to slits. This was the Jekyll and Hyde metamorphosis that had always thrown Julia for a loop. He could be like a Doberman in that way—placid one second, ferocious the next, triggered by the slightest sound. In this case, Erika was blowing the dog whistle.

To her credit, Erika held her ground. "The opposite is true as well," she said firmly. "If you did something to Fiona, you'd want someone else to look suspicious. And who better to target than an innocent high school boy?"

"Oh, spare me, Erika," David scoffed. "How innocent can he be after locking lips with a thirty-year-old woman who was drunk out of her mind? I have no reason to think Izzy would lie, and every reason to think it's true—or did you forget the lap dance Fiona gave your husband? I haven't seen a smile on Rick's face that wide since your wedding day."

Julia bristled. *Leave it to David to cut deep.* Unfortunately for Erika, he wasn't done.

"And thanks for basically accusing me of some kind of foul play—in front of the police, no less. Is that what you really think of me, after all these years?"

"I think we're all jumping to conclusions," said Baker. "I'm not suspecting anyone of anything right now. All I know is that an adult woman has been reported missing for a handful of hours. I'm just gathering basic information. We'll have a search team head out shortly, and we'll go from there."

"What if she doesn't turn up?" Julia asked. "What then?"

"Let's not get ahead of ourselves. Most of the time, these things get resolved on their own."

David puffed up with obnoxious vindication. "That's exactly what I've been saying," he declared, directing his retort to Julia. He hadn't wanted the police involved, and now that they were, he made it clear where he cast the blame. "This is all going to resolve itself, and we'll have wasted everyone's time and resources."

"It's not a waste," said Baker. "I'm just doing my job, and I've got one last question for Izzy. Did you happen to see Lucas acting aggressively toward Fiona? Was there any physical force? Did you hear any threats, coercion, that sort of thing?"

Izzy shook her head decisively, but her eyes drifted over to David as though afraid of his reaction.

Baker put David on the spot. "So, David, were you the last person to see Fiona? She did come back to the house with you after the fight?"

"Yeah, we went to bed together. And the 'fight' you keep talking about was just a little disagreement."

"And what time did you go to bed? And when did you notice she was missing?"

David appeared to calculate in his head. "It was probably after midnight. And then it wasn't until I got back from my run, maybe around eight o'clock this morning, that I realized she wasn't here."

"Was she in bed with you when you got up?" Baker asked.

"I thought so, but I was trying to be quiet and not wake her. I assumed she was there."

Baker nodded, but Julia could see doubt percolating in her eyes. "And the girl who ran out of here? Who was that?"

Julia spoke up. "That was my daughter, Taylor. But I don't know what upset her so much."

Baker nodded again, but this time, she conveyed compassion. "Young love," she said. "I remember it well . . . sort of."

Julia tried to get Erika's attention, but her friend wouldn't look her way. What was that all about? Did she have something to hide? Perhaps she was nervous that Lucas had lied to them, claiming he had never even spoken to Fiona. *In fairness, it's hard to chat when your lips are locked together.* But did Erika know more than she was letting on? If so, Julia couldn't fathom why she was keeping secrets.

Julia let her ruminations go, refocusing on her priority—protecting her daughter above all else. "I'll talk to Taylor and let you know if there's anything important to share."

"I'd appreciate that," said Baker. "Depending on how this goes, I may need to talk to all of you later, including Lucas. Here, take my card." Julia accepted the business card Baker removed from her wallet. "And what's your name?" Baker asked.

Julia gave the detective her information. Baker jotted it down and asked, "Anything else to add? Did you see anything out of the ordinary?"

Julia shook her head. "No, nothing really," she said. "You mentioned David and Fiona's argument, so I guess you already know about that. I only overheard some of it."

Erika wouldn't let an opportunity to deflect attention away from Lucas pass her by. "Oh, and don't believe David, that was hardly a *little* fight," she said to Baker.

Wisely, the nanny stayed in the kitchen as she stole glances up the stairs, likely wondering how the kids were faring without her.

Julia occasionally heard the stomp of little feet and soft giggles emanating from one of the rooms above. Luckily, the children seemed unbothered by the morning's events.

"Did you happen to hear the argument?" Baker asked Erika.

"Parts of it. And it was pretty intense," Erika said.

"Any idea what it was about? Oh, and your name, please."

"I'm Erika Sullivan. My husband is Rick Sullivan, and Lucas is my son. And David and Fiona had a big blowout about David sleeping with the nanny."

"Not me!" Izzy exclaimed as heads turned in her direction. "He slept with the other nanny—or not, because I don't know for sure. I don't know who he's slept with. I'm new here."

Poor thing is nervous as a fawn, thought Julia.

Baker tapped her pencil against her notebook. She gave David an assessing stare. "That sounds like an argument I'd remember," she said. "Now, I'm assuming the fight happened after the kiss, right?"

"Yes," Izzy said with confidence.

"And the boy who kissed Fiona, he's your son?" Baker asked Erika. "And he's how old?"

"He's eighteen and *allegedly* kissed," Erika clarified.

"Right, allegedly kissed," Baker corrected herself.

David strode into the center of the group. "Couples fight. People kiss. Sometimes people take off and then return, especially after a night like Fiona's. So like you said, Detective, unless the person vanished under suspicious circumstances, or you find her body in the water, God forbid, there's not much to do but wait this out."

Baker put her notebook away, preparing to leave. She paused to check out David's new digs once more. Julia could imagine what she was thinking. This modern, gleaming, glass-faced edifice looked entirely out of place compared with the neighboring homes.

"You sure do have a fancy place, Mr. Dunne. I assume you have a security system."

With that, David's whole face lit up. "I'm not thinking straight," he said, admonishing himself. "I've been so stressed I forgot the obvious. I guess I'm not used to the house yet, but yes, I have a brand-new security system with cameras, all connected to an app. I can see precisely when Fiona left, down to the second."

David took out his phone and got to work. Everything was online these days. Erika even bragged that her new smart fridge had a camera that allowed her to peek inside from the grocery store to see what produce was rotting.

Judging by David's sour expression, something other than fruit had gone bad.

He stood stock-still, gaping at his phone. He practically vibrated with unease.

The phone fell away from his face, his expression bemused. "It's gone," he said, almost to himself.

"What is?" asked Baker.

"The security camera footage—it's blank." He held up the phone, showing a square aperture—a video playback window which was entirely black. "It didn't record anything. Since midnight last night, the whole system has been out of commission. I just restarted it."

"Why would that be?" Baker wanted to know.

"I dunno," said David, his voice almost a whisper. "Maybe the internet was out, or it could have been a system malfunction."

"Yeah, a very convenient one," said Erika, echoing Julia's thoughts exactly.

Chapter 16

Izzy

Am I living under the same roof as a murderer?

I felt kinda badass, secretly investigating the unsolved disappearances at Lake Timmeny disguised as a prim and proper nanny. But now, I'm apparently working for a man who might have offed his girlfriend. Suddenly these cold cases don't feel so cold. If my mother, aka Ms. Drown-in-a-Tablespoon-of-Water, knew what I was up to, she'd drag me home by my ear like a bratty kid—back when you could do such a thing to bratty kids. While part of me is second-guessing my decision to be here, I can't turn back now. In fact, Fiona's disappearance makes me more determined to get to the bottom of things.

Detective Baker left to oversee the water search and rescue operation with a promise to follow up with David later—a pledge that, to my ears, sounded more like a threat. Julia and Erika departed without any pleasant goodbyes. I assume both went to check on their respective children. I'm sure Lucas will get a good grilling from his mother. Will he deny it all? Fiona isn't around to tell her side of the story.

As for Fiona, where could she be? We all hope she's not in the water, but the longer this goes unresolved, the more concerned I become for her well-being.

Everyone left, but David's still agitated. He paces around the living room, muttering expletives at his phone. I imagine he's trying to figure out what happened to the security system and why the camera was disabled after midnight. Was it an inconvenient technical malfunction or something else, something intentional? I understand that David might be putting on an act to fool everyone, including the police.

I don't stick around to see how he devolves. Instead, I head upstairs to check on Brody and Becca. It will be hard to hide a team of scuba divers from them, especially in a house with so many windows overlooking the water. I'll have to concoct a believable explanation for what they're doing and why.

While I didn't think I'd left them alone for long, I should have known that children don't need much time to make a gigantic mess. To my astonishment, they've converted their bedroom into a lunar landscape with white sheets stretched from wall to wall, pinned in place with chairs and a small desk that the kids managed to move by themselves. Since both are unscathed, I direct my attention to the scratches they've put in David's new hardwood floor, no doubt from shuffling the furniture around.

Apple cider vinegar mixed with olive oil can work miracles on the gouges (thank you, Grandma), but that will have to wait. I need to clean up this fortress and get the kids out of the way before the divers hit the water.

"Sorry that took so long," I tell them. "But everything's fine."

Sort of. Kind of. Liar.

The kids don't notice that I've returned without the promised treats.

"Welcome to Fort Brody!" he announces, emerging from a cave of white sheets, a pleased-with-himself grin stretching from ear to ear. For some inexplicable reason, he's wearing turtle floaties around each arm.

Not to be outdone, Becca crawls out from underneath the sheets on her brother's heels. "No, it's Fort Becca," she insists.

Before I know it, I'm dragged through a narrow makeshift tunnel into a fabric underworld. It's actually quite lovely. A broomstick placed strategically in the center creates a big top effect that gives me plenty of headspace and breathing room. Pillows galore are strewn about to make sitting more comfortable.

Becca even thought to bring her tiny tin tea set. She primly pours me an imaginary cup that I drink as daintily as possible, my pinkie finger extended for proper etiquette. I don't want to be rude and rush her, but we can't spend long drinking imaginary beverages. The divers will be on the scene any minute. I hear a boat motoring about.

"We'll have more tea later. We're going out for walk, so let's all use the bathroom before we leave."

Becca stays seated with her tiny tin cup and Brody heads to the bathroom first. I follow him out with a reminder to wash his hands. "I know, I know," he says.

I wait by the door, but when it closes, I feel someone grab my arm from behind. I'm so startled I gasp. Becca is still enjoying her tea, while my heart is now firmly lodged inside my nose.

I turn slowly to see who seized my arm. Part of me thinks (hopes) it's Fiona, but my face falls when I realize it's David glaring at me. I try to pull free, but he doesn't let go. In fact, his grip only tightens. His brown eyes look black, like a turbulent sea. I assume he's upset about the mess in the bedroom.

"I told the kids they could make a fort," I say preemptively. "But I promise I'll clean it up soon."

I don't tell him about the marks on the floor, not while he's clearly so volatile.

"I'm not worried about that. Look, Taylor is downstairs," he says. He might not be angry about the fort, but his tone conveys he's upset about something. I detect a low, menacing growl, reminiscent of a distant rumble of thunder. "She wants to talk to you."

Maybe my confession angered him more than I realized. I wouldn't have said anything if the police weren't involved. But I suppose David would have appreciated a heads-up beforehand. News of the kiss must have been a shock.

David glances over his shoulder when he hears a boat on the

lake. Does it make him feel sick to his stomach? Or does he already know what they're going to find?

I need to tread carefully. I don't know who I'm dealing with, and true crime podcasts tend to follow a familiar script. As the walls close in, the prime suspect becomes more desperate. They start acting out, behaving erratically, taking dangerous risks, and perhaps resorting to desperate measures. David's not there yet, but given the ugly twist of his mouth, it may not be long before he reaches a boiling point. Good thing Taylor's here, so I have an excuse to leave.

But David won't let me go. His cold, threatening eyes linger, his fingers pressing harder into my flesh. I study his knuckles, which are white and strained. My arm begins to ache in his grasp. If he crowds my personal space anymore, he'll be pressed up against my body. As it is, I can smell coffee on his breath and that musky odor I noticed after his run. He towers over me, blocking the hallway light like an eclipse.

"I want you to think carefully about what you share from now on, Izzy," he says. "You don't have the full picture. That stuff you said about Lucas makes me look bad. Real bad. You understand that, right?"

I nod like I'm under a hypnotic spell.

David continues. "I'm not the jealous type," he assures me. "And I'm also a very forgiving person. I know Fiona wasn't thinking clearly last night. I don't hold what she did against her. I'm not like that, Izzy. And I forgive you as well. I get why you told the police what you saw, but I don't need you filling Taylor's head with stories about me. I know how you teenagers are. Everything goes online the second you hear it, and I have kids and a business to think about. So let's keep it all quiet. Do I make myself clear?" I feel him tighten his grip ever so slightly, punctuating his point.

"Of course," I answer dutifully. The coldness in David's expression seeps into me. I can't help but imagine the hand that's pressed into my arm wrapped around Fiona's throat.

I strain to keep my face from exposing my fear. The last thing I want is for David to know I'm quaking inside.

He finally lets go. Instinctively, I pull back from him, rubbing my sore arm. He smiles at me warmly, like everything is fine again.

"I'll take the kids for a while," he says. "We'll grab an ice cream so they won't be here while the police do their search. You can take a break. Have a good time. And Izzy, remember . . . watch what you say."

Taylor's waiting for me downstairs. She hovers by the door, eager to leave even though she's just arrived. She's wearing long pants, a light T-shirt, and sneakers, not sandals. She's lost her effervescence. Her face is flat and expressionless.

I make a break for the door, hoping she has the same idea as I do and wants to go somewhere to talk.

I hear laughter and running footsteps overhead that sound like a stampede. The kids must be happy about their ice cream outing with Dad. He seems genuinely loving with his children. But I know the fear I felt upstairs wasn't in my head. David's an enigma, some kind of shape-shifter. He's rich and arrogant but also hardscrabble and street smart. His home is refined, but his gold chain and chest hair scream thug life. I don't know him well at all, and that only deepens my worry.

"Hey," I say softly to Taylor. "Are you doing okay?"

She nods, but it's hardly emphatic. "Can you take a drive with me?" she asks.

"David said I could have some time off. He's taking the twins for ice cream . . . get them away from everything going on here."

"Good," Taylor says, swinging her car keys around her index finger. "My dad said I could take the Defender. Let's go."

"Where to?" I ask.

"You'll see," she says.

I follow her out into a perfect, sun-filled day. The air is fresh with the smell of blooming flowers and warm, dry dust. Nothing is threatening about the bright blue sky and puffy clouds drifting over the lake. But amid all this beauty, a woman is missing, and I can't allow myself the simple pleasure of a lovely afternoon.

We get into the car. It's a luxurious ride. The leather seat caresses my skin. The dashboard has enough sophisticated electronics that this thing should be able to fly.

Taylor offers me bottled water, which I accept and drink greedily. She fires up Spotify—some pop song about love, loss, and a cheating ex-boyfriend starts playing. I wonder if it makes Taylor think about Lucas. Is that what she wants to talk about? *What did I see? What do I know?* Precisely what David doesn't want me to share. His words of warning come back to me, and my arm starts throbbing all over again.

Whatever Taylor wants to discuss, she's keeping it to herself. We silently cruise along narrow Vermont back roads, moving at a decent clip. Taylor is definitely on a mission. She has some specific destination in mind. But why keep it a secret? At least she's a good driver and very conscientious. She always keeps two hands on the wheel and looks comfortable maneuvering this big, expensive car.

"This is my father's real love," she tells me. "He's obsessed with this ride."

"I bet," I say, marveling again at the interior and how the upper class lives. "Why'd he let you take it?"

The verdant beauty of Vermont speeds past us at a dizzying pace. The greenery is so lush it's like I'm driving through a painting.

"He'll do anything I ask. You know—Daddy's little girl." Taylor sends me a telling smile.

"Oh yeah, I can relate," I say. "My parents are divorced and my father will basically buy me anything to pay off his emotional debt." We share a laugh that helps to break the ice. I take the opportunity to check in with her. "So how are you doing?" I ask.

"About Lucas, you mean?"

"Yeah, I'm sorry. I didn't intend for you to find out that way. I'm sure it was a shock."

"It's better that I know." Her voice has an edge that wasn't there a moment ago.

"I didn't see them do anything major, just a kiss," I feel the need to explain.

"He's not my boyfriend," Taylor says coldly and doesn't elaborate.

We drive in silence for a few minutes, with my gaze out the window, the music barely registering in my ears as my thoughts drift elsewhere. It's odd how worried I am about the kids. Is David going to feed them a good lunch? He is their father, but I wouldn't fill them up with so much junk that they won't have room for a couple of vegetables or some fruit in their system. And they must be wondering about Fiona. What's he saying to them?

Maybe it's the crisis, but I'm protective of these little rug rats all of a sudden. I'm like an undercover cop who's gotten too close to the subject of an investigation.

Eventually Taylor turns off the road, and we bump along a rocky lane. It's very shady. With the window down, the change in the air brings a sudden coolness to my skin. We don't drive far down this uneven route before Taylor pulls over abruptly, coming to a hard stop. "We're here," she says.

We get out at the same time and I follow Taylor toward a clearing. Soon we're surrounded by a wide expanse of tall, lush green grass dotted with wildflowers. The sun beams down on us with few trees to offer shade.

What stands out to me most is the lopsided rectangle of recently dug-up earth about the size of a tennis court. Sprigs of vegetation already pop up through the rocky soil. By this time next year, it'll be hard to tell the land here had ever been excavated. Flapping in a nearby tree is a strip of yellow plastic that catches my eye. It looks like the tail of some kid's kite caught in the branches. As I get closer, I make out black lettering printed on the plastic strip spelling out C-A-U. I'm not a huge fan of *Wheel of Fortune,* but if I had to buy a vowel, it would be an I or an O to finish the word: CAUTION.

Which is exactly how I'm approaching the dug-up earth. My steps are purposeful to avoid trampling over potential evidence.

"What is this place?" I ask, my voice slightly hitched. I think I know the answer. It's beautiful here, a grand vista overlooking a lush valley below, but a touch of melancholy hangs in the air.

A wicked gleam springs to Taylor's eyes. "This," she says, her dark smile spreading, "is the scene of the crime."

"The bones?" I whisper, feeling both confident and afraid that I'm right.

Taylor confirms with a nod. "Yup. This was going to be somebody's home. They were going to widen the road and build a four-bedroom house, until their contractor dug up a body. Now it's just been sitting here since the discovery. Seems like the owner has no interest in continuing to build on a grave site—bad feng shui, or something."

A shot of fear burns down my spine. That skull was somebody's somebody.

"Do the police know anything?" I ask as a shiver ripples through me.

Taylor answers with a shrug. "I mean, there's no positive ID on the remains yet, not that I've heard."

"So we don't know—"

"If it's connected to the vanishings?" Taylor asks, finishing my thought. "No. I guess it could be anybody—there are more missing people in this state than just the two women from Lake Timmeny."

This is my first time visiting an *actual* crime scene, and I'm all kinds of conflicted. When it's a podcast, it's like getting caught up in a story. But this feels real and deeply personal. The sunshine can't warm me. It's as if the smell of decay is somehow caught in the air and trapped in the sodden earth. Even though the bones are long gone, their presence surrounds us.

I feel I shouldn't speak, that this should be a place of quiet reverence and solemn contemplation, but I need to know more.

"Why did you bring me here?" I ask, wondering if Taylor notices the crack in my voice.

"You told me you're a true crime fanatic. Well, here's a true crime for you."

"I think we might have another back at the house," I say. "There's something super strange about Fiona's disappearance. I wonder if the divers have found anything yet. God, I hope not, but—"

"I'm sure they've got nothing," Taylor says. "No Lake Timmeny vanishing has ever been solved that quickly."

I eye Taylor with uneasy suspicion. "You're not thinking we should go all Scooby-Doo on this? I enjoy podcasts, but that doesn't make me an expert in solving crimes."

"Don't sell yourself short." Taylor pats my shoulder encouragingly. "I bet you know way more than you think."

The compliment makes me self-conscious. "I mean yeah, sure, I know *some* things. You have to secure the crime scene, identify all people present, and cordon off the area. Then you start talking to witnesses. It's a whole process." My gaze flickers to the piece of yellow caution tape still trapped in a tree branch. In my mind, I can see how the early stages of this investigation might have played out.

Taylor's face lights up. "See, you know plenty."

"But I don't have the bones, any physical evidence, or the case files . . . I have no idea how to do anything useful."

"I don't want you to work *this* case, Izzy," Taylor explains. "I brought you here in the hope that I'd inspire you to work a different one for me."

I squint in confusion. "What then?"

"I need to know the truth about Lucas. I have to know if he did something to Fiona."

My face burns hot. "Lucas?" I whisper.

"Yes," says Taylor. "If you had asked me last year, I'd have said I knew everything there was to know about Lucas Sullivan, but now . . . my head is spinning, and I don't know what to think."

"It was only a kiss," I remind her.

"That's all you *saw*," she shoots back. "Who knows what happened after that. Boys can be—*pushy*. Trust me."

David's warning rings loudly in my mind. I'm tempted to tell Taylor about the security camera blackout last night, but I keep quiet. Could Fiona have snuck out of the house to rendezvous with the enigmatic young musician next door? It didn't occur to me until just now that Fiona herself could have tampered with the system to get away with a late-night tryst.

"If I'm going to investigate, I need to know the whole story between you and Lucas."

Taylor sinks into a moment of quiet contemplation, staring at the upturned earth that was once an unmarked grave.

"I'll tell you what," she says, refocusing her attention on me. "I want you to go into this unbiased. But if you find out exactly what happened between them or if he has anything to do with her disappearance, I'll tell you everything. Honestly, I could use someone to talk to when I'm ready."

Well, shit. How can I say no to that? Whatever this is about, it's obvious Taylor needs a friend.

"All right," I say. "I'm in."

We shake on it, even though it feels wrong to make pledges at the site of a tragedy. Or perhaps that makes it a sacred vow.

Chapter 17

Julia

It would have been the perfect summer day if it weren't for the divers scouring the bottom of the lake in search of a body. Thankfully, after several hours, the dive team cleared out (as did the spectators), having found nothing.

But a K-9 unit was on the scene and on the hunt. The trained animal picked up Fiona's scent using a shirt David provided, but couldn't trace it beyond the property's perimeter. The paperwork requesting a cell phone ping was submitted. The ping itself, however, proved unnecessary, as David found Fiona's phone in a nightstand drawer. Indeed, it was out of battery.

Even so, who leaves without their phone?

It felt like everyone was doing their job, but each moment that passed was more tense than the last. Julia found herself pacing her kitchen instead of relaxing with a book. She hadn't even posted to any of her social media accounts that day, though she did her part to help with the search. While David, Christian, and Rick spent the afternoon scouring the woods, Julia and Erika kept watch over the twins as they worked their phones, contacting neighbors and uploading a pic of Fiona to the Lake Timmeny Community Page.

Every five minutes or so Julia would find herself thinking: *What the actual fuck? How was any of this possible? Does the lake really take them?*

On top of that, Fiona appeared to be an enigma. She had no

online presence. David didn't know any of her friends in New York City and couldn't get in touch with her parents if he wanted to.

Some boyfriend.

Julia checked in with local businesses, and sent those who agreed to help a picture to share online and in their stores.

So far, no luck.

Nobody had seen Fiona Maxwell. She wasn't in the water. She had yet to be found in the woods (not too surprising considering she hated hiking). And her car and phone were still at the house.

Technically the car belonged to David, so maybe that's why she left it behind. He could have reported it stolen. But if she snuck off, why wouldn't she take her belongings?

Did she flee in a blind panic? Did she leave at all?

Julia shivered at the thought of Fiona's body somehow hidden in a house made of glass.

But David wouldn't . . . he couldn't . . . could he?

The police had come. They'd seen no compelling reason to suspect foul play. All arrows pointed to a woman who was either accidentally lost or *wanted* to disappear.

Julia was distraught but remained determined to stay positive. Freaking out wouldn't do any good. If Fiona *had* taken off on David, Julia couldn't blame her. In less than twenty-four hours, she'd observed serious problems in their relationship. Lord only knew what went on behind those closed doors.

With nothing to do but wait, everyone desperately needed a reset, so they planned to meet at the lakeshore for sandwiches and drinks.

Julia was surprised when David joined them, with a pitcher of gin and tonic, no less. Years of friendship must have trumped Erika's earlier accusations, because he wasn't acting like she'd called him a murderer. He focused his attention on his kids, who played nearby in the sand. He pretended everything was normal, perhaps for their benefit as much as his. Still, things felt strange.

Christian and Rick relaxed on beach chairs after hours of exhaustive searching. Everyone was scratched, dirty, and riddled with bug bites. Erika and Christian appeared to have switched places. It was he who was zoned out on his phone. Was he working or just mentally shut down after their emotionally draining day? Probably the latter. They had a decent GM to mind the business while they were away, and if there was a crisis (other than the obvious), he'd have told her.

Meanwhile, Rick pounded his third Bud—or was it his fifth? Julia couldn't keep count.

"Baker said she's planning for a multiday search effort," he said. "They're setting up a command center down the road—tents, radios, specialized equipment, all that. They're keeping it away from the house because of the kids."

"Same with the reporters," Erika added. "There's been a few helicopters, and a couple news vans came around today, but Baker isn't allowing them down this far anymore since it's an . . . active search area."

Julia keyed in on the pause, which felt intentional, probably because her brain automatically filled the gap with the words *crime scene. Oh, David, please don't be that guy.* But it was good the reporters were going to stay away. Better for everyone that they did.

"The media won't stick around for long anyway," Rick continued. "They'll move on to the next story, probably tomorrow. A toddler at church has a longer attention span. They won't be back until she's found."

If she's found.

Julia set her hand on Christian's knee, breaking the spell his phone had over him. He was filthy and clearly drained from the strain of the day. Despite their problems, he had a big heart. He'd look for Fiona all night if it was safe to do so. She felt a surge of love and gratitude for her husband and for the life they shared. All the trite sayings used in times of crises felt true: *Life is precious. Savor every moment because you never know . . .*

"I love you," she whispered. When he whispered back the same, the devotion in his eyes filled her heart. Julia let go of the fears that had plagued her, the persistent gloom clouding her mind. They had their problems, but they also had each other.

Julia, trying to dispel some of the stress, stretched her legs and soaked up the scenery. A gentle wind created ripples that raced across the dark water before slapping against the canoes and kayaks latched to the dock. Under other circumstances, the hollow rhythmic sound of the lapping water would have lulled her into a meditative trance, but not today.

Everyone was doing what they could to distract themselves. For Christian, this meant returning to his phone. He wasn't a newshound or social media junkie. Julia couldn't say what kept him so captivated. But she had her own Instagram obsessions—*who was she to judge?*

"Do you think it's related?" Julia's voice was uneasy.

"You mean to the lake lore?" Erika asked.

"Well, yeah," said Julia. "Weren't we just talking about it? The other two disappearances were thirty years apart, and now it's been thirty years since Susie Welch went missing."

Julia's gaze drifted across the water to Susie's old house. It was a simple cottage with a wide front porch, perfect for enjoying sunsets. But now it didn't look so inviting. Even though a new family had moved in long ago, it seemed like a facade—a falsely cheerful front covering a dark history.

"How can they all be related?" asked Christian. "The perpetrator would have to be in their eighties by now, or even older."

"Maybe it's a copycat criminal or a father-son legacy team," suggested Rick.

"Sounds far-fetched to me," David said. "But not implausible. I read the *New York Post*. That rag is definitive proof that *anything* is possible, including father-son kidnapping tandems."

"Or mother-daughter ones," suggested Erika with a smirk.

"Right. We shouldn't be sexist," Rick agreed. "And we shouldn't rule out any possibilities. For all we know, the disappearances could be connected to a voodoo ritual, something handed down through generations."

Julia scoffed. "For what purpose? Do they need a human sacrifice for some witchy spell? That's outrageous."

"What, then?" Erika asked. "Why else would three women disappear from the same lake exactly thirty years apart from each other?"

Nobody had an answer. Music from Erika's house interrupted a brief, weighty silence. It was Lucas practicing his guitar, this time through an amplifier. None of the stressful events appeared to affect his guitar playing. Lucas's notes were crisp and soulful, yet Rick looked annoyed instead of proud of his son's talent.

"Has he even *seen* the sun today?" Rick directed his question to nobody in particular. "He should be outdoors, appreciating nature, maybe socializing a little. What's the point of coming to the lake if you're going to sit on your ass and do nothing but noodle on your guitar all day?"

"Cut him some slack, will you? It's been a rough day for everyone," said Erika. "He had a long conversation with the police, and it was very emotional for him."

"Oh, give me a break," grumbled Rick. "If he hadn't gotten his kicks with an older woman, he wouldn't have had to talk to anyone."

Erika tossed daggers with her eyes. "Way to show compassion, Rick. Here you are demanding I work less, and you're afraid that Lucas won't work enough. When you have the perfect balance figured out, please let me know. And if you'd actually take a moment to listen to your son's music, you'd know he isn't doing *nothing* with his time."

Rick balked. "I don't hear a successful future, I can tell you that much. That boy should go to college, or at least get a full-time job."

"Well, you didn't go to college. Why are you so judgmental of him?"

"Because the world has changed since we were that age, and I don't want him living in my basement."

Erika groaned. "If you're so concerned, why not let him work with you?"

"I'm not tossing him a rope," Rick said. "He can sink or swim on his own, as far as I'm concerned. I was barely encouraged to finish high school. Here he is, scholarship potential and everything, and what's he doing with his time? Singing his sad songs and living a pipe dream, that's what. And besides, he worked for me two summers ago. Remember that?" Rick's wide eyes suggested it didn't go well. "If he needs money, fine. Go and apply for jobs like people do in the real world."

Rick's beard only partially concealed a scowl, and his flinty gray eyes warned of a short fuse. Julia counted her blessings. Taylor might have fallen into a funk, but she was still planning on continuing her education.

Nearby, the children's playful banter reminded Julia that the world wasn't just full of problems. Wherever there was darkness, you could also find the light. But could they find Fiona?

"Maybe we should recruit a larger search party from the campsite," Christian suggested, without looking up from his phone.

Julia thought that made sense. Campsite reservations at the lake's southern end filled up quickly every year, so there was a potential small army of people to help scour the woods.

David pressed his lips into a fine line. "I think we're risking someone else getting lost," he said. "The deeper people go into the forest, the harder it is to find a way out, and cell service gets pretty spotty away from the lake."

Erika laughed. "David, imagine how that'll look on the *Dateline* episode—you telling us to sit on our asses and wait."

Julia almost spit out her drink.

"Back to that, are we?" David sighed irritably. "You've known me practically your whole life, yet you're hell-bent on labeling me some sort of killer. Thanks for the character assassination."

"You're the one who didn't want to call the police in the first place, and now you don't want to expand the search? I've represented guilty clients who have shown more concern. What am I supposed to think?" asked Erika.

"That I'm a good person who didn't do anything to harm my

girlfriend—who I love, by the way. And I'm worried sick about her."

"Yeah, that's what they all say," Erika clapped back.

Julia hated to admit it, but David was being oddly passive. Even so, she would reserve judgment, whereas Erika seemed to have her mind made up, and not in David's favor. She assumed Christian would take Erika's side. It was his idea to expand the search, after all. But to her surprise, he came to his friend's defense.

"David's right," he said. "There are thousands of acres of dense forest out there. How are we supposed to cover all that?"

"We're not," said Rick, tossing his support into what was now the Men's Camp. "This is a job for the police. They're trained to search for people. If Detective Baker wants our help, she knows where to find us. Meanwhile, we need to take a wait-and-see approach. They certainly don't want other people to get lost or hurt trying to locate her. For all we know, Fiona disabled the security camera herself so she could sneak off. As of right now, the police have no leads. If I were them, I'd think she left willingly, and if that's the case, I guarantee they will drag their feet investigating."

Julia shuddered. "Well, that's not an option," she said. "We can't just let her fall through the cracks in the system."

"What system?" Rick asked rhetorically. "It's nonexistent when it's an adult who runs away. At best, you get a haphazard series of starts and stops. Most of the time, the police follow a few leads here and there, and that's if you're lucky."

"You sound like an expert," said Christian as he popped the top of another soda.

"That's because he is. We've gone through this before."

All eyes went to Erika, except for Julia, who felt terribly guilty. She should have considered how Fiona's disappearance would be triggering for her friend, whose mother had vanished from her life.

"You've been looking for your mom all these years?" asked Julia, her voice soft with a blend of surprise and sympathy.

"We gave it a half-hearted effort for a while, but even if we invested considerably more resources, I'm not sure we could have found her," admitted Erika. "Like Rick said, there's no system for finding people who voluntarily vanish, none at all."

Rick took hold of Erika's hand. It was nice to see them put aside the snipes and disagreements, to show a more caring side of their relationship. Rick knew how hard losing her mother had been on Erika. Because she was so young at the time, all Cormac had explained to his despondent daughter was that Mommy had gone away and, hopefully, she'd call or write soon. But she never did.

Julia always thought that Erika had written her mother off. Her father became her world, and this lake, her sanctuary. When Cormac died of a sudden heart attack, not unusual for men his age, Erika had no time to prepare herself for his passing. *Was it really seven years ago already? It's hard to keep track of such things when you're moving at the speed of life.* But after the shock subsided, at least Erika had cherished memories with her dad to hold on to, and a parent for whom she could openly mourn.

"I thought you were too angry with your mom to want to look for her," Julia said. *Why hadn't Erika shared this with her?* Of course, Julia kept her own secrets, and sharing was a two-way street.

"Yeah, I definitely had mixed feelings, but she's still my mother," Erika said. "Even though she left when I needed her the most, I was lucky in many ways—my dad took good care of me, and we had a lot of family that stepped in to help. My aunt Evie lived in the apartment downstairs from us in New York and cooked dinner almost every night. And Uncle James popped over a lot back then. He and Dad were a riot together—a real comedy duo when they got going.

"But still, part of my history was missing. When I was younger, I'd yell at her, pretending she could hear me. I'd tell her I hated her for being so selfish, even though it wasn't that simple. But I wasn't about to waste money on a private investigator, not after what she'd done. So we tried a little on our own, hit a bunch of roadblocks, and eventually I decided to accept the situation, with all its unknowns. Enter mindfulness . . . it's not a cure, but it helps me cope."

It shouldn't be surprising that all their lives were messy and complicated, Julia thought. She contemplated how to accurately caption the five friends at the beach if she were to post a pic to Insta.

Time to play Guess the Malady! Match the problem to the person for the win. 1. Has mommy issues. 2. Conceivably did in his girlfriend. 3. Bordering on bankruptcy. 4. Ashamed of his son. 5. Losing touch with her daughter. Bonus question: Perpetually annoyed with her husband (pick any woman, no wrong answer). #blessed.

Julia's phone buzzed in her hand. *Don't look,* she told herself. *Be here now.* But it could be related to Fiona, someone returning one of the calls she'd placed. She checked and regretted it immediately. She didn't know which creditor was hounding her this time. She'd have to click the link in the tersely worded (read: threatening) text message to find out.

Oh shit. Well, there was nothing to be done about it right now. She'd wait until she was alone with Christian to sort everything out. Perhaps he'd been receiving his own batch of love notes. It would explain why he kept checking his phone like a teen waiting to hear from their current crush.

Julia put her phone away just as Taylor pulled into the driveway. She didn't know where her daughter had gone, only that she'd wanted to take Izzy for a ride. She was happy Taylor was making a friend and hoped it might help her get out of her recent funk.

The girls approached, but Taylor still looked solemn after the road trip. Izzy wasn't faring much better. She had distance in her eyes, rounded shoulders, and no pep in her step. If ever there was a case of the Summertime Blues, these two had apparently caught it.

Nutmeg approached, sniffing the girls intently. Clearly, the dog thought they had gone somewhere interesting.

"What's up?" Christian asked, putting down his phone to acknowledge the rest of the world. "How was the car? She drives like a dream, right?"

Julia resisted a groan. *She. Here he goes again, like the car has boobs instead of wheels.*

"It was fine. And don't worry, there are no scratches, promise," Taylor assured him. "Thanks for letting us borrow it."

"Where'd you go?" asked Julia.

"I took Izzy to see where they found the bones."

That one word, *bones,* charged the air. All heads turned in Taylor's direction.

"That's a pretty gruesome field trip," said David. "Why go there?"

"Izzy's into true crime, so I thought she'd think it was cool."

Considering Izzy's sober expression, *cool* might not be the operative word.

"What's happening up there, anyway?" Rick asked. "Is the new construction finished?"

Before Taylor could answer, Lucas erupted into a powerhouse solo that drew Julia's attention, as well as her daughter's. Julia saw something on Taylor's face that hadn't been there moments ago. It wasn't the same shock and hurt she had observed that morning. No, this was something else. A whiff of vulnerability? Perhaps. Longing? Maybe that. It was something significant, that much she knew, but Taylor was guarding her emotions like precious gems.

"Whatever construction there was, I think it's stopped," Izzy said. "There's some dug-up earth, but it's becoming overgrown."

David poured another G&T from the pitcher into his cup. "Yeah, I heard the new owner put a halt to the whole project until the police finished excavating the area," he said. "And he wasn't interested when he got the green light to continue. I guess he's superstitious. Weird."

Julia knew the look on Christian's face. He smelled an opportunity.

"Hey, that's a prime piece of real estate," he said.

Christian dove back to his phone and, a moment later, rocketed out of his chair with childlike exuberance. "Holy shit. That land is back on the market, and the price is a *steal.* He must really want out.

Dave, Rick, we should pitch in and buy it. I bet you anything it's the perfect spot for growing cannabis."

Cannabis? Julia scratched her head at that one. *Since when is Christian into growing weed? Didn't that go against his sobriety?*

Rick rose from his seat, but not the way a young man would. Julia swore she could hear his knees screaming. "Christian, get a damn grip, will you? Growing cannabis in Vermont is a bureaucratic nightmare. And besides, I think you have enough problems with the one business you're running into the ground. Don't try to latch us to your sinking ship, buddy."

Ouch.

With that, Rick headed toward his house, where Lucas continued to play a mournful tune on his guitar, echoing the sadness in Taylor's eyes.

Chapter 18

Izzy

I think I finally have the nighttime routine down. Brody and Becca brush their teeth without complaint, and I ensure they get their back molars (very important). Then we wash our hands, put on jammies, and read stories—no fussing at all.

Something has shifted since Fiona vanished. The kids are clinging to me for comfort, and I'm supporting them as best I can, though I wish I had someone to lean on as well. Fiona might not have been the kindest, but we slept in the same house last night, so she certainly isn't a stranger. And I know things about her that wouldn't appear in any news reports—like how she likes Greek yogurt, leaves her hair scrunchies around, and prefers all-natural soap. I refuse to use her soap, or move any of her belongings. It feels sacrilegious to disturb the items she left behind—not to mention they could be evidence.

I keep my focus on my job. There are kisses good night, and after all that sweetness, I spend the next hour or so trying to get them to stay in their beds, stop giggling, and finally sleep. While they can be maddening, they're both alive and well. Really, what more can anyone ask for? I set the same goals for tomorrow—*living children, relatively unscathed by the end of the day*—and that's that. Still, if this is parenthood, count me out—or at least give me a super helpful partner.

David certainly wouldn't fit that bill. He came back from the command center looking defeated and has been checked out ever since.

"Detective Baker is asking for no unauthorized search parties and to let the professionals do their job. A team from Northeast Search and Rescue is helping now. We would just be in the way."

I can't tell if he's upset or relieved to be off patrol, although I'd like to think he wants to be proactive. I want to believe he didn't do anything to Fiona. And yet, he was threatening when he warned me not to blab about him to Taylor. As I head to bed, I lock my door for the first time, reminding myself to be *very* careful.

In the morning, the kids sleep in. I'm surprised. Yesterday's events may have finally caught up with them. I head downstairs, half-expecting to see Fiona in the kitchen making breakfast, but I'm the first up and the only one there. I brew coffee because, Lord knows, nannies need caffeine. As I enjoy my hot, overly sugared beverage, I ponder the day's schedule from a comfy chair with a great lake view. As I take in the beauty of this idyllic vacation spot, I can't help but reflect on the underlying darkness. Across from me is Susie Welch's former house, and what should be a pleasant morning is marred by visions of bones and missing women.

I'm lost in thought when Taylor slips inside.

"Any word on Fiona?" she asks, a sprig of hope in her voice.

"None," I answer glumly.

"Lucas is going for a hike with his father. They said you could join them," she tells me.

I groan on the inside. "What? Go hiking with Rick and Lucas? Now?"

Taylor sends me an imploring look. "Yeah, Rick asked me to go with them, but I said you'd probably love to go on a hike, since you've never been to the lake before. I'll stay and watch the kids. I'll tell David I made you take a break to experience some of the area's scenic beauty. He'll be fine with it."

I'm aware I agreed to get to know Lucas better, but traipsing off into the woods with a potentially dangerous musician and his *Duck Dynasty* dad isn't high on my morning wish list. But since I don't see an easy way out, I agree to go. I'm sure David trusts Taylor with the kids as much as he trusts me. He's known her far longer.

In no time, I have on pants and a lightweight hoodie as part of my anti-tick ensemble, and off I go.

I come around the corner to see my hiking companions standing on the same patio where Lucas and Fiona had their tongue-wrestling match. Father and son don't seem particularly close. Lucas has his back to his dad. He's shuffling his feet, hands stuffed in his pockets. I don't blame him—I don't want to acknowledge Rick, either. He looks intimidating in camouflage pants, a matching shirt, and an orange vest. He's also holding a rifle.

I head back to the house to tell Taylor we'll try another way that doesn't involve weaponry, but Rick homes in on me with his hunter's eyes. "Hey, Izzy. Glad you're joining us," he says.

Busted, I turn around, resigned to my fate. I sidle up to Lucas, reminding myself not to be taken in by his friendly grin.

Meanwhile, Rick looks excited to kill something. It's puzzling, because I don't think it's hunting season until the fall.

He notices me eyeing his attire, and especially his firearm.

"We've got a coyote problem around here," he tells me. "More than a few local cats have gone missing. We have a year-round license to hunt them, so I hope we get lucky on our hike."

I'm hoping the coyote gets lucky.

"You should both put on vests," Rick instructs. "I doubt there are other hunters, but better safe than sorry."

Reluctantly I take one of the orange garments he holds out and slip it on like a smock. I look like a walking traffic cone, but it's better than being mistaken for a target.

Lucas puts his vest on, rolling his eyes at his father. It's probably more about the getup than his stance on killing animals. We fall into step behind Rick, who walks like a man on a mission.

The trail is easy enough to navigate, which is a relief. Dressed in camo, Rick looks like a soldier in the war movies my dad likes to watch. His eyes are ever vigilant, probing the dense woods for any sign of movement. Even though I don't know him well, I feel a duty to warn.

"I hope you don't shoot at anything that moves," I say tentatively. "Fiona might be out here somewhere."

"Don't worry. I work as a hunting guide. I know how to identify a target before I shoot."

I'm on a hunting mission myself, and my target is walking five steps in front of me.

We're heading up a slight incline, and already I feel out of breath. I'm pondering ways to break the ice when Lucas slows down. Before I know it, we're marching side by side on a path narrow enough for leafy branches to brush our shoulders.

"My mom gave me the fifth degree because of what you said to the police," he informs me.

I should have been prepared for this. I did rat him out, after all. Perhaps my preoccupation with the bones and the lake lore short-circuited my common sense. Then again, I have an impulsivity issue. And a bad-boy problem as well.

I try to read his emotions. His eyes are veiled behind sunglasses. His mouth is in a half smile, which is annoyingly ambiguous. He's either toying with me or letting me off the hook.

"Yeah, I'm really sorry about that," I say. I don't mean it, but maybe it will soften him up if I'm apologetic. "I just happened to be up on the deck and saw what I saw. And then the police started asking questions about Fiona, and I felt I had to be honest. But I'm sorry if—" My thought is cut short as I stumble over my words and the uneven terrain simultaneously. I fall forward, realizing a second too late that my foot has caught a rock jutting out of the ground.

Thankfully, Lucas is lightning fast. He shoots out a hand and seizes my arm just in time to save me from an embarrassing tumble.

Once I'm steady on my feet, he lowers his sunglasses, peering at me over the rims. His emerald-green eyes mesmerize me. Have I ever seen someone with eyes that color? They're flecked with gold, and the longer I stare at them, the more I can understand how Fiona crossed a line she maybe shouldn't have.

I'm here on a fact-finding mission, I remind myself. It's possible that Lucas has done something awful. Until I know more, I can't let myself get distracted.

"Are you okay?" he asks gently.

I stare at him, unable to find the words. It's those damn eyes, or maybe it's just all of him. Does the forest smell like sandalwood, or is it Lucas? Whatever it is, it's earthy, slightly sweet, and fully enticing. "You've got to keep your eyes open out here," he tells me. "You don't want to be chasing after those twins on crutches. Your job is hard enough."

I offer an uncertain laugh. "They're all right," I say. "I'm enjoying it much more than I expected."

I bite my bottom lip to stop from saying more. An experienced nanny would know what she was getting into, but Lucas doesn't seem to give it any thought.

"Your dad is kind of intense," I whisper, even though Rick is a good twenty feet ahead of us.

"Yeah. Try being his disappointing son."

"Are you two close?" I ask. This might be the icebreaker I need.

"Not especially. He threatened to send me home if I didn't come on this hike, not that I even care about being at the lake. I'd rather be playing gigs with my band."

"I'll have to check out your music," I say. "Are you on Spotify or anything?"

"Not yet. We're going to the recording studio soon, though. We just need a little more money. But my dad's acting like my life is basically over. He's pissed I'm not going to college next year, and he's taking it out on me every chance he gets—thinks I'm demonstrating poor judgment."

I try to suppress a laugh and fail.

"What?" he asks.

"I mean, I watched you kiss the *very drunk* thirty-year-old girlfriend of your next-door neighbor, so I think your dad might have a valid reason for questioning your judgment."

He throws up his hands. "Yeah, that was *not* what it looked like."

I raise my eyebrows at him.

"Okay, it *is* what it looked like," he confesses. "But I didn't kiss her back. I realized it was a bad idea and I pulled away. She took off. I don't know where she went after that."

He sounds convincing, got to give him credit. But I stuck around long enough to know he kissed her as much as she kissed him. *Right?*

Suddenly, I'm not so sure. At the time, I was overcome with surprise. I search my memory, but two scenes play out in my head: one with Lucas pulling Fiona close to him, and another where Lucas pushes her away. I can't say which is true. If I had stayed longer to watch, I would have known.

"I promise I'm telling the truth," he says, like I'm his girlfriend, and he's pleading his case. "She was drunk, and I'm not into her. She just caught me by surprise. If you talk to Taylor, you can tell her that."

My memory comes into sharper focus. Now I'm sure that I saw him kiss her back—with intensity. I can't say what happened after that, but I'm certain that Lucas is lying.

Chapter 19

Julia

Julia inhaled the scent of sunscreen, but it didn't evoke the nostalgic memories of vacation it usually did. It had been over twenty-four hours since they reported Fiona missing, and despite the efforts of the professional search and rescue teams scouring the woods and water, there'd been no sign of her.

She was heartsick. It didn't matter if Fiona was a close friend or not—she was a human being with loved ones who cared about her. The police promised to get in touch with her family, assuming they could find them. It wasn't sitting well with Julia that after several months of dating, David had no clue about her close friends or relatives. Either he was exceedingly self-involved, or he wasn't being honest.

Julia planned to go kayaking, attempting to infuse some normality into the day, though she knew she'd be scanning the shoreline for a body half the time. But to her surprise, Detective Baker had returned. This time, instead of one uniformed officer, four accompanied her. They arrived in several cop cars, all parked in front of David's glass house, their cruiser lights spinning but the sirens off.

They talked in a cluster, like a football team huddling to decide the next play. Julia heard Taylor and the kids frolicking out back, with Nutmeg barking excitedly. She guessed they were playing ball, one of Nutmeg's favorite games. The police, however, had no time for frivolity.

Had they come to collect David so he could identify Fiona's body at the morgue? That couldn't be right, because he was relaxing in his living room, sipping green juice from a tall glass. Julia could see him as clearly as if he were standing outside.

He was sweaty and shirtless, with a towel draped around his neck and white sneakers on his feet. Evidently Fiona's absence hadn't interrupted his workout routine.

Julia strode up to Baker, even though she could feel David's hard stare burning into the back of her neck. "Did you find something?" she asked.

Baker must have been sweltering in her dress slacks and blazer. She returned a neutral expression—neither a smile nor a frown. Julia found her lack of emotion unsettling. She had assumed Baker would welcome her as an ally. After all, she'd been the one who called the police. But upon reflection, it made sense that a metaphorical wall would be erected between them. They must not have answers yet, and until they did, everyone was a suspect.

"It's Julia Crawford, right?" said Baker, her voice as affectless as her body language.

"Yes, I'm Julia. Is there any news of Fiona?"

"None at all. We've deployed the dive team twice now, and added aerial coverage to augment the two K-9 units from the state police search and rescue division, who have already executed a comprehensive grid search of the woods. We've got nothing to show for any of it. But to be candid, we'd like to look in there."

Detective Baker directed a stubby finger at David's house.

He saw them, naturally. How could he not, with windows everywhere?

As if on cue, David emerged from within, having the decency to put on a shirt first. Never one to miss an opportunity to boast, he wore one with his new company's logo printed on the front.

But the cops didn't care what shirt he was wearing. They'd come looking for clues and must believe they'd find them inside.

Baker gave David a terse smile. It was the look a cat might offer a mouse before starting the chase.

David stood tall, signaling he wouldn't be easy prey. "Before you get into it," he said to Julia, "the police have already asked me. The answer was *no* then, and it's *no* now. I'd advise you to say the same about your place."

"*My* place?" Julia felt confused. She surveyed her home, half expecting to see the exterior draped with crime tape. But everything looked the same. Christian was probably still seated at the kitchen table where she'd left him, glued to his phone like he'd been since yesterday.

"They want to search my property instead of the woods—like I'm some sort of criminal. So I refused," David said. "They should look for Fiona in places she might actually be, which *isn't* my house. But apparently they'd rather waste their time here."

David's face flushed with indignation.

"Look, we can do this the nice way, or we can go through the court," Baker replied impatiently. "You have two cars, both registered in your name, that we need to search as well. And you have Fiona's phone."

David frowned.

"You can have the phone, but you're not searching my house or my cars," he said. "I know how the game is played, Detective. It's *always* the boyfriend, so you'll have confirmation bias from the start. You'll find something, I'm sure of it—either something you plant or something benign that you'll try to use against me. So no thank you. I politely decline your request."

David sneered, his eyes glinting with the steely resolve of a gunfighter. Julia wondered: *Was he right to be wary of the police, or was he hiding something?*

"We're not in the business of framing people," said Baker. "Don't you want us to do everything in our power to find your missing girlfriend?"

"I do," said David, "which is exactly why I want you searching the woods and the lake. That might actually be useful, instead of rummaging through my life in what I'm sure will be a game of Pin the Tail on the Donkey." He gestured toward his rear.

"If you have nothing to hide, David, then you've got nothing to fear," said Baker.

Her police colleagues maneuvered into a formidable blue line behind their boss. They eyed David with contempt.

"You should know, Mr. Dunne," said Baker, with the plastered-on patience of an exhausted mother, "that my next move is a warrant."

David refused to concede. He drew himself up to full height, his famous temper flaring, doing him no favors. "Yeah? Then go get one."

He turned and stormed off in a huff.

"Well, that didn't go well," Baker observed, unperturbed. She seemed to relish the challenge. "Maybe you can talk some sense into him," she said to Julia. "Getting a warrant won't look good for him in court, if it comes to that."

"I'll try," Julia said, shaken by the thought.

"Any chance he was raised by a cop? Abused by one?" Baker asked.

"No. Why?"

"It would be one explanation for his profound mistrust of the police."

"And what's another?" Julia wanted to know.

"That he's guilty of a crime," said Baker.

Julia was too keyed up to go kayaking. And she certainly wasn't up for snapping pics for Insta. She could see it now, posting a bright, smiling selfie captioned: *Great day for a search warrant.*

Ugh.

Instead, she changed into hiking clothes, found Nutmeg in the yard, and took her for a walk through the woods. A little pet therapy was in order. Nutmeg held up her end of the bargain.

After forty-five minutes of fresh air, movement, cherishing her dog's unbridled joy while she zoomed along the woodsy path, Erika's mindfulness practice tottering about in her head, Julia turned toward home feeling far more grounded. She hoped Christian would be there so she could update him on the new developments. He hadn't been home when she left for her walk, but perhaps he'd returned. She had a lot to tell him, and he could be a good listener . . . sometimes.

As she hung Nutmeg's leash on a hook by the door, Julia took off her trail runners and stretched her feet. Sitting down to decompress would be great, and she knew something that would help with that.

Julia headed for the fridge to get a bottle of wine, but stopped dead in her tracks.

There was Christian, her Christian, half slumped at the kitchen table, a tall glass in front of him and a half-empty bottle of whiskey by his side.

Chapter 20

Izzy

I'm hauling the added weight of Lucas's deception as we slog up yet another steep incline. With each step, my legs remind me that twice a month at the gym won't cut it. I figured we'd be gone a few hours at most, but that's not how Captain Coyote Killer likes to hike. From minute one, Rick has been a nonstop motion machine, taking us through a dizzying maze of intersecting trails. He's like a migratory bird able to find its way through thousands of miles of territory.

My muscles and lungs sigh with gratitude when Rick finally has the decency to take an extended meal break. Hopefully, David won't be livid at me for abandoning my post for most of the day, but Taylor assured me all would be fine.

We eat at the aptly named Overlook Pass. From our lunch spot on an exposed ledge, we can see Lake Timmeny far below. The water reflects like a mirror framed by lush greenery. Above, a hawk makes a looping circle, scouting its prey. A chipmunk scurries by, taking shelter under a nearby rock. Naturally, I'm rooting for the cute and fuzzy critter to make it through the day alive, but the hawk needs food, too, and now I'm battling with myself over the morals of the natural world.

But here I am, enjoying a ham-and-cheese sandwich, so I have no business passing judgment on anybody—except maybe Lucas.

"Beautiful," Lucas says. He leans back, taking it all in.

Rick grunts. "If you'd put down that guitar and leave your room more often, you could enjoy this view every day." He passes his son a sly look. "Though I guess you've enjoyed other pleasures recently."

His observation doesn't come across as playful ribbing. It's obvious what he's referring to, but is he reprimanding Lucas for inappropriate behavior, or could he be . . . *jealous*? It's difficult to say. His eyes are as dark and emotionless as I imagine the hawk's to be.

I can't stop thinking about Fiona. I care a lot more about what happened to her than what she and Lucas might have done in the dark. But Rick's displaying the same compassion for the missing woman that he shows for the animals he shoots. *Strange.*

After lunch, we finish the trail and reach the anticlimactic summit. While I feel invigorated from my time in nature, my mission is incomplete. Lucas has been untruthful, but I can't be sure there's anything nefarious behind it. It could be he's just embarrassed.

I need more time alone with him, so I'll have to get creative. Obviously, his dad is a powerful presence. That might be causing him to clam up.

The best idea I come up with is to lie, yet again. Here I am, questioning this boy's character because he told a fib, and I'm about to do the same. We're maybe two-thirds of the way down the hill when I shout, "Look! Over there—a coyote!"

Rick snaps to attention. "What? Where is it?"

I point to a particularly overgrown patch of forest some distance away. "He was over there. I just caught a flash of movement, and I swear it was as big as Nutmeg."

"Damn," Rick seethes. "Can't believe I missed it. Must be losing a step in my old age. I'm gonna try to track it down. Lucas, we've done this hike enough times that you know the way home, right? You can escort Izzy back?"

"Yeah, sure," says Lucas. He doesn't sound enthusiastic.

Rick is off in a flash, soon swallowed by the forest, as he races to catch his imaginary quarry. I've caught mine, but I have no idea what to do with him. We walk in an uncomfortable silence. The sound of leaves and sticks crunching underfoot is extra loud. I feel like an obligation Lucas has to lug around. He doesn't know me, we've hardly interacted, and he's unhappy that I outed him as a cougar toy. If something is going to happen, it'll be up to me.

"I wouldn't have said anything if I'd known you and Taylor were together." I'm speaking to Lucas's back because he's walking several paces ahead.

This stops him in his tracks. He turns to look at me, his penetrating stare making me flinch. "What makes you think we're together?" he asks.

"I dunno," I say. "There's been some weird energy between you two, so I figured something's going on."

Lucas stands taller and brushes his long hair away from his eyes. His full, soft lips are slightly parted, and once again that quiet intensity is drawing me in.

"Why are you so interested, anyway?" he asks. "You're kind of nosy for the new girl around here. Are you really a nanny, or some kind of undercover reporter?"

I gulp, but maintain a neutral expression. "I guess I'm just a nosy nanny." I laugh awkwardly. "But it's not like I don't have a good reason to ask questions. You're the one who kissed a woman who vanished the next day."

"What are you suggesting? That I did something to her? Think we met in the middle of the night for a hookup and now she's somewhere in the woods, buried under sticks and leaves for the *coyotes* to find?"

Shit. He knows I made up the coyote story, and he's probably figured out why. Note to self: Lucas isn't someone to be taken lightly. Best course of action is to redirect.

"You still didn't answer—are you and Taylor an item?"

His playful grin is even more self-assured than before. "Why? Are you interested?" He takes a step toward me.

His candor catches me off guard, and sadly, he's right. I am interested. Part of me hopes he is unattached (and not dangerous). I stop those thoughts before they can sprout roots. Getting involved with the subject of my inquiry (who is also still in *high school*) doesn't exactly meet my standards for journalistic integrity.

"I'm just curious, that's all. You've been cagey about it, and so has she."

"Maybe some things are better left a mystery," he replies, and leaves it at that. He turns away and resumes walking the trail.

We march in silence. I'm supposed to return with some breathtaking discovery that will meet Taylor's expectations, but all I've acquired is a blister on my right heel.

At least we're no longer going downhill. The flat ground is easier on my calves, but tall trees block my view of the lake, so I have no idea how much farther we have to go. It all looks the same to me.

Lucas has been quiet, leaving me to obsess over how I mishandled things. When he turns around, I think he's giving me a second chance.

"I have to pee," he says.

Not exactly what I was hoping for, but I actually have to do the same.

"You go that way, I'll go this way. See that rock over there?" He points to a sizable boulder, the top of which sticks up from the earth like an iceberg poking out of the water. "We'll meet there."

"Fine," I say, and I leave the path, bushwhacking to a secluded spot where I feel safe to go.

As I relieve myself, I try not to dwell on all the places ticks can hide. This is so much easier for a guy. I readjust my clothes and wander back to the path, trying to retrace my steps, but the sameness of the forest is disorienting. My heart rate ticks up a couple notches as I scour the ground for imprints my feet left in the soil or a branch I might have broken.

I think I'm headed the right way, but I also think I should have reached the main trail by now. I'm about to cry out for help, when to my delight, the vegetation thins and I return to what I'm sure is the designated meeting spot.

I look for the pointy rock and there it is. But I see other rocks that are similar, buried in the ground all around me. But no, I'm confident this is the right rock. So where is Lucas?

I wait. Maybe he had to do more than a pee. *Gross.* As the

minutes slip by, I grow increasingly anxious. I recall how Rick navigated these trails with ease and referenced all the times Lucas had done this hike.

Did he leave me here as payback?

"Lucas! Lucas!"

I race ahead on what I believe is the trail, but how can I be sure? Every tree, every rock, even the ground itself all looks the same as I remember, but different, too.

My anger at Lucas gives way to a gnawing fear. The trees loom over me, no longer peaceful; they've become threatening. The sky barely peeks through their dense branches. Dark shadows converge around me, obscuring the path. I check my phone. No signal. No way to GPS my way home.

Panic grips me. I run forward, continuing to call for Lucas. At some point, I realize that the path I thought I was following is gone. All that's there is thick undergrowth, a blanket of dead leaves and pine needles underfoot.

Will I become the next unexplained disappearance? I have a dim hope that Lucas is merely playing a sick game. I stop to listen, praying I'll hear an obnoxious giggle, something to signal it's a bad joke. But all is silent, except for the blood rushing through my ears. My terror deepens with each step to nowhere.

Walking isn't an option. I'm running now, even though I remember something about staying in one place if you're lost. But I keep hearing another voice—this one as irrational as it is demanding, telling me to move, that the right trail is just ahead, and all I have to do is keep going to find it.

My head whips around as I plunge through branches that claw at my face like an attacking animal. I'm moving too fast, but I can't slow down. Fear makes me reckless. Every step, I hope, will reveal a sign, some familiar marker, anything to orient me, but it never does.

I realize too late that I should have been watching where I was going. My foot strikes something hard. At first I'm not sure what happened. All I know is I'm unexpectedly flying through the air. The next instant, I land hard on the ground. Pain rockets up my arm, but my ankle takes the brunt of it. It swells almost immediately, like an inflating balloon.

I try to stand, but when I put weight on my foot, a sharp, stabbing sensation shoots through my leg. I brave a step and it's not pretty. The pain is intense enough to make my eyes water. I have to sit down. My ankle continues to swell.

I want to scream at myself for all the terrible decisions I've made. Coming to the lake, visiting the site of old bones, opening my big mouth to the police, lying to Rick so I could be alone with the boy who's abandoned me.

What now?

Tears, that's what. They streak down my face, gracing my lips with their salty aftertaste.

Irrational fears arise—or maybe not so irrational. What will my parents think if I don't return? How would my disappearance alter their lives? I'm not ready to become anybody's ghost. I have too much to do, and now I'm getting angry. I won't let Lucas beat me, but I can't walk, and I worry what will happen when night falls.

So I do what any smart, levelheaded, partially college-educated young woman would do in my predicament. I scream—as loud as I can. My throat turns raw from the effort, but I don't let up.

I'm howling like a madwoman when I hear something rustling in the trees. My heart swells more than my injured ankle, filling with relief. But fear coats me anew as I worry I've summoned nothing more than a creature, perhaps a bear with teeth and claws that will tear me to pieces. Or worse . . . a predator who preys on young women . . . whoever or whatever is at the heart of the lake lore.

It's moving toward me and causing too much of a disturbance to be a small animal. I brace myself, holding my breath, worried that giving myself away would be the worst thing I can do. But it's too late. Something is heading this way quickly. I grab a nearby stick; it's a flimsy weapon, but it's all I have. I'm ready to scream again, this time to scare it off.

As I brace for the end, to my delighted surprise, an old woman appears from behind a thicket of bushes. She's dressed in a bright teal fleece and dark jeans. Her face is heavily lined, and despite the protection of a lavender adventure hat, her skin is deeply sun-kissed, as though she's seldom indoors. She appears as comfortable in this landscape as any animal living in the forest. Her long, flowing gray hair, coarse and silvery like a horse's mane, makes me think of the legendary wisewomen. As she moves closer, I see concern in her wide, luminous blue eyes. She carries a walking stick in each hand, her knuckles gnarled like the knots of a tree branch.

A sob escapes my throat as she lowers herself to my level.

"You're hurt," she says in a raspy, age-worn voice. "Are you lost as well, dear?"

I nod, over and over, unable to muster any words. She brushes my cheek, her touch filled with kindness. "Well, you're not lost anymore. I'll fix you a splint and we'll get you out of here. Are you staying at the lake?"

I nod again, my voice still locked somewhere inside.

"Well, you're in luck. I live there as well. My name is Grace Olsen. What's your name?"

I smile slightly as I answer her question. Fate is a funny thing.

Chapter 21

Julia

Julia felt a dozen emotions in a matter of seconds. Anger. Sorrow. Disbelief. Then the rush of feelings gave way to pure shock.

While the amber tones of the liquid in front of Christian looked like maple syrup, the Maker's Mark label made it evident the contents weren't for pancakes and waffles.

Where Christian got his hands on a bottle of whiskey was a question for later. She never kept anything stronger than wine in the house, and that only after years of Christian's sobriety, when she could finally believe his assurances that he was comfortable having alcohol around. Which raised the more pressing question: Why would he throw his sobriety out the window after all they'd been through?

An electric current coursed through her body and out of her mouth in one panicked, disbelieving yell: "Christian, what in God's name are you doing?"

He barely moved. For a moment, Julia feared the worst—had he swallowed a handful of pills with his drink? Eventually, though, his hand went to the bottle, and she watched him pour another splash into his glass without so much as a glance in her direction.

Was this about the bank accounts—the passwords he had changed without informing her? Was there more going on than she realized? She never had the chance to confront him because of the chaos with Fiona. Now she was afraid to learn the truth.

"Christian!" she cried. "Answer me, what are you doing? You're drinking!"

Finally, he looked at her, his eyes so red they were glowing. "Yeah, no shit. Do you want some?" The words slurred together—*doyawannsum*—as he teetered on his chair.

Julia stormed across the room and grabbed the bottle off the table, barely resisting the urge to club him over the head with it. Instead, she poured the contents into their ancient kitchen sink. She saw her life going down the drain along with the alcohol.

"I take that as no," he slurred. "But you gonna regret that."

Bad grammar. Barely able to hold his head up. He was blotto.

Julia thought she might pass out from the adrenaline rush, but collected herself enough to sit beside her husband.

He fixated on her with those awful bloodshot eyes, drooping with remorse. The smell emanating from him was potent, but it was still his face, the same mouth Julia had kissed thousands of times. Seeing him like this was both familiar and strange, an unwelcome visitor from the past.

She gripped the table's edge to keep upright, but the room spun anyway, her world tilting at an unnatural angle.

"Christian, you need to tell me what is going on. Where did you get the whiskey, and more importantly, why are you drinking it?"

His hand unsteady, Christian slowly raised the glass to his lips and drank again. Julia didn't have it in her to knock it away. Instead, she watched him finish the contents in one long gulp.

In the ensuing silence, a worst-case scenario occurred to her: he was about to confess to murdering Fiona. It would be Christian, her beloved husband, who would lead the police to the body. *But no. That was insane. He couldn't have. He wouldn't.* Still, he hadn't answered her.

Confronting a drunk with anger was as effective as debating people online. So she asked again, in a patient voice, tempering her fury by touching his hand.

His eyes were so wounded that she felt injured herself. Her face softened, giving Christian the security he needed to open up.

"I didn't get it," he said, as if she should know what he was talking about. "It didn't come through."

He picked up his phone from the table, staring at it morosely, as if the device had somehow betrayed him. His face knotted up. Julia thought he might burst into tears, but instead his lips curled into a vicious snarl. His forehead blanketed into deep creases, red splotches erupting on his neck and cheeks.

In one swift motion, he cocked his arm back and thrust it forward. The phone flew from his grasp, sailing across the room, where it slammed against the wall over the stove.

Julia jumped at the sound of the impact, but Christian didn't flinch. Perhaps he'd wanted a more dramatic result, but the phone fell to the ground mostly intact, save for the splintered screen. Whatever he was trying to get out of his system hadn't been purged, and Christian winced in agony.

"Christian—Jesus Christ. What didn't come through?" Julia asked. "What is happening?"

"The loan," he sobbed, burying his face in his hands. "We didn't get the loan."

"What loan?" Julia was baffled. They hadn't sought any loan, none that she knew about. "Is that why you've been obsessively checking your phone? Were you waiting to hear from a bank? What on earth did you apply for? What kind of shit mess did you get us in?" Her anger was rising again.

"They said it was guaranteed. I was preapproved. That's exactly what he told me. Pre . . . a . . . proved. What else does that mean?" He reached for the bottle, no longer there, and then tried to drink from the glass he'd already emptied.

Julia felt like she might explode. "Christian, I have no idea what you're talking about, but you're really frightening me."

When he met her eyes, they were filled with tears. But dammit, she knew he was crying for himself. Shame radiated off him. He turned away from her because he couldn't bear the indignity, and that gesture alone told her all she needed to know. The news was bad. Really bad.

"I've lost it all," he blurted out. "I thought I had it under control, Jules, I really did. One more loan, that's all I needed . . . Then

I could have shuffled the money around until business picked up. I was right there. I had it all figured out. Fuck!" He slammed his fist against the table, then grimaced, swallowing hard as if he'd downed another burning shot of whiskey. "I'm so, so sorry."

Of all the words that drunkenly spilled from his mouth, Julia focused on the three most important ones.

"What do you mean, *lost it all*?" Mounting pressure in her chest painfully squeezed at her heart. Unable to breathe, she felt her whole world caving in. It was like being buried under a crush of bodies, a mishmash of all the creditors who'd been hounding her for months.

It had been Julia's greatest fear—that Christian would move so fast and recklessly that her hard-charging husband would forget when to apply the brakes. His explanations and excuses wouldn't matter. The final result would still be the same: the twisted wreckage of their lives would be scattered about, and the black box that held all of Christian's horrible choices would reveal precisely how he'd brought them down.

Lost it all.

"The loan was supposed to pay off the line of credit. I maxed it out, but now I've defaulted."

"Christian, what line of credit? I don't understand." God, talking to a drunk was like trying to follow a bouncing ball.

"The HELOC," he finally spit out.

HELOC. Got it. Home equity line of credit. Making progress. But this made no sense. Christian couldn't get one of those without her signing it too, since her name was also on the deed to the house.

As that thought came to her, another struck, this one so unsettling that Julia nearly had an out-of-body experience. She envisioned herself strangling her husband, her hands wrapped tightly around his throat, squeezing the life out of him.

Their primary residence was available for a line of credit only with her authorization, but the lake house was held in a trust, along with other cash assets, and Christian was the trustee. They'd set it up that way because they'd lumped an inheritance from Christian's family with her assets to safeguard these resources for Taylor down the road. At the time, picking Christian as the trustee had seemed like the most sensible choice. He was the finance guy.

A wave of nausea rose. "Christian, what about the money? We had money in that trust."

"Long gone," he said.

Her whole body trembled. "The HELOC—which house did you use for that?" But she knew—of course she knew.

"Tell me you didn't just lose my family's lake house. Tell me, you son of a bitch."

Christian crumpled in his chair, the final admission like a weight he could no longer shoulder. His obvious remorse meant little to Julia at this point.

"*How could you?*" she shouted, her cheeks burning. "You took out a line of credit on *my family home* without consulting me first?"

"I knew you wouldn't approve."

"Damn straight, I wouldn't," she snapped.

"I just needed a cash infusion to keep the business alive until things turned around. And then I would pay off the other loan, and we'd be fine. You wouldn't have even known about it. The projections looked so good. It was low risk. I can't tell you how sorry I am, Jules."

She hated him using her nickname. It made her skin crawl.

Now the call from the Purdy School made much more sense. She couldn't believe it. In all their life, despite all the drinking, the affair, and his streak of poor choices, she'd never even considered that he could do something this deceitful and hurtful.

"What have you done to us, Christian?" she said.

"Please forgive me, Jules."

Julia coughed out a disbelieving laugh. "Forgive you? Christian, I can't stand the sight of you."

"Please, I'll figure this out, I promise. I love you so, so much." His desperation only made Julia feel more out of control. Her entire body thrummed with fury.

"I am beyond devastated," she said. "I am so angry I'm scaring myself. This is a betrayal on a whole different level than what you did before. I certainly can't address this when you're drunk, and I don't want to see you after you sober up, either. This might be my last two weeks on this lake for *my entire life,* and I don't want you here anymore. You make me so sick I could scream. You can sleep in the guest room. And keep away from Taylor. I don't want her finding out right now that you tossed your sobriety and my home in the trash. After you sleep it off, you can get in your precious Land Rover and get the hell out of here."

Without giving Christian a chance to respond, Julia stormed out of the kitchen. She could hardly hold back the tears that poured out as soon as she reached the bedroom, where she slammed the door and locked it behind her.

Chapter 22

Izzy

One moment, I'm lost without hope. The next, I'm having a warm cup of tea in Grace Olsen's home. My leg is elevated with a bag of ice draped over my ankle. The swelling frightens me, but I think the ice is helping. My ankle is big, misshapen, purplish, and so unfamiliar I can't bear to look at it. It's like I have someone else's body part attached to me.

Grace assures me it isn't broken. She seems certain, so that's a relief.

Her home itself feels healing. It's as though I've stepped into some kind of fairy-tale apothecary. There are exposed wood beams throughout and a few old-fashioned windows with lots of small panes that let in plenty of natural light. Herbs hang drying on the walls. The room smells of lavender and lemongrass. From the living room I can see into the kitchen, which is stocked with mason jars full of dried goods—beans, barley, lentils, and an assortment of loose teas, nicely displayed on wooden shelves that are as misshapen and varied as the trees they came from.

I've concluded Grace is some kind of naturalist. She uses a large mortar and pestle to create an aromatic-smelling herbal poultice (her word, not mine), which she rubs all over my injury. Whatever it is, it smells delightful, like it came from an exotic spice shop. Perhaps there's turmeric in the mixture, for the whole paste has a yellowy-orange tinge.

Grace lists the ingredients: "It's made of onion, ginger, dandelion root, garlic, turmeric, and several other herbs I can't name because they're part of an ancient family secret."

Turmeric! I enjoy a sense of pride. I try to guess what the other mystery ingredients might be. My mind goes to something witchy: small toads, eyes of newts, things I've read about in storybooks. Whatever she's applied, it seems to be working. I take a peek, and the swelling is down considerably.

Grace trades her hiking clothes for a billowy patchwork skirt and white top. She's accented her outfit with a colorful string of beads and dangling earrings that plink ever so slightly as she moves about, tending to her patient. I wonder where she acquired her skills. I was impressed with her quick thinking in the woods. She fashioned a splint from two sticks latched together with a belt, then used her teal fleece to pad the injury. That's what enabled me to walk out of the forest. I should return the light jacket to her, but it's keeping the ice bag from freezing my skin.

It took us an hour to reach her small house hidden in the woods off the main road. If I had been uninjured, the trek would have taken half that time; that's how close I was to the house before Lucas left me for dead. I can't count the thank-yous I uttered on our way back, but it was plenty.

The decorative lamps scattered throughout the room are perfect for reading, as is the worn and weathered couch, with a multicolored afghan draped over the back. She has a cozy little book nook stocked with paperbacks and hardcovers, inviting me to settle into one of her comfy chairs and get lost in a story. Several nice rugs, a few of which are the classic farmhouse oval design, are scattered about, but nothing is upscale. It's all very modest, with signs of wear and tear, which is how I'm accustomed to living. It's homey.

But it feels lonely, too, despite the orange tabby cat purring at the foot of my chair. Winston, her feline companion, appears to be the only other inhabitant of the house. I mean, yeah, the cat-lady trope can definitely paint a picture of isolation, but it's something more. The knotted pine walls are filled with framed pictures of Grace's family, all from so long ago. They're photos from her childhood, and this woman must be in her seventies, judging by her gray hair and kind, but wrinkled face. The images look aged as well, like vintage postcards, yellowing, and set inside tarnished frames. It's a family of five. I remember the brother, Tom, from the *Globe* article I sourced, and I'm certain the beaming girl in the bikini decorated with gingham checks must be Anna. She's standing next to her younger sister, who's looking at me from the photo with the same bright eyes I saw when she saved me in the woods. The sisters appear radiant, like they're living their best lives.

But there are no recent pictures on display. If Grace never had a family of her own, maybe she's clung to the one she once knew, from a time before sorrow swallowed joy, back when her beloved sister was a fixture at the lake.

"More tea, dear?" Grace asks, preemptively heading to the kitchen to heat the kettle.

It would feel rude to decline.

"I did get in touch with your employer—what's his name, David?" she calls from the other room.

Grace saunters back to the sitting area, and I nod as I shift position slightly. It's enough to send a sharp twinge through my injured ankle. I prop it up on a pile of pillows set atop an ottoman in front of my chair. The cat lurks nearby, eyeing me like I've stolen his favorite lounging spot. Twice now, I've had to redirect him from licking the paste off my leg.

"He was very relieved to know you're safe," says Grace. "I guess a whole group was out looking for you. I told him I'd drive you home after we get that swelling down. I was surprised, though—he offered a reward, like I'm returning a lost pet or something."

I harrumph in my head. *A pet? At the very least, I'm a service animal.*

While I don't complain about David, I do share that I'm not the first female to go missing from his home this week.

"I heard about that woman, Fiona. It's terrible," Grace says as she brings me my drink. Her hand is shaky. The teacup clinks against the saucer as she sets both on an antique table within reach. Grace's eyes are strained like she's holding something back.

"Unfortunately, I haven't seen her. It's so distressing. A third missing woman . . ." Her voice trails off as she gets lost in thought. She peers at me as though just remembering I'm still in the room. "I'm sorry. I don't want to scare you. I'm sure you're safe. It's probably just a bizarre coincidence."

She doesn't know I've read about her online and searched her sad history for my own investigative purposes. But this is exactly who I need to talk to, and I can't miss this opportunity. I gulp, preparing to push her a little more.

"Three women vanished from this lake, *including* Fiona?" I say, playing dumb. "Do you know anything about the others?"

Grace's mouth slips into a frown. "One was my sister, Anna," she says, pointing to a picture on the wall, confirming my earlier suspicion. Heartbreak invades her eyes.

"I'm so sorry," I say. "You were close?" It makes me queasy to ask questions I know the answers to, but I must build rapport.

"The closest," she tells me. "I sometimes miss her more now than I did when she first disappeared. The longer I go on, the more I realize how much life she didn't get to experience." Grace releases a sad sigh. "But that was a long time ago. I have memories to comfort me, especially in this place, our old home. Never thought I'd be a year-rounder, one of the hearty few. But I love the quiet solitude of winter almost as much as I do the summer. This land has healing powers. Speaking of, how's your ankle?"

I move the ice away and see that the swelling has subsided. The pain is better, too.

"I'm not surprised," Grace says. "That concoction is quite potent. People don't trust herbs enough. What we need to heal is growing all around us. My family doesn't like me living out in the woods alone, especially because my memory isn't what it used to be. I do have a nephew who checks on me, but that isn't enough to appease my family. They want me to move. They don't understand how important it is for me to be close to nature. Besides, I'm worried my memories of Anna will fade like all my others if I leave the lake."

"You and Anna lived here year-round?"

"No, this was a summer place for us, but when I inherited the house, I had it winterized. Not much has changed from when we were kids. The furniture is mostly the same. But after my sister went missing, my parents stopped vacationing here. They sold off anything that reminded them of her. I understood why, but I was the opposite. I liked having her things around. They reminded me of her and a better time in our lives. Over the years, I've found some of Anna's belongings my parents sold or gave away to antique shops and thrift stores in the area. Anytime I saw something, I bought it, but it's been a long time since that happened."

My heart is heavy. I don't have any siblings, but I can imagine the pain of losing someone so close to you.

"Who was the other woman who went missing?" I ask, my stomach tightening. Another lie, since I likely know more about the second disappearance than Grace does.

"She was a young girl named Susie Welch. I was in my forties when she disappeared, so I didn't know her well, but I was living at the lake at the time. My parents had passed by then." Grace pauses, and I allow her space to connect with that difficult time.

"Everyone at the lake looked for Susie, myself included. It was like Anna all over again. That's when the lore started—murmurings that *the lake takes them.*"

I don't tell her that I've heard the lore. "Do you think it's a coincidence that three young women disappeared from the same lake exactly thirty years apart? Is the lake cursed or something?"

Grace focuses on her tea as she answers. "The world is full of mysteries. Nature is powerful. It takes as easily as it gives. We must respect it, always." She dabs her eyes with a napkin. "Maybe it is the lake and not a person. The coincidences are hard to explain. All I know for sure is that you shouldn't go digging, Izzy. Some secrets are best left alone."

I smile weakly, knowing good advice I won't take when I hear it.

Silence settles over us. I look around for something to keep the conversation going. This place is like a time capsule. A grandfather clock stands in the corner of the living room, with a glass front that allows me to peek at the weights and pendulum that help it keep time. The end table is adorned with lace doilies under antique crystal bowls, one filled with hard candy.

The shelves are stocked with old books and all kinds of knick-knacks—a choirboy figurine, a ceramic cat and dog, other vintage glass animals, and a set of old-fashioned teacups. I wonder which of these items belonged to Anna, and if Grace recovered any of them on her quest to reclaim her sister's possessions. I find myself taking a mental inventory of everything, and that's when I see it. A shock reverberates through my system.

It's a small wooden box with decorative metal edging and a delicate clasp. I can see the intricate pearl inlay that ribbons around the bottom, and I recognize the repeating pattern of vines and flowers. I *know* this box, or at least one just like it. I've seen it before, but obviously not in Grace's home. But where? I can't place it. The answer is dancing just out of reach, like a terrible itch I can't scratch.

Grace follows my eyes, perhaps noticing I'm spellbound.

"It's beautiful, isn't it?" she says. She carefully takes the box off the shelf, cradling it in her hands like she's holding a valuable piece of art. "It belonged to Anna. Such a precious keepsake. It's the last piece of hers I found. I got it at an estate sale nearby—bought it for three dollars, something like that. I just love it." She hands the box to me, then asks if I'd like some tea.

I point to my cup, which is still pretty full.

"Oh, my bad. There goes my memory again. Lucky for you, I don't seem to forget my way around the forest, but I do forget a lot of other things these days. I'll go make myself a cup."

She ventures to the kitchen, leaving me alone to examine the box and hopefully jog my memory. It feels *important* somehow. I admire the craftsmanship, but I want to have a look inside. I try to lift the clasp, but it's stuck. Maybe the tiny hinge has rusted with age. I try one more time to loosen it, but I use too much force. The entire clasp separates from the wood in one piece.

I panic and look toward the kitchen, hoping Grace hasn't seen what happened. Luckily, she's still busy making her tea. But what am I going to do? She rescued me, and here I am, repaying her kindness by breaking something that means the world to her. My hands shake vigorously as I try to put the clasp back in place, but the glue is old, and it lost a tiny screw that I can't find.

I hear Grace returning from the kitchen. Panic floods my chest. Before I know it, I'm shoving the box into my backpack. Maybe she won't notice, or maybe she'll forget, her memory issues working in my favor. Then I can fix it and return it, and she'll be none the wiser.

Grace approaches, displaying a hint of concern. "Are you feeling well? You look peaked."

She dabs my forehead with the same tea towel she used for her misty eyes.

"I'm fine," I say breathlessly, trying to keep my heart inside my chest.

"How's your ankle feeling?"

I show her that I can move it fairly well, but perhaps adrenaline has blocked my pain receptors.

"Oh, good. I like to see that kind of mobility. Let's get the paste cleaned off, and I have a crutch you can use. I think it's time to get you home, dear," Grace says with concern. "You've been through a lot and need a good night's sleep."

Grace gets the crutch from a closet and does not mention the box that seems to have vanished into thin air. As soon as I'm cleaned up, Grace helps me to my feet. Whatever she's done seems to have worked. I can put more weight on my injured ankle than before.

"I recommend wrapping your ankle in an Ace bandage, and staying off your feet as much as possible," she says. She sounds knowledgeable, and I don't dare argue. But more important, the crutch has given me an excuse to come back, so I can bring the box once I fix it.

"Sure thing, and I'll return the crutch when I'm better," I tell her, finding a smile now that I have a plan. "But I'm sure the twins I'm looking after won't let me lounge around."

Grace escorts me to the door. "In that case, I'm going to give you an herbal treatment to take daily. Just mix it with water. It will help with the swelling. It's bitter, but a pinch of sugar will help it go down."

I don't tell her that she's essentially quoting Mary Poppins. I'm too ashamed of being a lying thief to associate myself with the greatest nanny of all time. But I promise to set things right. And I wonder if everything that's happened to me—my injury, my rescuer, and the broken clasp—all happened for a reason, because this box means something.

I just need to figure out what.

Chapter 23

Julia

For one brief moment, Julia believed all the awful events from the day before were simply nightmares. Perhaps Christian *hadn't* downed half a bottle of whiskey and made his heartbreaking confession. She peeked out the bedroom window. As the early morning light seeped into her eyes, clearing her thoughts and vision, she realized it was all true. Christian was driving away. It must have been the sound of the engine that woke her. She could see his taillights fading into the distance like a sad wave goodbye.

She'd asked him to leave and was still beyond livid, but Julia wasn't prepared for the deep loneliness she would feel in the aftermath of his departure. Her stomach turned into a bottomless pit.

The anger was easier to sit with, so she held on to that. She wasn't sure what to say to Taylor, and she had no idea what the path forward looked like. She recalled a favorite AA saying of Christian's—one day at a time—but even that felt daunting. She'd have to break it down further, into hours, perhaps minutes.

After her shower, which did nothing to wash away the negativity, Julia trudged across the dew-covered grass to Erika's house. She picked up the smell of freshly brewed coffee.

"Where have you been, stranger?" Erika said. "Are you feeling better? Taylor said you were sick, so we didn't bother you with all the news. Did you talk to her this morning?"

Julia had left a note for Taylor last night, letting her know she wasn't feeling well and was going to bed early. It wasn't a lie.

"No, Taylor was still sleeping when I left the house."

"Well, you won't believe what happened while you were out of commission. Lucas lost Izzy in the forest."

"What?" Julia's face widened with shock and surprise. "Is she okay? She's been found, right?" Her question came with a deep pang of guilt for having powered off her phone last night in an attempt to shut out the world. But she had hardly slept a wink. Instead, she lay awake ruminating, fuming all through the night.

She heard Taylor come home from David's, where she had been watching the twins. Christian stayed in the guest room, and Julia was glad he had kept his distance.

"Yes, Izzy's fine, thank God. The Olsen woman down the road found her in the woods before it got dark and bandaged up her ankle. I guess she sprained it pretty badly. Lucas was a wreck—he thought he had killed her. I blame Rick for leaving them alone to chase down some animal. What a dumbass. Sometimes he has his head so far up his butt, he could give himself a colonoscopy."

"Oh no! That's awful. But I'm so relieved Izzy's okay. What a nightmare."

"Tell me about it," said Erika.

"Is there any news on Fiona?" Not only was Julia out of touch, she was barely holding it together.

"No, no updates . . . it's all so crazy, but . . . what's going on with you?" Erika's tone and expression shifted to one of concern. "Is everything all right? You look an absolute wreck. Are you still feeling sick?" She took Julia by the arm and guided her to a cushioned chair at the breakfast nook.

Julia noticed Erika's laptop open on the counter and caught a flash of a legal brief she was editing. So much for her pledge to turn it off on vacation. But Christian was a stark reminder that old habits die hard.

Julia's jealousy over her friend's renovation work now seemed trivial to her. All she wanted was a sober and honest husband, and to keep the run-down lake house that felt like a beloved family member.

"Do you want coffee?" Erika was already pouring Julia a cup, as well as another for herself. "Talk to me. What's going on?"

There was no graceful way for Julia to bridge the gap between small talk and the deeper stuff. "Christian is drinking again," she said morosely.

Erika set her mug down hard enough to splash coffee onto the countertop. Her eyes widened. "He's what?"

"Yeah, I came back to the house yesterday after walking Nutmeg and found him totally sloshed at the kitchen table, pounding Maker's Mark like it was Gatorade."

"Jesus, I'm so sorry," Erika breathed. "Where is he now?"

Julia pushed through the profound tightness in her throat. "Gone. I told him to sleep it off in the guest room and leave when he sobered up. He was driving away when I woke up."

Julia needed a hug, which Erika provided intuitively. They might have kept a few secrets from each other, but this was what true friendship was all about. You could stain their favorite sweatshirt, breeze in and out of each other's lives, but when the shit hit the fan, they'd be right there with you.

Erika asked, "Do you know why he started up again?"

Julia's tears threaten to fall. She willed herself to stay composed. She wasn't ready to come unglued just yet.

"You know we've been having financial problems," she began. "But even I didn't know how bad it was. Christian applied for a loan that didn't come through. He was counting on it. I guess the stress put him over the edge."

For a moment, Julia feared being judged for letting things get out of control, but instead she read true compassion in Erika's eyes. Yet Julia couldn't bring herself to reveal the biggest news of all: that she was in danger of losing the lake house. She didn't know how she'd tell her parents, either. Even in her forties, she wanted to call her mother, cry on the phone, and lean on her for support. But some shame was too much to put into words, and saying it aloud would make it all too real.

Erika took hold of Julia's hand.

"I should have seen this coming. We've been under so much strain with the business."

Julia caught herself. This was Christian's fault, not hers. She understood that life was full of risks. Terrible things happened all the time: tree limbs fell on unsuspecting motorists, ocean currents dragged swimmers out to sea, and a bad oyster could ruin a vacation. But when she said, "I do," she didn't expect her husband to turn into a walking tsunami.

Who did this man think he was? *Fine if he wants to drive himself over the cliff, but he should at least stop the car and let his family out first.*

"Do you need money?" asked Erika. "We've put a lot aside for college. We're still hoping Lucas will use it, but Rick and I can help out a little."

Julia squeezed her friend's hand. "Oh my god, no. Thank you for offering, but this mess isn't yours." She fell quiet for a time. "I wonder where he got the Maker's Mark. Do you think he keeps a secret stash?"

"The Liquor Outlet, probably."

"Maybe, but I only left for a dog walk and that store is a good distance away. I don't think he could have left and come back without my noticing," said Julia.

Erika blanched. "I hope he didn't snag it from us," she said. "We've been keeping the liquor upstairs in the old playroom until Rick finishes the bar. I know we have one bottle of it. I remember seeing it when I was making the Lake Escape drinks. Do you want me to go look?"

Julia was up on her feet. "Do you mind if I do?" she asked. "If it turns out my husband was also sneaking booze out of your house, I want to be the first to know."

Chapter 24

Izzy

Brody and Becca hover over me as I lie on the couch. They assess my injured ankle, which I've propped up with a stack of pillows. Their grave expressions suggest amputation might be in order.

"I think you need medicine," Brody says.

He puts an empty Dixie cup to my lips and forces me to drink. I grimace, pretending it tastes as bitter as Grace's herbal concoction that (surprise, surprise) continues to help with the swelling and pain. Even the bruise is far less purplish than yesterday, and my mobility has improved, though I limp when I walk without Grace's crutch. I'm surprised how good it feels to be back with the twins. My time in the woods made me keenly aware how much I'd miss the people in my life, these two included.

Last night I was too tired to confront Lucas about abandoning me on the hiking trail. Believe me, I'd like nothing more than to take the tourniquet Becca has inexplicably latched around my arm and tighten it around Lucas's scrawny neck. But I'll get an explanation from him, even if I have to resort to threats of violence.

"You have a fever," Becca tells me after placing her clammy little hand on my forehead.

"I do?" My voice carries the appropriate degree of alarm. I might not be a trained actor like my roommate, Meredith, but I know how to stay in character.

"Yes, and it's a high one," Becca says. "I think you're going to die."

"Well now," I say, holding back a laugh, "I think your bedside manner might need some refinement."

Both kids eye me with confusion. "What does *re-hine-man* mean?" asks Brody, mispronouncing the word.

"It means you're both wonderful doctors, but there's always room for improvement," I tell him. Even when I'm on the precipice of death, my nanny know-how is as sharp as ever.

Before the children have a chance to start amputating my injured limb with a wooden spoon, David comes downstairs, sunglasses on. He's not trying to be cool—it's simply a matter of practicality with so many windows and so few shades. Even at this early hour, the sun is like another guest in the home.

"Kids, why don't you get your bathing suits on, and we'll go for a swim," he tells them. He's already wearing his blue trunks.

Without giving me or my ailment another thought, the children dart upstairs to get changed. Doctors these days—so distractible.

I'm hoping David will move along as well and leave me be. But no such luck. He comes over and sits on the chair beside the couch.

"I'm so sorry," I say, preempting any disapproving remark he might toss my way. "I'll be back on my feet tomorrow. And Taylor promised she'd help out all day. You can pay her instead of me."

"I'm not worried about that," he says without a smile. "It's not your fault you're laid up. Accidents can happen anytime, anywhere, to anyone." His voice is flat, lacking any trace of kindness. With his sunglasses on, I can't tell if he's sending me a veiled threat.

His warning about talking to Taylor still nags at me. Does he harbor a grudge about what I told the police? It's obvious David has a strong aversion to people nosing into his business.

"I appreciate your concern," I say. "Grace told me you were really worried."

When he finally removes his sunglasses, I immediately wish he'd put them back on. His stare could freeze a penguin.

"Of course I was happy to know you were okay," he says. "Two women missing from my home wouldn't look good for me, would it? Now listen, Izzy. I need you to get better so you can take care of the kids. I have work to do while I'm here, and I'm paying you good money to keep them out of my hair. But more important, I need you to be very mindful going forward. I'd certainly hate for there to be any more . . . mishaps."

The way he emphasizes the last word sends a chill down my spine.

Did I hear him correctly? It sounds like he's trying to send me a not-so-coded message: next time, it won't be a clumsy fall I have to worry about, but David himself.

In a blink, his fractured smile morphs into something I'd have to call charming. His eyes hold a touch of warmth. "You keep that ankle elevated," he tells me with what seems like caring. "We need you back at one hundred percent as soon as possible. The twins are counting on it—and so am I."

He pats my uninjured leg before standing to go. If he noticed me flinch, he didn't care. I'm speechless and completely confused by his contradictory behavior. But I don't have time to dwell on it for long, because Taylor arrives flaunting an extra-wide pearl-white smile that feels falsely cheerful.

"How's the patient?" she asks.

I confess to being in pain, but leave out the part about getting another glimmer of David's sadistic side. Since I'm stuck here with him, I'm better off trying to keep the peace.

Taylor's expression shifts. "My mom wants to talk to me about something. I think she and my dad got into a huge fight. He's gone. Took the car. But she's not home right now, so I came to check in on you while I wait for her to get back."

"I'm sorry about the fight. I hope it's nothing too serious. And I'm glad you're here," I say. "I could use your help with something."

We wait for the twins to head outside with David before Taylor helps me to my bedroom upstairs, where I show her the box that I ostensibly stole from Grace's house.

"What's this?" Taylor asks. She sits on the edge of my bed,

turning the box over in her hands, opening the top to stroke the empty, velvety interior.

I tell her how the box felt important to me, and how Grace said it belonged to her sister, Anna. I describe my panic when the clasp broke and my ill-thought-out decision to take the box to have it repaired, hoping Grace's memory lapses would allow me to sneak it back onto the shelf without her ever knowing it was gone.

"I need a tiny screw and probably some glue. I don't have the right tools."

Taylor gives the box and clasp a close inspection. "Honestly, Lucas would be better at this than me," she says. "He's really meticulous with his guitar repairs. I've seen his tools, and I'm sure he has a screw small enough for the clasp." She hands the box back to me with a bemused expression. "But why couldn't you take your eyes off this?" she asks. "It's just a box. It's pretty and all, but it's not *that* nice."

"There's something about it," I tell her. "Something familiar. I just wanted a closer look. I didn't plan on taking it. It means so much to Grace."

"But why does it mean so much to *you*?"

I flop onto the bed, landing hard enough to jostle my ankle. "I wish I knew," I say with a sigh. "It's like I've seen it before or something, but for the life of me, I can't remember when or where, and it's driving me absolutely crazy."

"Why don't we try hypnosis?" Taylor suggests, as if she does it all the time.

"You know how to do hypnosis?" Call me skeptical.

"No, but, like, I'm sure we can figure it out," she says. "It's got to be on TikTok. You can learn anything there."

Before I can say *dumb idea,* we're watching short videos on how to perform hypnosis, and afterward, even she agrees it would be a waste of time.

I ask Taylor to grab my iPad off my desk. I'm glad it's fully charged, because I want to search for boxes like the one in question.

Taylor does the same, but on her phone. If we can figure out what era it's from or where it was made, perhaps that will jog a memory. It certainly can't be any less effective than hypnosis.

Soon I'm scrolling through pictures of boxes: big ones, little ones, some that look like the one I have, but most don't. I refine my keywords with no success, trying the names of different woods and textures. There's no make or model, no identifiers on the box whatsoever, so that makes it even harder. I'm about to give up when Taylor thrusts her phone in my face. There's a wood box in the picture, but not an exact match.

"Look at this room," she says with a laugh. "Totally eighties."

It was true. The colors were vibrant—eclectic blues, hot pinks, and neon greens. The clothing styles on display in the many posters covering the walls, along with a cassette player parked next to the wooden box that had caught her eye, marked the era well.

On closer inspection, the box is nothing like the one I took from Grace. But still . . . there's something here, something important I can learn from this image. I just know it. Since it's not the box, perhaps it's the time period that matters—the eighties, like Taylor said. Then it hits me, and now I think I know why I was so drawn to the box at Grace's house in the first place.

My breath catches in my throat. Can it be true?

I use my iPad to log in to our family iCloud, where we uploaded all our old photos. I know it's here. I've looked at the picture I'm searching for a thousand times. It hangs on the wall in our living room, haunting my mother, and our home in equal measure. My heart pumps like I'm doing intense cardio.

Eventually, I find it. I zoom in. It's hard to believe my eyes: a box that looks *exactly* like the one in my lap is also right there in my family's old lake house back in the 1980s, the same era as the picture that jogged my memory. It's resting on an end table, with my mom standing beside it. Her hair is something to behold—huge bangs that appear to defy gravity and curls that never quit. She's posing in a denim miniskirt and a concert T-shirt with the words *Duran*

Duran above what must be a rock band. One arm is decorated with bangles, and the other is lovingly draped around her sister, my aunt Susie—or Susie Welch, the second woman to go missing at Lake Timmeny—a kind and beautiful soul whom I would never have the chance to know.

THE LAKE, *SUMMER*

The surface of the lake glistens, rejoicing in the warmth of the summer sun, while the depths remain cold, dark, foreboding. Beware all who wade too far, who underestimate its power. All life must feed. And the water lives, it breathes, it *takes* . . .

Chapter 25

Julia

Julia went straight for the closet where Erika said she kept the liquor. The bottles were easily accessible and neatly arranged on a large shelving unit off to the side. No big shock: the Maker's Mark wasn't there.

She sank to the floor, despondency washing over her. He *was* desperate enough to steal from their friends.

The idea of Christian restarting his sobriety, getting his first twenty-four-hour medallion (again), and going back to AA meetings—two, maybe three a day—was too much to bear. For Julia, it meant a return to endless worry, fretting anytime she got close enough to smell his breath, and living in constant fear of another relapse. It felt like a crushing weight pressing down on her, even though this was all Christian's doing.

But shouldering the burden always fell to the woman, didn't it? If she were the drunk, she'd have to pick up her own damn pieces. Christian—Mr. I-Lost-Your-Lake-House—wouldn't be her knight in shining armor, that was for sure.

Julia thought about taking a final selfie next to the makeshift liquor cabinet and trying her hand at a pithy caption that would summarize her state of mind.

My husband fell off the wagon, yet I'm the one who got run over.

Or maybe . . .

When life gives you lemons and your alcoholic husband steals whiskey to make a whiskey sour, call a divorce attorney. #nojoke #referrals-wanted

Thoughts of Taylor sprang to Julia's mind, returning her to the here and now. She *couldn't* fall apart. She had to be a stable parent and a strong role model for her daughter. God knew Christian wasn't capable of filling that role.

Julia got to her feet, straightened her clothes, and dabbed tears out of the corners of her eyes. She would figure this mess out and *not* lose her family's lake house in the process.

As she was heading for the door, Julia tripped over a shoebox, but caught her balance thanks to a rolled-up carpet propped against the wall. It was the brown rug that she and Erika had talked about only days ago, the one they both disliked.

Julia unfurled the carpet and pressed her fingers into the chocolate-brown piling. The sensation transported her elsewhere, memory engulfing her, pulling her under. The feeling was so sudden and disorienting that for a moment, Julia wasn't sure which way was up. She swam back in time, years, then decades, until the sound of Erika's old music box filled her ears, and the taste of sticky sweet rock candy coated her tongue. Sunlight streamed in on what seemed like a glorious summer day.

Before it became a storage room full of dilapidated boxes, old fans, sneakers, stacks of books, and retired beach gear, this was the playroom where Julia and Erika spent countless hours with their Cabbage Patch dolls, a Lite-Brite set, and Erika's art kits.

On that particular day, she and Erika were engrossed in a game of Hungry Hungry Hippos, but stopped when they heard voices downstairs. They couldn't tell what they were saying—the voices were raised, but muffled by the closed door. Who was there? Cormac, of course, but who was he talking to? Something kept nagging at Julia as she probed her memory.

Erika—who was four at the time, if that—tried to open the door. Her tiny hands turned the doorknob, but it wouldn't open. Without warning, she burst into tears. Was the door locked from the outside?

Julia remembered other loud noises and was sure she'd heard something crash. She'd tried the knob as well, but the door wouldn't budge. Julia pulled with all her might, as if she might rip the door off its hinges. The walls felt like they were closing in. The air took on a thick, oppressive weight.

Erika cried for help. They took turns pounding on the door until their tiny hands were red and raw. Tears filled their eyes at the thought of being imprisoned inside the room forever.

Julia didn't know how long it was before help finally arrived. It could have been five minutes or an hour. All she knew was that it had felt like an eternity.

When Cormac finally opened the door, Erika was so upset she kept crying for her mother, who'd already abandoned her some time ago. Eventually, the girls downshifted from full-on panic into soft whimpers. Cormac's big broad smile softened his harder features. His skin had a healthy glow, coated with a sheen of sweat that stretched across his balding scalp, matting together what remained of his sandy brown hair.

He told the girls they were foolish for being frightened, that the door was simply stuck, that they should have pulled harder, and that everything was fine. He patted the top of Erika's head with his large, calloused hand, smiling down at her. *Silly children,* he kept saying with his eyes.

It was strange how parts of this memory were so clear, but others remained vague and out of reach. Julia recalled how she burned with shame that day. She'd never felt trapped before, and the experience shook her to the core. However, for Cormac to say it was nothing only added to her distress. She didn't know what to believe.

Erika was so upset, Cormac had to carry her downstairs. She buried her face in his barrel chest, her legs clinging to his ample belly like a monkey.

When they reached the living room, Julia's mind was still whirling. Cormac got the girls water and a snack. They ate in front of the TV while Cormac stayed in the kitchen, whistling as he did the dishes. Something still felt off to Julia, but she didn't trust her feelings. Cormac had said everything was fine.

But it wasn't fine. No, something *was* different. She was sure of it. And now, after all these years, Julia realized what it was. When the girls got downstairs, the beautiful red area rug in the living room was gone, without explanation—the floor where it had been lay bare.

A few days later, the ugly brown carpet appeared in its place and stayed there until recently, when Erika replaced it with a gorgeous red carpet similar to the one that disappeared the day the playroom door inexplicably got stuck.

Chapter 26

Izzy

I have a terrible game face, but I do everything possible to keep my reaction to a minimum. I am sure the box that once belonged to Anna Olsen somehow ended up in my aunt Susie's possession, and it eventually made its way back to Grace.

I can't let Taylor in on my secret. If the truth gets back to David about why I wanted this job, why I had Lake Timmeny in my Google Alerts, everything I've come here to accomplish will be in jeopardy.

I shut down the iPad before Taylor sees the telltale photo.

"No luck," I say with a sigh. "I guess I'll never know why I was so obsessed. But I have to fix the clasp and return the box to Grace. Would you mind asking Lucas to come over with his tools?"

I know I should be wary of the boy who essentially left me to die, or at a minimum wanted to scare the crap out of me in some petty revenge plot, but I need this box fixed, and he's the boy for the job.

"We aren't really talking," Taylor says. Her loaded look implies the subtext: *You haven't learned anything helpful about Lucas and Fiona.* That's true. All I managed to do was get lost and injured.

"I'll text him," I say. "Just give me his number."

Taylor appears hesitant. "Are you sure you want to be alone with him?"

"Based on how he acted in the woods, he couldn't wait to be rid of me. I highly doubt he's going to force himself on me." I don't mean to be crass and crude; it just sort of comes out.

A look comes over Taylor's face. It's more than sadness. Even if I weren't a naturally empathic Pisces, I would pick up on her pain. Lucas has obviously hurt her, but how? This is more than just a broken heart. A chilling thought occurs to me: Is it possible he could have *assaulted* her? It certainly would explain why Taylor suspects Lucas of doing something nefarious to Fiona.

I wonder . . .

Maybe Lucas knew I was investigating him, and left me to die in the woods before I could learn the truth. I want to think otherwise, that it was just a bad breakup. He and Taylor have known each other for years; could he really do that to her? Unfortunately, I know the answer. We're educated about it on campus all the time. Rapists come in all forms. Often, it's the person you know best, the one you trust the most, who takes what he wants without consent.

Is that what happened? Was it a drunken night at the lake, with Taylor in no condition to say yes? Perhaps the Fiona incident is a mirror of her trauma. I've read that sometimes victims doubt their experiences and recollections after an assault. Could Taylor be questioning her memory and I've been tasked with getting the answer?

I've experienced something similar before. My mother's trauma affected memories of her childhood. Everything was always vague when she talked about it. *I think we were there. Maybe we did that.* It was all conjecture. Fear filled her memory gaps, overshadowing any and all positive feelings she tried to conjure from her past. Everything became a potential threat. Nothing was safe because a part of her was forever trapped in a time when the danger was so real, it had reached out and taken her sister.

I've heard about generational trauma, where post-traumatic stress disorder can actually be passed from parent to child through DNA. I think that's what happened to me. It's why I keep seeing the children wandering off into the lake. Perhaps my suspicion that David is a predator is simply my fear response kicking into overdrive. My nervous system is always on high alert, and that's probably at the root of my impulsivity. Whenever I feel out of control, or want to fix something, I react too intensely and make rash decisions.

I'm sure as time goes on, I'll become just like my mother, where all risks are to be avoided, and romantic relationships are just an invitation to disaster. I know in my bones that I must solve the mysteries of the lake or I'll spend my life worrying when the next shoe will drop and mistrusting kindness when I see it in a man. No matter who I meet, I'll always be looking for the darkness.

Taylor texts Lucas's contact info to my phone. "Just be careful with him," she says.

"After the shit he pulled in the woods, he should be careful with me," I reassure her.

As soon as Taylor leaves, I grab my phone to message Lucas, but I write to my mom first. I've been terrible about staying in touch. I don't want to cause her more stress, so I don't tell her about my ankle. At this point, I'm so far from the truth that I don't know how I'll ever make my way back. But I stick to my story and send a bland message that simply says: *Love you, miss you! Having a great time and learning a ton. Let's talk soon!* I add a heart emoji so she knows I care.

It takes her all of twenty seconds to write back—she's probably been checking her phone obsessively and trying not to bother me. My mom doesn't want to be stifling. She just can't help herself. One day without a message, and she'll think I'm in a hospital; two days, I'm in a morgue.

Miss you SO much! she sends. *It gets lonely here, but I'm happy you're having fun and learning. Call when you can so we can really catch up. XO. Mom*

She always signs her messages like I won't know who they're from. Gen X. They do the silliest things.

When this is over, and I break open the cold cases of Lake Timmeny, Mom will understand and forgive my deception. She will have the closure she needs and the healing she deserves. I'm counting on that to justify my lies.

I text Lucas and ask him to meet me upstairs in my room.

Hopefully, I won't regret that decision. I need to stay off my ankle, and I also want to prove that I'm not afraid of him.

It's not long before I hear footsteps approaching. Lucas pokes his head through the door.

"How are you feeling?" he asks, sounding genuinely concerned.

This attitude is way better than the cocky bullshit he was pulling in the woods.

"I'm fine, no thanks to you," I grumble.

He looks appropriately contrite as he enters, carrying a plastic tool kit in his right hand, like a doctor paying a house call. He's got that same lock of hair falling in front of his eyes that I've come to consider the signature Lucas look. He might seem all innocent in his Henley T-shirt and dock shorts, but he's not fooling me.

"You left me for dead out there!" I glare at him hard, though I doubt I'm very threatening.

I move to the edge of the bed, wincing when I turn my injured ankle. I want easy access to the crutch leaning against a wall, which I can easily convert into a weapon if Lucas decides he wants to finish the job.

"Left you for dead?" He looks and sounds wounded. "What on earth are you talking about? Did you hit your head when you fell? I spent ages searching for you. You walked off the trail, Izzy. You must have. I don't know where you ended up, but it wasn't anywhere near our meeting spot."

Here's where *my* memory isn't so clear. I have a sudden nagging suspicion that I might not have accurately retraced my steps. It seemed to take a lot longer than it should have, and I recall being disoriented. Perhaps I confused one rock for another. I mean, really, I'm no geologist. But I'm also not ready to give Lucas the satisfaction of being right.

"I kept screaming your name at the top of my lungs," he continues. He sounds sincere and highly charged, like he's still upset about it. "When I couldn't find you, I ran the whole way back to get help. We searched all over, but couldn't find a trace of you."

I now feel compelled to give him the benefit of the doubt, but I still have many unanswered questions. Did he assault Taylor? What went down with Fiona after I stopped spying? And why did he lie to me about not kissing her back?

Since we're being candid, I try the straightforward approach. "Taylor won't talk to you. I've seen it myself, and I want to know why. What did you do to her?"

Lucas's eyes go wide. He looks more confused than angry. "What did *I* do?" The high pitch of his voice is rife with indignation. "What the hell do you think of me? First, you interrogated me about Fiona, and now you're accusing me of doing something to Taylor? Why? Do you think that because I'm a *guy*, I must be guilty of something? I mean, have you ever stopped to think that maybe I'm hurting, too? Like, maybe I didn't want Fiona to come on to me, and I don't understand what's up with Taylor? Did you ever once consider, even for a second, that I might not be such an asshole?"

That gives me pause. Sadly, the answer is no. It hadn't crossed my mind that Lucas could be a good guy.

I shift my attention to the box on the bed. Here I am, wanting his help and accusing him simultaneously. That has to feel shitty.

"You never did anything to Taylor?" I ask.

A murky sorrow clouds his eyes. He's protecting something, but what?

"Why don't you go ask *her*," he says testily. He moves to go. He'll leave, take his tools with him, and I'll be stuck with a broken box and no way to fix it.

I soften my expression. "I'm sorry," I say. "For accusing you. Maybe it was an accident and you did try to help find me."

"Maybe? I broke down when I thought I'd lost you. I was convinced something awful had happened."

"You sound like my mother," I say, which earns me a smile.

"She worries a lot?" he asks.

"If worry was an Olympic sport, she'd have a stack of gold medals."

Now I get a laugh, and the lightness in his eyes eases some lingering doubt. There's more to the story of Lucas and Taylor than either has shared, but I won't push. I need his help, and as the saying goes, you catch more flies with honey. However, who really wants more flies? Either way, I'm letting it all go. I might not have the answers I'm looking for, but I have a gut feeling I'm not in danger.

I reach out my hand. "Truce?"

He grudgingly steps forward, and we shake.

"Yeah, truce. Give me the box," he says.

Lucas sits next to me on the bed. I pick up that underlying scent that's uniquely his, and it sends my mind reeling . . . but there's unresolved business between him and Taylor, so I push the feeling away.

Lucas turns the box over in his hands, examining it keenly. "Where did you get this?" he asks.

I go for a half-truth. "It belongs to the lady who rescued me. She let me borrow it, and I accidentally broke it."

He opens his plastic toolbox full of guitar picks, wire cutters, strings, and little wrenches. There are tiny compartments containing small screws that look perfect for this purpose.

"This is easy," he says. He takes out a screwdriver so small it could have come from a dollhouse. He uses two drops of glue, applied with extreme precision, to ensure the metal sets tight against the wood, then turns the screw, securing the clasp. When it's all done, he holds up the box to examine his handiwork. It looks fine to me, but he's very thorough. He opens the lid and feels along the inside with his fingertips, making sure the screw didn't poke through the wood before tightening it one last time.

As he brushes his hand along the spacious interior lined with red velvet, I notice a shift in his eyes. He looks puzzled. He takes out a different screwdriver from his tool kit—this one a small flathead—and wedges it into the narrow gap between the front of the box and that velvet liner.

"This has a false bottom," he says, intrigued. He applies light pressure, and the bottom lifts up. We peer into the exposed compartment and see something white resting within. There's faint lettering on the back, like a watermark. I can make out the word *KODAK*, set at an angle and printed repeatedly across the paper.

"What's this?" he asks, but I know the answer. It's a photograph; I'm familiar with the brand name. They make instant print cameras, but this picture is way old, judging by the faded markings on the back and the slight yellowish tinge to the paper. It reminds me of my mom's old photo albums, before she digitized and uploaded them to the cloud.

I carefully remove the photo from the hidden compartment. Lucas doesn't know I have a connection to the lake, and likely to this box, and it needs to stay that way.

The paper feels smooth against my fingers, its finish glossy. Lucas and I exchange wary glances because we're invading someone else's privacy. But I have to know. I turn the picture over to see what's on the front.

My heart leaps to my throat as I peer down at an image of my aunt Susie. I'd know her anywhere. She's about my age in this photo, meaning it must have been taken shortly before she disappeared. And it was captured here, at Lake Timmeny—I recognize the front porch where she's standing. I've seen the house behind her with my own eyes, from across the shore.

She's wearing denim shorts, and pink bathing suit straps show from underneath a white halter top. Her freckled, sun-kissed skin glows with youthful radiance. Long blond hair falls like a curtain over her slender shoulders. Even at such a young age, she looks like my mother. She has the same basic features—the signature Welch family round nose (which sadly I didn't get), and sparkling blue eyes that are as crisp as the sky on the day this photograph was taken.

She has her arm draped around the shoulder of a boy. Her fingernails are painted the same dark tint as the lake. Her sunny smile tells me she's in love. It's in her eyes, too, an unmistakable light that burns bright. But as for the object of her affection, he is an enigma.

I can read nothing in his eyes and gauge nothing from his features because someone took a black marker and scribbled him out. The blackout is crudely done, thick lines made in crazed zigzags that cover his face, disguising him completely.

I can feel the haste, anger, and raw emotion that went into obliterating him from the image. I don't need to be an experienced investigator to deduce that something happened between these two. The picture was found in a hidden compartment, in a box that had been in my aunt's room, so she must have been the one who blacked out his face.

But why?

While I have no idea who I'm looking at, I can guess he's about Lucas's age. He doesn't have the build of a grown man, and his olive-toned skin pokes out from beneath a Nirvana T-shirt and tan surf shorts that descend below the knees.

"Whoa. It's like a horror movie prop." Lucas says it lightheartedly because he doesn't know the black ink covering this boy's face might be hiding a monster.

I feel a wave of nausea. It's too much to process, more than I can bear. My thoughts are bouncing around as if my mind is a pinball machine.

When was this taken?

Who is the boy?

What did he do to my aunt?

I notice one small detail that eluded me before, and something clicks. My blood freezes as I focus more intently on the photograph—specifically a small, seemingly inconsequential piece of jewelry the boy is wearing.

That day in the kitchen when David returned from his run, only to find out that Fiona was missing, he pranced about shirtless, leering at me over the rim of his glass of orange juice, basically forcing me to look at his bare chest and the thick gold chain he wore around his neck—a piece of jewelry the same color, size, and shape as the necklace that the boy with the blacked-out face is wearing in the picture with my aunt Susie, taken not long before she disappeared.

Chapter 27

Julia

It was after sunset, and the croakers were louder than usual. The starry night blinked down on Julia, a solitary figure by the firepit, with her wineglass as her only companion. She savored her petty revenge—indulging in the very activity for which she had ostracized her husband. She, too, drank out of need, the alcohol quelling her storm of sorrow.

Dinner that evening was different from the boys' usual grill-a-thon. Everyone ate in David's backyard, at the picnic tables near the campfire. David made tuna salad sandwiches, and Erika cooked a pot of mac and cheese that the twins gobbled down. Julia had contributed some wine for the adults and juice for the kids. She wasn't up for cooking.

While Izzy had a limp and moved at half power, she managed to keep pace with occasional help from David. Meanwhile, Taylor was back in the house, glued to her computer, watching something mindless on Netflix. Julia checked in with her several times, but left her alone when she insisted she was fine.

Tomorrow night, Erika planned to take Taylor into town for a movie, just the two of them. It was Julia's idea; she wanted to give her daughter a respite from the family drama. The sojourn would also offer a chance for unfiltered girl talk, which Julia had encouraged. Without her mom around, perhaps Taylor would open up about her father's relapse and sudden departure from the lake. Julia, however, was stuck here for the duration.

The smell of the campfire made her feel extra lonely. Christian should be here, his strong arm wrapped around her, pulling her close. She'd rest her head on his shoulder, the night orchestra of the humming insects and the crackling fire playing in her ears.

She stoked the dwindling embers, arguing with herself about calling him. Christian wasn't checking on her, so why was it incumbent on her to call him? Although she was reeling with anger, if she was honest with herself, she was also worried. Was he still drinking? Had he gone back to AA? Called his sponsor? People often did crazy things when they were financially desperate. When addiction was thrown into the mix, their behavior could be *wildly* unpredictable. She didn't think he was suicidal, but she couldn't be sure.

An instant later, her anger returned, stronger than before.

What would she say if she called? *Sorry I haven't reached out, Christian. Sorry I don't seem more caring. Sorry. Sorry. Sorry.*

No. Fuck that.

Instead, she drank. The fruity taste of wine caressed her lips and tongue, sending a buzz to her brain that traveled to every cell in her body until she hummed from the inside out. Christian did this to himself, and he should be the one to call, pleading for forgiveness and promising to find a way out of this mess—and not an empty promise, for once.

She inhaled the air. The lake smelled different at night, somehow fresher and richer. Daunting as it was, she had to believe in herself and her ability to rebound from this disaster.

Her financial advisor was on the job. He'd figure out what, if anything, could be done. Maybe they could mediate with the bank, liquidate other assets, or sell the business (if anyone would buy it).

But that wasn't what mattered most. What she wanted was Christian, or something akin to the man she *thought* he was up until yesterday. For good, bad, ugly, or worse, he was still her husband. Even though this was her childhood vacation home, Christian had embedded himself into the fabric of the place. He'd painted the interior more than once and fixed the door that constantly flew open in a strong wind. He had replaced every window and cleaned every gutter. He'd hung the WELCOME HOME sign at the front door that greeted them upon each arrival.

Even gone, he haunted this land. Her thoughts flickered back in time, to when everyone was much younger. The kids were finally tucked into bed and sleeping. The group had reconvened around the firepit, drinking and relaxing. David, so youthful, went on about his newly formed talent scout business, and some new girl in his life whose name was lost to the past.

Back then, Erika and Rick sniped at each other less, and Julia and Christian connected more. The mystery and magic of those early days of parenthood acted as a soothing balm, obscuring the slowly forming fissures in their respective marriages. The laughter never seemed to end, and it was always Christian who made the wittiest remarks, leaving everyone in stitches. But that was when he was still drinking, and his lack of a filter made their conversations all the more entertaining. This was what meant the most to Julia—her friends, her husband, time together as a family, and loving the lake life. In those days, the rest of the world didn't exist when they were here.

"Hey, there." The deep, baritone voice from behind caused Julia to jump.

Rick's bearded face appeared, lit by the fire. The dying embers rose up, casting him in a mischievous glow.

"How are you doing?" he asked casually, as though her world wasn't falling apart.

Whatever. She'd prefer time with Erika, but she could see her friend through the window cleaning up from dinner. Funny that Rick didn't feel a need to help his wife, but Julia wasn't offering, either, so who was she to judge?

Rick dragged a chair over, twisted off the top of his beer, and gulped some down. "I'm really sorry about Christian," he said. "That's a tough one. I don't know all the details, but Erika told me enough. Just sucks."

Oh, Rick. He never pretended to be a deep thinker, so leave it to him to sum everything up so succinctly.

"It sure does," Julia concurred.

"Hope he's doing better," said Rick, which created an opening for Julia to share more, but because she hadn't checked on her husband, she couldn't answer him. Instead, Julia offered a strained smile and a soft "Thank you" for his concern, and left it at that.

"I just came from the command center. Day three, and still no sign of Fiona. Not sure how much longer Baker and company will keep up the effort." Rick's tone was grim and filled with uncertainty.

"And nothing about her family and friends?" Julia inquired.

Rick shrugged. He hadn't heard about or seen anyone from her close circle at the command center.

Why aren't her people on-site, tracking progress, holding vigil . . . something?

The stark lack of support filled Julia with a painful realization: Fiona must be truly alone in this world. Perhaps her parents were no longer alive, or they had turned their backs on her.

Whatever the circumstances, Julia endured a tremendous pang of sorrow as she pressed her fingers to her temples, which throbbed from layers of worries and wine. *Christian. Fiona. The Glass House. Her lake house*—or what might be her *former* lake house. *The business. Their money*—or lack thereof. And there was Taylor's shift into a different orbit, emotionally and soon physically, when she'd make them empty nesters.

Would Julia even be in that nest with Christian, or would she be on her own? Divorce seemed like a distant land, a journey too long and fraught for her to navigate. No wonder she felt displaced. The earth hadn't just moved under her feet; it had opened like a giant gullet, swallowing her whole.

"What else did Baker say?" she asked.

"Not much," said Rick. "As far as the police are concerned, it's still a missing persons case, not a criminal investigation."

Here she was, wallowing in her misery, when Fiona should have been the top priority.

But what could she do? She wasn't a search-and-rescue expert. Still, she felt like she should do more to help. Fiona existed somewhere on this planet, even if only as a corpse, and she deserved more than Julia sitting around having a personal pity party.

They fell into a pensive silence as Rick downed more beer. "What do you think happened to her?" he asked. "The police seem to be going in circles."

"They've searched the lake. Searched the woods. What's left?"

"Search the house," said Rick, sliding his gaze over to the glass house and arching his eyebrows.

"You don't think . . . ?" Julia couldn't finish the thought. The fire popped and crackled as if the flames wanted to chime in.

"We don't know what went on between those two," Rick said. "And they *were* fighting . . . drinking a lot . . . and, well, you saw her that night."

"What are you suggesting?" asked Julia, losing patience. If he wouldn't say it, then she would. "You think David did something awful to Fiona—that he's hiding his crime, maybe hiding her body, is that it?"

Rick returned an apathetic shrug. "Your words, not mine. You know I love Dave. He's my buddy," said Rick. "But it's weird, right? And Erika's the one with legal expertise, and even *she's* wondering."

Julia could count on one hand the number of in-depth, heartfelt conversations she'd had with Rick over the years. It was odd how much she could relate to Erika on a soul level and yet have almost no connection to her spouse.

"I just don't believe David would ever harm anybody," said Julia, while simultaneously recalling all the times she'd seen his anger get the better of him.

"Then why not let the police search the house?" asked Rick. "Why make such a fuss if he has nothing to hide?"

"He's worried about confirmation bias," said Julia, surprising herself with how quickly she came to David's defense.

"Or maybe he did something in a fit of jealousy," Rick countered.

"You really think David would kill Fiona over a drunken lap dance? I think his ego is stronger than that."

"Yeah, probably. But we never know what goes on behind closed doors."

Julia silently stewed. *With friends like this . . .* "I think I know David fairly well, and I don't believe for one second that he did anything to his girlfriend." Anger surged through her, a welcome reprieve from the lingering self-recrimination. "In fact, I'm going to go check on him, see how he's holding up . . ." She stood to go. "I don't think we've been giving David nearly enough support. Maybe instead of tossing out accusations, you should be the buddy you say you are and be there for him."

Off she went, leaving Rick with no opportunity for a retort. She marched purposefully, but as she walked away, she noticed Taylor pass by their kitchen window. Julia paused, coming to a realization. She was in no shape to comfort David tonight. She would check on her friend, but it would have to wait. She had to focus on herself and her daughter before she could help David with his troubles. She continued on, now heading for home, away from the glass house. Maybe Taylor had the right idea and they could watch something mindless together.

It certainly wasn't a solution to her problems, but she knew, like the standard instructions about applying an oxygen mask on an airplane, she had to help herself before she could help someone else.

Chapter 28

Izzy

I've been a bundle of nerves. Finding a hidden photo inside the secret compartment of a mysterious box is one thing, but discovering it's a picture of your long-lost aunt from yesteryear is something else entirely. Add to that the possibility that my boss is responsible for her disappearance, and it's a recipe for high anxiety stew.

It can't be a coincidence that two out of the three missing women from Lake Timmeny possessed the same box with the secret compartment. But what does it mean? More important, what did David do to my aunt Susie? The raw anger that went into the black marker scrawled across his face will haunt me forever.

What little shut-eye I got last night was plagued with horrible dreams of someone carting me off into the woods. It was a man, but he was faceless, almost shapeless. I could feel his tight grip around my wrist as I grunted and strained against his efforts. He tossed me like a trash bag into a waist-deep hole he'd dug into the ground. The landscape looked vaguely familiar, similar to where the construction crew dug up those human remains. But now it was *me* lying inside that hole as my kidnapper dumped shovelfuls of dirt from above.

The mix of soil and gravel rained down in a steady stream, coating my body like a layer of concrete, spilling into my mouth, and filling my throat as it buried the scream I couldn't release. I jolted awake just before more bits of earth covered my face entirely.

Drinking my morning coffee, I try to shake off the lingering feeling of doom that the nightmare left behind. I feel desperate for the familiarity of a hot cup of java, but I'm also struck by the irony that this calming morning ritual is actually bad for my frazzled nervous system. *Oh, well.* This is no time to give up caffeine.

I'm pleased to find my ankle is much better. There's hardly any swelling now, and I can walk with just an Ace bandage, thanks to Grace's special paste. Even so, I continue to use the crutch. I don't want David to think I can fully resume my duties—the more he's occupied with the twins, the easier it will be to investigate him.

The question is *how*?

It's not like I can ask my mother if she knew a man named David Dunne and if he and Aunt Susie ever hung out at the Shack together. My mother would have some questions for me, namely: "Where the hell are you?" and "What are you doing?"

I could rifle through David's dresser drawers while he's busy with his kids, but what would I find? People don't hide their secrets under piles of socks and underwear anymore. These days, we keep our lies and deceit, our embarrassments and dark truths, close to us at all times, locked in our phones and laptops, safe from prying eyes. I'm no computer hacker, so I feel stuck.

With my investigation stalled, I focus my efforts on my paying job—after all, I am still David's employee. The twins don't know that I suspect their father of being a killer. They want to play with LEGOs, watch cartoons, and eat Fluffernutter sandwiches, because one apparently cannot have enough marshmallows while on vacation. After doing all that and more, I take them to the beach for some outdoor fun.

I limp behind as they race ahead, reminding them to stay out of the water until I get there. I feel so much closer to the children now than when I started, which makes it easier to envision eighteen different tragedies unfolding simultaneously, all involving some variation of drowning.

A tablespoon of water is all it takes, as my mother would say. I can feel her fear and worry invading my brain like a virus.

The kids go into the water while I stand watch. Even though they're just splashing in the shallows, I insist they wear floaties. A water rescue with my injury might not go so well. It figures that when actually *in* the water, Brody objects to wearing the inflatable turtles around his arms. But I insist, or else he'll have to play on the shore, and that's that. By now, I've earned enough nanny respect that he doesn't push back.

After our water fun, we make sandcastles. The wet sand is disturbingly reminiscent of the dirt from my dream. High above, a hawk circles. I wonder if it's the same bird I saw during the disastrous hike with Lucas and Rick. How a bird can spot its prey from such great heights is miraculous. I feel a duty to make my young charges aware of this soaring spectacle.

"Look," I say, pointing. "That hawk is searching for a fish from way up there."

Brody cranes his neck skyward, using his hand as a visor. "How can it see a fish from that high up?" he asks with genuine interest.

My heart swells with appreciation for their pure, endless awe and wellspring of curiosity. I must remind myself that the children aren't their father. They don't have poisoned blood. Their DNA isn't tainted. No matter what their father may or may not have done, I won't label or judge them. In fact I feel all the more protective of the twins, knowing David could be dangerous.

"All birds of prey have incredible eyesight," I tell Brody. Out comes my phone, and a quick Google search later, I have details to share. "Hawks have eight times better vision than people. But their eyesight isn't as good as an eagle's, which can spot something to eat from over two miles away."

"How do you know that's not an eagle?" Becca asks.

Leave it to the five-year-old to make me question myself.

"I think eagles are larger than hawks," I say, squinting into the sun to see if this bird is on the smaller side, and indeed it is.

"I want to be an eagle when I grow up," announces Brody. He begins to imitate his newly adopted spirit animal, extending his arms like wings as he dips and dives about the beach.

"I spy, with my eagle eyes, a fish from miles away!" he shouts delightedly.

I'm about to start a game of I Spy when a jolt of inspiration hits me. It's the magical kind, like a gift from Mary Poppins herself. Let's call it *supercalifragilisticexpi-inspiration*, which I define as a burst of genius that has the power to change everything.

A line from the movie pops into my head. "Why do you *always* complicate things that are really quite simple?" Mary asked Bert, her dear old friend and skilled chimney sweep.

Why indeed?

Thank you, Mary.

I don't need to be a highly skilled computer hacker to break into David's phone. I just need my eagle eyes to peer over his shoulder while he's unlocking his device so that I can steal his passcode. Will it be easy? No. But it's my best shot at uncovering his secrets—a picture, a note, a clue—something that will link him to the disappearance of at least one of the missing women from Lake Timmeny. And I'll have plenty of opportunities to score the prize because, as is true for everyone these days, David's phone is essentially fused to his palm. He'll unlock it more times than I can count, and with some luck, I too will get my fish.

It's dinner at last. David makes pizzas, and the kids go bonkers for them. I guess they've had their fill of hot dogs and hamburgers. They've been running around amped up on an early sugar high because their thoughtful nanny decided to make banana splits before the meal was served.

"Special treat," I said as I drowned the ice cream in hot fudge and heaped on the whipped cream and butterscotch sauce. I had asked David to pick up the ingredients at the store, fully intending to use it as part of my arsenal. Sugar-high twins plus a hobbled nanny will help keep him distracted. Naturally, I play up my injury anytime I catch David looking.

One thing I didn't count on was Lucas getting in the way. That boy is everywhere. I can't seem to shake him, and he's like bug repellent for David since he was caught swapping spit with Fiona.

I go to the picnic tables, and Lucas follows me there. I'm plating pizzas for the kids, who can barely sit still long enough to eat them, and I have Lucas breathing down my neck. How am I supposed to stay close to David this way?

"Should we give the picture to the police?" Lucas whispers.

The boy's not dumb, I'll give him credit for that. He recognized the house in the photograph; then he sourced Susie's picture on the internet and found her missing persons poster. I wonder if, like me, he's thinking the bones from the construction site could be what's left of my aunt, and we just discovered a piece of evidence.

I pull him aside as discreetly as possible. "I'll handle this," I say.

But perhaps I'm keeping it all too closely guarded. Maybe I should let Lucas in because two sets of eyes are better than one. I debate with myself how much to share. *Can I trust him?*

I'd rather have Taylor as an ally, but she went into town with Erika. Lucas is my best option, especially since he's already involved and practically begging to help. Besides, David is now connected to two missing women, knocking Lucas down on my suspect list.

The upbeat music around the campfire brings little joy to the evening meal. There's no more Christian or Fiona. It's just Julia, who is morose; Rick, who is being his usual grouchy self; and David and the twins. It's not easy to slip away unnoticed, but I manage to get Lucas alone by the water.

When I'm sure the coast is clear, I take out the photograph, which I've been carrying with me for safekeeping.

"Look at this chain," I tell him.

He studies it carefully, but it's clear he doesn't recognize it.

"David wears one just like it," I say. "It's the same one, Lucas, I'm sure of it. I think the boy in this picture is *David*."

Lucas knits his brows, clearly unconvinced.

"Girls notice jewelry more than guys, even rockers who wear ankh pendants."

He blushes, touching his ankh, which dangles from a thin cord around his neck. "Point taken, but what do we do?" he asks.

"If you really want to help, first you have to promise to keep this quiet. We don't want to spook him. Who knows what he might do if he gets scared. That detective is on him already, and she's not letting up."

"I can keep a secret, don't worry. So what's the plan?" he wants to know.

I tell him my big idea to use my eagle eyes, but Lucas finds a flaw in my thinking.

"Doesn't his phone use FaceID?"

"Shit," I mutter, but joy sparks anew. "But he's wearing a hat and sunglasses. Maybe he'll need to enter his passcode anyway."

Lucas brightens. "Let me get the code for you," he suggests. "I have something with better eyesight than anybody here." Lucas holds up his phone. "Ask David to take a picture of you and the kids, and I'll record him over his shoulder. He'll be so focused on you he won't notice me."

Smart thinking. We head back to the campfire, our plan in place.

I slip back into nanny mode upon our return, grateful to see David has kept his hat and glasses on.

"Kids, let's take a picture together for your father," I tell them. "The light is perfect."

This isn't a lie. The horizon is brushed with a brilliant shade of orange, almost as if the sky is on fire. "David," I say, as cheery as the cherry on top of the kids' banana splits, "can you take a picture? The light is beautiful."

David is more than happy to oblige. I broaden my smile, praying that David doesn't notice Lucas hovering close behind him. The kids are more observant than their father. Brody points at Lucas, but I subtly shake my head and send him a telling smile. *We're playing a trick on Daddy,* my twinkling eyes say. Now it's a game and the kids buy in without additional prodding.

"Look at me, Daddy!" cheers Becca.

"No, me," Brody insists.

David's all smiles as he takes out his phone. It feels like a bomb is about to explode inside my chest, but I manage to stay bright for the camera. I think I see him enter his passcode, but I can't be sure.

He takes a few pictures, checks, and is pleased enough to show me the results. As expected, they're as cute as can be. But more important, Lucas sends me a discreet thumbs-up, and I know we've scored.

"Nice pics," says Lucas.

David whirls around, but thankfully Lucas had stashed his phone in his pocket.

"Right," David grumbles at him. He has no warmth for Lucas. Maybe it was just a drunken kiss, but I don't think David is as forgiving as he says he is.

I'm curious how he'll react when he gets exposed.

Chapter 29

Julia

Everyone settled back at their respective homes after dinner, except for Taylor and Erika, who hadn't yet returned from the movie. Julia was restless; she found the walls of her usually comforting lake house strangely confining. She could use a friend to talk to and promised herself she'd check on David—no time like the present.

Izzy directed Julia to the second floor, where she could see David sitting, looking handsome in shorts and a short-sleeved button-down shirt that revealed his gold chain. It had once belonged to his father, so she understood why he always wore it, but she had never liked the look. It reminded her of a sleazy street thug in a gangster movie.

He lounged on a cushy deck chair, soaking up the soft jazz music wafting from hidden speakers. The deck was lit in blue, colors that David could change using an app on his phone, a feature he'd bragged about at dinner that first night.

She found nothing appealing about the nightclub aesthetic or the house in general. But in Julia's mind, David wasn't as harsh and uninviting as his home. Sure, this place was pretentious, and David could be the same. He was forever trying to be bigger than his britches—he'd had champagne wishes and caviar dreams even back when they lived off beer and fast food. But Julia told herself that just because David could be a pompous jerk at times, that didn't make him a killer.

"Mind if I join you?" she asked.

David gestured with his tumbler toward the empty chair beside him. "By all means," he said. He sipped his whiskey as if there was nowhere in the world he'd rather be, but Julia knew him well enough to see through his false front. His eyes were weighty with worry. There was a nervous edge to him, like a man waiting for the other shoe to drop.

"Izzy let me in. She's tucking the kids into bed. She's so good with them. You're lucky to have her."

"She's a keeper," he said, but Julia wasn't convinced he was being sincere.

Either way, she was done with the pleasantries. "I'm sorry for everything that's going on, David. I know it hasn't been easy."

"You think? I'd say it's absolutely *fucked.* Do you have any idea how bad this looks for me, Julia?"

"Right now I'd say it looks a whole lot worse for Fiona."

David brushed this off quickly and returned the focus to himself. "Oh, come on now. I'm sure she took off. I just can't believe she'd do this to me. My cheating girlfriend intentionally goes missing, and now I'm a person of interest in her disappearance," he said.

"Isn't there someone you can call, David? Anyone in her life she may have mentioned?"

He frowned with regret. "She was always cagey about her family, so I didn't press it. Thought I was being polite . . . and I don't know her friends. We were in that new phase of a relationship—you know, when all you want is to be alone together. I don't know who to call. The police will have to figure that out."

"Speaking of which, maybe you should let the police look around the house? It might help. I was talking to Rick earlier, and he—"

She stopped before saying too much. David's cold stare filled in the blanks.

"He thinks I did something to her, doesn't he?"

Julia cleared her throat uncomfortably. "He didn't say that, not exactly."

David laughed under his breath. "He doesn't have to. I know what he's thinking. Maybe you are, too. Is that why you're here, Julia? To accuse me? To grill me? Are you wearing a wire?"

"A—a what?"

"A wire. Didn't you watch old cop shows? Did Baker put you up to it? Wouldn't put it past her."

"No, nothing like that," said Julia. "I just came to check on you. I'm concerned, that's all."

"Maybe I should frisk you before we talk."

Julia returned an uneasy laugh, trying to make light of his comment. "I'm not wearing a wire," she said.

"Who said I'd be looking for a wire?"

He sent a coy smile, his tone shifting, hunger sparking in his eyes. It gave Julia a surprising tingle in her chest. She laughed him off again.

"Oh my god, David. You have a mental illness, you know that? This is serious business we're talking about. People are getting suspicious because you're not cooperating fully with the police."

David brushed it off. "And what about you?" he asked. "Do you think I had something to do with that woman's disappearance?"

The words stung—so harsh the way he said *that woman,* as if she was nothing to him.

"I know you," was all Julia could think to say.

"Not really an answer," he countered.

"I just think you could let them search your property," she said.

David sank back in his chair, resigned to the ambiguity. "Why? So I can be their fall guy? No thank you. Fiona took off on me," he repeated. "Or she died in the woods, and some hiker is going to eventually stumble across her body. It's as simple as that."

"How heartfelt," said Julia, unable to mask her disgust.

"What do you want from me? It's not like she's the mother of my children or we've been together for years. She's a new girlfriend, I barely knew her. And just for the record, I've been defying Baker's orders by going out in the woods every day to search for her. We've got her picture all over the news, in town, on social media, and nothing has turned up. In a week, she'll be forgotten. In ten years, they'll find her alive or as another pile of bones some construction crew digs up."

"Friendly advice: Don't say that to a reporter."

"You don't know her like I do," he said. "She's pissed because she thinks I'm screwing around, and she's got *major* trust issues. I wouldn't put it past Fiona, not for one second"—he holds up a finger for emphasis—"to pull a disappearing act, just to fuck with me. Who knows, she might have snuck off to meet Lucas. Why isn't Baker looking at him?"

Julia thought this sounded ludicrous. David didn't sound sure of it himself, so she allowed him to vent.

"Either way, I can't care what everyone else thinks. Honestly, I don't even care that much about her anymore, because Fiona screwed around with my security system, and then she left me. I'm sure that's what happened because that system doesn't glitch, and we should have found her by now." David went quiet, letting that harsh truth land like a gavel.

Then, in a much softer tone, he added, "But I do care about you. You've got a lot going on. How are you holding up?"

This was how it had always been with David. He could be callous and selfish, but as soon as he reached out, even a little, Julia would find herself opening up. His one small gesture of concern brought back all the complications of their lifelong friendship. She wanted to be honest with him, to spill all of it and have her friend help hold her together. But it was never that simple with David.

She wished she could say, *I'm doing absolutely shitty.* That summed it up. But she couldn't seem to answer him. The words were there, dancing on the tip of her tongue, but her thoughts were a jumbled mess.

Julia stood up to see if that would help, but instead, she felt lightheaded and dizzy. She walked to the railing and leaned over, inhaling the fresh night air. The lake was perfectly still, like a black mirror lit from above by a half-sized moon. What she wanted was to call Christian and tell him to fix it, fix it now, all of it—the money, the business, his drinking—and get her house back immediately.

What she did instead was cry. A sob burst from her lips, so unexpected that it frightened her. She covered her face with her hands, trying to hold it in, but all she managed was hiccupping gasps as her tears spilled out.

David came up behind her. He wrapped his arms around her waist and pulled her against his body. She sank into him, letting his touch comfort her, soaking in his tenderness, allowing it to calm her nerves.

"Hey, hey," he said, brushing her hair with his hand and shushing her like a baby. "Easy now. What's going on? Talk to me, Jules."

Only David and Christian used that nickname. Maybe that was why she always found it soothing. She pulled away, peering back over the railing. She had a flash of falling; knowing her luck, she'd break a leg, not her neck.

"He's lost it all," she said, keeping her back to David. She wanted to look out over the water, a scene as familiar to her as the *Mona Lisa* or *The Starry Night,* something equally immutable, as fixed in her reality as a calendar year. The thought of losing her lake house struck such a deep chord that it triggered a burning anger, and when she turned to face David, he involuntarily stepped back.

"What do you mean, he lost it?"

The words Julia had been unable to find moments ago came quickly, without a filter. She left no truth untold. She told him about Christian's drinking, the failing business, the loan that fell through, how he gambled the lake house and lost. She said it was the end of everything.

When she finished, David's astonished look said it all. He wordlessly guided Julia back to her chair as he took the one opposite her.

The depth of caring in David's gaze felt like an embrace. No matter how others perceived him, at that moment, he was there for her, present and whole, like a safety net. His warmth assured her he'd cradle her fall, though Julia knew his helping hand often came with a catch.

"I'm glad you told me," he said before knocking back some more of his drink. "If Christian were here, I'd throttle him."

"Why? That wouldn't get my house back."

"True," said David. "Violence seldom solves anything."

Seldom, not never. She wondered if it was a turn of phrase or his truth.

He continued, "But Christian isn't your problem, Julia—you know that, don't you?"

"What do you mean? Of course Christian is the problem here." Was David trying to blame *her* for this calamity?

"The drinking is his cross to bear, not yours," David clarified. "And while it might affect you, you could always walk away, divorce him if you want, free yourself from the burden, easy as that."

"Divorce is never easy, David. You know that better than most. Your ex would have clawed your eyes out if she could."

David smirked. "Debbie still might. But what doesn't kill you makes you stronger."

While she didn't agree with his oversimplification of divorce, Julia was curious about David's take on her situation. Christian had finally texted, so at least she had proof of life. But for all his rambling pleas for forgiveness and promises that he would stay sober and go to meetings, she wasn't anywhere near offering absolution. She had no clarity on how she would move forward.

"So what *is* my problem, if it isn't Christian?"

David's smirk was reminiscent of a magician's expression before a big reveal. "Money," he said blandly. "You, my dear, have a *money* problem."

"Well, no shit," said Julia. "Christian's torched us."

"And you can blame him all you want, but what good is that going to do you? You can't expect the person who caused the problem to fix it."

Julia didn't respond.

"If Christian knew how to get you the money," David said, "you wouldn't be in this mess. The mistake you're making is thinking that *he* can fix it and *you* can't."

Julia squinted at David, as though he were dim. "If I could get the money, I would. I'm not an idiot."

David stretched his legs out long. "No, of course not. You're just caught up in fear, which blinds you to possibilities."

"And what possibility am I missing?" Julia was losing patience. She wasn't in the mood to be toyed with.

David pointed to himself and said, "Me," as he finished the last sip of his drink. "You didn't ask *me* for the money. Look around, Julia." He gestured toward his grand mansion as if he had personally constructed it, forged every bolt and rivet with his hands, and turned sand into the glass she peered through. He'd undoubtedly spared no expense; Julia could see that. The floor was of the highest quality, the windows had triple panes, and none of the furniture required assembly instructions.

"We're not talking about pocket change," Julia said. "Are you suggesting you'll just give me the money and make it all better?"

"Something like that," David answered cryptically.

Julia didn't like his tone—it raised hairs on the back of her neck. She folded her arms across her chest, having caught a sudden chill. When she saw a spark of desire catch in David's eyes, her icy shiver became an Arctic plunge.

"No," she said defiantly, keeping her arms folded. "I'm not a whore."

David pretended to act aggrieved. "I certainly don't think of you like that. We seem to have an opportunity here to . . . help each other out. You want something, and I want something—*again*."

Julia got flustered, stammering, "What we did was stupid and thoughtless, and—"

"Fucking amazing," David said, cutting her off. "You were everything that night, Julia. Don't think for one second that I haven't wanted a replay."

Julia's muscles went weak. Her thoughts drifted back to that day at the lake seven years ago, when she knocked on David's door, the old sturdy pine one, painted a shade of green that blended with the surrounding forest. She was dressed in a tight-fitting top and a loose skirt that would give him easy access to everything she came to offer. She'd invited herself inside and didn't say a word before she kissed him hard on the mouth. He hadn't met Debbie yet. The twins weren't born, so they had the house to themselves.

"Whoa," he'd said, pulling back, but only after he explored her with his tongue. "I think you might be mistaking me for your husband."

She didn't laugh or crack a smile. Instead, she leaned into him and traced a path up his inner thigh with the tip of her finger while nibbling at his ear. She whispered, "Take me upstairs."

But they didn't make it that far. Another man might have asked questions or tried to douse the flames with the cold water of reality, but not David. Instead, he turned her around, grabbed her by the hips, and pulled her against him. He reached under her shirt, lifting her bra, exploring her, his touch igniting her desire. She guided his hands under her skirt, showing him exactly what she wanted. David didn't need much direction. Their bodies were in sync, breathlessly grasping for each other as he entered her from behind, right at the base of the stairs. She pushed against him, moaning, greedy, knowing it wouldn't last nearly as long as she wanted, but David surprised her. He slowed down, using his fingers in just the right place, sending waves of sensation through her body until she went over the edge, losing all control.

"I like your idea about going upstairs," he said afterward, a wicked gleam in his eyes. He took her by the hand, leading her to the bedroom. He touched her more slowly, gently, her passion rising again. When she was ready, she pushed him inside her, desperate with longing. She no longer wanted him to be gentle. She couldn't get enough, and she knew he felt the same—wanting more, needing more—until they finally came together in a shuddering, glorious release.

"This won't happen again," she told him as they lounged naked in his bed. Christian was hiking with Rick, so she'd have time to shower and change before he returned.

"Understood," said David, who'd asked no questions, so it felt incumbent on Julia to explain.

"He cheated on me with some random woman he met on a business trip. This was payback."

David nodded languidly. "I'm honored," he said, his tone indecipherable. Again, no questions asked, a clear signal that he'd take whatever she gave him and seek nothing more. This wasn't a surprise. She knew David well enough to guess how he'd react to her advances. He was a man who wanted what he couldn't have, and he could never have Julia, even though he had idolized her for years, decades even.

He *had* had a brief fling with Erika when they were teenagers. Young love often doesn't last long, and it faded for him before it did for her, but luckily their friendship endured. Julia had never fallen for David's ways like Erika had. She'd remained the unobtainable one, which made Julia all the more desirable in his tangled logic. It made her someone to protect, respect, and admire, though only from afar. He was like the Mob in that he had a code, something which she understood about him. He wouldn't expose her or beg for more; he'd never mention it again, even in private. Instead, he'd follow Julia's lead because *that* was the gentlemanly thing to do.

But now he was asking or offering, because the situation had changed, the stakes had risen, and she was a helpless fish bleeding in the water, attracting him—the hungry shark.

"One night with you, and I'll make all your troubles disappear," he said.

Julia rose from her chair. She knew what she should say: *No, absolutely not, that's not an option.* But the words that came out surprised even her.

"I'll think about it," she said.

Chapter 30

Izzy

I have to admit, Lucas pulled off an impressive feat of cinematography. When we viewed it frame by frame, we got the numbers: 585429. But now comes the hard part. How will I get David's phone? He carries it with him everywhere.

I could sneak a peek when he's in the shower, but I'd have to follow him into the bathroom. *No thanks.* It's so frustrating, I want to scream. How could I be so close, yet still a world away?

All hope feels lost, but then an idea occurs to me. People often use the same password for their various devices, so even if I can't get to David's phone, I might still be able to access whatever secrets he keeps on his computer.

He is out on the deck with Julia, engaged in what looks like a pretty intense conversation. This could be my chance. I'm grateful I've got my nanny world under control. One good thing about a sugar rush is that, after the high, comes the crash. I've never had an easier time putting Becca and Brody to bed. Both were sound asleep before I read the last page of *Frog and Toad Are Friends.*

I head up to David's office on the third floor, quiet as a thief, to have a look.

Fear ratchets up inside me. I try to slow myself down. When I'm this revved up, I can easily make stupid, impulsive decisions. I must be careful. I hear my mother's worried voice banging in my head like a drum. *He'll catch you. He'll hurt you. You'll be the next Susie Welch.*

I remind myself of the promise I made to end my family's generational trauma once and for all. Which is why, before I know it, I'm lurking about in his private sanctuary. With David on the deck below, I should be safe to turn on the lights—for a minute.

The office is spacious, neat, and off-limits to the children. In the center of the room is a fancy rug resembling a multicolored abstract painting. It's not my taste, but not much is in this house. There's little wall space designated for books, even less for pictures, but the ones he's chosen to hang are all nature photographs. I'm most fond of the flying owl swooping across a golden meadow.

David's desk is like a big modern sculpture. The top is a large piece of glass (surprise, surprise) supported on thick, angled legs made of sleek black metal. It's uncluttered—no random piles of papers like my mom's desk at home. It's basically a huge surface area to hold a large display monitor connected to an external keyboard, a wireless mouse, and a laptop computer propped open on a metal stand.

A mug on the desk advertises the electronic components company that made David rich, but apparently not rich enough to shut down the talent scout business. Or maybe he just likes having a convincing pickup line for women, like when he tried to recruit me.

Every fiber of my being tells me to go. But I'm also stupidly stubborn. The computer monitor shows a black screen. I move the mouse an inch and watch the display spark to life. The desktop image is of a snowcapped mountain—more generic nature images for David. I'm prompted to enter a passcode.

Adrenaline floods my body, and I'm hyperaware of my surroundings, hearing phantom sounds like footsteps and breathing right behind me. My legs shake. My palms are sweaty. It's like I'm having a spontaneous anaphylactic reaction. My windpipe constricts as my skin gets all prickly. Every breath feels like a small victory, a lifeline.

Will this work? It's a long shot, but I have to try something. I enter the numbers Lucas recorded: 585429.

And . . . holy shit—it works.

But I immediately regret it. I might not know exactly what

David does for work, but I'm now painfully aware of what he likes to do in his free time, and all I can say is "Ewww."

What greets my eyes on his massive high-resolution computer monitor is a web page filled with box after box, row upon row, of pornography. We're talking a whole lotta porn, with all the moves on display in small preview windows.

It's not like I haven't seen fleshy entanglements before. In this day and age, you can't avoid it. It's not my thing, but I do understand that without sex, none of us would be here, and I'm ready to put this unfortunate discovery into the same category as David's taste in furnishings—to each their own.

According to the cheesy graphic in the top right corner, the name of the website is All Access Sex, and it claims to be the hottest amateur porn hub on the internet.

Upon closer inspection, the "amateur" part appears to be indisputably accurate. David's affinity for high-end products apparently has its limits. The videos are poorly lit, the people look like regular folks, nobody is airbrushed, and certainly none of them are porn stars. I had no idea this sort of thing was a fetish, but evidently it is, and my boss is into it. I want to scrub my eyeballs and brain, but no can do.

However, my success emboldens me. I glance over my shoulder to ensure the coast is clear before using the mouse to minimize the sordid web page. I now know where he keeps his "piles of paper," as his desktop is littered with digital files and folders. All his documents are sorted by type, with handy labels beneath the icons for easy identification. One digital pile is for Documents, another holds his PDFs, and there's one for Movies, but the collection that catches my eye is the one labeled Spreadsheets.

Since David is so fixated on money, perhaps I'll find something worthwhile hiding in numbers, not letters. I click on the spreadsheet icon, which expands into a bunch of individual files. I scan the titles. Most of them are meaningless to me, but the one that draws my interest is named AAS-PL, and it's dated recently. I hearken back to an Accounting 101 class I took to satisfy my math requirement as a freshman, and note it's finally paying off in real life. PL could stand for profit and loss, and that makes this document of keen interest.

I open the Excel file and see a simple accounting spreadsheet delineating revenue, overhead, and profits by month. The revenue is broken out into credit card types, and the expense section includes subcategories for hosting, content, and payroll.

It seems legit enough, but I soon make another connection. The subtotal line is labeled AAS Profit/Loss, which matches the name of the file, but it could also be an abbreviation for All Access Sex.

I'm wondering if David's not just a visitor to the amateur porn website, but its purveyor. Could his talent scout business be a front for a different type of venture? Filming people doing what nature intended isn't exactly "talent," but whatever . . .

Instinctively, I snap a picture of his accounting log with my phone and return to digging. There are other spreadsheets with more cryptic names, and perhaps there are other websites David the Pornographer owns. But before I can start looking, my ears pick up the sound of footsteps, and this time, I'm sure it's not my imagination playing tricks on me.

With a quick mouse draw and fast fingers, I have just enough time to quit Excel and hit the lock screen command before I hear a voice behind me.

It's David, and he sounds pissed. "What are you doing in here?" he growls from the doorway.

I whirl to face him, but my mind goes blank. His stare bores into me from across the room. I open my mouth to speak, to explain myself, but no words come out. I'm busted—*big-time.*

David approaches, and judging by his expression, my punishment is going to be severe.

Chapter 31

Julia

Julia left David's house in a daze. His salacious offer swirled in her mind. Could she? Would she? Was she despicable for even considering it?

The night sky proved gloriously clear, but her vision was not. A cloud of dust encapsulated her thoughts, casting everything in a dim, hazy glow.

Home was dark, no lights on. It was a strange sight. She was used to some activity at the lake at all times, but now she felt deeply alone. Across the way, she could hear Lucas playing his guitar, but otherwise, all was quiet. Erika's car wasn't parked out front. It might be a while before she and Taylor returned from town.

Reflexively, Julia looked for Christian's beloved Land Rover. Of course it wasn't there. She should be relieved. After all, she'd sent him away. But instead, she felt a profound sense of loss and confusion. Why did she feel so loyal to him? He had deeply betrayed her twice now, yet if she accepted David's offer, it wouldn't be to exact revenge. She'd learned her lesson the last time. She got no lasting satisfaction from her actions, no sense of justice. And this time she risked losing her self-respect, too. Who knew what long-term damage that would do?

Since her home looked uninviting, Julia detoured to the lake, where she took off her shoes and waded into the water up to her ankles. She peered up at the night sky. The light from the star they'd wished upon twenty-five years ago reached them, but no wish had been granted. The trio were nothing like they had once been.

She said prayers this time, one for guidance and the other for forgiveness. When she'd had enough, Julia exited the water and walked through the sand carrying her shoes, headed for the familiar path back home. The light was dim, but she could find her way blindfolded. This place was like an extension of herself. She could no more let it go than she could cut off a limb.

As if she needed further reminders of her predicament, Julia's phone chimed with yet another auto-generated text message from one of the creditors hounding her.

Julia, this is Advanced Account Resolution reminding you that you owe a minimum of $500 for your repayment plan. Click here to pay, or call during business hours to speak with a representative.

Julia considered responding in the language of one of her Instagram posts:

Sorry for the delay. I just need to have sex with my neighbor before sending you the money. Hope I'm not too old for the oldest profession, LOL! #MyHusbandIsAThief #MyMoralCompassBroke

Instead, she continued on the path until she found herself back in David's yard. With a sigh, she peered up at his second-story deck. He was no longer outside, bathed in blue light, but she could see the back of him in what she thought was his office on the third floor. *Who has three floors at a lake house? David, that's who.*

A host of descriptors came to mind, none very flattering. But of all those that popped into her head—*narcissistic, arrogant*—one that simply didn't fit was *killer.* Julia was almost sure of it. She'd seen him with Fiona. Her radar would have gone off if something were that deeply amiss. Were they a toxic couple? Definitely. But David had been in and out of toxic relationships his entire life. None of them had ever ended in murder.

Julia had a good instinct for people and thought herself a good judge of character, but then again . . . maybe not. Her husband, her trusted partner, had completely blindsided her . . . *twice.* Perhaps that was the problem—she was too close to Christian to suspect him of wrongdoing. She liked to think she had a different perspective on David, a little distance that allowed her to see the whole man clearly.

But now, with her business struggling, her marriage failing, and her relationship with Taylor strained for unknown reasons, Julia could no longer rely on her intuition. Come to think of it, had she ever been able to?

She thought back to her childhood, specifically the incident in the playroom. Something about that memory still felt amiss. She replayed it again in her mind, seeking clarity. They had heard loud voices. Erika went to the door to see who was downstairs. She tried to open it. The door wouldn't budge. Erika panicked and started to cry, and Julia soon joined in after she couldn't open the door either. Had they been wrong to be so frightened? Cormac assured them that sometimes that door got stuck, and they just didn't pull hard enough. All these years later, Julia still didn't quite believe it. The door had never been stuck before. But instead of doubting Cormac, she had doubted herself.

Is that where it all started—her nagging self-doubt that kept rearing its head in different ways? She'd shelved her concerns about investing in the VR gym, letting Christian's exuberance override her better judgment. She had done the same with their finances. "I've got this," Christian told her on many occasions, and since he was the finance major in college, she rationalized her decision to let him steer the ship. But if she were honest with herself, she had always worried about shouldering that responsibility alone. And here she was again . . . actually considering David's offer, ignoring her inner wisdom, and handing her problems over to someone else to fix.

She sighed. Julia wasn't sure what she should do, but she knew one thing for certain: questions about David would haunt her, especially if they were intimate again. How could she ever be with someone she suspected of murder? She couldn't—that was the answer. She'd have to dispel any suspicion before she could even consider his proposition.

That was great in theory, but how could she do it in reality?

Julia continued her walk around the house, lost in thought, when she stubbed her toe hard against an unknown object.

She almost screamed, but managed to swear under her breath while hopping on one foot to extinguish the fire in her toe. It was too dark to see the culprit. Julia turned on her phone's flashlight, and was even more annoyed when she realized she'd run into one of David's stupid new lawn ornaments. This unappealing cold stone orb probably cost more than Julia owed the collection agency.

All of David's lawn ornaments were ridiculous, the same as his house. *Rich people with too much money,* Julia thought—especially the nouveau riche, not accustomed to wealth—*do stupid things, like buying a new girlfriend a damn Porsche.* A Cayenne GTS, at that. Whether the car was under his name or not, it was still unbelievably extravagant.

But . . . that gave Julia an idea.

She could see the Porsche from across the lawn.

She wondered . . . the police wanted to search the car and the rest of his house, but David refused. Julia, however, wasn't the police. She was his friend—potentially with benefits—and not subject to the same rules and restrictions.

She slowed down. Adrenaline swam through her veins, momentarily numbing the pain in her toe. David was busy in his office. Erika and Taylor were still out. Nobody would see her.

The car was unlocked. Not a surprise at the lake where crime was nonexistent, unless you counted possible abductions and maybe murder. The interior light came on, causing a brief panic. Julia quickly found the button to shut it off and used her phone's subtler flashlight.

The interior looked pristine—not so much as a crumb. The seats were made of buttery soft leather. The dash was sleek and probably ultramodern when powered on. Christian would certainly envy this ride.

She started her search by checking the glove compartment, finding nothing other than the manual and registration—which was in David's name, as expected. She was careful that her feet and hands left no telltale marks behind as she checked under the seats and behind the visors.

Nothing.

Forget signs of blood; this vehicle showed no signs of *life.* Fiona had been very protective of her car around the kids, and perhaps it was her nature to keep it fastidiously clean. David might have already detailed the vehicle to remove anything suspicious, but Julia didn't remember the car ever leaving the driveway.

After scoping out the little compartments in the door and front console, Julia was convinced there was nothing more to see. But bodies usually end up in the trunk, so she closed the car door as quietly as possible—but only after she triggered the latch that opened the back of the Cayenne GTS. The inside of the trunk was as clean as the rest of the vehicle. The only smell that hit her was the scent of a new car and rubber from the extra floor mats.

Julia was about to end her search, but decided to check under the mats to be thorough. She lifted them off the carpet and, to her astonishment, finally found one trace of human activity. It wasn't much, a small slip of paper, but it was something. Using her flashlight, Julia realized she was looking at a dry-cleaning ticket. She wasn't familiar with the place, but the business address was in a town in Vermont, south of here—maybe a couple hours away.

What was Fiona doing with a dry-cleaning tag from a place that wasn't anywhere near her apartment in New York City? She hadn't mentioned having ties to the area.

Julia didn't have time to ponder the implications. Car lights flashed down the road, signaling Erika and Taylor's return from their girls' night in town.

Julia stuffed the ticket into the pocket of her jeans, closed the trunk quietly, and hobbled back to her house as quickly as she could on her still-sore foot.

Chapter 32

Izzy

I asked you a question, dammit! What are you doing in here?"

I cower as though David's words have been thrown at me. Holding my breath, I wait for the worst.

He grips the doorframe like he's holding himself back. Maybe he's afraid of what he'll do if he lets go. But now he takes that step.

My first thought is to seek shelter—flight, not fight—if only I had somewhere to go. I move out from behind the desk, now standing at its side, thinking I'll leave, but David is blocking the only exit.

I consider screaming, but who would come? Becca and Brody? By the time anyone arrived who could actually help, I'd have the life squeezed out of me and David's fingerprints all over my throat.

"Izzy, answer my question," he says, advancing slowly.

Instinctively, I step back, only to bump into his desk. I hit the glass top hard enough to make the computer monitor teeter on its stand. I search for something I can use as a weapon. There's a pen, but I'm too frightened to make a move.

He comes to me without hesitation, stopping only a foot away. I don't like how hard he studies me, as if he can view my secrets, extract them from my mind one by one.

"This is my private office. And these are my private things. You have no business being up here."

My breath quivers. David's shoulders are clenched like he's

ready to pounce. He feels as dangerous as a live wire. "Well? I'm waiting."

I've never been great at coming up with excuses on the spot. I open my mouth to speak. I won't be able to walk out of here without some sort of explanation. But all I manage is sputtering gibberish. "I . . . I . . . was . . . just—"

That's when Mary's words of wisdom to Bert come back to me. *Why make simple things complicated?* Why indeed.

"I misplaced my phone charger. I was hoping to find one up here I could borrow." Luckily, the lie rolls easily off my tongue. It's a logical reason to come into the office, after all.

I notice David soften slightly. His face goes slack and his shoulders release. He's processing my excuse like he wants to believe me, but that could be wishful thinking.

"A closed door should tell you to *stay out.*"

He leans down, pressing his hand against the desk. His greasy palm leaves a streak on the otherwise pristine glass. I gulp as he reaches for his mouse. He must want to check if I've been snooping. Did I lock the screen down? My memory is a blur. If not, we're both in for a huge surprise. He moves the mouse ever so slightly. His computer monitor sparks to life. Thank God, it brings up the lock screen with the background picture of that mountain. The password field is empty. There's no evidence I was in there clicking about.

Whew.

David isn't satisfied. He stands in front of me, assessing me anew. I'm reminded of the many times I've felt claustrophobic in his presence—in the kitchen, in the hallway outside the kids' room—but this is a thousand times worse.

"I don't want you coming in here ever again, Izzy. Do I make myself clear?" His hard eyes bore into me. "I don't have much privacy as it is." He motions to all the glass. "And that's by choice. I'm really an open book. With me, what you see is what you get."

What I see is his face scratched out with a black marker.

"There's a reason I built a third floor just for me, and that's so I could have *some* privacy, which you've just disregarded."

He invades my personal space in a tit-for-tat way, leaning in extra close. I'm layered with fear. I think of a dozen ways I'll fight him off if he attacks. I'll claw his eyes. Kick him where it hurts. I'll scream and punch. In my mind, I'm a rabid wolverine, so look out, asshole, you will not make me disappear, too. *You have no idea who you're messing with!*

But that's just fantasy. In reality, David reaches out and grabs my arm like he did before, only his grip is much stronger this time. His fingers gouge into my flesh until it burns from the pressure.

I can't move. It's as if someone has driven nails through my feet. My legs are as stiff as tree trunks. I don't dare protest—I'm raw with fear over what he might do. David bathes my face with his hot whiskey breath. His grip softens, but his expression remains rock-hard.

"Do you think I'm a fool, Izzy?"

I think you're a pornographer and a kidnapper and probably a killer. But wisely, those words stay inside my head.

"I don't know what you mean," I squeak out.

David leans in more, almost touching his lips to my cheek as he speaks. "I know you're lying to me."

A sudden rush of fear coats me anew. At last, David lets go of my arm. He rests his hip against the desk, which creates a narrow pathway for me to escape, but something tells me that trying to get away would only make matters worse. With or without physical restraint, I'm trapped.

He sends me a crooked grin. "I was in a bind when I hired you," he says. His posture is more relaxed now. "But I'm not an idiot. You're not an experienced nanny. You're an overqualified babysitter, at best. Believe me, I've seen enough professionals to know the difference. Why are you here? What is it you're after?"

"Nothing. I just really needed a job." My voice is barely there.

"You wanted a job for two weeks watching five-year-old twins so badly that you lied to get it? I pay pretty well, but you're not making *that* much." He peers into my eyes long enough to make me recoil. "No, I don't think that's correct," he continues. "I don't think that's right at all. You're still not being honest, Izzy."

He pulls back, far enough for me to see him transform right before my eyes, a wolf becoming a man. When he smiles, it's in an understanding way, as if all is forgiven. "But we're here, aren't we?" he says. "We're in this together. And we're going to make the best of it because I plan to stick around . . . for Fiona . . . and that means you need to help with the kids while we're sorting all this out. And I'll be watching you, Izzy, very carefully, every move, every minute of every day, I'll have my eyes on you. I've *had* my eyes on you."

He looks greedy. His lips blossom into a self-satisfied smile. A fierce chill rips through me, because I know what he means. This house, with all its glass, has yet another way to strip away my privacy, and he's been using it to watch me this entire time.

Cameras.

Chapter 33

Julia

It was a two-hour trip south to Bennington, Vermont, the town where Fiona inexplicably did her dry cleaning. Julia had never been there before, but after finding the receipt in the Porsche, she felt compelled to investigate further.

Bennington, a town of roughly fifteen thousand, was situated near the borders of Massachusetts and New York. It was a straight shot down Route 7. Julia would normally have enjoyed the rural scenery, covered bridges, and quaint towns she passed through along the way, but she was too caught up in her own troubles to pay much attention.

It had been a grueling morning with Taylor, who wasn't interested in talking about her time with Erika, and she vehemently refused to discuss anything relating to her father. Julia's attempts to connect at the breakfast table were met with a mix of indifference and defiance.

"I don't want to talk about Dad. He keeps asking me about you, and I shouldn't be in the middle," Taylor grumbled between bites of her blueberry muffin, a breakfast treat from a local bakery that never went light on the butter. "I've read that it's supposed to be bad for my mental health."

Julia knew she was being goaded into an argument, but didn't take the bait. "I believe you're confusing your father's relapse with divorce, and that's not our situation," she said. "You're not in the middle of anything, but the whole family *is* affected, and I want you to be able to talk about your feelings. Naturally, we should be supportive of your dad, but his sobriety is his battle. I'm more concerned about *you.* Did you and Erika talk about it?"

Taylor's expression was a blank canvas. Julia could project whatever emotions she wanted onto it, but Taylor wasn't about to reveal anything.

"Like, yeah, we talked," she said. "But what do you want from me? This is between you and Dad."

And with that, Taylor abruptly left the table.

"What are you going to do today?" Julia called out as she walked away.

"Be bored," Taylor called back, stomping up the stairs.

Guilt kept Julia from calling out her daughter's thoughtlessness for leaving her dirty breakfast dishes behind. Taylor's barb had stung. The lake wasn't a place for boredom. The kids had always loved being here. They never complained about having nothing to do. Their lake activities had always been enjoyable and family-centered. But now it was none of those things. Those days were relegated to the past, to old Instagram posts and the few associated likes and comments that could only hint at the real magic those pictures had captured.

Although Taylor's words left a mark and Julia felt a strong pull to call Christian—to talk it out and share the burden as they usually would—she couldn't lean on him right now. Besides, she might say something she'd later regret—like the truth.

"Don't worry about a thing, hon," she imagined herself confessing. "I'm just going to let David have his way with me . . . yeah, in bed . . . and we'll get ourselves back on track financially, so no big deal."

She fantasized about making a sex tape, too, so she could torture Christian with it later. Then she'd divorce him, and in the end, she'd get both houses and the car, and Christian would be left to find a buyer for the business and pay back all the debt he'd incurred. But this was nothing but pure fantasy, and nobody—not Erika, not Taylor, and certainly not Christian—could *ever* know the whole truth if Julia went through with the bargain.

Julia was, however, honest with Detective Baker about her discovery. Before starting her drive to Bennington, she stopped at the search and rescue station down the road from the lake house. As Rick predicted, the media were gone. Fiona was already yesterday's news. There wasn't the usual crowd of searchers, either—only a handful of police and an equal number of trained volunteers were on hand. The thermos of coffee Julia had brought would be more than enough for this skeleton crew, and it earned her a round of thanks, although Baker was the least smiley of the bunch.

"We're probably going to make this our last day," the detective said morosely. "My team says it's unlikely she's out there. There are no signs of her. She's left no markers, no scent trail of any kind—nothing for us to follow. We have another K-9 unit from Rutland coming to help, but nobody is optimistic. Any luck getting your *friend* to cooperate? We'd really like to search the house for clues."

Evidence, you mean, thought Julia. It wasn't lost on her that she and Baker had similar aims. Both wanted David either cleared of wrongdoing or not, but for strikingly different reasons.

"No, he's not going to budge. I guess you'll need to get a search warrant, if you can," Julia answered before showing Baker the dry-cleaning ticket. "I found this in Fiona's car. It's from a place in Bennington, Vermont. I don't think David or Fiona have ties there, so it's curious."

Baker barely gave the dry cleaning ticket a passing look. So much for Julia's detective work. "I guess you don't know Fiona all that well," she said. "That's where she's from. We've already told the Bennington PD to be on the lookout. So far, nothing."

Julia was nonplussed. "David should have known that. You'd think that her being from Vermont would have come up in conversation before they came here. He thinks she's from the city, meaning Manhattan, or at least that's what he told us."

Baker eyed Julia as if she was being dim. "Yeah, you would think. He either didn't pay much attention during their conversations, or David keeps a lot of secrets. I know which one I'm betting on. The best way you can help is by convincing him to let us search his property."

Julia screwed up her face. Baker would need probable cause to get a warrant, and for that she needed evidence that a crime had been committed. Good luck there. Fiona was a ghost who had left no trace behind.

"Every thirty years," Julia said under her breath.

"I'm sorry, what?"

Julia decided not to say more. Baker might know about the lake lore, but better she focus her efforts on David.

"I'll do my best to help out," she promised, knowing she'd have little sway.

Baker didn't want to keep the dry-cleaning ticket, which showed Julia how little she thought of her discovery. But for Julia it was a lead, a breadcrumb to follow.

Downtown Bennington was what most people expected from a quaint Vermont town. Main Street evoked the nostalgic feeling of days gone by. Old brick buildings lined a broad road of mom-and-pop stores interspersed with bustling cafés, art galleries, and enough Americana charm to satisfy the most discerning tourist. A scattering of flower boxes added a splash of color, as did a long array of American flags set out in anticipation of the Fourth of July.

While this dream town was home to the elite Bennington College, it also housed a dark underbelly. According to Julia's research, Bennington was among the ten most dangerous cities in Vermont. Most of the crime was related to drugs and gang violence, and the northern section was considerably less secure than other areas. Of course, the dry-cleaning business Julia came to check out was located in the not-so-great part of town.

Julia had no trouble finding parking, since several shuttered businesses meant plenty of empty spaces. Thankfully, Kelly's Cleaners was among those still in operation. She double-checked that the key fob had locked the car doors. It would be hard to explain how her trip to see a financial advisor (a white lie she'd told) ended with Erika's car being disassembled and sold for parts.

Relax, she urged herself. This was still Vermont, after all. Plenty of green spaces and several thriving businesses were nearby, including a convenience store and an Irish pub that, surprisingly, had quite a bit of foot traffic before noon.

Kelly's was like any dry cleaner. It had that pervasive chemical smell of who-knows-what they put on the clothes to get them clean, and a huge conveyor belt system that delivered garments cocooned in plastic bags. An older woman with a hard-bitten face and sallow skin greeted Julia with a joyless glare as if a customer was the worst part of her day.

"Can I help you?" The woman's froggy voice betrayed a smoking habit. Sure enough, Julia picked up a faint whiff of tobacco that even the powerful chemicals couldn't mask.

Julia produced the receipt from her pocketbook with the store's name printed on the top.

"I'm supposed to pick up for a friend, but someone may have already done it. Could you look? It's for Fiona Maxwell."

Julia was relieved her voice remained steady. The clerk didn't bat an eye. Kelly's might not be the most upscale establishment, but it had a computer system.

"Sorry you went out of your way. Someone got it already," the woman said after squinting at the computer screen for a moment.

Julia feigned disappointment. "Oh, no worries. I guess we had a miscommunication. Glad it's taken care of. Just curious . . . do you know when that was?" Calculating backward from the clerk's date, Julia deduced that Fiona had likely snagged her clothes on her way to the lake.

"Did Fiona pick them up herself? Do you know her?"

The clerk's eyes narrowed. She stood straighter. "You ask a lot of questions. What are you getting at?"

"I'm a friend of Fiona's. You know she's missing, right? She was staying at a lake house two hours north of here, and she vanished. Nobody can find her."

The clerk acted more suspicious of Julia than concerned for Fiona.

"I know Fiona, but I don't know you, and I'm not answering any more of your questions. I like to mind my own business. I suggest you do the same."

The clerk retreated to the back room without a goodbye, leaving Julia flummoxed. Why the strong reaction? Instead of expressing worry, the woman had seemed defensive and . . . *frightened*? Julia couldn't make sense of it.

Back outside, she didn't know what to do next. She could visit the local police, but what good would that do? It was unlikely they'd share information, since she wasn't family. Baker said Fiona was from here, so what kind of family and friends wouldn't bother with a missing persons poster? Julia hadn't seen any in store windows or on telephone poles. It was either extremely sad or extremely strange, or perhaps both.

The drive to Bennington was long enough for Julia to be hungry and tired. The Irish pub down the street called her name.

The Black Rose was just what Julia expected—dark and dreary, with a beer smell perfuming the air. An oddly enticing aroma made her crave a basket of fries and a drink. A healthy diet was hardly her top priority.

She ignored the stares of several patrons, all old men nursing beers, to grab an empty stool at the far end of the bar, near an old-fashioned jukebox that she couldn't believe still worked. It played a song from the Foo Fighters, a tune Christian especially loved and would sing out of key at any opportunity.

It's so sad . . . what an idiot.

The menu she perused had a tacky residue, a thin film of old grease that made her question ordering food, but hunger beat out her misgivings. It occurred to her that if the old stereotype held true, the person best in position to help her was the man asking what she wanted to drink.

"Do you have white wine? And I'll take a veggie burger, too," she said, still craving the fries, but knowing she'd regret that choice later.

The bartender took her menu and put in the order. He was the opposite of David—fair complexion with a Lincoln beard. The look made Julia think of a leprechaun, an observation she wouldn't dare share, especially in an Irish bar. She'd say he was middle-aged, in his mid-fifties, with a wrinkled face, weathered and worn from too many stories and late nights. Short and stocky, he had a body shaped like a keg and wore a flannel shirt with rolled sleeves, showing off his tattooed arms.

When he returned with the wine, Julia was ready with her phone. He put the pinot grigio down in front of her before directing his attention to the image Julia shared, a picture she'd taken at the campfire. She pointed to Fiona, who looked ravishing in her small top and red wrap skirt, the magic hour's golden light casting her in an angelic glow.

"Do you know this woman?" she asked.

He gave her a wry smile. "Oh yeah, sure, that's Fiona Maxwell," he said, speaking with a Boston accent she didn't expect this far from home. "Nice shot. My cousin was a friend of hers back in high school. They were theater geeks together. I saw a couple of her local shows."

"Oh, I didn't know she acted."

"Acted like a pain in the ass mostly." He chuckled. "That girl had a nose for trouble, but that's not unusual around here. I think Fiona had big dreams of becoming a Hollywood star or something. She and her best friend, Bella, poor girl."

"What happened to Bella?" Julia couldn't believe she was finally getting some information.

"Sad story there. She killed herself about five years ago. Her fiancé dumped her just before the wedding. She didn't take it well. Fiona found her in the bathtub—you can figure out the rest."

Julia's hand reflexively went to her mouth. What a horribly tragic story. She felt heartbroken for both women and Bella's family, too. Fiona wasn't just David's sexy fling. She was a young woman with a life full of hopes and dreams—and loss.

"Do you know that she went missing?" Julia asked.

The light in the bartender's eyes went out as if someone flicked a switch. "No, I didn't hear that," he said. "When?"

"A few days ago. I just met her while on vacation at Lake Timmeny. The police have been searching for her. I expected it to be a bigger deal down here where she's from, but I haven't seen one missing person poster yet."

The bartender didn't look surprised. "That whole family is *extremely* private—they don't air much of anything, good news or bad."

"I don't get it. A woman is missing. And even if the family is private, wouldn't the police be putting the word out?" Julia couldn't fathom such a lackadaisical response to *any* emergency, let alone one of this magnitude.

"It's, umm . . . complicated," said the barkeep, assessing the room, wary of prying ears. Luckily, the bar was relatively quiet. Even so, he dropped his voice. "Fiona's circle isn't the type you want to get involved in. It's more like the kind you want to run away from."

"What do you mean?" Julia asked.

"These people, Fiona's family, they do business that isn't exactly on the up and up. I shouldn't really get into it, not here, but Fiona's father—his name is Jim Tracey." The bartender looked uneasy, as if he'd just said Voldemort's name aloud. "But everyone around here calls him Jimmy T."

"Tracey?" Julia squinted her eyes. "But Fiona's last name is Maxwell."

"Yeah, she was divorced but kept her married name, probably because Tracey carries a lot of connotations in town."

"How so?" Julia's curiosity kept rising.

"Her dad, Jimmy T, is kind of old-school, if you know what I mean—like he's connected, organized crime, the Mob, all that. Jimmy made a small fortune working the smut trade in Times Square before Giuliani cleaned it up in the nineties. I lived there before and after, so I saw the transformation myself. It definitely got sanitized, but business is business, and Jimmy T kept his hands in things. You seem like a nice lady. I'm only telling you this so you'll get away from here and *stay* away."

"What do you mean, he kept his *hands in things*?" Julia prodded.

The bartender sighed, but he could tell Julia wouldn't give up easily.

"I told you about Fiona's best friend, Bella, right? That she killed herself? Well, it was because an old boyfriend of hers sold a . . . um . . . *private video* of them to a porn website that had a lax vetting process. The video was uploaded, unbeknownst to Bella, to the internet for all to see. So the night before the wedding, her bitter ex sent a group text with a link to the video. The would-be groom was included, and boy, was he ever pissed, so much so that he couldn't go through with the wedding. You've heard the term 'revenge porn,' right?"

Julia nodded.

"That's what this was. But the guy who uploaded the video didn't know that Jimmy T *owned* that website. It was a carryover from his Times Square business—and Jimmy didn't like that the FBI showed up asking questions about it. Illicit digital content crosses state lines, so it gives the Feds an opening to investigate. I mean, porn is legal and all, but only when both parties consent. The website went dark, but I doubt Jimmy T got out of the business."

"Did the guy who posted the revenge porn get arrested?" Julia sure hoped the answer would be yes.

"No, he had a little slip and fall from a bridge. Ended up in the Walloomsac River with his neck broken. Terrible accident, if you know what I mean." A shadow crossed the bartender's face.

"Oh," said Julia, getting a much clearer picture.

The bartender glanced at the photo of Fiona again. "I know that guy, too," he said, pointing to David, who sat beside Fiona around the campfire.

Julia almost recoiled. How would this man know David?

"Not sure how you got involved in this mess," said the bartender. "But that guy there"—again, he pointed to David—"helps

Jimmy T run his businesses. Like, he recruits girls and manages a bunch of these adult websites for him."

Julia's blood went cold. Before he got lucky with his investment in the electronics company, David boasted about his talent scout business to anyone who'd listen. Was that the talent he was seeking—naked girls for adult entertainment?

"He'd come in here a lot, so I know him well enough," the bartender said, not sounding happy about it. "And he said the strangest thing to me. After Jimmy T put the heat on him for being sloppy about the Bella thing—it was his job to verify the content had the proper consent—he got all drunk, loose-lipped, and started talking shit about his boss—which is dangerous, but whatever, this guy's ego was too big to care. He told me they didn't know who they were messing with. He even bragged to me about knowing how to commit the perfect murder—a surefire way to never get caught. Naturally I asked him how, and he answered with a riddle. I'll never forget it. He said: 'How do you shoot someone without ever pulling the trigger?'"

"How?" Julia wanted to know.

The bartender smirked. "Beats me. He never did say. And it's not a hitman—that was my guess. He just smiled with a look of superiority. Listen, it's not my place to give advice, but if I were you, missing person or not, I wouldn't go around asking questions about Fiona, or her family, or their business in this town. It's not safe. Do you understand?"

His eyes drilled into her, driving his point home.

"Got it." Julia finished her pinot grigio in one big gulp. "Thanks for your time. I think I'll take that sandwich to go."

Chapter 34

Izzy

I need to talk to someone or I might burst. I can't carry all these secrets by myself anymore. I have only one logical choice for a confidante: Taylor. We bonded over Fiona's passive-aggressiveness at the start of this vacation; she entrusted me to investigate Lucas (sort of, since she didn't confide the full story); plus, she's the only female around who is close to my age.

So Taylor it is.

Before I track her down, I have to take care of the kids. There seems to be no limit on the amount of cereal or the number of cartoons they can consume.

David acts like nothing happened at all. He drinks his orange juice standing as close to me as he did last night; his gold chain glittering before me like a cruel taunt.

"I went for a run this morning, doing my usual non-sanctioned hunt for Fiona, and saw one of the cops on the trail. He told me today is the last day of the search."

His voice is flat, like he's describing what he had for breakfast. This guy changes faster than New England weather, which makes him mercurial and dangerous. He's clearly trying to tell me something with his easygoing attitude and newfound willingness to keep his shirt on indoors.

I get his message loud and clear: if I play along, follow his rules, and don't make trouble, he'll let it all go. And maybe I should oblige. But I keep wondering if I should give my DNA to the police so they can match it to the bones. Was it David's hand on the shovel that buried my aunt's body? If I were a Magic 8 Ball, I'd say, "Signs point to yes."

As afternoon nears, David settles in to watch *Moana* with the twins, and I find Nutmeg resting on a patch of shady grass outside with Taylor lounging nearby on a yellow Adirondack chair, writing in her journal. She's wearing white shorts and a cozy sweatshirt because the lake air is a little cooler today. Even though the sun isn't as strong, I keep sunglasses on to hide the dark circles under my eyes. Sleep was elusive last night.

"Working on a new poem?" I ask.

Taylor nods. "Yeah. I've had a lot on my mind. I'm really worried about my dad."

"I can imagine," I say. I don't ask to read what she's writing. If she wants to share, she'll offer. Instead, I take the box out of my backpack to show her the repair job. "I have a few hours off," I say. "I was going to return this to Grace, but I could use some company. Want to come along?"

Taylor studies the clasp. "He did a good job fixing it."

"He did more than that," I say. "Let's walk. There's a lot to talk about."

Nutmeg comes with us. We set off at a quick pace down the same path we took to find the Shack.

As soon as I start talking, I can't stop. I'm going so fast, I'm breathless. I don't hold anything back. I tell her about lying to get this job so I could investigate my missing aunt, finding her picture in the secret compartment of the box that had once belonged to Anna Olsen, how David's face was blacked out, how Lucas helped me steal David's passcode, and what I saw on his computer before he threatened me.

Taylor is stunned. She shakes her head as if to clear her mind.

"Izzy, I'm so sorry. If I knew you had a close connection to the lake lore, I never would have taken you to where the bones were found. That must have been horrible for you."

"It's not your fault," I say. "And thanks for caring. Really. I came here to learn more, so you did me a huge favor. But you know who isn't doing me any favors? David. He caught me snooping around his office. Luckily, he bought my bullshit excuse for being up there, but he knows I've never done this job before. And he basically implied that he's been watching me—that there are hidden cameras in the house."

'Cameras?" Taylor is rightly horrified.

"Yeah, I'm showering in the dark from now on, that's for sure. Hopefully he doesn't have one in the office because he'll know I was lying. But my biggest concern is that I think he's a killer, and I'm afraid he might actually try to hurt me."

"That's insane, Iz. What are you going to do?"

What I do right then is start to cry. Hot tears spill down my face and my shoulders shake. I'm surprised by the sudden outburst of emotion. Taylor pulls me in close and hangs on until I regain my composure. I wipe my eyes with the back of my hand, and by the time we reach Grace's little house tucked off the beaten path, I'm fully recovered.

From a distance, I see Grace gardening in her front yard. As we get closer, I hear her humming a melancholy tune. I feel sorry for interrupting her solitude, but I'm on a mission. Nutmeg lets out an excited bark that gets Grace's attention. Her kind and wizened face lights up when she sees me approach.

"I brought you this," I say, handing her the crutch.

Grace leans it against the house and smiles warmly. "Told you that poultice works wonders. And who's this cutie?"

Nutmeg rises to place her paws on Grace's denim top, leaving prints on the fabric, but Grace laughs it off as she brushes away the dirt. She scratches the dog behind her ears.

"This is Nutmeg," I say. "And I brought my friend Taylor. We're both staying at the lake."

"Hi, I'm Grace."

"We've actually met before, a couple times, but it's been a while," says Taylor, shaking Grace's hand.

A trickle of sadness seeps into Grace's tired eyes. "I'm sorry for not remembering," she says.

"I think I should be apologizing," I say, slipping my backpack off my shoulder. I undo the zipper, take out the box, and hand it to Grace, unable to meet her puzzled gaze.

"What's this all about?" she asks, her forehead wrinkled with confusion.

"I accidentally broke the clasp when you let me look at it, so I took it back to fix it. I should have said something to you when it happened, but I was too embarrassed. Anyway, it's fixed now, and I came to return it."

"I hope you weren't that upset about it. This thing is older than I am. I'm sure it's as fragile as me, too." Grace punctuates her comparison with a quiet laugh. "Honestly, I didn't even notice it was gone. That's my memory again. But I'm glad to have it back. Thank you."

"There's more," I tell her.

When Grace peers into my eyes, an understanding passes between us. Her recollection might not be what it once was, but I get the feeling that she knew about and still remembers what was inside the secret compartment. "Come in," she says, taking me gently by the arm. "I'll fix you both some tea and get Nutmeg a bowl of water."

Chapter 35

Julia

Julia drove back to Lake Timmeny in a daze. David, her dear friend, was a low-budget pornographer. Even worse, he was partially responsible for a young woman's death and was also connected to the Mob. What the hell? In her mind, Julia kept seeing a young man splayed out on the rocks in a river, his neck twisted at an unnatural angle, a tangential casualty of David's shady occupation.

Jimmy T's dealings weren't on the up-and-up. That's what the bartender said, but what did that mean exactly? Everything Julia knew about the Mob, she'd learned from *The Sopranos.*

At a rest stop on the drive home, Julia took out her phone and did some research. Sure enough, she came upon a series of articles dated five years ago confirming the death of a young man found in the Walloomsac River with his neck broken. It was deemed an accident, but Julia knew better. Maybe she could help rewrite history, go to the Bennington police, and tell them about her conversation with the bartender. But his words of warning came back to her with force.

Don't ask questions about Fiona or her family in this town. It's not safe.

She wished she hadn't come looking for answers, because all she left with were more questions, including the odd riddle that David had recited about committing the perfect murder.

How do you shoot someone without ever pulling the trigger?

Julia had no idea, but was that what he'd done to Fiona—somehow shot her without firing a weapon? David's connection to his missing girlfriend wasn't simple or straightforward. There was far more than jealousy to stoke Fiona's fires. She may very well have a motive for revenge, and David a reason to keep her quiet.

It was a bright and clear afternoon when Julia returned from her sojourn. Somehow, in her absence, the surrounding greenery had lost its vibrancy, and the lake's sparkle had dimmed to a dull shade of gray. She found Erika at the shorefront, entertaining the twins.

"Thanks for the car. Why are you with the kids?" Julia asked as she handed Erika her keys.

"David gave Izzy some time off and then regretted it, so I came to his rescue. He's working in his office."

Julia peered into the glass house, spotting David seated at his computer on the third floor. Fortunately, she couldn't see whatever explicit images might be on his monitor. She wanted to tell Erika everything about her trip—what she'd learned at the Black Rose. But sharing all that would probably mean confessing her own secrets, including the loss of the lake house and David's distasteful offer to fix her money troubles. The only picture she could post to Instagram to capture her current state of mind would be a mushroom cloud exploding over the New Mexico desert.

"Where are Lucas and Rick?"

"Rick dragged him to see Champlain College. I don't know what kind of bribe he used to convince him to go," she said.

"Or threat?" suggested Julia, which got a smirk out of Erika.

Nearby, Brody and Becca splashed at the shoreline without a care. Erika watched them from under the brim of her sun hat. "I miss those simpler days, don't you?" she said.

"Little kids, little problems," answered Julia, reciting the familiar parents' maxim.

Somehow the aphorism jarred something inside her. Suddenly an answer to her troubles that had once seemed so elusive became stunningly clear. The best way to address her problems was to shrink them down to a manageable size. It was so simple, so effective—and yet so easy to overlook.

You don't tackle a massive project all at once—you break it down into manageable steps. You turn a big bite into many small ones. It was as if the way forward had been magically downloaded into her brain.

Back in her house, Julia called her financial advisor, who didn't answer, but she left a voicemail. The next call she made was to Christian.

She endured a pang of sadness at the sound of his voice, but girded herself for what she had to do.

"Hey, I'm so glad you called," Christian said. If he had been a wine, she'd describe him as genuine with notes of remorse and full-bodied sadness.

"How are you doing?" she asked without much cheer. "Are you sober?"

"Not a drop since the lake," he promised. "I've been going to two meetings a day."

"Good," said Julia. "I'm glad to hear it."

Even though she meant it, she was still surrounded by his betrayal—swallowed by it, actually. She could forgive him (maybe), but she couldn't escape what he'd done. Even if she left him, she'd still bear the scars of losing the lake house. Time would not heal that wound. She'd be forced to relive his deception in her constant yearning to come to a place where she no longer belonged.

"Listen to my words carefully," Julia said. "I still love you, though I'm not entirely sure why. I'll have a therapist help me unpack that down the road. But while you are sober—and you need to *stay* sober—you will find a buyer for our failing business. I don't care if we leave cash on the table. You will get this albatross *sold,* and then you will use that money to save my house. Do I make myself clear?"

"Crystal," Christian said. "I know my apology rings hollow, but believe me, Jules, I feel sick about what I've done. I've never been so sorry in all my life."

"Not even after you screwed that stranger?"

She heard his sharp intake of breath. "I know you well enough to understand that this is even worse."

He's not wrong there.

"Honestly, Christian, I don't care about your apology. Right now, I care about this house—all the memories I have here—and Taylor's school. And I do care about our family. I know you have an addiction, and maybe that's manifested in some sort of gambling problem involving our assets. You certainly have a problem with truthfulness as well, but you need to sort all that out yourself. The bottom line, Christian, is you need to fix what you've broken. I mean it. Fix it *now*."

Julia ended the call without a goodbye, feeling strangely energized. Surprisingly, empowerment felt more intoxicating than Erika's Lake Escape cocktail.

She turned her attention to her laptop, where she found her résumé in a folder that would have been covered in dust if it hadn't been a digital archive. It was strange to see an accounting of her life before she climbed aboard Christian's entrepreneurial rocket ship to nowhere. Now it was time to get back into her own vehicle. She was good at running organizations and loved nonprofit work, but her skills were portable. She could look for work in the corporate world that might pay better. It wasn't going to save the lake house, but it would give her back some of her dignity. After Julia fired off her résumé to a few choice contacts she found on LinkedIn, she heard a knock at the door.

She went to answer it, but hesitated when she saw David through the window, standing on her doorstep holding a bottle of wine in each hand. She steadied herself before opening the door. He greeted her with a smarmy smile.

"Erika is with the kids, Taylor and Izzy are off somewhere—we've got some time," he said with a glint in his eyes.

Julia didn't invite him in.

"I went to Bennington to look for Fiona," she told him.

David seemed genuinely confused. Julia put it together quickly.

"You didn't know she was from there, did you?"

"What? No. She's from New York City." David sounded quite sure of himself.

"You can check her high school transcript if you'd like, but I happen to know for a fact that she's from Bennington and does her dry cleaning at Kelly's, at least according to the ticket I found in the Porsche."

Julia had never seen the color drain from someone's face as rapidly as it did from David's. He might have passed out if she told him Fiona was also Jimmy T's daughter, but she held that ace close to the vest. It was possible he already knew, but she suspected he didn't. He wouldn't have let a woman with a vendetta get that close to him. Besides, with David's Mob connections, she felt safer keeping some information to herself. However, other tidbits were too compelling not to share.

"And I've also found out that you, David Dunne, are into underground porn. I know that your talent scout business is nothing but a front for illicit adult websites." Julia couldn't mask her disgust. "Revenge porn? Really, David! How could you?"

He stammered, looking like a fool, his jaw moving but no words exiting his mouth.

"Let me be blunt," Julia continued, her tone clipped. "My body is hereby and forevermore off-limits to you. And if I find any videos of our past escapade on one of your websites, I swear to God, I will use a hot poker instead of the law to teach you a lesson *so* instructive you'll be shitting out of a catheter for the rest of your life. Do I make myself clear?"

For the second time in less than an hour, a man answered her question with the same single word: "Crystal."

"I can't trust you, David. And don't bother trying to defend yourself, because I'm not interested. I'm solving my own problems from now on. I don't need your coercion, your money, or anything at all from you. Somehow, some way, I promise I will come out on top, and I'll do it on *my* terms."

With that, Julia closed the door in David's face, and for the first time since coming to the lake, she finally had something to feel good about on vacation.

Chapter 36

Izzy

I love anything with ginger, but can't bring myself to drink the tea Grace pours. I'm too nervous. My hands are so shaky, I'm afraid I might drop the mug and break something else of hers.

Meanwhile, Grace's home enchants Taylor, who doesn't seem anxious at all. With wide eyes, she takes in the dried herbs decorating the kitchen walls, the rough-hewn shelves lined with glass jars reflecting the afternoon light, the exposed wooden beams overhead, and the faded rugs where Nutmeg has found a comfortable resting place. (Winston, Grace's tabby cat, has likely found a dog-free spot elsewhere.) It feels like we've stepped into a fairy tale—though not one destined for a happy ending. At the moment, I believe my boss is a murderer, and I have no way to prove it.

I don't know how to begin.

Thankfully, Grace jump-starts the conversation.

"So, Izzy, did you notice anything unusual about the box?" Her voice cuts through the air. Her eyes are fixed on me, waiting for my response.

I recall the understanding that passed between us, but apparently, she wants confirmation that we're on the same page.

"Yeah, I noticed something," I say, my focus drifting out the window. "Actually, Lucas found the hidden compartment when he fixed the clasp."

Grace nods, but her expression reveals nothing. "Lucas is the boy who left you in the woods?" she asks.

"I don't think it was intentional," I say. "And I guess it was kind of fortunate, because I wouldn't have met you otherwise . . . and I wouldn't have found the photograph."

Grace grimaces ever so slightly.

"Do you know who it is?" I ask.

"Susie Welch, the second missing girl," Grace answers quietly.

"She's my aunt." My words come out heavy, though I instantly feel lighter for saying them. The more people who know my story, the less burdensome it becomes. The relief encourages me to keep going, and I tell Grace my real reason for being at the lake. "I never imagined I'd end up working for the man who might be responsible for her disappearance."

Grace is still as a stone while I reveal details about the necklace. "Oh my," she finally says. Her expression remains grim. "David Dunne has a reputation around these parts that appears to be well-earned—and now he's got a missing girlfriend, am I right?"

"Yes. Fiona Maxwell, the third woman to vanish from Lake Timmeny," I say.

Taylor's eyes darken. Looking at Grace, she asks, "If you knew the picture was in the box, why didn't you show it to the police? They might have been able to identify David years ago."

"Oh, trust me, I showed them the photo when I first got the box back. And the police weren't interested. They said it looked like a bad breakup, but they were certain it was unrelated to Susie's disappearance. Don't ask me why; I couldn't explain it then or now. So I put the picture back. I didn't know what else to do with it, and it felt like it belonged where I found it. Honestly, I forgot all about it until now. It's just . . . I don't like to think about that tragedy because it reminds me of Anna—it brings me nothing but sadness."

I pull the defaced photograph from my backpack. "Since it's my family, I'd like to keep it, if that's all right with you—unless the police need it."

"That's yours to have," says Grace. "I get it. I have a hard time parting with Anna's belongings."

Shame warms my cheeks. I didn't dig up any bones, but I might as well have, because I'm unearthing painful skeletons—not only for me, but for Grace as well. I can barely imagine what this will do to my mother when I finally confess where I am and why. But I can't stop now. I've come too far, and we're too close to getting answers.

"Don't you think it's strange that a box with a secret compartment is connected to two women who went missing from the lake, but decades apart from each other?"

A shadow sweeps through the room.

"It's more than strange," Grace admits. "But I got an odd feeling from the police, like they knew something they weren't telling me. It was more than a brush-off. But I didn't know what to do about it. Honestly, I was scared."

Taylor bites her bottom lip. "What do you mean, you were scared?" she asks.

Regret fills Grace's eyes. She rises from her chair slowly, as if resigned to some fate. Off she goes, departing for another room, with no explanation.

Grace returns, holding a piece of blue-lined paper, the kind you'd find in a school notebook. She hands the paper to me, though I await her nod of permission before unfolding it. The paper is yellowed with age and smooth to the touch; my fingers glide across its surface. I'm filled with trepidation.

"When we were little girls, Anna and I used the box to pass secret notes to each other. It was like playing spy." Her eyes brighten at the memory. "Eventually we outgrew the game. Boys were on my mind by that point, and evidently on Anna's as well. The day she went missing, I checked the box on the off chance she'd left me a goodbye note. I found that inside."

She points to the paper, which I cradle like a fragile egg.

"It's a letter from Anna," Grace explains. "She left it in the secret compartment, just like when we were young. I never told anybody about it. Wouldn't even show it to the police, and you'll see why when you read it. Anna was my older sister, my hero. Whatever she said, I did. It was as simple as that. And it was her final wish that I honor her request and keep this to myself. I didn't think anyone would ever see it, but I didn't anticipate the box falling into someone else's hands."

"How did that happen?" I ask.

The speed at which Grace answers proves some aspects of her memory are still as sharp as ever.

"One weekend when I wasn't around, my parents had a yard sale," she began. "A lot of Anna's belongings were sold off. Someone in your family must have bought the box that day. Unfortunately, your aunt must have found the hidden compartment and the letter inside, because the very thing my sister worried would happen to me, happened to her instead.

"When I bought the box back years later, I was amazed to find the letter still inside along with the photograph you discovered. As a precaution, I put the letter in a fireproof safe so nobody would ever find it again, but I'd still have it in case the time was right to share it. I guess that time is now. These secrets have been buried so long, and so many people have suffered—including you, Izzy, and your family. I don't know if I'm putting you in danger by showing you this, but I think you should decide for yourself what to do from here."

It feels like I'm holding a lead in Susie's disappearance that's so hot it could leave blisters on my fingers. I unfold the paper with extreme care. It's dry and fragile. I worry it might tear. My eyes rake up and down the page. The handwriting, in blue ink, is feminine and near-perfect cursive. I don't think I could even write my name with such precision, but Anna composed an entire letter that's as easy to read as any typewritten page.

Taylor stands behind me, looking over my shoulder like a classmate who didn't study for the test.

The paper is dated June 8, 1965, the day before Anna Olsen went missing. I read it aloud in case Grace wants to hear, though something tells me she has it memorized.

My Dearest Sister,

If you find this letter, it means I couldn't come back for it, and it's doubtful I ever will. There's something I have to do, and it's all I've been thinking about. The time has come for me to take action. I guess you should know some things that I've been keeping from you, Mom, and Dad.

First, I'm pregnant.

I know I never told you about my boyfriend, but he's the love of my life, and we're meant to be together, now and forever. But I have two big problems. One is that he's married. Please don't judge. I had no idea when we got involved. I only knew that he was everything I ever wanted in a man and more. Being together makes me feel so alive. I know I should have broken things off when I found out about his wife, but how could I? I was already deeply in love. I can't deny what's in my heart.

He told me he's going to get a divorce and that we'll be married, only it's not happening fast enough for this baby growing inside me. I can't be an unwed mother. I can't support a baby on my own, and Mom and Dad will probably disown me if they find out.

The other problem is, the man I love has become involved with the wrong crowd. He's part of some gang in New York, and I think they work with the Mafia. He never talks about what he does for them, but I know it's dangerous. He's trying to get out. He's a good man, really he is. It's just hard to leave once you're in over your head. But we'll sort that out after we're together, and we'll start a whole new life as a family.

But I'm worried. If he won't tell his wife about us, then I have to, because this baby is coming, and I need him to be with me. Who knows what threats she'll make, and what information about his business and associates she might share to keep him from leaving?

I need to be careful, which is why I'm writing you this note. This is a risk I have to take. I'm not afraid of my boyfriend. I know he loves me. But his connections are another matter.

If anything happens to me, I don't want you taking any risks yourself.

Grace, you can't tell Mom or Dad any of this. Not ever. It's too dangerous for everyone. If someone comes after me, they could very well come after you. Just know I'm doing this for the baby and myself, and I love you very much.

Your devoted sister,

Anna

A heavy pall settles over the room, a silence born from sorrow and pain. I feel it deeply in the pit of my stomach, and it seems Taylor does as well—she's on the verge of tears. Her arms are crossed over her chest, her face strained as though trying to contain her emotions. I'm not sure why the letter impacted her so profoundly, but I have no doubt that it has.

I can't take Anna's letter for myself. It's an archive from Grace's life, an artifact with her sister's handwriting, something she would want to safeguard. But I ask if I can take a picture of it. I don't know how I'll use it, what significance it'll have or how it might help my cause, but I know that my aunt read this letter—and soon after that, she vanished.

Grace gives her permission, but issues a warning. "You know what I'm worried about, don't you?"

"You think my aunt Susie showed this letter to the wrong person, is that it?"

"Yes. And that maybe she was killed by the same person who took my sister. Killed because she learned the truth," says Grace.

My head spins at the thought of Aunt Susie becoming embroiled with the Mob. For an aspiring podcaster about all things criminal, all that I know about organized crime is that it hasn't gone away. Wherever there is an opportunity to make money, people band together to find ways to get it, legally or otherwise.

"I won't put myself in any danger," I assure her, though I'm thinking: *Here I go with another piecrust promise.*

Grace's tone is parental. "Follow your heart, but, Izzy, please watch your back."

I stand to go.

"I've got to get back to the kids," I say. "Thank you for helping me with my ankle, and for everything else. I'm sorry again about taking the box. If I find out anything, anything at all, I promise I'll let you know."

Taylor seems out of it. There's a faraway look in her eyes, a halo of sadness surrounding her. Grace is an empathetic, intuitive type, and I think she's noticed, like I have, that Taylor's gone pale.

"You look unwell. Perhaps you both need to go home and take a rest. It's a lot to absorb. And thank you for being here, and for sharing," Grace says. "Please, please, don't be strangers. I'm making vegetable soup this evening for my nephew, Noah, who comes to check on me from time to time. We'd love to have you join us. Or come back another time. You're always welcome."

She pulls me into a warm embrace, but when Grace reaches for Taylor, her hug is barely reciprocated. Taylor is completely withdrawn, her mind elsewhere.

I can't imagine what's worrying her to this degree, but on our way out, as we walk along the well-worn path, Taylor pulls me to a stop. Her eyes are pleading, glazed with tears. She takes my hand, giving it a squeeze.

"Izzy, there's something I need to tell you." Her voice is a nervous whisper. "I could really use a friend right now. I guess the letter was a sign that I shouldn't deal with this alone anymore."

"Deal with what?" I ask.

"I've been keeping a secret. Something that changes everything."

Chapter 37

Julia

Julia buzzed with a fresh surge of energy. Shutting David down had awakened a dormant part of herself. Her growing confidence felt addictive.

She would be okay regardless of how the situation unfolded. The loss of her business? Fine. Losing the lake house? Why would she want to live next door to that asshole anyway? So what if Taylor needed to go to public school? Julia went to one, and she turned out fine—a few minor hiccups aside.

The first step on her new journey was to embrace reality. She had stopped at a bookstore on her way back from Bennington. Chapter one in the book on mindfulness she had purchased suggested that in order to grow, she needed to accept her situation as it was, without attaching judgment to her story. And that meant taking full ownership of the role she played in the cratering of her life. She had joined Christian's business willingly. She'd endorsed the private school they couldn't afford, believing, as her husband did, that it would be in Taylor's best interest. And she, nobody else, had agreed to give Christian signing authority over the family trust, which included the lake house. Julia had gotten herself into all these situations, and she intended to get herself out of them.

Now, that was a post that would get a lot of likes: *Your happiness depends on your actions, not your wishes.*

She brought a piece of paper to the kitchen table and began to write a list of worst-case scenarios:

Go broke, file for bankruptcy.

Julia had no idea about the ramifications of bankruptcy, but they couldn't be good. Taylor would have to take out college loans (if they could get them), and good luck paying those back. But she tempered her anxiety with reminders that these were worst-case scenarios, not inevitabilities.

Which led her to . . .

Divorce Christian.

What would she have after splitting their assets? Julia did some mental math and came up with not enough.

The next item didn't make her feel any better.

Sell the house.

Not the lake house, but her primary residence. She could buy a condo or rent if it came to that. Julia couldn't remember the last time she'd paid rent. It would have been over twenty years ago. Bonus: can always move to a less affluent town. Taylor wouldn't be in public school long enough for it to matter.

On to . . .

Lose the lake house.

This one was crushing. But what could she do? Actions, not wishes, right?

Looking over the options (none of them ideal) moved her to pour a tall glass of wine. She'd need to watch herself to make sure a new item doesn't get added to the list:

Develop a drinking problem.

But that could be tomorrow's concern. She took a sip, and then another.

Outside, she heard peals of laughter coming from the twins. Julia went to the window. There she saw Brody, Becca, and Erika playing catch with Nutmeg in David's yard.

A wedge of sadness slipped between her ribs. It had always been the three of them at the lake together—Erika, David, and her—and now it was undone, a shared history unraveling before her eyes. No amount of wine, no list, could lessen the ache of the immense change that time had wrought.

Julia returned to her wine just as the front door flew open. Taylor walked in with a weighty aura. She was followed closely by Izzy, whom Julia was pleased to see walked without a limp.

"Mom, we need to talk," Taylor said.

Julia cringed. When a teenager requested a conversation, it was generally for one of two reasons: they wanted money or there was big trouble. From her daughter's body language, Julia guessed it was the latter.

"Of course, honey. Come. Sit down."

They gathered at the kitchen table. Izzy's leg bounced while Taylor fidgeted in her seat. Julia feared she was about to have more items to add to her list. Since nobody took the initiative, Julia got the ball rolling.

"What's going on with you two?"

Taylor's gaze slid over to Izzy. "Maybe you go first," Taylor said. "I . . . I need a minute."

Julia's maternal instincts kicked in. "Is this about Lucas?" she asked.

Her daughter's pained expression was answer enough.

Every fiber of her being told her a dire revelation loomed on the horizon, but Julia would have to wait, because Taylor insisted Izzy begin.

"She needs to know about Susie and Anna," Taylor urged.

It took Julia a moment to place the names. "The missing women? The lake lore? Why? What have you both been up to?"

Izzy released a resigned sigh. "It's the real reason I came here," she confessed. Her words hung in the air.

The revelations she delivered over the next several minutes left Julia speechless.

"Once I read about the bones, I set up a Google Alert looking for job opportunities. I just knew I had to come here and learn more. What better way to investigate my aunt's disappearance than during a two-week stay right across from her old house? And before you get mad, I got my CPR certification and took an online first-aid class, so I wasn't completely irresponsible. Plus, I read a ton about nannying and watched *Mary Poppins* enough times to have it memorized."

Mary Poppins? Despite the shock, Julia couldn't suppress a smile.

"That's quite inventive of you, Izzy," she said. "It *is* Izzy, right? I mean, is that your real name?"

"Yes, I'm Isabelle Greene, like I told Detective Baker. And my mom is Lauren Greene, but she was Lauren Welch until she married my dad. They divorced, but she didn't want to take her old name back. There were too many painful memories attached to it. I don't know if she's ever been diagnosed, but I think my mother has suffered from PTSD ever since her sister's disappearance. That's why I became a true crime junkie. And I got the idea that if I could figure out what happened to my aunt, it would somehow help heal my mother's heart."

As the news sank in, vague memories began to congeal in Julia's mind, forming an increasingly vivid picture. Lauren and Susie Welch—the girls from across the lake. She had played with Izzy's mother as a young girl. As a teenager, she'd done vodka shots in the Shack with both Welch sisters. How crazy was that? She hadn't thought of Lauren Welch in ages, not since the family abandoned the lake house shortly after the disappearance.

But then again, the lake lore was always about the missing, not those left behind.

"I've been investigating Fiona's disappearance as well. Taylor asked me to find out if Lucas might be involved."

"Lucas?" But then Julia caught on. "Right, the kiss."

"I don't think he did anything to her, and he's actually been helping me . . . Taylor, too." Izzy cleared her throat uncomfortably. "Anyway, we've discovered some concerning information."

Izzy took a Polaroid picture from her backpack and placed it face up on the kitchen table in front of Julia. She told the craziest story about a box that had once belonged to Anna Olsen, but had ended up with Susie Welch.

"This picture was hidden inside a secret compartment. I'm certain the boy in the photograph is David. He was involved with my aunt, and judging by the blacked-out face, it didn't end well."

Julia stared wide-eyed and open-mouthed at the image before her. She recognized David's gold chain, which had belonged to his father. She even remembered that ratty old Nirvana T-shirt he had worn until it was threadbare. She knew David and Erika had hooked up back in the day, but she wasn't aware he had a relationship with Susie. Of course, David had pursued everyone, Julia included. And growing up, he had spent more time on the lake than Julia. Her parents always had to leave to get back to work, but David could spend his summer with Cormac, his ever-grieving mother a shadow of herself. Had Julia missed an entire romance between David and Susie Welch?

"There's more." Izzy told Julia about Anna's letter to her sister Grace and the strange coincidence of two women hiding secrets inside the box before they went missing.

Julia thought things couldn't get any crazier until she read Anna's letter, which Izzy had saved on her phone. The story was heartbreaking, but the mention of the Mob nearly took Julia's breath away.

Izzy's leg was bouncing up and down fast enough to shake the table.

Julia cupped the nanny's hand, and the leg movement slowed. "This is all very disturbing," she said. "Especially since it's the second Mob reference I've heard in one day." She revealed David's connection to a gangster named Jimmy T and his association with an underground website that also had a tragic link to Fiona Maxwell.

Izzy's eyes danced as she absorbed all the information. "I've seen that website. I got the code to his computer and searched through it. I know I shouldn't have, but the Polaroid changed everything."

"What? How?" Julia was equal parts impressed and concerned.

"Don't ask," said Taylor, and Izzy didn't offer, so Julia chalked it up to kids and technology and left it at that.

"So you saw a porn website on David's computer, but he could have just been watching it. What made you think he's running the site?" Julia crinkled her nose.

"There was a spreadsheet," Izzy explained. "It was obvious from the entries that he was making money from it. It looked like a lot of homemade stuff, which could easily include revenge porn—but I only got a quick look because he caught me, and, well, it was kinda scary. He threatened me . . ."

"Oh, Izzy, this is *way* too dangerous," said Julia, whose shoulders sagged with the weight of this news.

"So let's review," she continued. "We have a sketchy adult website—not that there are many non-sketchy ones—the Mob, a revenge porn suicide, three missing women from the same lake, a secret letter, and a Polaroid picture of your aunt with my neighbor in what appears to be a relationship gone sour. I'm afraid to ask what else you wanted to tell me, Taylor."

The room went so silent that all Julia could hear were the distant sounds of the twins playing in the yard next door.

Taylor inhaled deeply, closed her eyes, and released a sigh of surrender. "I don't know how to tell you this, so I'm just going to come right out and say it. I'm pregnant."

The moment she made this announcement, a piercing scream erupted outside.

Chapter 38

Izzy

We jump from our chairs, the scream frightening us all. It's so powerful that I wouldn't be surprised if Grace Olsen heard it at her house. And it's not Brody or Becca. This scream undoubtedly came from an adult female with a strong voice.

I race to the kitchen window with Julia right behind me. Taylor squeezes in beside me, her bomb drop momentarily forgotten.

Julia doesn't know the whole story yet, but on our walk back from Grace's place, Taylor told me everything. Lucas is the father, and thank God I was wrong about him. It wasn't rape; there was no sexual assault of any kind.

She's in love with him, but completely freaked out by the pregnancy. She hasn't even told him yet, she's so afraid. Apparently she and Lucas have always been close, and he carried a torch for Taylor for years, but she hadn't reciprocated his feelings. Lucas had always been stuck in the dreaded "friend" category until a couple of months ago, when they went on a college tour and spent the whole weekend together. In addition to touring schools, Taylor shared her poetry and Lucas put it to music.

A deeper bond formed, and Taylor found herself falling for him. They spent a night together, and now they have a big problem. It explains a lot about the odd dynamics I've observed. Now I know why he lied about kissing Fiona. He loves Taylor, and doesn't understand why she's become distant. But that's for sorting out later.

There's an even more pressing issue, namely whatever the disturbance is in David's yard.

The scene completely puzzles me. Erika has both hands on a piece of fabric, the other end lodged firmly inside Nutmeg's mouth. They're playing tug, which is a fine game between a human and a dog. But why the shriek? It's just a piece of clothing, a shirt or something of that sort, nothing to get crazy about. But Erika *looks* crazed. It's as if she's in a fight to the death, while Nutmeg couldn't be happier.

"Drop it! Drop it!" Erika yells, but Nutmeg won't release her prize. She digs her hind heels into the soft earth, giving one firm yank after another. Erika tugs in the opposite direction, pulling on what I now think is a tank top with spaghetti straps. She pulls so hard that her sun hat dislodges from her head, freeing a cascade of red hair that falls past her shoulders. At this point I can see Erika clenching her teeth.

Julia's hand flies to her mouth. "Oh my god, is that . . . ?"

Instead of finishing the thought, she races out the back door toward Erika and Nutmeg. Taylor and I follow.

By the time we arrive, the tug-of-war is over. The loser, Nutmeg, has found a new distraction and is contentedly chomping on a tennis ball. At the same time, Julia examines the article of clothing Erika extracted from the dog's mouth. I sidle up close. Erika smooths out the fabric of a soiled off-white tank top. Even though it's dirty and ripped in places, I can make out a misshapen rust-colored stain on the shirt that definitely *isn't* mud.

"That's Fiona's," Julia stammers. Erika is basically electric. I feel vibrations radiating off her in waves.

"Nutmeg went for the ball under David's porch, and she came out holding this," Erika explains breathlessly. "At first I didn't think anything of it, but then I saw it was covered in blood, and I screamed."

Blood. That's my cue to get the kids out of the way. I shuffle them into the house just as David is coming outside. He approaches Julia and Erika, so perplexed that he doesn't acknowledge me or his children as we slip inside.

I set them up in front of the TV near a window (no shortage there) so I can keep an eye on them. I venture back out to find David has encroached on Erika, his hand extended. Obviously, he wants the tank top.

Erika is absolutely panicked. She backs away, clutching the soiled garment to her chest.

"It was under your porch," Julia tells him. "It's Fiona's. I remember her wearing it the night you two fought outside. And now it's covered in blood."

"That makes no sense," says David.

Julia stares him down. "It makes perfect sense if you did something to her and tried to hide the evidence."

"Maybe you wanted to keep it," suggests Erika with disgust. "Some sick token of what you did."

"What *I* did?" David scoffs. "Are you out of your mind?"

Hmmm . . . maybe not. I've seen enough murder shows to know that killers often keep mementos of their crimes.

Julia has her phone out, and I think I know who she's calling.

"You're going to have to explain all this to Detective Baker," Julia informs him as she places her call. "And we need some space from you. Whatever excuses you have, you can give them to the police."

Great. So I'm stuck in Murder Man's house guarding his kids? This job does NOT pay enough.

Thankfully Julia comes to my rescue. "Izzy, why don't you bring Becca and Brody over to my house. We'll all wait this out together."

Chapter 39

Julia

Julia was at a loss for words. She had found her voice with Christian and David and needed to do it again, right here, right now, with Taylor. But she had a layer cake of crises to tackle, with the frosting of a teen pregnancy covering a looming divorce, potential financial ruin, and a murder investigation involving her longtime friend. It was the unwritten rule of motherhood to always know the right thing to say and precisely how to say it, so Julia would find a way.

To an outside observer, the scene inside her home would have appeared perfectly normal. Izzy was in the living room watching a video with the kids. To his credit, David hadn't protested when she told Izzy to bring them over. He must have realized it was the right decision, but he would probably blow a gasket when his ex-wife Debbie came to collect them. Julia had taken it upon herself to see that Becca and Brody departed the lake as soon as possible. At least not all of her rational mind had gone out the window.

If things got heated between David and his ex, she figured Detective Baker would be on-site shortly to run interference. She could keep that pot from boiling over.

Baker was getting a search warrant. With the discovery of a bloody shirt, she was confident it would happen quickly. Brody and Becca didn't need to see the police ransacking their home and likely carting their father off in handcuffs. Izzy would keep them occupied until their mother arrived—which might be some hours from now, depending on New York traffic.

But who was going to help Julia?

Erika had pulled a vanishing act when Rick and Lucas pulled down the drive, back from their college tour. She had left to update her family on the disturbing new developments. Julia was on her own.

She decided to think less and feel more. Tamping down her anxiety, she let go of parental judgment and simply opened her heart to her daughter's plight.

"Sweetheart, how are you managing with all this? And I have to ask, who is the father?" Julia could guess the answer, but she couldn't be sure. But still, pieces of a puzzle finally snapped into place. Julia gave Taylor's hand a supportive squeeze.

"It's Lucas," she said softly.

Julia didn't mean to gasp, but couldn't stop herself. It was just as she suspected, but hearing it confirmed tilted her world.

Taylor's face twisted. She looked as though she could drown in the worry brimming in her eyes.

Once her daughter began talking, it was as though a dam broke, the words pouring out of her in rapid succession. Her story came so fast it was difficult for Julia to follow. She heard everything, but couldn't process it in real time, absorbing it all through a filter of shock and confusion.

"Erika got two rooms, one for us and the other for Lucas. But we stayed up late working on a song together. He's a great guy. I've always known that, but he's really grown up a lot. I just started to see him *differently,* you know? He loves my poetry, and it was magical how he put it to music. I found out I actually have a decent singing voice. And he told me that he's had a crush on me for a long time. Honestly, I always knew, but he hadn't said it out loud. He was so caring, so vulnerable. Anyway, one thing led to another and I don't regret it, except for, well . . . here we are. I love him, Mom, I really do, and I know he feels the same way. I realize

I've treated him terribly this summer. He doesn't know yet. I just couldn't handle it all."

"I'm not surprised." Julia squeezed her daughter's hand again.

"That's why I hoped he wasn't coming to the lake. I wasn't ready to tell him. I can't manage my own emotions, let alone his. I needed time and space to sort it out. And then the whole Fiona fiasco happened, and when I found out he kissed her . . . I guess I got scared. I wondered if I really knew him. I thought maybe I was wrong about everything. I started to question my own judgment. I even feared he could somehow be involved in Fiona's disappearance. I know that sounds crazy, but I've been a wreck. He's upset with me because I've been ignoring him, and he has no idea why."

"That's why you asked Izzy to investigate Lucas? You needed to know for sure?"

Taylor confirmed with a nod.

"I understand." Julia's voice shook. "Can I ask, how far along are you?"

"About two months, but I only found out a few weeks ago."

Taylor's tears revealed that her heart overflowed with concerns for the baby, Lucas, and her future. Julia moved her chair next to Taylor's, wrapping her arms around her daughter.

"I'm confused," she said. "You're on the pill." Julia was careful to keep her voice inflection neutral. She didn't want Taylor to interpret her inquiry as chastising.

"I accidentally left them at home. I didn't think a few days would make that much of a difference . . ." Taylor broke into full sobbing. Julia could tell she was trying to keep it as quiet as possible so she wouldn't call attention to herself. "I don't know what to say to Dad. He's going to be so disappointed in me." Thoughts of her father were enough to pull the damper off the volume control.

"Your father is in no position to judge anybody, especially his daughter. It's going to be okay," Julia said. "We'll figure it out—together."

She fell quiet, allowing her daughter to release all her pent-up emotions with a cleansing cry.

"Do you think he'd make a good father?" asked Taylor, her voice shaky, her breathing shallow. "He has a big heart, but he's a little ungrounded, a big dreamer—I mean, he's a musician." She made it sound like a one-way ticket to poverty. "In my heart, I know he cares about me, and he's kind and loyal, but being a father is a totally different thing."

"I don't know if he'll be a good father," said Julia, who wasn't surprised that Taylor was contemplating having the baby. Also unsurprising was Taylor using the same descriptors for Lucas that Julia would have selected: *ungrounded, a dreamer . . . but kind and loyal.* Like so many of life's problems, Taylor's question had no clear answer.

She could see why her daughter had kept everyone in the dark. Christian especially would have struggled with the news. He had an outdated way of thinking when it came to relationships and marriage. He wanted his daughter to find the kind of guy who would take care of her, even if that sent Taylor the wrong message about relationships and her ability to be self-reliant.

And now there was a baby on the way that was half wannabe rock star. Julia wasn't ready to hear Christian's reaction to this news, so she had no plans to call him just yet.

"I'm glad you told me," Julia said, trying to be as reassuring as possible. "And we don't have to solve it all right now. But we will, I promise. This won't be easy, but you're strong and you'll figure it out, with lots of people by your side who love you unconditionally."

Taylor managed a weak smile.

And everything Julia had said was true. They couldn't address it all that instant. There were other matters to contend with, namely Detective Baker and her team of police officers, who had just arrived on the premises.

After another quick hug, Taylor headed upstairs, understandably needing time to regroup. She took Nutmeg with her for company and comfort. Julia didn't kid herself into thinking her assurances had eased her daughter's heavy heart.

Setting her worries aside, Julia stepped outside into a muggy, overcast afternoon to see what was happening. David stood in front of the glass house, his hands locked on his hips, squaring off against Baker, who looked imposing in her suit and sunglasses.

Debbie was still en route, so Izzy would have to do the yeoman's work of keeping the twins distracted until she arrived. That girl was a true gem. She might not have any nannying experience, but she more than made up for it with qualities that mattered most in child-care—an open heart and common sense.

And common sense told her that David wasn't going to easily sidestep the consequences of his actions. *Innocent until proven guilty, my ass,* thought Julia. How was this her friend? How was any of this possible? Julia couldn't wrap her mind around it.

Erika, Rick, and Lucas showed up, all three looking equally shocked, and for good reason. Five police cars were parked in front of David's house, all flashing strobe lights.

David braved Rick's disdain as the two locked eyes.

Rick shook his head, giving his beard a tug with one hand. "It's just unbelievable," said Rick.

Julia directed her attention to Lucas. "Yes, it is," she said in a low tone, passing him a glance.

Erika took notice. "What's that all about?" she whispered to Julia.

"You and I need to talk later," Julia said somberly. "And you're going to need every last bit of your mindfulness training . . . But first things first. Do you have the shirt for Baker?"

"Yeah, it's in a plastic bag in my kitchen."

Julia returned a subtle nod while, from a distance, she watched David study what she presumed was the search warrant. What could he do but step aside and let Baker's crew in?

They entered his home, carrying boxes and bags for gathering evidence. Julia noticed that they all wore purple latex gloves to preserve the integrity of what was now a possible crime scene.

David marched over to Julia and Erika, his eyes simmering. Baker came up on his heels, anticipating trouble.

"I heard from Deb. Thanks for calling my ex without telling me. You've both shown what kind of friends you *really* are."

Julia stood tall. "I wouldn't piss off Erika if I were you. She might be the only attorney willing to take your case. And I'm sorry if you think I overstepped my bounds, but the twins don't need to be here right now. You can argue that point with Debbie if you'd like, but I did what I had to do. I can't trust you, David. I don't even know who you are anymore."

David pulled back as though he'd been shoved. "If I'm such a bad guy, Julia, why haven't I spilled your secrets to Christian? Hmm? I certainly could do that, gladly—especially if I were as detestable as you say."

Julia burned inside. "You wouldn't dare."

"Stay out of my business, and I'll stay out of yours," David replied, an insincere smile plastered on his face.

Julia could only imagine what Erika was gleaning from this exchange, but she didn't have the bandwidth to care.

Baker took David aside, distracting him with paperwork. It was all handled professionally, Julia observed. Emotions might have been running hot, but Baker did her part to keep them from boiling over. From what Julia could tell, David was being treated fairly. Baker allowed him to wait out the search inside his home, likely because he was being cooperative. Otherwise, he would have done the same as Julia and watched from a distance.

Thanks to all the windows, it was like looking in on an ant farm—seeing the busy workers going up and down the stairs, searching through drawers, checking all the rooms, and investigating closets and under beds. A part of Julia sympathized with David for this invasion of his privacy, but the bloody clothing under his porch had forced her hand.

Julia heard a ding from inside her pocket and pulled out her phone. Christian. What timing he had.

You probably don't want to hear from me until I fix some of this mess, but I promise I'm working on it. And I learned more information about that property that's for sale. Please call me. It's important.

She silenced her phone and shoved it deep inside her pocket. The last thing she needed was to listen to Christian's wild pot farm scheme. Julia couldn't ignore him forever, but she certainly wouldn't deal with it now.

She turned her attention to the underside of the porch, which had been cordoned off with yellow tape. A CSI team was working the area (yes, Lake Timmeny mustered one). Glibly, Julia thought of an Insta caption.

Lucky us! Netflix is filming a new crime drama right here at the lake! They've even cast us in the production. Erika and I are the horrified onlookers, and David is our guilty AF former friend suspected of murder. And in other news, my husband is high as a kite at his new weed farm. #goodtimes #funinthesun #lovethelakelife

Unfortunately, after the police exhausted their search, Debbie still hadn't shown up. Izzy was doing a good job keeping the kids occupied so they didn't have to watch the cops cart off boxes of personal belongings containing computers, phones, clothes, and other items of interest.

David followed the detective's crew out of his house. Julia watched him climb into his blue Mercedes—though not before sending Julia a death stare she fully expected. He rolled down the car window after turning on the engine.

To Baker, he shouted, "Let's get going, please. I've got things to do, and this will be nothing but a waste of my time."

Julia was confused. Was David going in for questioning? He certainly wasn't being arrested. Julia had to know. She approached Baker, who was huddled with her colleagues, likely comparing notes on the search.

"Is he going to the police station?" Julia asked.

"Yes, he is," said Baker. "I used something we call 'police judo' to convince him to come chat with us. It helped that his attorney is vacationing not too far from here. He's going to meet us at the station as well."

The development surprised her, but Julia was glad to know they were making progress. "What about Fiona? Is the house a crime scene now?" she asked.

Baker's slim smile bent into a frown. "At this time, I can't really say. We did recover a gun from the property, though I don't know any more than that. But I would like to have a quick word with the nanny, Izzy. Is she available?"

Julia asked Erika to take over kid duty to allow Izzy to join them outside. When she emerged from the house, Izzy looked like an anxious survivor of a natural disaster. Her curls were unruly, her steps as tentative as her expression. Julia decided to stay close by for moral support.

Baker's demeanor remained relaxed. She conveyed nothing but support and caring, so it didn't appear the young nanny was in any trouble. "Izzy, I just want a quick word with you, if I may." Baker looked to Julia. "It's a private matter."

Izzy brushed off the dismissal. "She can hear it, whatever it is," she said.

Baker straightened. "Very well. I know who you are—we did some investigating. That's kind of in our job description, you know?"

Izzy's face flushed. "So you found out I'm related to Susie Welch?"

Baker nodded her head enough times to imply that and more. "Izzy, my father was a police officer here in town many years ago, and I followed in his footsteps. This is hard to share—hard to say, but I think you have a right to know."

Izzy's hand gripped Julia's. "Yes?" Her voice was subdued.

"My father remembered your boss—David Dunne from back then. There was a charge against him related to your aunt—an accusation, more accurately, of rape."

Izzy cupped her hands over her mouth, and then she let them down slowly. "That's why she blacked out his face," she said in a daze. "He . . . he raped her."

"Well, not according to the law," said Baker. "You see, my father actually interviewed your aunt. He said she gave a very credible and emotional account. But then something happened, and the police captain told my father not to pursue it. He said Susie was a regretful teenager who'd willingly gone too far. My dad didn't believe it, not for a second. But there wasn't anything he could do, and the case was dropped."

"Why are you telling me this?" asked Izzy.

"Because I want you to know that I believe my father's instincts were accurate and that your aunt was telling the truth. I understand those times were different; women often weren't believed and feared coming forward, but I happen to know there was also some corruption in the police department decades ago. It's better now, but I have reason to believe your aunt's case wasn't handled appropriately. I don't know why, but I intend to find out. I want you to know that I will seriously consider David as a suspect in both her disappearance and Fiona's. I'm truly sorry your family hasn't had closure or justice for your aunt, and I will do whatever I can to set things right."

Chapter 40

Izzy

I promise myself I won't cry.

I plan to hug the little rug rats and say my goodbyes, and that will be that. It's not like I've been their caregiver since infancy, and suddenly we're all done. I've known Brody and Becca for less than a week. And while it's been quite an eventful number of days, I've been a temporary visitor, nothing more. I wasn't present for their first steps, first teeth, first day of preschool, or any other important milestones. I'm barely a blip on the radar of their young lives.

And now, the time has come to go our separate ways. It's as simple as that. And this should be a nonemotional farewell.

I recall Mary Poppins's departure at the film's end. She offered a nod full of steely resolve toward the Bankses' home, then unfurled her ubiquitous black umbrella and, without a word to the children, set off for the skies.

She did cast Bert a knowing albeit wistful look, offering faint acknowledgment of their special bond, a subtle light dancing in her eyes. And with that, she was off to her next assignment.

This, I vow, will be me. I'm off to what's next, with a quiet resolve and pleasant adieus.

I approach Brody and Becca, now with their mother Debbie, who has no idea I've conned my way into her children's lives.

Debbie could be any random woman, as far as I'm concerned. She and I have had our one and only interaction for this lifetime. Our paths will never cross again.

"Thank you for everything," says Debbie, addressing me in a neutral tone as she climbs into her Lexus. This woman oozes quiet luxury the way others do sweat. "The children spoke quite fondly of you."

The children she referenced do not follow their mother into the car. Instead, they glue themselves to my legs. I've got one on each side, like little koalas clinging to a eucalyptus tree.

"Come with us," Brody pleads. "We love you. We want you to stay with us forever."

A small lump forms in my throat, nothing more. I remain in full control.

"Thank you, Brody," I answer crisply. Still on the clock, I feel a duty to nanny him. "I need you to be very well-behaved for your mother," I say. I intentionally leave David out. Brody can take scissors to his father's wardrobe for all I care.

As I understand it, the kids were told that their dad had business to attend to, so they had to leave the lake early. They didn't make a fuss. At first, I thought they were profoundly adaptable little beings, but I found out they were headed to Debbie's mother's house—where there's a pool and the promise of an arcade and chocolate cake. So much for attributing superior coping skills to them.

Becca peers up at me, her big, wide puppy-dog eyes shimmering beneath a thin coating of tears. "Thank you, Izzy, for being our friend. I love you." She wraps her arms around me like she will never let go.

And that's it. That's all it takes. There's no magic umbrella to whisk me away. Nope. I'm stuck right here, ill-prepared for this moment, and there's no preventing the waterworks that spill out of my eyes.

A pit opens in my stomach, so deep I fear it will swallow me whole. The cry that emanates from this well of sadness is the result of the most genuine, loving feeling I've experienced in ages. Like miniature radio antennas, the little ones pick up on my sorrow and start to cry as well. In a matter of seconds, the three of us are a huddled, blubbering mess until Debbie honks the horn, breaking the spell.

"Kids, let's go. In the car, please," she calls out through an open window. "Grandma is expecting us."

We wipe our eyes at the same time. I help them into their car seats, adjusting their buckles and making sure everything is secure. This gives me one last chance to ruffle Brody's hair and brush Becca's cheek.

I can't believe how close we've become since that initial car ride. "No fighting over the stuffie," I say, patting Becca's tiger on the head. Brody promises to comply, though it helps that he's clutching a stuffed bear.

I remind them what a fun time they will have with their mother and grandmother and force a huge smile on my face.

I have no idea what will happen to these two precious beings. They didn't ask to have a rapist and murderer for a father. But there are killers in the news every day, and many of them have children. It's my hope that whatever befalls David, they will be as resilient as it's possible to be. All I want is for them to have a happily ever after, but since I can't make magic happen, I simply say a silent prayer and hope for the best.

I close the car door. It shuts with a click. Becca blows me a kiss through an open window, and I return one to her. To my surprise, I swear I feel something magical fly off my palm. It's as if my wish somehow became tangible, carried on the wind, sticking to them like a fountain of gold glitter, coating their clothes and hair with my love and best wishes.

And that's it. That's our final goodbye. They wave to me as Debbie drives away, and then they are gone.

I'm stuck with a pervasive feeling of sadness. It's for the children, Aunt Susie, and myself as well. I feel directionless. I've accomplished what I came to do. I've solved the disappearances of Lake Timmeny. A man here at the lake murdered his pregnant paramour, Anna Olsen, to keep his double life as a Mob fixer safe, and David took my aunt's life to keep her from pressing rape charges against him. It's her bones that were unearthed in that field. I'm sure of it, and so is Detective Baker. She took my DNA for comparison, but it will be weeks before we have confirmation. The Fiona mystery remains, but I'm confident it was my former employer and not the lake that took her.

In my mind, the case is closed, albeit with a few unanswered questions. I should spend some time here doing interviews, taking pictures, and tying up loose ends for a wrap-up episode of the podcast I plan to produce, but really, all I want to do is leave. This mission was my fuel, and now I'm depleted. Part of me worries that my future podcast about my family's tragedy is disturbing an ancient burial ground, like I'm doing something sacrilegious with this obsession of mine. But Aunt Susie doesn't have a voice anymore, so I feel compelled to speak for her, to let the world know who David Dunne really is.

I wander around to the back of the glass house, where I stare at the lake for a time. It's a quiet and serene afternoon. My eyes follow the path of a snow-white egret that's found a good fishing spot near a strip of land that juts into the water. I enjoy the peace and solitude. Lucas isn't playing music for once. Taylor is hidden away in her room, exhausted, I'm sure, from her emotional day. Julia is over at Erika and Rick's place. With so much to talk about, they could be there for hours.

As for me, the urge to leave before David gets back from the police station—if David gets back—is compelling. Perhaps they'll arrest him, and he'll have to spend the night in jail before his arraignment. A quality crime reporter knows the proper procedures for criminal processing, which is how I know he could also return at any moment. I can't be near him if he shows up, but where do I go? He was my ride to the lake, and the others aren't packing to leave.

I can probably stay with Julia and Taylor and catch a bus in the morning. That way, I can wrap up a couple of things. Afterward, I can keep an eye on everything from a distance and, hopefully, see David held accountable for his actions through the media. I've had enough close contact with murderers for one summer.

But what a hypocrite I'm being. Here I am, wanting David to be held accountable for his actions while avoiding taking responsibility for my own. I resign myself to what I must do. Honesty might be the best policy, but that doesn't make it easy.

I take out my phone and call my mother.

"Hey, dear, I was just thinking of you," Mom says.

Her voice tears a hole right through me. I should have been up-front with her from the start, but just the mention of Lake Timmeny would have sent her anxiety skyrocketing. However, I can't avoid her any longer. Who knows when some of these developments will hit the mainstream news and spread all over the internet?

"Hi, Mom," I say, the words rubbing against my dry throat. "How are you?"

"Oh, fine. Nothing new here. How about you? Are you getting a lot of articles written? Anything published yet?"

My lie bites back at me with venom.

"No, Mom. Nothing published. But I have a question for you. I've been thinking about Aunt Susie, and I'm wondering about something . . . Did she ever say anything about being assaulted by some guy at the lake?"

The line is so quiet I can't even hear her breathing. "Mom?"

"I heard you," she says, her voice harsh. "What are you up to, Izzy? Why are you asking me this?"

"Did she, Mom?" I press again. "Was she—raped?"

"Yes," she blurts out. "She was, if you have to know. It was some good-for-nothing boy who lived in the house across from us. And he got away with it, too. I thought Susie was brave to go to the police and speak up for herself, but nothing ever came of it.

"Your grandmother and I spent years trying to get someone to investigate her rapist after she went missing, but the police insisted there was no connection—and no rape. The case was basically dropped. There were rumors about corruption in the local force, and Susie said something about an Irish mobster in the area—but we don't know for sure if that was the reason we were stonewalled.

We never got to the bottom of it, but the police weren't going to pursue charges against that boy, that much was clear.

"But how do you know this, Izzy? Why are you asking about Aunt Susie? What are you up to at the newspaper?"

I can't swallow. I can hardly breathe. The pressure building in my chest feels extraordinary. I can't bear it a second longer.

"Mom, I'm not at the newspaper," I say, barely getting out the words.

"What?" Her voice rockets in surprise. "What are you talking about? I don't understand."

"I lied to you because I knew you wouldn't let me come to Lake Timmeny. That's where I am now—at the lake. I got a job working as a nanny for a man named David Dunne."

It's like I can feel my mother's heart stop through the connection. Then she takes a short, sharp breath, and I do the same. For the second time today, tears stream down my cheeks. I feel so much shame my skin is on fire.

"Oh my god, Izzy, you don't understand; that man is dangerous!" Her words clap back, shrill and urgent.

"I'm fine. I'm safe. Please don't worry. I'm not staying there anymore," I say through a choked-back sob. "I'm so sorry, Mom. I just wanted to help you. I know how traumatic losing Aunt Susie was for you, and you've never been able to move past it. Your anxiety is like a third person in the house. And it's been getting to me, too. I'm living your fear, and it's affecting my life. I thought if I could figure out what happened, I'd give you some closure and maybe help you get better—and help myself in the process."

"Oh, Izzy . . ." But she can't finish the thought.

I know there are different degrees of pain, for I've experienced several of them throughout my life. A cut is at one level. A broken bone is at another. A broken heart, another still. And I'm afraid I've broken my mother's heart by telling such a calculated and manipulative lie.

Eventually, my mother says, "Izzy, Izzy, Izzy," in a disappointed tone that only my mother can deliver like the zing of an arrow. "I really wish you hadn't done this."

"But why?" I shoot back. "Someone needed to keep digging. He killed her, Mom! He did it to keep her silent. And we can't just let that go unpunished. I know I can't. Susie needs us to speak for her and get the justice she deserves."

But now I'm wondering how my relationship with my mother will change—if I've done more harm than good. Mom and I are close, in a way, but there's always been a strange distance, too, as though Susie's memory formed a wall between us, preventing my mother from being fully present. Mom made it her mission in life to make sure I was safe. She was the order in a world of chaos. It was always my father who did fun things with me. He took me camping, taught me how to fish, and showed me how to shoot a basketball. While Dad was the moon circling high above, casting his majestic glow, Mom was the planet Earth that kept me so grounded I often forgot she was the rock I stood on.

But I'm not forgetting her now. I had hoped this investigation would bring us closer. I want her to know I love her and care about her suffering. And that I'm old enough now to do something about it. We can be a team, not just a mother protecting her daughter. Would she—could she—understand?

"I'm coming to get you right now," she says.

Guess that's answer enough.

She can't see me shake my head, but she hears my firm denial.

"Mom, no," I tell her. "I'm fine. I'll get a ride to the bus station tomorrow. David is at the police station being questioned, and I have a friend I can stay with tonight. I'm safe, and I need at least another night here. I started this on my own, and I have to see this story through to the end. Your blessing would mean everything to me, but I'm staying regardless. I'm so sorry for hurting you, Mom. I hope you can forgive me."

The line goes silent and still.

"And, Mom . . ." I say, summoning my courage. "Why didn't you tell me about Susie being raped?"

"That's not something we ever needed to discuss," she answers sternly.

"But it's our family's history."

"No, Izzy, it's not. It's hers—it's Susie's. It's not yours or mine. It's hers alone."

"But that's not why you kept it from me, is it? You didn't want me to know because you always want to shelter me from life. Don't you understand that the more you try to keep something from me, the more I'm going to want to go after it?

"You can't keep me safe from the world, not while I live in it. If you want me to be honest with you, then I need you to trust me. Have some faith in me. Let me fall. Let me get hurt. I'm not going to drown in a tablespoon of water."

"But you could," she says.

"Right," I say, exasperated. "I could. But I'd rather die swimming than watching life pass me by from the safety of the shoreline."

Mom clears her throat and, thank God, she laughs. "Stop being so dramatic," she tells me. "You're not writing an exposé about me. And no matter how persuasive you are, you're still in big trouble."

"You can't send me to my room anymore," I remind her.

She sighs. "I guess that's true." Another sigh. "I love you, Izzy," she says emphatically. "And while I'm extremely upset about what you've done, you're right. You're not a child anymore. And it's true, I can't control everything you do—it's simply impossible. But I just ask that from now on, if you want honesty from me, I expect the same from you—about everything. No more keeping big secrets from me."

"Deal," I say. "And I promise I'll head home in the morning, don't worry."

While this is all well and good, and my mother and I have fixed something about our relationship, I still have an empty place inside me. "Mom, I need to know how you feel."

"Feel?" she parroted back. "I told you. I'm pissed off. And rightfully so."

"No, not that, Mom. About him. David Dunne."

Her exhale fills my ears. "Well, if I'm being honest, Izzy, I feel a profound sense of relief knowing that son of a bitch will end up where he belongs, thanks in part to you."

There. That's what I needed to hear. The empty feeling is gone and I understand something I didn't before. A podcast can inform and entertain, but only people can heal your heart.

Chapter 41

Julia

There'd be no more grilling. No cocktails, no boating, swimming, lounging, or hiking. The vacation was over before it really even started. But in the grand scheme of things, what did it matter? A woman was missing, most likely dead, and one of the Lake Gang was responsible. That trumped all.

The stress of the past few days had short-circuited Julia's taste buds. Sitting in Erika's living room, she picked at the sandwich her friend had prepared, but it tasted like cardboard. Rick's freshly popped popcorn was stale as old bread.

Taylor wasn't eating, either, though probably for different reasons. Before she went to Erika's house, Julia checked in on her daughter, who was isolating in her room. Taylor assured her she was fine, but wanted to be left alone. Julia respected her need for space, but they still had another person to talk to—Christian. Julia didn't have it in her to respond to his last text message, and whatever pot farm scheme he was concocting would obviously take a back seat to the current crisis.

"Do you want to be the one to tell him, or should I?" she'd asked Taylor. "Give it some thought, but we have to call him soon. He's your father and needs to know what's going on."

Taylor's whole body sagged. "I'll tell him," she said, her voice hardly above a whisper. "I just need a little more time."

Julia gave her shoulder a supportive squeeze.

Taylor asked, "What's going to happen to David? And will Izzy have to leave the lake?"

Julia couldn't say. It was more uncertainty they'd have to sit with, which was never comfortable. Erika and Rick were stuck in the same uncomfortable waiting place, but at least they knew how to pass the time: drink. Julia joined in with a glass of wine, pretending to eat her sandwich, all while seated under the ever-watchful gaze of Cormac Gallagher's stoic portrait and the heads of many dead deer.

"I'm too sick about David and Fiona to stay here any longer," Erika stated. "My caseload feels more relaxing than the lake at this point."

She didn't know the half of it. Julia had revealed nothing of Izzy's relationship to Susie Welch. It wasn't her place to share, which meant she hadn't told Erika or Rick about the Polaroid, or Anna Olsen's letter, either. And she couldn't broach the topic of the pregnancy until Taylor told Lucas herself. She was dreading that difficult conversation, but it had to be addressed soon.

"I just can't believe it," said Rick, who seemed far more relaxed than was appropriate, but shock could do that to a person. He stuffed popcorn into his mouth, some falling onto the new rug that had replaced the brown one Julia despised.

There it was again—the rug, what was it about the old brown rug that bothered Julia so much?

"I see it all the time in my law practice. Good people getting caught up in the heat of the moment, too much alcohol, one bad decision, and their lives are ruined," Erika said matter-of-factly.

"Well, I'd say Fiona got the worst of it," said Rick. "Poor girl."

"Of course," Erika agreed. "It's just, as a defense attorney I tend to think of it from the client's perspective."

Julia was aghast. "This isn't some unknown client and random victim, Erika. It's David and Fiona we're talking about. Our long-time friend and a woman we saw alive and well, in her prime, just days ago. Now there's nothing left of her but a bloodied shirt. It's horrifying."

"I know, I don't mean to be crass. But I've seen a lot of terrible things in my line of work. It can be easy to depersonalize it." Erika coupled her observation with an apologetic look. "And you're right. It *is* horrifying. Guess you never really know what's in somebody's heart."

Or head, thought Julia, wishing she better understood what Erika was thinking and feeling.

Even after playing with the twins and bagging up the bloody evidence, Erika didn't have a crease in her summer capris or a stain on her crisp white blouse. She appeared cool and collected. Did the law really harden you to that extent? Erika had screamed at first, but soon after her composure kicked in like a well-honed muscle. Rick was the same. What this unlikely couple had most in common at the moment was their cavalier attitude—first toward the glass house and now regarding these disturbing new developments.

With David's secrets out in the open, Julia wondered again what Erika and Rick might also be hiding. Then again, who was she to judge? Julia couldn't be fully forthcoming without revealing information about Izzy, the depth of her financial woes, and her trip to Bennington.

In thinking it over, it was the Mob aspect that bothered Julia the most. In a short period, the Mob had come up twice—and both times, there was a connection to the lake lore.

Obviously, David had nothing to do with Anna Olsen's disappearance; he hadn't even been born. But could Jimmy T have been a resident of Lake Timmeny? That was an unsettling possibility, though it was probably a stretch.

Curious enough to google him, Julia got up to excuse herself. "The wine actually isn't sitting well with me. I'm going to make some tea. Anybody need something from the kitchen?"

Erika and Rick declined. The drink was beside the point. Boiling water and steeping tea should give Julia time to do some research without her absence being noticed. She sat herself at the breakfast bar, lost in her phone, barely hearing Lucas playing guitar upstairs or Rick and Erika's faint conversation wafting in from the living room.

Julia had done a cursory exploration of Jimmy T after the Bennington trip. She ended up with little, but now she narrowed her focus. She remembered the name the bartender gave her: Jim Tracey. But because of his association with porn and crime, Mr. Tracey had done an exemplary job of keeping his face off the internet, even when she added 'Lake Timmeny' to her searches.

He had no social media presence, and according to the court appearances that Google indexed, no arrest record, which made it unsurprising to find no news stories written about him. Jimmy T played it clean for good reason. Low exposure made it easier to run his rackets. And if he had a couple of connections to the local police, as the bartender implied, any slipups could easily become cover-ups. That would explain why David's failure to monitor for revenge porn had enraged him. There were some ramifications even Jimmy T couldn't control, including the FBI investigation and the media spotlight following Bella's death.

Julia came across others with the name "Jim Tracey" as she searched, but she doubted they were *the* Jimmy T. She felt stuck, and, no surprise, caved in to her compulsion to check Instagram for a distraction.

However, the thought of Instagram gave Julia another idea. Jimmy T may have kept his photo from ever landing on the internet, and Fiona's social accounts were nonexistent. But Fiona did have a best friend who might have an active account in memoriam.

Finding Bella's last name and the link to her Instagram page didn't take long. Luckily, the profile wasn't set to private. Bella, like Fiona, had been an aspiring actress and used social media to promote herself. There was no shortage of both personal and professional pics on her account, and Julia started to peruse images of this young woman's short life.

Bella was a raven-haired beauty with caramel-colored eyes and a fresh-faced appeal that was tailor-made for show business. Her last post was from her family, announcing her passing with a headshot that Bella probably would have selected herself, if only she'd been able.

Julia kept a close eye out for photos of Fiona with her dad in the feed. Jimmy T cared enough about his daughter's friend to allegedly toss the man who had betrayed Bella off a bridge. It seemed conceivable he could be in one or more of Bella's pics—a group shot, most likely. If she got lucky, Julia could put a face to the name and maybe uncover something to link the notorious gangster to Lake Timmeny and Anna Olsen.

Bella's posts were nothing extraordinary, a bunch of the usual shots—dinner with friends, out at concerts, pictures of her cocktails, Bella on the beach showing off a youthful figure. Fiona was featured in many of the posts, looking dazzling and full of vitality, but her handle, @FeistyFiona, went nowhere since her profile had evidently been deactivated at some point.

Bella, however, kept posting up until the end. There were several pics of her with a handsome young man with thick auburn hair. In one, his arm was draped around Bella as she showed off an impressive diamond on her left hand, gazing into the camera with bright eyes and a brilliant smile that spoke of a future full of promise. Julia realized, with a knot in her stomach, that this must be Bella's beloved ex-fiancé.

She kept scrolling, losing hope as she went through years of Bella's life in reverse chronological order, all her trips, her haircuts, sunsets, books she'd read, movies she'd seen, plays she'd performed in, and parties she'd attended.

It was disorienting to watch someone who had passed on move away from their death. Only she knew Bella's time was short and her joy on lease. The knowledge burdened Julia in a way that infused each image with a palpable weightiness. She felt intrusive, like a macabre voyeur.

But she was glad she stuck it out, because near the end (or

beginning, actually) was a fresh-faced, very young picture of Bella broadcasting a big smile on her graduation day from SUNY Albany. And there, embracing her in a half hug, was Fiona also in cap and gown, with two men on either side of the young women who Julia assumed had to be their proud fathers.

The caption read:

Our dads didn't think we'd pull it off! #jokesonyou #wemadeit #ontothenext #love #apprecationpost #ohtheplacesyoullgo

Bella stood next to a handsome fellow in his fifties, and, if the post was to be believed, the man next to Fiona must be her father, Jimmy T.

Julia was expecting a frightening mobster—square head and jaw, muscular and imposing—but what she saw surprised her.

Jim Tracey was the dad-next-door type. He had an average build and was fortunate to have a thick head of dark hair touched with silver. His most distinguishing characteristic was his bushy, mouse-brown mustache. It gave him an approachable air, which he augmented with a pair of tortoiseshell glasses that magnified his soft blue eyes. He was dressed for the occasion in a light gray sport coat over a white collared shirt, no tie. To Julia, he looked like a workingman, not a thug and pornographer—certainly not some gangster who might have masterminded the not-so-accidental death of Bella's ex-boyfriend.

What struck Julia most wasn't this man's unpretentious demeanor and dapper style of dress. It was the shocking realization that he was currently staring at her out of two separate pictures.

Almost in a daze, Julia stood up and held her phone next to a framed photograph hanging on the kitchen wall across from her. It was an image of Cormac Gallagher taken years ago, holding a fishing rod on the dock he had built himself. His fishing companion stood beside him, grinning ear to ear—a dark-haired, handsome, mustached man Julia knew from her childhood, but who she now realized bore a striking resemblance to the much older gentleman celebrating his daughter's graduation.

Julia's mind went blank for a second, but soon enough restarted like a frozen computer. Fiona's father, Jim Tracey, might be known in some circles as Jimmy T, but to Erika, he was always Uncle James.

Chapter 42

Izzy

I might feel better after talking to my mother, but I don't know how Taylor feels after talking to hers. I return from the lake to find the door to Taylor's house shut. I'm sure it's unlocked, but I knock anyway. I hear a few faint barks from Nutmeg, but nobody comes to greet me, so I let myself in.

"Taylor?" I call out.

Her muffled reply drifts down from upstairs. Nutmeg greets me when I enter her bedroom, panting with excitement as I give her a satisfying scratch behind the ears. Taylor is sprawled on her bed, her eyes fixated on her phone, mindlessly scrolling through a social app. I recognize the automatic finger flick.

"How are you holding up?" I ask as Nutmeg jumps onto the bed and cuddles next to Taylor.

This is my first time up here. The room is painted light pink, and the furniture is worn and secondhand. She's decorated the walls with a few framed prints, but there's also a poster of Katy Perry and one of Katniss Everdeen from *The Hunger Games.* It's a younger girl's sanctuary, left untouched because she either outgrew the need to have the decor match her age or she's taken solace in the memories of simpler times.

"I'm okay. Thanks for checking on me," she says, though her quiet voice and downcast eyes contradict this assertion.

"How'd it go with your mom?" I ask.

"Way better than I expected," Taylor says, though without cheer.

"But now I have to tell my dad. He's going to lose it." She puts down her phone, sending me a sad half smile.

"Maybe he'll surprise you like your mom did," I offer hopefully.

Taylor's expression conveys her doubts.

I take a seat on a desk chair across from the bed. "I was afraid my mom would try to strangle me through the phone, but I told her everything—where I am, why I came here, and what we found out about David and Aunt Susie."

Taylor perks up. "Whoa. How'd that go?"

"She's pissed," I admit. "But I think, in a way, she's also relieved. She needed closure, and now we've got some. It feels like I've ended the family curse. I don't know if they'll find any evidence that David killed my aunt, but we're all hoping he'll at least be held accountable for Fiona. That'll be some measure of justice."

"You think she's dead?" Taylor asked.

My thoughts flicker to the dream I had about getting buried alive, a faceless figure gripping the shovel that piled on the dirt, bit by bit, until it covered my entire body.

"She has to be," I say.

"But why bury the evidence on his own property?"

"They feel a compulsion to keep a trophy close by," I say, echoing Erika's earlier observation. "These guys get off on thinking they're smarter than everyone else."

"Sometimes they are," Taylor says darkly. "Anna Olsen's killer got away with it."

We pause, a quiet moment of reverence.

"That reminds me," I say, "my mom said Susie told her about an Irish mobster in the area."

Taylor's eyes go wide. "She did? Does that mean Susie showed her the letter?"

"I don't think so," I say. "She didn't mention the letter on our phone call. And I've never heard of the Irish Mob. That detail wasn't in Anna's letter, but my mom definitely said the mobster was Irish."

"I haven't heard of the Irish Mob, either," Taylor says, frowning.

Simultaneously, we grab our phones and start googling. Taylor fills me in about the Winter Hill Gang out of Somerville, Massachusetts, founded by Buddy McLean, though the most famous member was Whitey Bulger. He spent years on the run before he was caught, eventually dying in prison.

I focus on New York and learn more about the Westies, who hailed from Manhattan's Hell's Kitchen. This group was nasty with a capital N. They covered all the crime bases—drugs, illegal gambling, and contract killings—and they were best known for their ruthlessness and reliance on *extreme* violence. And as an interesting side note, I find out they even formed an alliance with the Italian Mob, who gave them the highest praise a gang could receive—"f'ing crazy," according to one top-level capo. With the backing of the Italians, the Westies spread their influence north to Times Square, their power growing in proportion to their brutality.

"I don't get it," Taylor says. "What are the Westies doing in Times Square? Isn't it just a big tourist trap?"

I'm with Taylor. All I know about Times Square is that it's full of chain restaurants and mangy Elmos that pressure tourists into pricey photo ops. But there must be something to it, so I keep digging.

After some time clicking and reading, I come across an article detailing the Mob's focus on the sex trade in 1970s New York City, which was only a few years after Anna Olsen fell off the face of the earth. Evidently, these gangsters made big money off porn, pimps, and prostitutes.

I let Taylor in on Times Square's smutty past.

"Wait, porn was in movie theaters?" she asks.

We swap incredulous looks.

"Guess it got cleaned up, but probably not until after the Mob made a lot of money selling sex," I say. "Don't you think it's interesting that the Irish Mob seems to be connected to this lake, to two of the three disappearances, and to the sex trade? And we happen to know that David has a shady porn business."

Taylor quietly absorbs this information.

"It feels like all of this is connected to David somehow, but that can't be," she says. "He's not old enough to have even known Anna."

That gets me thinking. "Well, what if David had a connection to some Irish gangster who lived at the lake back in Anna's day. Know any Irish guys David was close to?"

Taylor sits up straighter.

"Cormac," she says with dismay. "Cormac . . . *Gallagher*. He became David's surrogate father after his real father died. And David was like his personal assistant or something. My parents know more about it than I do, but Gallagher is an Irish name, right?"

"Could there *be* a more Irish one?" I ask. "And he's got a redheaded daughter. How Irish is that?"

We look at each other, dumbfounded.

"We need to talk to Lucas, pronto," I say.

"Nutmeg, you stay here," she orders. "We'll be right back."

Finally, there's something that propels Taylor out of bed in a flash.

Chapter 43

Julia

Julia stumbled out of the kitchen in a daze. She had forgotten all about her tea, and although she'd only drunk half her glass of wine, the room was spinning. She was trying to remember Uncle James more clearly, but his image was a blur. She recalled him often wearing a hat and having a genial smile, but otherwise her memories were murky and elusive.

He must have stopped coming to the lake when she was in her teens. But she'd been distracted at that age by boys and friends and hadn't paid much attention. She didn't think there'd been a falling-out, since Cormac had kept a picture of Uncle James on the wall.

A disturbing thought hit her like a punch to the gut. The playroom. During the all-consuming fear of being trapped inside a locked room, Julia recalled hearing the sound of voices and a loud crash. Had there been an argument, some sort of struggle? And then, when they were finally let out, the red living room rug was gone, exposing the hardwood floor underneath.

What if . . . ?

It was horrifying to even consider . . . but Julia thought she finally understood her aversion to the brown rug that had appeared soon after. Subconsciously, she'd always known something was deeply wrong, and now she could see it in her mind: a very Mob-like image of a body rolled up in a bloody red carpet, being discreetly carted away.

It felt surreal to finally piece together what happened, after so many years of confusion and self-doubt. Erika's father was a salesman, a vague enough job to be anything—including a criminal, a fixer, or maybe even a hit man for the mob. Julia supposed that Jimmy T *could* be the man Anna Olsen referenced in her letter—but she'd made it clear her gang-affiliated paramour *resided* at the lake, which pointed to Cormac. And with her memory coming into sharper focus, Julia's doubt was washed away.

It all fit, even the timing. It was in their teens, after David's father died, that he became Cormac's errand boy. If David acted as the go-between for the two gangsters, it would explain why Uncle James stopped coming to the lake. That could be how David first got involved with the Mob, James Tracey, and the porn trade. But what did she know? She'd been young enough not to ask questions, and Uncle James, aka Jim Tracey, aka Jimmy T, was relegated to a vague memory and nothing more.

The picture of Cormac and Jimmy T in the kitchen revealed another disturbing connection. Erika likely had known Fiona *before* this vacation started. Sure, there was an age gap, but with such a close friendship between their fathers, those two must have crossed paths on more than a few occasions. And yet they had acted like perfect strangers. How David's relationship with Fiona factored into all this was yet another question.

Julia staggered into the living room, determined to get some answers.

Erika took one look at her friend, and her demeanor shifted instantly. *Was that fear in her eyes?* "Are you all right? You're deathly pale," Erika asked.

Julia faltered. "Did you know her?" she said in a bleak whisper.

"Know who? What are you talking about?"

"Fiona," said Julia, narrowing her gaze.

Erika flinched, betraying herself. Her complexion dulled. Her brilliant eyes lost their glimmer.

So it *was* true.

Julia shifted her attention to Rick, who looked like he'd taken a hard slap across the face. He knew as well. He must have been in on it. But in on *what,* exactly?

"Uncle James is Fiona's father."

Erika switched to a stony expression. "I have no idea what you're talking about," she said, her tone forced. She obviously wasn't the actress Fiona had been.

Before Julia could confront her further, the front door flew open, and Taylor and Izzy strode in, apparently on a mission.

"We need to see Lucas. Is he upstairs?" Taylor asked, her speech hurried.

Julia nodded, noticing that Taylor and Izzy avoided eye contact with the two homeowners. They knew the name Jimmy T, but had they somehow connected the dots back to the Gallagher family?

Both kids bounded up the stairs without seeking permission.

Rick got to his feet. He approached Julia slowly, steadily, like a wolf closing in. Julia's blood went cold.

Erika bolted from her chair, barricading herself between Rick and Julia.

"No, don't," she said, pressing her hands against her husband's chest to hold him back. "It's not her fault. She's done nothing wrong."

"But she knows," he said.

Julia didn't like the nervous flutter in his voice. She suddenly regretted letting her daughter and Izzy enter the home. Hopefully they'd be safe upstairs, but that didn't help Julia.

Rick shoved Erika aside as if she were an empty paper bag. What did he plan to do? Julia froze, not knowing if she should fight or flee.

Before she could make a move, the front door came open for the second time in as many minutes. Julia swiveled toward the kitchen, surprised to see David make an appearance.

His face was plum-colored. He stormed into the living room, skin shimmering with a thin coating of sweat. His eyes were so wide they were primarily white.

"Good. Just the two people I was hoping to see," David said, gesturing toward Erika and Rick. "Where is Fiona?"

"I . . . don't know," Erika stammered.

"Bullshit!" David spat. He shook his head in disbelief. "Blame is on me . . . partly," he said, his tone softening. "I was too distracted by my hot new girlfriend to bother looking into her background. If I had, I would have found more lies than truths. You know what Detective Baker told me?"

Julia held a breath.

Oh, shit.

"She said that Fiona's father is Jim Tracey from Bennington, otherwise known as your uncle James. You must have known that your dad put me to work with Jimmy years ago. Cormac and I were like family, but with Jimmy, it was always business. I knew nothing about his personal life—I never met his family.

"But *you* were like family to Jimmy. You know what that means, Erika, don't you?" David inserted a long pause that put Julia on edge. "You would have met Fiona at some point. For all I know, you even babysat her! So where is she? What did you two cook up and why? You're going to tell me what the hell this is all about, right here, right now."

"Or what?" Rick braved a step forward.

David was ready. With one swift motion, he snatched a rifle from the gun rack mounted to the wall directly below Cormac's portrait, and aimed the weapon at Rick's chest.

"I'm pretty sure this is the gun you use when you go coyote hunting," David said. "And I believe you were the one who told me that armed intruders don't wait for you to load your weapon. Do you follow your own advice, Rick, and keep a loaded gun on the rack?"

David hefted the rifle higher. He squinted as he stared down the barrel, taking careful aim.

Rick swallowed hard, but otherwise he didn't move a muscle.

"I guess that's my answer," David said. "Sit down and stay out of this," he ordered.

Julia saw murder in her friend's eyes. Rick must have seen the same, for he obliged without protest, parking himself in the closest chair. He might be bold, but he wasn't stupid.

"Now, *you.*" David swiveled until he had the rifle aimed at Erika. "Where is Fiona? I just spent hours getting grilled by Baker, who is convinced I killed her.

"Funny that *you* found the bloody shirt under my porch even after there was a K-9 unit nearby," David continued. "So start talking, Erika. Because I'm running out of patience."

Julia hadn't realized fear had a smell, but a new odor permeated the air, something harsh and pungent.

"I . . . I don't know what you're talking about," Erika said, stumbling over her words, but she regained her composure quickly. "I don't know anything about my father's business and didn't know Fiona until you pranced her around like your new trophy," she insisted. "I think I met Uncle James' daughter once when she was a baby, so there's no way I'd recognize her as an adult decades later."

Erika looked so confident, Julia started to believe her. Was it really that simple? A bizarre coincidence? But no, she had seen her friend's fear. It was brief, but it was palpable.

Julia should have expected that the commotion might draw the teens, who surged down the stairs in one thunderous stampede. She felt as if she were moving through molasses. Her cry of warning got lodged in her throat, like those terrible nightmares where you watch tragedy unfold, paralyzed and unable to stop it.

By the time Lucas reached the bottom step, David had the gun pointed at his chest. Wisely, Lucas came to an abrupt halt. Taylor screamed as she foolishly stood beside Lucas, putting herself in harm's way and thinking with her heart rather than her head. Thank God Izzy had the sense to pull Taylor away as she moved to stand next to Julia, though Lucas remained stuck in place with the gun trained on him.

Rick jumped to his feet. David didn't even bother looking his way.

"Stop right there, Rick, because I have nothing to lose," he said.

Julia watched David's finger tighten on the rifle's trigger.

"Stay back," she warned. "He means it."

Rick froze, following the order.

"If you take so much as a step in my direction, I will shoot," David threatened. "Maybe the gun isn't loaded, maybe it is, maybe there's one in the chamber that you didn't check for—are you willing to gamble your son's life?"

The bravado drained from Rick's face. Erika visibly trembled, her confidence gone now that Lucas was in the line of fire.

"Don't test me," David continued. "I'm a dead man walking if I don't find Fiona. Jimmy T isn't going to let this slide. No place will be safe for me, and that includes prison. So you're going to tell me where Fiona is, right here, right now, or it's your son who will pay the price. You decide."

"Don't hurt him, David, please," Erika begged. "Put the gun away." She dropped to her knees, hands clasped in front of her. "Leave my son out of this. I promise, I'll tell you everything."

Chapter 44

Izzy

The air is so thick it's hard to breathe. All eyes rest on Erika, who is on her knees, her face a knot of agony.

"Talk," says David.

I watch him closely. He's a time bomb, a threat that grows with every second that ticks by.

Unfortunately, Erika seems to have lost her voice at a most inopportune moment. She manages to get to her feet, but she's not saying a word. The gun stays on Lucas.

In the silence, I find myself moving toward David, not away. I know I should be afraid—terrified, in fact. But I've reached some kind of breaking point. This man has put his mark on my family for long enough. I won't let him control the narrative any longer.

"Let him go—you can have me instead," I say, stepping in front of Lucas.

Julia's eyes go wide. She can't believe what I've just done. Honestly, I can't believe it, either. Taylor gasps, but I'm not budging. I've set my sights on David while he glares back at me.

It's on.

"Susie Welch is my aunt," I announce, mainly for David's benefit. The shock that spreads across his face delights me.

"She's your aunt?" David squints as though he can't see clearly. "You sneaky little bitch. I knew you weren't telling me the whole story, but I never would have guessed *that.* I suppose you get what you pay for. I *was* desperate for a new nanny after Fiona figured out I was sleeping with the last one." He smirks like he's proud of himself.

"Nice. Way to keep it classy," I say. "And you had *no* chance with me, by the way, I can assure you of that. I only wanted this job to investigate what happened to my aunt. I found out quite a lot, too. I know what you did to her, and I have every intention of exposing you for her rape and murder. So, if you have to hold someone accountable, it should be me. Let Lucas go. He has nothing to do with this."

I sound a lot braver than I feel. Inside, I'm quaking. I've never had a gun pointed at me, and the feeling is far more frightening than I anticipated. But here I am, being dangerously impulsive yet again, skipping the filter of logic and reason and going straight from thought into action.

I steal a glance at Lucas, who appears conflicted about being rescued. Instead of relief, his eyes are full of confusion. We look at each other, and I try to make it clear he doesn't have to be the big strong man. I've got more skin in this game than he does. Besides, he has more pressing concerns—namely the baby he doesn't know about.

I shift my focus ever so briefly to Taylor, and when I do, Lucas seems to get it. He might not know all the facts, but he's sensitive enough to understand that this is best for her, and that's enough for him. Lucas moves aside.

David doesn't object.

"Go ahead and play hero if that's what you want," he says. "Your aunt's charges against me went nowhere. And good luck sending me to jail now that she's not around to tell her side of the story." He addresses Lucas directly. "Stay where I can see you. If your mother doesn't give me the answers I need, this rifle will be pointing right back at you."

Welp, my heroism hasn't really changed anything. Lucas and Taylor are still in danger. Hopefully, Erika will pull it together and get us out of this jam.

David turns toward her, expecting the same. My body relaxes, but only a little.

"You're my worry, not the damn nanny," he says, addressing Erika. "Now, answer me . . . where the fuck is Fiona, and what the hell are you both up to?"

A ragged inhale and exhale help Erika to settle. She appears more composed, while my blood pressure is skyrocketing.

Erika turns to Rick, sorrow etched on her face. "I'm done," she announces. "Enough is enough. Whatever the punishment, whatever the consequences, we're going to face this together."

Rick holds up a hand in protest. "What? No. We didn't agree to this."

"It's over," Erika declares with authority. "I can't risk anybody else getting hurt. It's the right thing to do. We should have done it ages ago. I'm going to end this once and for all."

Rick says nothing, though anger ripples off him.

Erika tunes out her husband's objections to focus on David. "You did this to yourself," she tells him like a mother scolding her child. "You started the whole chain of events when you came to me for seed money to invest in your electronics company."

"NewPulse?" David is surprised.

I remember being in the kitchen when David, shirtless and sweaty, tossed me a blue tee with his company's name emblazoned on the front. I can't figure out how an electronic components company could connect to Fiona, Jimmy T, Aunt Susie, Anna Olsen, Erika, and the Mob, but color me curious.

"When Rick and I wouldn't give you the money, what did you say, David?"

He smiles wickedly, eyeing Erika down the long black barrel. "I said I've kept your secret all these years, but there could be an expiration date on my goodwill."

"That's not goodwill, that's a threat," says Erika.

David chides her with his eyes. "I needed some help for a once-in-a-lifetime opportunity, and you laughed me off, told me the business would go nowhere. But with NewPulse, I saw what you didn't—a golden goose. I knew better." He chuckles softly to himself. "I couldn't go to the bank—they don't like guys who make most of their money under the table. And I'll be honest, I couldn't go to Jimmy for the cash because he was still pissed about Bella. So, I went to the next best source—you. Jimmy told me how much Cormac left you in his will, and you're a well-paid attorney on top of it. So yeah, I asked you for the money. Hardly a crime."

"You blackmailed us," Rick shouts.

"All you had to do was give me the cash and it would have been over. But my lifelong friends with their hefty bank account couldn't be bothered. What was I supposed to do? I needed the money. And lucky for me, I had the leverage to get it. The bones changed everything. I gave you a choice—pay me or pay the piper. I think you picked wisely," David jeers.

"And then you took our money and went and built that monstrous glass house blocking our view of the lake, just to lord it over us." Erika's fire sparked again, if only momentarily. "Of course we were nervous when the remains were found, but there wasn't anything to trace it back to us except the gun, and that was easy enough to get rid of.

"You, however, were a different story. We couldn't let it go on. You were too big a threat. First, it was the money, then the house—who knew what was next? You could have come after us for the rest of our lives."

David's callous shrug suggests that Erika was right.

"I wasn't going to let you push us around forever," she continues. "I'm not very religious, and I certainly don't deserve forgiveness, but it was Jesus who said, 'The truth will set you free.' It's time for the truth."

David appears smug, like he knew he'd win the standoff.

I'm waiting for Erika to address him with her big reveal, but to my astonishment, she advances toward me. I have no idea why or what she's about to say.

David follows her with his weapon. She's standing so close that the gun is essentially pointed at both of us.

"Izzy, I'm so sorry," she says, her voice cracking from emotion. "Many years ago, when I was very young and foolish, I shot and killed your aunt Susie."

Chapter 45

Julia

Julia couldn't believe it. She hoped she misheard, but no, Erika repeated it for Izzy's benefit.

"I'm the one who killed your aunt . . . and I can't tell you how sorry I am." Tears streamed down Erika's face, long salty lines that carved a winding path down her cheeks, which were flushed as red as her hair.

David didn't react, which was revealing. He must have known; otherwise, what leverage would he have had to get Erika to pony up the money for his business investment? At last Erika's ho-hum reaction to the glass house made perfect sense. It wasn't her newfound mindfulness that keep her cool, calm, and collected. She was acting the whole time. But there was still so much Julia didn't understand. And how did Fiona factor into all this?

"Not a day goes by that I don't regret it, that I don't think of her and what I did. But I swear to you, Izzy—it was an accident. We only meant to scare her."

"We? Who is *we*?"

Erika shifted her attention to Julia, who had asked the obvious. But before she could answer, the front door burst open yet again, and a man Julia had seen twice today, only in pictures, strutted into the house, taking command of the room.

James Tracey bore a vague resemblance to the person Julia knew in passing from his infrequent sojourns at the lake, but he looked very much like he did in the snapshot on Bella's Instagram feed, only a little older and thicker around the middle. What remained of his hair had gone mostly silver, his prominent mustache matching in color. He wore the same tortoiseshell glasses Julia had observed in his photo, and a crisply pressed collared shirt, but no sport coat, this occasion being less celebratory than the one shared on social.

Even without the sartorial enhancement, he looked more like a retired insurance adjuster than a gangster with a murderous past. But Julia could see the edge underneath. Here was a man who could switch on the cruelty the way one would turn on a TV. A twist of his mouth, a slight narrowing of his eyes was all it took to transform him from the avuncular man of Erika's youth into a killer.

Izzy barely took notice of him. She'd slumped to the floor, Erika's words no doubt tumbling through her head, as they did in Julia's.

I shot and killed your aunt Susie . . .

Erika, not David.

David, too, was in shock, but most certainly because Jimmy T had sauntered in with an air of complete authority. He lowered the rifle immediately. Judging by the fear in his eyes, he didn't dare point a gun at his boss. The two sizable men who had followed Jimmy T into the home might have provided some added incentive. Both had buzz cuts and close-set eyes, hard looks that could have been perfected in prison. They wore large suits and were built like football players. It was hard to tell where their necks ended and their shoulders began.

"David, I'm not going to mince words," Jimmy said. He didn't bother to acknowledge Erika, the woman who'd grown up calling him Uncle James, in any meaningful way. Jimmy's focus was reserved exclusively for his protégé, his demeanor calm and confident despite walking into a room with people held at gunpoint. Perhaps he'd become inured to anything that whiffed of violence.

"I'm here for my daughter," he said. He had a powerful baritone voice that demanded respect. When this man spoke, you listened.

"Jimmy, what are you doing here?" Julia thought she heard David stutter.

"I just told you, dumbass. I came here for my daughter. Now where is she?"

The goons accompanying Jimmy T moved on David like two walls closing in.

Suddenly David remembered he had a gun. He backed up a step so he had proper distance to take aim. He picked Tweedledee over Tweedledum, but both men put their hands up.

"You know what you're doing is dangerous," said Jimmy. "Listen to me, you're going to put that gun away and tell me where my daughter is. You can shoot one of these guys, but the other is going to snap your neck." Jimmy's voice was like ice. "Where . . ."

Blood lust sparked in his eyes. "Is . . ."

He balled his hands into fists as he took a threatening step forward. "Fiona?"

David lowered his weapon a second time, but then it was as if he suddenly snapped awake. He turned, aiming the gun not at the goons or Jimmy, but at Erika.

"She's Cormac's daughter, calls you her uncle. You leave now, or I shoot."

Jimmy was unfazed. "David, you hurt her, I'm talking so much as a scratch, and I'll rip your throat out," he warned.

"I don't know where Fiona is, so I'm dead anyway. Get out of here, Jim. Give me time. I'm trying to find her."

Before Jimmy had a chance to answer, the sliding glass doors in the living room shattered. Julia's eardrums nearly burst from the cacophony of breaking glass. Shards sprayed in all directions, but thankfully, nobody stood near enough to get cut.

Two men, dressed in navy blue windbreakers with 'FBI' stenciled on them, stormed in through the broken doors with guns drawn. Julia wrapped her arms around Taylor, shielding her from the onslaught.

"Down, down, down!" The agent pointed his handgun at David's head.

David got the message. He relinquished his weapon without protest, dropping to the floor with his hands clasped behind his head. What choice did he have?

Jimmy threw his hands up with a look of annoyance like some jackass just spoiled a surprise party.

"Agent Cody and Agent Fulton. To what the fuck do I owe the pleasure?"

Both agents were like thinned-down versions of Jimmy's muscle guys, with wiry builds, close-cropped hair, and the steely stare of ex-military men.

"Did you bring handcuffs for me?" Jimmy asked the agents, not showing a drop of concern. Julia guessed guys like him didn't get ruffled even if they were riding in the back of a police car.

"Nah, Jim. You're under surveillance, not arrest. Lucky for these folks, we followed you right to a crime scene. Unlucky for us, our cover is blown, so you can relax—for now."

"Not until I find my daughter," Jimmy said.

A moment later, Detective Baker, wearing a bulletproof vest over her button-down shirt, strode into the living room through the busted door, her gun drawn. Other police soon joined her, but the angry look she cast behind her wasn't directed at anyone in uniform.

"I told you to wait outside," she barked.

"I'm sorry, but this is my family."

The voice was as familiar to Julia as the man who entered. Christian rushed to her side. He pulled Julia and Taylor into a hug. The three of them huddled together in a collective embrace.

Julia let go of all sense of betrayal for the moment as she melted against Christian, allowing him to hold and comfort her. Taylor buried her face into her father's shoulder.

One of the agents—Fulton or Cody—cocked his head in confusion. "Hey, are you local cops clairvoyant or something? We didn't even have time to call it in. This guy was going to shoot." The agent pointed to David, who was lying on the floor, handcuffed, and not taking it well.

"Call it lucky timing," said Baker. She pointed to Christian. "The husband came to the house, saw what was going on inside, and phoned it in. Guess he didn't see your car parked nearby."

"Well, we're kind of undercover," said the agent. "At least we *were*."

Julia touched Christian's cheek as though he might not be real.

The police and FBI were busy sorting out David and Jimmy, so the two of them had a chance to talk in low voices.

"I can't believe you're here," Julia said to him.

"That's what happens when you don't reply to my text messages," he said, finding a half smile. Then, more quietly, he whispered in her ear, "We have to talk. Rick's family used to own the land where the bones were found. I was doing research because the guy who wants to buy our business—"

"Wait, you found a buyer?" Despite the full-throttle excitement, Julia found room for an extra burst of energy.

"Yeah, but that's not important right now. Our potential buyer is looking for property in Vermont, so I did some research for him. That's how I found out. It bothers me that Rick never told us. Worse, he lied about it when I asked him. Obviously he's hiding something." His voice was still low as he glanced toward their friends to make sure they couldn't hear.

"Oh, they're hiding something, all right," said Julia with a nod. "Erika killed Susie Welch."

"*What?* Jesus," Christian murmured, the blood draining from his face. "For real?"

Before Julia had a chance to elaborate or press Erika to do the same, everyone was ushered out the door by the police and FBI, Jimmy T and his thugs included.

Outside, Christian pointed to the new arrivals. "Who are those guys?"

"Long story," said Julia. "But that's Erika's Uncle James . . . turns out he's Fiona's father."

"Wait, so does that mean Erika . . . ?"

She had to give Christian credit. He was a quick learner. "That's right . . . she knew Fiona before any of us, David included."

"As soon as I found out about the land, alarm bells went off in my head," Christian said. "I remembered how bothered you were by their lack of a reaction to the glass house. And you're right. It did feel . . . off. I couldn't stop worrying that you and Taylor could be in a really bad situation, so I decided I had to check on you. I didn't tell you I was coming because I didn't want you to try and talk me out of it."

"I'm glad you listened to your intuition," said Julia.

"Well, I wasn't exactly a hero. The FBI got here first."

"Ever hear the expression, it's the thought that counts?" Julia hugged her husband again, holding on extra tight. "We have a lot to talk about. Whatever happens between us, please know I'm really happy to see you."

And that was true. Having his support meant everything right now, especially with her two oldest friends caught up in something nefarious. David's blackmail scheme meant he knew about the murder. He must have. But why didn't he ever come forward?

He might now if he wants to try for a plea deal, Julia thought. Potentially, he could give up Erika and Rick to lessen his punishment. But for the moment, the cops didn't know about her confession. At present, David was the only one guilty of a crime—threatening people with a gun.

But Julia knew what Baker did not. Erika and Rick had a story to tell, and they weren't even being questioned.

That was about to change.

Chapter 46

Izzy

This is why you don't rush childhood, why kids should be allowed to hold on to their precious belief that the world is full of magic.

Let's go fly a kite . . .

The song lingers in my head, even though I know better. Fairy tales are the product of imagination. The real world is full of monsters wearing the masks of our friends and neighbors, hiding lies, secrets, and betrayals that go back generations.

I came to Lake Timmeny hoping to solve the cold cases and break the cycle of anxiety for my mom and myself. Mom could stop worrying about everything in life, and I would stop acting first and thinking later.

But maybe I *wasn't* being impulsive when I confronted David. Perhaps because I had finally learned the truth, I was facing my fears rather than simply reacting to them. By coming here, I've learned there's a difference between trusting my inner wisdom and simply responding mindlessly to stressful situations.

I feel a deeper sense of freedom, like I achieved some kind of victory. I'm not sure how it will all play out, but I know I've set some wrongs to right. Now, the healing can begin. I may always be Frizzy Izzy, the girl who doesn't think things through, but I love her regardless, and I'm damn proud of the woman she's become.

But what about Erika? What's her story? Why did a loving, caring mother and friend kill my aunt? I have to know.

More police have arrived. I'm told this is a local matter, and the FBI is clearing out. David is in the back of a cop car. *Good.* I hope he never walks free again.

Lucas is talking to his parents, but even from a distance, I can tell it's a painful conversation. He looks unmoored, like a boat adrift on the ocean. Erika reaches out to hug him, but he pulls away. It saddens me, regardless of what she's done. While I still don't have all the facts, my instincts tell me that Erika and Rick were being truthful. They didn't mean to hurt Susie. For what it's worth, it wasn't intentional.

Taylor beckons Lucas away and he can't leave fast enough. I've been watching her as well. She's been talking with her dad, overwrought with emotion. I'm sure she's told him everything, and now I wonder if Lucas is about to get the *second* biggest shock of his young life.

Nearby, Jimmy T and his two thugs are busy with Detective Baker, which gives me an opportunity to finally confront Erika.

I don't have to go alone. Julia joins me in silent understanding, and together, we approach Rick and Erika, huddled by an oak tree. Every muscle in my body tightens. A wool blanket draped across Erika's shoulders keeps her warm in the night's chill, but I need something to cool me down.

"Why?" I say to her, my voice breaking. "Why did you do it?"

Erika shuts her eyes, "Izzy . . . I can't imagine what you're feeling right now."

"I'll help you," I say. "I'm feeling fucking angry and hurt, and very, very confused." My entire body, my whole being, is burning with a mix of rage, adrenaline, and heartache.

Julia steps forward. "Erika, before Jimmy barged in, you said, 'We only meant to scare her.' What does that mean?"

Erika looks at Rick, who walks toward the shoreline, motioning for us to follow. We fall into step behind him.

There are so many police vehicles, fire trucks, and ambulances parked out front that night has become day. But Rick has brought us to a secluded spot at the water's edge that's covered in near darkness. It's the perfect place for a private conversation.

"I don't expect you to forgive us, but let me explain." Erika's voice is soft and heartfelt. "Rick and I planned it together. We had to do something to make Susie stop, for her own safety. It all started when David wanted Susie to drop the rape charges. He told her that he was connected to the Irish Mob and that it made him untouchable. He even said that he had a couple cops in his back pocket because of his connections."

David. Why does it always come back to him?

"But he didn't know that Susie had found evidence—a letter written by Anna Olsen—that basically foretold her death and pointed the blame at a mobster living at the lake."

"I know about that letter," I say.

Erika looks surprised but continues. "Your aunt knew that David worked for my father, which meant his mobster connection had to be Cormac—the same man, she deduced, who got Anna pregnant and then silenced her."

I don't say anything. Erika keeps talking.

"Susie came to me and told me about the letter, what David did to her, how my father and the Mob were protecting him, and her plan to expose my father—go to the FBI if she had to—unless I could convince Cormac to stop shielding David. For her, it wasn't so much about Cormac and Anna; that was in the past—she wanted David to face the consequences of his actions, and she would threaten Cormac to see that justice was served. I knew all about my father's so-called *business*. More importantly, I knew he was capable of *extreme* violence. I believed the letter was real and that my father *had* murdered Anna Olsen to protect his life and guard his secrets. And I knew he'd do the same to Susie in a heartbeat."

I hear a splash nearby, a fish jumping to catch a meal. It's interesting how other species kill only to survive, but not us humans. No, we find all kinds of reasons to take a life that have nothing to do with biology. Greed. Ego. Hatred. Jealousy. The list goes on. If only we were as simple as a hungry fish—satisfied after a meal, and then back to living in peace and harmony with its environment.

Erika pulls the blanket tighter, her body quivering like the ripples in the water.

"Your aunt didn't understand the danger she was putting herself in. I didn't have any power over my dad. If he felt threatened, he would react. My father was with the Westies, one of the most violent gangs ever: kill first, ask questions never. That was how they operated. I tried to talk Susie out of it, but she wouldn't listen to reason. So, I came up with a plan to scare her straight."

I piece it together in my mind. It was as if I could stand in Susie's shoes and feel what it was like to be a young woman full of grief and rage, suffering from a profound injustice. All it took was a chance yard sale purchase of a decorative box with a secret compartment to change her fate. At some point, Susie took an old Polaroid of her and David, blacked out his face in anger, and placed that picture in the box along with the letter, cementing a bond between two strangers, two victims, the first two disappearances at Lake Timmeny.

It made perfect sense why my aunt Susie approached Erika and not the police with what she knew. Obviously she couldn't trust the *local* authorities, so she went to her next best option—a fellow lake kid who also happened to be the daughter of the man she could bring down.

"Rick and I had gotten together that summer," Erika continued. "I needed someone's help, and I felt like I could confide in him. I told him about my dad and he agreed something had to be done.

"We arranged to meet Susie at the Shack so we could talk it out. When she got there, I begged her to give me the letter. I told her she was putting herself in grave danger by threatening to expose someone as powerful as my dad. When Susie wouldn't comply, I took out the gun. It was Rick's idea to use it as a last resort.

"We planned it all carefully, including the pistol I would take from my father's collection. I needed something small and lightweight that I could conceal. The gun wasn't loaded—we had checked and made sure. I swear to you, we only meant to scare her, nothing more. The plan was that I would pull the trigger *only* if

Susie refused to give me the letter. We figured one moment of true terror would convince her to back down, that she would realize the next time it would be Cormac Gallagher confronting her, and the shot would be for real.

"Susie wouldn't hand over the letter, and I did as we had planned. I fired. The gun wasn't loaded. We triple-checked the magazine—it was empty. But we never checked the chamber—didn't think of it—and that's where the bullet that killed Susie must have been. It hit her in the chest. We tried to save her, but we didn't know how, and she died so quickly."

Erika's composure fractures as tears slip from her swollen eyes. Even in the low light, I can tell her complexion is gray. Rick's isn't much better. They are reliving the worst moment of their lives, and I'm convinced that Erika's sorrow and regret—Rick's too—are genuine.

"We buried her on Rick's property—his family's hunting grounds would be safe, or so we thought. We cleaned up as much evidence as we could, removed all the blood from the scene, disposed of our clothes. Susie vanished, and the investigation into her disappearance went nowhere. We were in the clear. All we had to deal with was our guilt, and the sick feeling that has followed us for thirty years.

"We thought that was the end of it. But then, Rick's family sold the land, without telling us. We got nervous, fearing someone would find Susie's remains. But we couldn't remember exactly where we had buried her. That night we'd been in a fog. We were both in shock, so we never marked the spot.

"Then our worst nightmare came true. Someone else unearthed our terrible secret. I tried not to panic, but we were so scared. We never did find the bullet that killed her. We assumed it was lodged in her body. But I knew the police wouldn't be able to trace a bullet back to us without the weapon. So, we felt relatively safe.

"That is, until David approached us, demanding money for his new business opportunity. I told him I wasn't interested. But David wouldn't take no for an answer. He said: 'I know whose bones those are, and I know who put her there.'

"He recounted that night to me, moment by moment. He knew it all, every awful detail—what we did, how we acted, things I said to Rick, words I'll never forget no matter how hard I try. There was no doubt he was a witness."

Erika shakes her head in a slow sweep of dismay.

My hard stare drills into her. "My grandmother died not knowing her daughter as an adult, not even being able to bury her. My mother became a shadow of herself, always living in fear. You took a lot more than one life that day."

Erika's eyes again fill with tears. "We didn't mean to hurt her or anyone else. It was an accident. We've never forgiven ourselves."

She buries her head in her hands, sobbing uncontrollably. Rick places his arm around his wife's shoulders for comfort.

"I never understood your relationship with Rick or why you gave up your art for law school," Julia says. "But now I do. It wasn't love that brought you together. It was trauma. And you became a defense attorney to absolve others of guilt because you couldn't do it for yourself. But I don't understand why David was there that night."

"He told us he came to have a beer at the Shack. He got there at the wrong time and saw what went down." Even Rick's thick beard can't hide his pain. "When he blackmailed us, we were shocked by what he knew—all those years he kept quiet, but he knew. We paid him what he wanted, and we kept paying when he came back for more, all while trying to find a way to end it. Our bank accounts were getting low, and he was building his huge house."

While all of this is revelatory, it still doesn't explain Fiona's involvement, so I ask Erika about her. The regret rolls off her tongue like a great unfurling wave.

"I've known Fiona for a long time. I lied about that," Erika admits. "We were never close because of our age difference, but I met her several times over the years. And Fiona knew all about me. She came to me looking for advice. She wanted to escape her life and get away from Jimmy T for good.

"She told me about Bella and what her father had done to that boy they found in the river. It wasn't the life she wanted—a world full of violence, always looking over your shoulder and trying to stay one step ahead of the law. She said something that I know to be true: it's hard to leave the Mob when you know too much.

"I had managed to build a life apart from the family business, but I couldn't really leave it completely until my father died. Fiona didn't have that kind of out, and Uncle James kept an iron grip on her. She was stuck, and I wasn't sure how to help.

"As we kept talking and getting to know each other better, she realized I was friends with David. She knew he was one of her father's employees—the one Jimmy held second-most accountable for Bella's death.

"And that's when I came up with my idea. Fiona wanted to disappear, and I wanted to be free from David. I realized we could both get what we wanted, and David could get what he deserved.

"Revenge for Bella wasn't really on Fiona's mind, but when she heard my plan, it became an added bonus. The timing couldn't have been better—thirty years since the last disappearance. We would tie it into the lake lore and start to build evidence against David.

"It was all carefully planned, and Fiona was more than willing to play her part. We set up a supposedly chance encounter in a coffee shop, and Fiona worked her charm. Everything was in place—missing girl, bloody evidence—but we still needed a smoking gun to make it all work."

Julia's face comes alive. "Baker told me that she found a gun in David's house . . . I didn't think he owned one. Did you two . . . ?"

"There are no registration or licensing requirements in Vermont," Rick says. "The police can't trace ownership. David could say the gun isn't his, but he can't prove it. Possession is nine-tenths of the law."

Wow. I'm horrified, but also somewhat amazed by the plan they managed to execute.

"You planted the gun used to kill my aunt in David's house," I whisper. "And what about the bloody shirt?"

"Fiona planted the gun," says Rick. "And Erika put the shirt under the porch after the search ended. It's Fiona's blood from a small self-inflicted cut to her hand."

"And now both bits of evidence are with Detective Baker," says Erika. "Rick and I had talked about planting the gun on David long before Fiona got involved, but it was too risky. Calling in a tip after all these years would seem suspicious. However, a missing person and a search warrant—and suddenly David looks like a careless killer responsible for the deaths of two different women."

Her words sting with the finality of a bullet.

"Fiona must have messed around with the security system as well, so it wouldn't record her leaving the house," I mutter.

Erika nods slightly. "We gave Fiona the rest of the money we'd earmarked for David, along with the fresh start she wanted. People don't look for the dead like they do the living, and Fiona would most certainly be presumed dead. We got what we needed out of the deal, too—freedom from David, and from a past that's been haunting us since we were kids."

I'm stunned, unable to move, my brain rushing to make sense of this intricate web of deceit.

"The police will want to speak to all of us," Erika says, wringing her hands. "Izzy, I know what you heard tonight is incredibly painful, but Rick and I have been talking, and we'd like you to consider something. We have no right to ask anything of you, I realize that, but . . ."

Erika's anxiety makes me uneasy. I have no idea what's coming. I'm glad Julia's here. She puts her arm around me, while coolly assessing her friends. I can't speak. I don't really know how to address my aunt's killer, but Erika doesn't wait for my invitation.

"David's going to tell the police that I killed Susie. If that's corroborated, he will walk. He'll probably get a light sentence for threatening us with a gun, and the rape charges will never resurface. He'll pay no real price for his crimes. But if it's just our word against his, with the evidence we planted, he will likely go to jail, for Fiona *and* for Susie. The police don't have to know that Fiona's alive. We can all deny that I made my confession, deny all of

David's allegations. And when they match the bullet they recovered from Susie's body to the gun in David's possession, you can finally have some justice for your aunt. He might not have pulled the trigger, but he *did* rape her, and he set everything in motion that led to her death. She's gone, while he's continued to live a life of privilege and exploitation."

Rick steps forward. He looks broken. This tough, manly man is a shell of himself. "I know it's a lot to ask, but now you have the truth. It's up to you what you do with it."

I look to Julia for guidance, but her eyes are veiled. I get the sense she's giving me the space to decide for myself. It's my call.

As if on cue, I see Detective Baker heading over. Her complexion is ashen and her expression grim. She might be a rugged Vermonter, but she's human and has her limits.

"Heck of a night," she says.

Is she competing for the Understatement of the Year Award?

"Yeah," is all I can think to respond.

"I heard you put yourself in front of that rifle, Izzy . . . that must have been terrifying."

"Actually, for once I wasn't afraid," I say.

"David is telling us an interesting story," she says, diving right in. Her eyes, like two stones, are fixed on Rick and Erika. "He seems to think the bones we have belong to Susie Welch, Izzy's aunt. And that you, Erika, shot her with your father's handgun, which you then planted in David's house for us to find. He also believes that Fiona is alive and well, that you and she orchestrated her disappearance to make him look guilty of her murder." Baker sends them a thin smile.

"I've been a cop for a long time, and I can't say I've heard a tale as wild as this one," she declares, clearing her throat. "Bottom line is, I've got a job to do—and I need to confirm if what David is saying is true. What's your side of this story?"

Erika and Rick's pleading eyes are on me. I sense an earnest desperation that's hard to resist.

Their words run through my head. This could be my one and only chance for justice. David has the money to buy himself out of trouble. Maybe he'll serve some time, but not much. Erika is right. If he didn't assault my aunt, Susie would be alive today. How dare he walk away with only a slap on the wrist?

Julia says nothing. Maybe she would keep the lie going—David has caused so much harm—or perhaps she'd come clean eventually. But for right now, the choice is mine to make: live or die, thumbs up or thumbs down. I am the emperor at the Colosseum with the power to decide one man's fate.

It's not lost on me how Lucas will grieve. And Taylor will ache for Lucas, which will cause Julia and Christian to suffer alongside her. We are all links in some amazing chain. It's not like David's gold chain. This one you can't see or necessarily feel, but it's wrapped around us nonetheless. These links go back days, years, even generations, intertwining our lives. Our actions have consequences; our words matter, connecting us in unexpected and profound ways.

I'll never know the exact repercussions of my decision, how many lives I'll impact, or whose trajectory I'll forever alter.

"And the truth will set you free," I say to Erika, using her own words against her. She looks at me with such vulnerability that I almost break. Almost. But no. I cannot.

"I came here for the truth," I tell Detective Baker. "I came to find out what happened to Susie. I came here for my mother. I know how lies can destroy lives, and I can't be a part of that. If I'm going to investigate anything, it has to be with integrity.

"What David said is true. Those bones belong to my aunt Susie. Erika shot and killed her thirty years ago. It was an accident. I know she's sorry. Rick helped to cover it up. And her father, Cormac Gallagher, was a gangster who murdered Anna Olsen because she threatened to expose him. I have the proof. And there's more . . ."

The wind howls. A lone owl announces its presence from a

nearby shadowed tree. But I hear something else, a sound like no other: a soft clink of a hammer on steel, the blacksmith at work, forging a new link in my ethereal chain, one that binds me to Lake Timmeny, now and forever.

Chapter 47

Julia

An ominous, empty feeling had replaced the comfort and familiarity of the lake house, like a hole where a tooth had been extracted—something you obsessed over once it was gone. Julia was grateful she had Nutmeg by her side. The dog was her loving companion—a warm, reliable presence in her otherwise upside-down world.

Izzy had left by bus days ago and, through text messages, Julia learned she and her mother were doing well. Their reunion had been tearful but healing. She had told Julia about her hopes of starting a true crime podcast, which she would produce only with her mother's blessing.

Julia sipped hot herbal tea from the screened-in porch, peering at the lake through David's glass house. A swath of moonlight illuminated a patch of water as smooth as an ice rink. There was hardly a breeze. Sunset had been hours ago, yet the nighttime air carried the lingering remnants of the day's humidity. All signs of the season were on full display. Yet it was a summer unlike any Julia had ever known.

For as long as Julia could remember, Lake Timmeny had been her safe place, a soothing balm for the soul. While she was facing many types of loss—property, friendships, maybe a marriage—there were gains as well—namely a future grandchild.

Taylor and Lucas decided to have the baby. It was heartwarming when they made the announcement. Taylor glowed with youthful optimism, slightly tinged with trepidation. Naturally, she was nervous about the path ahead but felt certain she was making the right choice. It was endearing—Lucas talked about baby names and the instruments his future child would play. They were inexperienced, idealistic, and probably overly romantic. But they were also in love and had the best of intentions—though Julia wasn't sure how practical their future plans were.

They fantasized about becoming partners in parenting and music—her poetry combined with his songs.

Maybe they'll have a hit that will bring a huge windfall. Or, more likely, they'll wake up to the realities of raising a child. But who knows? It wasn't her place to judge Taylor's life choices. Her job was to guide and support.

Julia had made a slew of impractical decisions herself, and now she was looking to return to her passion for nonprofit work. She certainly wouldn't steer Taylor away from what lit up her life, be it poetry or something else—not now, not after all they'd been through.

Still, there were far more questions than answers. How would Taylor finish high school and be a new mom? What about college? How would Lucas contribute to his young family's financial future? He was now taking college seriously and considering a career in music education. Julia hoped this would offer him stability while he and Taylor pursued their songwriting passion. Julia was pleased to see he could be a practical dreamer.

No matter what happened, Julia would support her daughter as only a mother could. Speaking of mothers, Julia wished she could call her parents to unload her troubles, but they were older now, and she didn't want to burden them—other than to share the exciting news about their great-grandchild. Other than that, she was on her own.

It would be easy to let all her losses define and overwhelm her, risking a descent into self-pity. She inhaled the night air as crickets serenaded her from the darkness, their chorus blending with the croakers' song. Other than that, she listened long enough to realize that, for a brief moment, the sounds of nature had genuinely soothed her. It was fleeting, but she noticed a brief absence of sadness.

What had brought about that rare moment of peace? It wasn't a specific thought but rather the lack of one—her focus on Nutmeg, her surroundings, the feel of the cottony blanket on her lap, and the spicy taste of tea lingering on her lips. It provided her with a momentary respite from the pain.

She recalled Erika's pledge to practice mindfulness. She and Rick would need all the help they could get.

Erika and Rick's house stood silent and still, its darkened windows a reminder of all that had transpired. Detective Baker had arrested Erika for the homicide of Susie Welch. Rick had been charged with crimes in connection with the improper disposal of a body and evidence tampering. Both were arraigned at the county courthouse and posted bail, where David had done the same. And like David, neither wanted to stay at the lake now that their reputations were in tatters. The media hounded them with a vengeance.

Lucas felt different about leaving. He needed space and time to process everything and asked if he could remain with Julia and her family for a few days until they headed home. That was welcome news to all, especially Taylor. One thing was certain, Lucas would be in for a roller-coaster ride—and not just because there was a baby on the way. His entire identity, what he thought he knew of his family, had been completely upended. Therapy was a must; thankfully, Lucas was open to the idea. And Julia and Christian would support him as best they could.

Julia brought her attention back to her breath. She knew the basics of meditation. She felt the air swim into her lungs, delivering life-giving oxygen. Next she concentrated on her exhalation, slow and steady, like a gentle release of tension. She did it again with the same degree of focus, continuing until she had counted fifteen breaths. In that time, she felt her anxiety slowly ebb. She was okay. For those breaths, at least, she was present, safe, and whole.

Julia now understood she didn't need the lake house to achieve this calming effect. She had what everyone else had, house or not: one day, one hour, or maybe just one minute. *That's all anybody ever has—this moment, the here and now.* She had read somewhere that depression was rooted in the past and anxiety was nothing but a worry for the future. That was good for Instagram, but Julia was done with social media. The apps were deleted. She didn't have the energy for public sharing anymore, and no longer cared about the false reinforcement it provided. She had to focus on her daughter and her husband . . .

Christian.

Why had she given so much of herself away to him? As she considered this, a single word came to mind: trust. It wasn't about faith in another person. No, this went deeper than that. Julia often pushed aside her instincts, she realized, to follow the lead of others. At the root, she didn't believe in herself enough, nor did she *trust* her inner guidance. And with this sprig of insight came another, something she could trace back to childhood.

Her mind flashed again to the locked playroom at Erika's house. Julia had taken Cormac's account as gospel despite the gnawing feeling in her stomach. Raised voices. A door that was never stuck before suddenly wouldn't open. A missing carpet.

After all these years, Julia finally started to listen to her intuition. She revisited that day, realizing the thing still troubling her wasn't another detail like the missing rug she'd forgotten, but rather the order of events she'd misremembered. That one slight change—switching *A* with *B*, which event happened first and which was second—was profoundly significant. She'd always believed the locked door made Erika burst into tears, but now she was *sure* Erika started crying when they heard the *voices* downstairs, and that was before she ever tried the door.

What voice would likely cause a small child to cry?

A missing mother's, of course. That explained why Erika had called for her in the aftermath of the locked room incident. Julia now believed that Erika's mother had returned for her daughter—and had left in a rolled-up carpet that served as a makeshift body bag.

Julia would call Erika later to share this new insight. Self-doubt might have made the old Julia distrust herself, but not anymore—she was ready to speak her truth.

This applied to Taylor as well. They were in for quite the ride together, and Taylor would need all the help she could get—and that included up-front honesty. As a mother, Julia had constantly feared doing or saying the wrong thing, as if her daughter were a live ordnance that might explode in her hand. She had allowed moments of their togetherness to be clouded with insecurities of not doing enough, not being enough, or not saying the right things.

But it wasn't too late to change. That was the beauty of the breath. Each one gently reminded her that she was still here, that she had another chance to make her inner world calmer, more centered. She thought of Christian, who even after his relapse, opted for that one-day-at-a-time mantra rather than a lifetime of self-recrimination. Despite all his mistakes, she appreciated the wisdom behind his intentions.

Her thoughts seemed to have summoned him, for Christian joined her on the porch with a can of diet soda.

"Beautiful night," he said, taking the seat beside her.

Julia inhaled deeply. "Yes, it is," she said.

He looked at her longingly. She took in his handsome face, the luminous yearning of his eyes, and felt love for this man who had deeply betrayed her. She had choices. She could question that feeling, doubt herself, or sink into it. Would this love come and go, like her breath?

"Taylor and I had a good long talk," he said. "She's obviously nervous, but she's so strong and resilient—just like someone else I know."

Again, his eyes bore into her, beckoning Julia to him, but she held back.

"Are we okay?" he asked. "Jules, I know I've screwed up royally—but I love you, I love us. And now, with a baby on the way . . . well, I don't want us to lose everything we've built together. I'm pretty sure I can make this sale happen. Our buyer is very interested in the business, and he has the experience in the fitness industry to turn it around. Maybe we could even—"

"Don't say it," Julia said, holding a hand up to stop him. "We're not taking on a partner. I'm out, Christian. I've started my job search in earnest. My résumé is out there, and I'm already getting leads. Women on the Move wants to interview me next week."

Christian didn't know about the global nonprofit that worked to advance women's economic empowerment and reduce gender-based violence around the globe, so Julia briefed him.

"VP of Global Programs. Sounds right up your alley. You'll be amazing," he said. "I hope you get it. They'd be lucky to have you. But what about us? Do we still have a future? Julia, I don't want to divorce."

Instead of panicking about making a decision, Julia returned to the breath. With her eyes fixed on the stars spread out across a black canvas, she took a deep one, held it, and then let it out slowly. This went on for a while as Christian waited patiently beside her. Finally, she felt grounded enough to address him.

"I've read about something for situations like ours," she told him. "It's called a postnuptial agreement. Basically, it's like a prenup for married people. It details exactly how we'll divide the finances if we separate."

Christian's eyes filled with tears. "Please don't say it, Jules. Give me a chance."

"I am, Christian. It's a postnuptial. I'm not filing for divorce. We'll meet with a lawyer and draft one I'm comfortable with." Oh, it felt so good to use her voice. Julia didn't want to stop.

"What you did was a profound betrayal. This house was not yours to give away. I don't care what your reasons were. I don't care how scared or confused you were. You violated my trust in a way I can't easily forgive. I don't know if I will ever be able to find my way back to where we were before, but I know this is the first step. Step two is counseling, which we need to start right away."

Christian bowed his head, a man resigned to his fate. "But, Julia, is there a real chance for us? Or is all this just leading to . . ."

She cupped his hand. "There's always a chance. I still love you," she told him. "But we're going to have to take it a day at a time, one moment at a time. You know that approach better than most."

"I understand," he said, unable to mask his disappointment.

They held hands like an old married couple, which technically they were.

Julia's phone lit up on the table beside her chair. She looked; it was a message from Izzy, who wrote:

I got my mother's permission to produce the podcast. I know you're busy, but I hope you'll be able to work on it with me. Something about Susie's death has been bothering me, and I think I know what it is. Can we meet?

Julia was about to respond when Izzy sent a follow-up message.

And FYI, I might be back at the lake soon. I went to see Grace one more time before I left and ran into her nephew, Noah. Turns out he's her grandnephew. He's funny and handsome, and, well . . . we have a date next weekend. It's time to give a nice guy a chance, right?

Izzy added a couple of blushing emojis, and Julia couldn't help but smile.

While it was difficult to find the right words with Christian, Julia had no trouble answering Izzy.

That all sounds wonderful. And I'd love to help.

Epilogue

The Vanishings at Lake Timmeny
EPISODE 5: One in the Chamber
Announcer: Meredith Underwood

Previously, on *The Vanishings at Lake Timmeny* . . .

Erika Sullivan

It's my word and Rick's against the world, really. We know what we did that night. I pulled the trigger. I took a life. But I never meant to harm anybody—I was only trying to help. We were young and foolish for sure, but that doesn't mean I had malicious intent. Unfortunately, my thoughts aren't evidence. What was in my heart doesn't leave a trace.

Izzy Greene

From Gold Glitter Productions, this is *The Vanishings at Lake Timmeny*, and I'm your host—and witness—Izzy Greene, with Meredith Underwood, my college roommate and associate producer. We're at a critical point in the story, and for Erika, if nothing changes, she will most likely be charged with murder, among other felonies for her efforts to frame David Dunne for the crime.

If you need to catch up, now is a good time to listen to past episodes because, spoiler alert, I think there is a serious mitigating circumstance that could dramatically reduce Erika's culpability, and I'm going to try to prove it. Erika's lawyer declined to be interviewed for this podcast, but I don't think we need her testimony to make our case. The state ballistics team concluded the gun recovered from David's house was indeed the same weapon used to kill my aunt Susie. Disclaimer, I am related to the victim of this story, one of three women who disappeared at the lake. We have a statement regarding firearm forensics from Detective Baker, the lead investigator on the case.

Detective Baker

Handguns and rifles are manufactured based on blueprints that specify their configurations. This is known as rifling. The spiral lands and grooves built into a firearm's barrel leave an identifiable imprint on the bullet. The different rifling techniques make each barrel unique, so a trained examiner can determine if a given bullet was fired from a particular gun. We're sure we have the murder weapon in our possession.

Izzy Greene

Erika claims she checked the gun to make sure it wasn't loaded, which might reduce the murder charge to manslaughter. But can we prove it? Her lawyers will talk motive, how Erika feared for Susie's life because she knew her father was dangerous. Julia Crawford sensed the same from earliest memories. Cormac always made her nervous, but it wasn't until recently that she fully understood why. For more details, make sure to check out episode 4, where we talk about the playroom incident.

Julia Crawford

I can't prove that my memory isn't flawed. The voice we heard that day could have belonged to a stranger. The carpet may have been thrown out because of a spill. But I highly doubt it, just like I now doubt that Erika is the one most responsible for Susie's death.

Izzy Greene

There's no way to prove Julia's take, but it raises several interesting questions. The door to the playroom where the girls were trapped doesn't lock from the outside. Julia and I both confirmed that fact. You can block it with a chair, so the doorknob turns, but no matter how hard you pull, you can't get out.

So what if Erika's mother had taken off for her safety, but returned for her daughter?

It's common knowledge that it's hard to leave the Mob when you know too much. David Dunne had that very problem. He got in over his head as a teenager, and that was that. The Mob essentially owned him. Now he's likely viewed as a liability by Jimmy T and his crew. If David gets hit with a murder charge, he might be tempted to plea out in exchange for information on Jimmy T, which leaves him in a very precarious position. Then again, David's commitment to truth-telling isn't exactly sacrosanct.

Which brings us to this week's episode titled, "One in the Chamber," because Erika is sure the bullet that killed my aunt was *intentionally* hidden inside the chamber of the gun used to kill her.

Rick Sullivan

I come from a family of hunters, so we know our way around firearms. Erika was also raised around guns. She and I planned everything carefully. I made sure the gun we were using wasn't loaded. I even double-checked it *that* night. We just meant to scare her. Nobody expected a live round to fire.

Izzy Greene

And this is where the bartender comes in. Yeah, I know we haven't brought him up since episode 3, when Julia went to Bennington to search for Fiona. Honestly, we might have left it there, if not for something David Dunne said when he was holding us hostage. It really stayed with me. I asked Julia if she remembered it the same way I did.

Julia Crawford

I remember David had the gun aimed at Lucas, and he warned everyone that there could be a bullet in the chamber that Rick hadn't checked for.

Izzy Greene

So how does this comment relate to our bartender? Well, in that episode, we discussed his rather odd quote when speaking with Julia.

Julia Crawford

The bartender told me that David didn't appreciate getting berated by Jimmy T over the Bella situation. He didn't think he should have been blamed for the revenge porn, which had put unwanted attention on Jimmy's operation. David tried to build himself up by bragging to the bartender that he wasn't someone to mess with—that, in fact, he knew how to commit the *perfect* murder. He didn't confess to killing anybody, but he did say the strangest thing . . . a riddle.

Izzy Greene

The riddle was: *How do you shoot someone without ever pulling the trigger?* I asked Detective Baker for her answer.

Detective Baker

I suppose if you hid a bullet in the chamber of a gun, someone might think the weapon was unloaded, and if they pulled the trigger, they could unwittingly shoot someone.

Izzy Greene

When I told Baker what David said to the bartender at the Black Rose, her expression darkened.

Detective Baker

That's what we call circumstantial evidence. It doesn't prove that David knowingly put a bullet in the chamber of the gun that killed Susie Welch, but it does suggest it's a possibility, and he certainly had motive to kill her because she was threatening him with rape charges.

Izzy Greene

Which brings us to one other question. How would David have known which gun Erika was going to use?

Julia Crawford

I think there's a simple answer—he could have easily overheard Rick and Erika planning the confrontation at the Shack. We all hung out there. Maybe he showed up at the right place but at the wrong time for Susie. He also worked for Cormac, so he had access to the house and his guns.

Izzy Greene

That's the part that bothers me the most: Detective Baker doesn't seem to think we have enough evidence to charge David Dunne with my aunt's murder. It's hard to believe he didn't hide the bullet in the chamber of the murder weapon, hoping Erika would silence Susie for him. There are too many unsettling coincidences for that not to be true. If he was simply a witness to Susie's murder, why did he keep it a secret for thirty years? Why make up that bizarre riddle? And why reference a bullet in the chamber when he held us all at gunpoint? No, David was there that night to make sure his plan worked.

It may be circumstantial evidence, but I think it's more than enough to instill doubt in the jury at Erika's trial. And we're putting our theory out there in the hopes that someone with information will hear this podcast. Maybe David bragged to others, like he did to the bartender, about how to get away with murder.

As we mentioned previously, David Dunne is a father. I know his children, having cared for them as their nanny. Their mother and I have stayed in touch. She shared her thoughts on David's involvement.

Debbie Glasser

I was in shock when I found out about the charges—I *still* am. But naturally my concern is for my children. I'm happy to share that they're both doing well. They don't understand everything that's happened, but they still have fond memories of the lake, though what they talk about most is Izzy. They have supervised visits with their dad, which makes them happy, and they were also glad to see Izzy again.

Izzy Greene

That was a great day for me. And they recently sent me artwork they created at school—a hand-drawn picture of the glass house where we all lived for a few short, but eventful days. I love that drawing, because it reminds me of the innocence of childhood and what I meant to these two young souls. But it also breaks my heart, because I know what I must do, and David is their father.

I'm not a professional investigator. I don't have many resources at my disposal. But I'm committed to seeing justice served. I won't stop my quest for the truth until I reach my goal.

This leads me to Fiona: she may be even more determined than I am. There's been no trace of her online, through banking, credit cards, or any of the usual means. Erika told me she delayed planting the bloody shirt to give Fiona extra time to get away. A young murder victim attracts a lot more national attention than an adult woman who is simply missing for a day or two.

Maybe something happened to her that we don't know about, but she is bright, bold, and supremely resourceful. It's possible she successfully pulled off a disappearing act in a day and age when it's nearly inconceivable to fly under the radar and off the grid. There's a quote from Mary Poppins that relates: *Everything is possible, even the impossible.*

Dear Erika,

Greetings from somewhere beautiful. Please don't look at the postmark to try to find me. I had a handsome gentleman mail this from his next destination. But the gorgeous turquoise water pictured on the front is an accurate representation of my view each morning. The nights here remind me of the lake, full of stars and the peaceful sounds of gentle waves lapping against the shore. You've probably been wondering if I'm doing okay and if I got what I wanted. You'll be pleased to know it's even better than I dreamed. I'm never coming back, and I'm confident my father won't be able to find me. You helped me live my best life and I wish the same for you.

With Love and Thanks, Fiona

Excerpt from the *Burlington Standard*, Vermont's Largest Independent Newspaper

MAY 5

In a plea deal with the state district attorney's office, manslaughter charges have been dropped against Erika and Rick Sullivan of Greenwich, Connecticut. They have pleaded guilty to charges of improper disposal of a body, and were sentenced to time served. Lawyers for the two former defendants said only that the family of Susie Welch fully supported the plea agreement, and that everyone involved is relieved to put this tragic event behind them. No further comments were given.

Excerpt from the *Burlington Standard,* Vermont's Largest Independent Newspaper

JUNE 29

Police are still searching for David Dunne, who failed to show for his scheduled court appearance in relation to criminal charges stemming from an incident that took place one year ago at Lake Timmeny. Dunne, facing several years in prison for criminal threatening with a loaded firearm, had been out on bail and staying at his lake house. Police attempting to serve the arrest warrant found a pair of running shoes belonging to Dunne by the lakeshore near his home, but there was no sign of Dunne.

A neighbor, Grace Olsen, who is the sister of Anna Olsen, the first local woman to go missing from Lake Timmeny back in the 1960s, told police she wasn't surprised by the news. "There are rumors spreading that he had a more direct involvement with the murder of Susie Welch. And he ran with a rough crowd. Did he vanish of his own volition? Did the Mob decide to silence him? Or did *the lake take him,* to even the score? Perhaps we'll never know."

THE LAKE, *AUTUMN*

The lake breathes a long yawn, each wave against the shoreline now sounding like a satiated sigh. It is ready. It has fed. The lake prepares for its long, deep slumber. It will take rest, before the cycle begins anew . . .

The Lake, a series of seasonal poems by Taylor Crawford, winner, Scholastic Arts & Writing Awards

Acknowledgments

Thank you for reading *The Lake Escape*. My simple goal with these books is to take you on a wild ride while keeping it light, breezy, and a whole lot of fun—just like a memorable lake vacation. I grew up spending my summers at the ocean in Falmouth, Massachusetts, but water is water, and I felt I could capture the essence of lake life by drawing from my childhood experiences on the Cape. As I often do, I created Lake Timmeny to keep the story free from geographic details and constraints that a real location can impose—so don't bother trying to find it on any map. I also invented "The Lake Gang." While I never vacationed with other families the way Julia, Erika, and David did, imagination is a wonderful thing.

I do, however, have a gang that has my back with every story—I call them "The Book Gang." This gang is loyal, steadfast, whip-smart, and without them, I couldn't deliver on my pledge to entertain and enthrall at a high level.

My thanks and gratitude go to my gang at the Jane Rotrosen Agency—especially Meg and Rebecca. I'm also deeply grateful to my team at St. Martin's Press, starting with my intrepid editor, Jen Enderlin, who paired me with an incredible group of marketers and salespeople, including Erica, Brant, Katie, and Christina. I also want to acknowledge the cover artists, production team, sales force, and everyone who supports the creation and distribution of books. Reading is vital to our culture, and I'm forever grateful to play a role in it.

My early readers—Colleen Joyce, Sue Miller, and Judy Palmer—were instrumental in shaping the novel and providing much-needed course corrections, much like GPS guiding a hiker. For subject matter expertise, I turned to Ben Adams, proprietor of Wicked Weaponry in Hudson, NH, and my go-to guy for all things firearms-related, as well as Police Captain Jon Tate, who provided details on law-enforcement procedures. Thanks also to Lauren Mello, who consulted with me on real estate matters.

But my north star remains Kathleen Miller, who supports me in every capacity—from plotting to writing to revising. I would truly feel lost without her.

I also want to thank my children, as well as my friends and family, who help keep me sane as I tap away on the keyboard. Most of all, none of this would be possible without you, dear reader, so thank you for diving into the lake with me.

I hope we share many more reading adventures together.

With thanks and gratitude,
—Jamie Day

About the Author

Jamie Day lives in one of those picture-perfect coastal New England towns you see in the movies. And just like the movies, Jamie has two children and an adorable dog to fawn over. When not writing or reading, Jamie enjoys yoga, the ocean, cooking, and long walks on the beach with the dog or the kids, or sometimes both.